NEW YORK 1609

Also by Harald Johnson

Mastering Digital Printing, Editions 1 & 2
Digital Printing Start-Up Guide

The Manhattan Series (eboooks)
1609 (Book 1)
1612 (Book 2)
1625 (Book 3)
1640 (Book 4)

NEW YORK 1609

A Novel

Harald Johnson

P

PHOOZL, LLC

Charlottesville, Virginia

Published by Phoozl, LLC, Charlottesville, Virginia
http://haraldjohnson.com

Cover image, a computer simulation of Manhattan island
(seen from the southwest) at 2:00 p.m. on September 12, 1609:
© 2009 Markley Boyer / The Mannahatta Project /
Wildlife Conservation Society
https://www.welikia.org

Cover design, maps, and book design/formatting by Harald Johnson

This is a work of historical fiction. Apart from actual (real) people,
events, and locations included in the narrative, all other characters,
dialogue, events, and locations are the product of the author's
imagination or are used fictitiously. For more details, see
"Notes About the History" at the end of this book.

ISBN 978-0-692-11525-1

First Edition

to my wife, Lynn—for your love, patience, and partnership

Contents

►◄

What follows is based on true events.
Events as written by Europeans.
But they didn't tell the whole story...

Prologue

THE TWO HUNTERS COULD SEE IT WOULD NOT GO WELL.

They sat on the high bank, bundled in skins and eating parched corn, and watched the canoe with three aboard approach from the west—from the island.

The rain had stopped, but the gale at their backs was still gusting. Whitecaps roiled the gray, cold waters below them, and a continuous roar from both wind and sea, not unlike a waterfall, thundered.

"Worst time to attempt this passage," the taller of the two shouted in their Munsee dialect.

The other man grunted agreement while he chewed his corn and pulled his beaver cloak tighter against the north wind.

The tide was turning at this spot they called Monatun, just east of Mannahatta. Here three salt rivers and waterways converged into one channel. Currents from different directions raced and collided. Waves rammed into each other and shot spray high in the air. Deep whirlpools spun and sucked, and a standing wave spanned the treacherous water route.

The hunters could do nothing to change what they knew was coming—they would be silent witnesses.

The man was in back, a woman in front, and in the middle a boy who had seen maybe eight or nine winters. The man paddled furiously and yelled instructions to the woman, her eyes wide with fright. The boy remained motionless, as if in his dreaming

1

world, his small hands grasping each side of the canoe.

As they entered the violent stream, the paddlers' efforts had little effect—the canoe was pulled into the standing wave that blocked its path. The man tried to angle them up and over the wave, but the heavy canoe flipped like a small twig, its occupants launched into the icy water and swept along with the main current.

The wind then caught the lip of the canoe and sent it sailing against a large boulder that jutted out from the water. It broke into splinters with a loud crash.

The man and woman flailed and tried to swim to shore while being carried on by the chaotic flow. They quickly disappeared under the water's choppy surface.

The hunters' attention went to the boy. He was not helpless like his parents. He was not fearful. He struggled in the water, but with a fixed determination.

He held a rope, and while he bobbed toward the jutting rock, they could see him purposefully and skillfully tying the end into a large knot.

Just as he passed the boulder, the boy threw the rope over it. The knot slid into a crevice, and when it did, the rope pulled taut. The boy naturally swung to the rock's downstream side, and slowly—hand over hand—dragged himself up to, and finally onto, the boulder. There was a flat area on top where he curled up and lay still while the water churned around him.

The hunters now stood, their eyes fixed on the boy.

"He has strong Breathing Soul," the taller native said.

The other nodded and spoke up to be heard over the wind. "The Manetuwaks watch over him. You saw how he danced with the water. He is marked, that one."

They stood motionless, studying the boy on the rock, the wind whipping around their fur mantles. Then the hunters grabbed their bows, bags, and quivers and started down the long slope to the water. They would help the marked boy.

Part One

The Visitors

1609

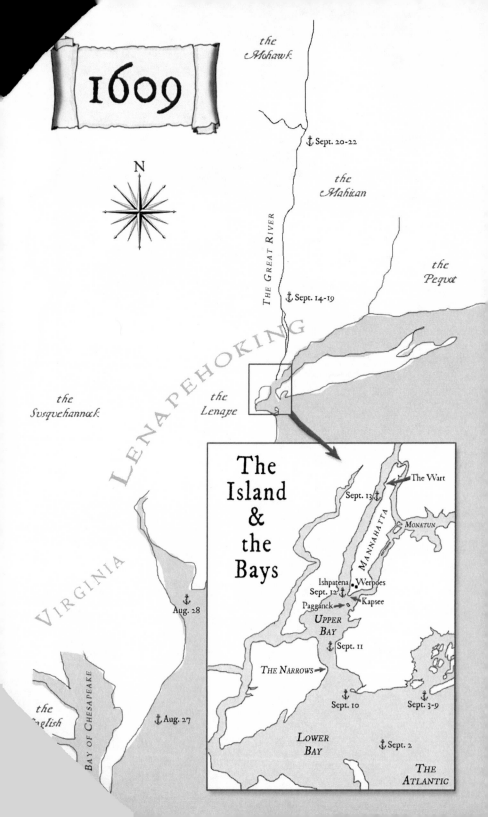

One

AH, THE DUTCH, HE MUSED AS HE INSPECTED THE CORRIDOR. Black and white tiles alternated in the pattern of a draughts board. And not a spot of dirt to be seen.

The floor was scrubbed and polished until it gleamed like one of the brass bells on his ships. It squeaked when he walked to the end window and looked down at the cobbled street. Also well scrubbed. And smelling of the strong soap they used to keep the vermin and plague away in Amsterdam. Not like his London streets. There, they hosted a daily gauntlet of trash, filth, and human waste one tried his best to avoid.

No, these people were clean. Neat. Practical.

A tall door creaked open and a small man with spectacles leaned into the hall and announced, "They will see you now."

The meeting room of the Dutch East India Company, the world's first and largest joint-stock corporation, was as sober as the men seated at the long wooden table. There was no gilt, no silk on the walls, no vaulted ceiling painted with cherubs. It was all business. And business he was here to do.

With his interpreter, he sat on one end of the table while the eight directors of the Amsterdam Chamber of the Lords Seventeen crowded around the other. He wore his most subdued doublet and breeches, yet he still felt like a peacock compared to the somber directors in their long black coats with the incongruous white, lacy collars. These no-nonsense men would

5

decide the next phase of Henry Hudson's life.

The greetings and pleasantries were thankfully short, and they proceeded quickly to the matter at hand. The group's slender, pale leader glanced at his co-directors and back to him, tipping his head slightly. "We have decided to support your April expedition."

He handed the contract and sailing instructions to the man with spectacles, who walked to Hudson and placed them on the table before him.

Hudson held in a smile while glancing over the contract's two short pages. The ship, route, men, provisions, and his payment were all in order. Months of negotiations had come to this. He would be making his third trip to find an alternative water passage to the Indies. One way or another, he would secure his fame on this voyage. But he wondered—

"I see no mention of trading, Christianizing, or the claiming of land."

The director pulled at his pointed beard and glowered. "Meneer Hudson, we are only interested in your finding the fast route to the South Sea, to Cathay. That is our goal here. We are not interested in other adventures, or in settling colonists, or in Christianizing the Wilden, the savages." He fixed his stare on him. "Your task is to find us the new passage over Russia and report back earliest when you have done so. Are we understood about this?"

Hudson looked into the older man's sharp blue eyes and nodded. "We are." As he signed the contract, he knew that once on the water and underway, *he* would be the master and captain of the ship, and *he*—the most experienced explorer of the North Atlantic—would decide how this voyage would proceed.

▶◀

The 80-ton *Half Moon*, a three-master with six sails and a crew of 16, including his 18-year-old son John, sat at anchor in the bleak, gray harbor at Novaya Zemlya in the Arctic Ocean. It was now mid-May, more than four weeks into the voyage, and it was obvious to everyone on board that the passage over the top of the world to the Indies would not be found this way. The ice ahead was solid, and the howling winds cut through their clothes like a frozen knife.

Hudson smirked to himself. So much for the Temperate Arctic Theory proposed by the "experts" back in Amsterdam and London who had never gotten their feet wet.

The men were huddled around the hot stove in the ship's cramped forecastle when he entered. He knew if he wanted to change direction and sail west to America, the decision would have to be made now. And he wanted—no, he needed—the crew's consent. It was essential they be on his side, excited and willing to take on whatever lay ahead.

Ignoring the potent smell of men who hadn't bathed in the weeks since they left Amsterdam, he started.

"I have proposals to present you. For the relief of our current situation."

"Would that include sailing straight ahead into the ice?" an English swabbie yelled out to much amusement. The crew, though a mix of Dutch and English, all shared the same seaman's humor and a basic understanding of each other's languages.

"No, I have a better idea," Hudson said calmly. "Two, in fact."

"Let's hear 'em," shouted another. "I vote against freezing to death."

"Aye to that," murmured several others.

Hudson carefully watched the men's reactions while he laid out the two options. The first was sailing southwest and across the North Atlantic to find a top passage through or around the new continent. The second was to travel farther south to Virginia in search of a mid-America passage, which Captain

John Smith had hinted at in one of their letter exchanges.

Neither option included returning directly to Amsterdam. He was counting on a conniving crew that would not want to head straight back to port with nothing to show for it.

Every man knew a longer voyage would present opportunities for plundering and thieving, whether or not they reached the Orient. And all knew their ship was well fitted with armaments and munitions to do the kind of raiding that was on their minds.

"Which way is warmer?" asked one of the Dutchmen, only half in jest. Many of the Dutch had already sailed the long way around Africa to the Indies and were used to warmer climes. But it was the offer of stolen booty that would surely make the difference.

"The southern route is warmer," said Hudson with a small smile and a lingering pause to indicate his preference. "And with more time for whatever may come our way."

"And what might that be, Master?"

"A bit of trading, no doubt," he said with the immobile face of a card player. "There are Wilden along that shore, I'm told."

The crew laughed loudly in unison. They knew from experience and from numerous dockside tales about the Indians of the New World who could be stripped of their furs. And their women.

One of the English crew members stood and announced, "Aye, Sir. I'm one for going to see the wild men, the savages." The others noisily joined in with their affirmations.

Hudson scanned his ragged, smelly crew and gave a quick nod. "Good. The southern route it is then. To the savages!"

Two

Corn Planting Moon

The sun was long asleep, but Dancing Fish made his way up the flank of the ridge with little effort. Light from the moon's half disk shone strongly enough for the boy-turned-man to see the twisting path ahead.

He finally stood at the edge of the cliff and looked down at the black water of the pond. The grip of fear was gone. He had worked hard against it since the drownings.

A cool breeze nipped his skin, and he smelled the smoke from many fires. Dense forest ringed the area, and in the dim light he could make out the longhouses and wigwams that clustered in the clearing near the pond's southern shore. This was their summer camp on the island—Werpoes. Where the families of the Manahate band had come for all his 15 sun cycles.

He knew the large pond well. Fed by an underground stream, it flowed out both north and east through marshy channels to the two rivers. Xitkwe was its name. Deep Water. No one, not even High Limb, had touched its bottom lying in mystery beneath the high point where he stood. Tonight, he would try again. He would satisfy his curiosity and be the first.

The last frost was behind them, but the pond kept its memory of winter well into the corn planting season. The chilly water would help him remain under longer, slowing his heartbeat. He would reach his goal tonight. He felt the truth of that.

Standing motionless at the edge, clad only in his short

apron and starting to shiver, Dancing Fish looked up to the two bright stars that were his departed parents. They winked back at him. Then he spoke out to his Manitto—his Guardian Spirit—the silvery perch. "Fish, watch over me while I dive and enter the deep water. Assist me in my small quest."

He took three long breaths to fill his belly then raised his hands over his head until they touched, fingers clasped together. He flexed his legs and took another short inhale of air.

Then Dancing Fish leapt into the night.

He plunged into the water head-first, his hands ripping a hole through the surface that his body slid through. When his downward movement slowed, he started the undulating motion he had seen dolphins make in the great waters.

He pinched his nose and relieved the pressure in his ears as he sank deeper and deeper. His eyes were open but all was black. He felt only the cold water pressing harder and harder while he descended. He had a strong need to breathe but pushed it aside.

A worm of doubt wriggled in his mind. Then his hands dug into the stiff mud of the bottom. He was surely ten or twelve body lengths under the water, where no one had been before. He thanked his Manitto and looked up to the surface. He could see the Corn Planting Moon as a small, bright spot in the clear water.

Positioning his feet, he grabbed a handful of mud and pushed hard against the bottom to start his ascent.

He finally emerged from the depth and into the night air, which he took in with long, deep gulps. With his mouth wide in a smile, he slowly kicked his way to the bank, his head toward the winking stars. He had done it.

And he was not alone.

"What are you doing?" demanded his new father, standing at the edge of the pond.

Dancing Fish could hear the irritation in his voice.

Two Winds grabbed him roughly by the arm, yanked him

out of the water, and pulled him toward the longhouse.

▶◀

Dancing Fish sat by the central fire wrapped tightly in his bea-
verskin cloak. He watched Kong, his dog, happily gnawing on a
rabbit bone while he soaked in the warmth of the smoky longhouse they shared with five other families. Drinking his flower
tea, his teeth soon stopped their uncontrollable clicking.

Rock, his best friend, poked him with his elbow. "You really
did it? You touched the bottom?"

Dancing Fish nodded. "Give me your hand." He placed
some of the still-wet mud into Rock's chubby palm. "Here's
your proof."

Rock massaged the mud with his fingers. "Amazing" was all
he could say.

Dancing Fish felt great pride in his accomplishment. But
not his new father, who rarely approved of anything he did.

"Why do you have to be different?" Two Winds asked as
he added more wood to the fire, then sat next to him on the
reed mat. Yellow Flower, his aunt and now his new mother, sat
nearby, watching but not saying a word.

"No one dives into Xitkwe at night," he said. "It's dangerous, and it serves no purpose. It is not done."

Dancing Fish was about to reply with a tart tongue, but he
held back. What was the point? Here was the beginning of the
same conversation he had had with his new father since they
adopted him after the accident that had turned his parents into
stars.

The drownings had been seven sun cycles past, and he still
felt apart from his new family, standing on the outside. This
man was nothing like his real father, who had encouraged him
to think his own thoughts. Here, with a new father and mother,
and with most others in the band, what was done was always

what had been done. There were rules that had to be followed, roles to be observed.

But he wanted more out of life. He was curious about everything. Why did the geese fly in the shape of an arrowhead? Why did the tulip tree grow straight but oaks not? Why did the Great River flow backward at times?

He swallowed his private thoughts and answered Two Winds. "I'm sorry. I just wanted to do it. To see what the bottom was like. To be the first one."

A new voice joined the group. "Being the first one is not always the best way," said Hard Stick, the clan's Matron and his grandmother. People made room for her while she eased herself down to sit on a stump. She leaned heavily on her cane for support, but her old bones still crackled.

"The first down the path in war is always killed," she said. "The first fish in the net is always eaten. Do you see?"

"Yes, Matron," he said. He didn't agree, but it was not his place to argue with the Sakima of the band.

Another took his seat by the fire. "Don't be so hard on the boy, all of you."

It was Thundercloud, his uncle. A great man who was the War Chief of the band. As his dead mother's brother, he was in charge of his upbringing. But his new father, who had no children, also felt responsible. So the two men were joined in raising him to be a man.

"Some are chosen to follow a different path," Thundercloud said. "Look at me, boy," he commanded.

He faced the well-muscled man with the plucked head of a warrior, his skin glistening from the sunflower oil. "I'm no longer a boy," Dancing Fish said stiffly.

"Yes, yes, we know. But you were only recently made a man, so you're not yet fully formed. There is much you don't know. However—"

He felt the eyes of the important man piercing his flesh,

probing, searching.

"Do you believe in the Spirits that influence all things?" the War Chief asked. "The Manetuwaks? The Two Souls? Tell me truthfully."

He paused for only a moment. "Yes. But I also believe in the will of the mind. A mind that is free."

He heard murmurs and Thundercloud clapped his hands to silence them. Then he leaned toward him. "Have you been chosen, Nephew? Has the Great Spirit Kishelemukong spoken to you? Or the Lesser Spirits? Have they blessed you with special dreams or visions?"

Dancing Fish knew why his uncle was asking this. After he had survived the deadly waters that drowned his parents, many started calling him "the marked boy" when the story was told by the two hunters who returned him to the village. Which meant that some thought he was a sorcerer. That he was aided by Matantu, the Evil Creator, who invaded his Dreaming Soul. They whispered about him.

But others thought of him as lucky, brave, and special. Someone who had seen the very face of death and pushed it away in the swift currents. They listened to what he said.

He answered his uncle firmly, "In my dreaming worlds, I am different. I don't know if it's because of the Great Spirit or the Sky World, but I am always different from others."

"And in your wakeful world, too, Dream Maker," his new father said, shaking his head. "We are not individuals here. We are a band. We work together."

Ants also work together, he thought. And I am not an ant.

Three

HUDSON POURED HIMSELF ANOTHER BRANDY. HE SAT IN THE Master's cabin, writing in his log, thinking about the voyage so far. They had been four months at sea, the last three bouncing down the coast of America controlled by the French, moving ever southward.

The melancholia had descended upon him again, heavy and dark. The smallest setback or failure seemed to set it off. He wasn't sleeping, and the isolation and sadness were overpowering. *Fear and sorrow without just cause*, he wrote in his log.

He drank the warm aqua vitae potently infused with blue borage flowers he kept in a small tin. These two friends soothed his spirits and allowed him a brief escape from the worries. But he was careful to stay in his cabin. He couldn't let the men see this weakness, which came and went like a summer storm.

This was now a renegade mission once he had turned around in Russia. Although the crew was initially supportive, he could see the tension and apprehension building among them. Having few prizes or plunder after so long sailing must have been the trigger of the earlier episode.

They were anchored off the French territory of Norumbega when two canoes of natives appeared, intent on trading. Unfortunately, the *Half Moon* had little to trade and turned them back. Hudson had asked, but the directors in Amsterdam thought it unnecessary to stock the ship for such a circumstance.

The Dutch, of course, had no idea he would end up on the other side of the Atlantic. But now they were meeting Indians almost every time they anchored, and these natives were used to trading.

So on this occasion, after the natives had been refused, a group of the crew, led by ship's mate Robert Juet, quietly rowed to shore in the small boat with muskets and attacked the Indian village. They killed and injured several of the naturals and took away what they could carry. When questioned by Hudson later on the ship, Juet pointed to all the furs and French goods taken from the pillaged community. "Now we have something to trade with," he said triumphantly, holding up a French knife for all to see.

Hudson understood the motivation but was surprised by the brutality. He would have to watch Juet and the others closely. Juet had a clear disdain for the savages, perhaps due to his father's death at the hands of some years earlier in Jakarta. And this was a cause of concern, for they were sure to meet many more natives as the voyage proceeded.

▶◀

They finally reached their southernmost goal when they came to the wide entrance of the bay of Chesapeake on August 18. Before them was the Kings River where Englishmen were struggling to survive at the Jamestowne settlement. But they spent little time there before sailing north again along the coast.

Hudson was more interested in the large section of shoreline that had been virtually ignored by both the French and English—although there were rumors of some having scouted the region. Sitting roughly between latitudes 37 and 41, this was the area of exploration on which Hudson now set his sights. He felt he could be close to something important.

On September 2, after days of frustration probing bays and

fighting contrary currents, the *Half Moon* steered near land at latitude 40 and found a large body of water with a great stream flowing from it. Hudson could see the distant entrances to three rivers that caused the surge, and he anchored to the northeast of a sand spit that guarded the bay's entrance. While he waited out the night—listening to the booming of waves tumbling into shallow water and the creaking of the ship as it rolled with the swells—Hudson's skin tingled with anticipation. Was this the head of the passage he sought?

A thick mist came with no wind at first light, and they could do nothing but sit at anchor. Finally, near ten in the morning, a south breeze flushed away the fog, and the ship heaved to the north and across the mouth of the broad bay. By afternoon, they were sheltered inside an inlet, surrounded by a magnificent forest of oak and pine trees. A strong pine scent perfumed the air, while birds of all descriptions clamored and flew from limb to limb.

No sooner had the ship anchored when the naturals came alongside in their dugout canoes. They seemed frightened and anxious at first, but before long were eager to trade their oysters and tobacco leaves for a few knives and the glass beads the ship now had on board.

As trade items were passed up and down, Hudson noticed how strong and healthy the natives looked, much more so than his own crew. Their teeth were straight and white, their muscles firm and full of strength. They were dressed in the skins of animals, although barely. Their bodies were mostly naked and exotically painted and tattooed.

Old men and boys, and all women, wore their black hair long—some straight, others braided. Men of fighting age had their hair completely shaved, leaving only a single lock or a crest on the crown of the head.

Hudson stayed at anchor another day for repairs and trading, but on the fifth he went ashore with several from the ship and took a walking tour of this new land. They were immediately met by a group of Indian men, women, and children who stood in a large crowd and sang at the top of their voices in the strangest of rhythms.

"Such a racket they make," Hudson whispered to his first mate Cornelis Klock, a Dutchman who shared some of Juet's opinions.

"They do, Master," said Klock. "But what of the passage? Do we proceed?"

"Tomorrow. We'll start our explorations in earnest."

Four

DANCING FISH COULD SEE THE RIPENING MOON SLIDE PAST the dark smoke hole at the top of the longhouse. It had been a long day of squash harvesting, and the clans had come to the fire and eaten their fill of roasted deer meat and stewed succotash. Now they drank their tea and smoked their pipes.

He sat close to the fire, holding his tea in one hand and scratching behind Kong's ears with the other. He observed those around him.

In the group were the ones he both loved and disliked the most. His strongest feelings were for Willow, who sat to one side. Her striking oval face framed shadowy, dark eyes and generous lips shaped like a bow. Her black hair was tied in a single braid that reached to her long, muscular legs. Her lightly greased skin shone in the flickering firelight.

Then there was High Limb, of his own Turtle Clan. Named for his height—and his arrogance—he had been initiated into manhood at the same time as Dancing Fish and Rock. High Limb was the Matron's grandnephew and therefore a distant cousin. But he felt superior, and he constantly intimidated and bullied the others when he could get away with it. With his hair singed off in the manner of a warrior—a distinction he was still in training for—he caught Dancing Fish's eye and made kissing motions with his puckered mouth. Dancing Fish pantomimed a favorite obscenity and turned away.

The stories soon started, and many took their turns telling them. This was a favorite time for Dancing Fish, especially when the stories told of daring feats or of strange people in far-off lands.

He asked Long Pipe, the Holy Seer, "Elder, will you tell the story of the Seven Fires?"

The Seer, a frail wisp of a man, known for his special insights more than his words, scowled. "We only talk of the Seven Fires Prophecy in winter. The story is too important."

Dancing Fish pressed. "Elder, if it's important, how can it be told too often?"

He saw Long Pipe frown and look to Hard Stick, who finally pulled on her cane to stand.

"Alright. As your Sakima, I will tell the story of the Seven Fires," she said.

Hard Stick wavered after the effort of standing. He noticed how old she looked. Her face was furrowed with deep lines, her eyes clouded and watery like oysters in their opened shells. Her white hair hung down in two long braids that started to swing as she began to walk around the communal fire in the longhouse. People moved out of her way to clear a path while she dodged the sacks of dried meat and grain that hung from the ceiling poles.

After retelling the old story of how their land was formed from the back of a giant turtle that rose from the sea, she explained the era of the Seven Fires. How the Lenni Lenape people—the Real People—closely watched time. They measured it by the position of the sun, the stages of the moon, and the passing of the seasons.

"The ancient ones developed a calendar to warn the People of Lenapehoking and our band—the Manahate—of things to come," she said, pausing to rest. "This calendar came in the form of a medicine wheel or round hoop. There were cycles inside of cycles. Fourteen sun cycles for each of the four

19

directions. Fifty-six cycles was a life walk, the age of an Elder. And the Creator Spirit, Kishelemukong, granted two life walks or 112 sun cycles for each Fire. Seven Fires stretched end to end—784 sun cycles. So became the prophecy of time for the Real People."

Dancing Fish swiftly worked out the numbers in his head for confirmation.

She continued. "And a new prophet appeared for each Fire to foretell what the People should watch out for and what they should do.

"We are now in the Fourth Fire," she said, walking ever more slowly with the full attention of all who heard her gravelly voice. "The Fourth is the central Fire. The one directly opposite the starting point of the wheel more than 300 sun cycles ago. The Fourth Fire is also special because there were two prophets who delivered the message. Like the good and evil brothers, the two prophets told two different stories, one good, one bad."

"I'm the good prophet and Dancing Fish is the bad," High Limb blurted out, cackling.

"Silence!" demanded Hard Stick, whipping her cane around and cracking it over High Limb's knees. He yelped and everyone laughed.

Stupid oaf, Dancing Fish thought, catching Willow's eye and playful smile.

Hard Stick continued her hobbling walk. "The first prophet warned: *You will know the future of our people by the Visitors from the East. If they come wearing the face of brotherhood, then there will come a time of peace and prosperity for all. These Visitors will carry no weapons and come only bearing their knowledge and a handshake, and they will join us in a mighty nation.*"

She stopped to straighten her back and bend it to crack its bones. "But there was a second prophet. He said: *Beware if the Visitors from the East come wearing the face of death. If they come with weapons of war and filled with hatred, take heed. Their hearts may be full of greed for the riches of our land. If they are indeed our brothers, let them prove it. Do not accept them in total trust."*

No one made a sound after hearing this. Finally, Dancing Fish asked the question everyone was thinking. "When will we see the Visitors?" He had heard talk of strange men or Spirits— he knew not which—visiting Lenapehoking in the time of his parents and earlier, but getting any details was like water slipping through his fingers: nothing to hold onto.

Hard Stick focused on him and nodded. "We are at the point of prediction," she said. Supported by her cane, she looked over the group and moved her right hand across all of them as she turned in a circle. "We are exactly at the midpoint of the Fourth Fire. We must pay attention to the warnings of the prophets and be on guard for these Visitors."

She hesitated when her gaze met his. "Dancing Fish, can you do something for me?"

"Yes?" he said, curious.

"When you set your Dreaming Soul free tonight, make a memory of it. And in the morning, tell us of it. I feel it will be an important dream."

Low talking filled the longhouse. The families then slowly moved to their partitioned areas for sleep. Remembering his dream instruction, Dancing Fish lay on his bed of reed mats covering fresh hemlock boughs, pulled a deerskin over him, and was asleep within moments.

He had several dreams, most of a minor kind with little importance. But the final one left him panting and sweating. And worried.

▶◀

The smell of dandelion tea opened Dancing Fish's eyes, and he looked up to see not only his new father and mother but also Thundercloud and Hard Stick. They all stared at him.

21

"Tell me about your dream," the Sakima instructed, leaning on her cane.

Dancing Fish propped himself up against one of the poles supporting the longhouse and sipped his tea. He looked at Yellow Flower, his new mother. She signaled with her eyes and he began.

"I dreamed I was swimming with my Manitto, the perch. We were happy in the water." He paused and shuddered, thinking of what came next.

"Continue," Hard Stick said.

He saw it all again. "Suddenly, there was a bird. It was white. And very big. With a mouth full of teeth." He could feel his lips trembling and bit into them. "The huge bird grabbed my Manitto and, and . . ."

Yellow Flower reached over and touched his arm. "Don't stop," she said. "It'll be fine."

He took a deep breath to still his trembling. "The bird started eating my Manitto. There was blood everywhere. Then, no perch."

Tears blurred his eyes. Then he saw many more people standing and staring at him. No one moved, no one spoke.

Five

On September 6, after giving the morning's church service, Hudson watched as quartermaster John Colman, his friend and most trusted officer, rowed west in the shallop with four others. They were to measure depth soundings and take stock of the land and the water. Juet and Klock stayed behind on the ship while a blazing sun rose into a cloudless blue sky.

The boat finally returned the next morning from the opposite direction. And a shocked Hudson was shaken to see that it bore the dead body of Colman and two injured crew members. As soon as he had seen to the wounded and to sheltering Colman's corpse from the sun, a saddened Hudson had the two uninjured sailors brought to him on the ship's main deck to determine just how this could have happened. Juet and Klock looked on.

"We followed land west and then north to a fine opening between two headlands," one of the Dutchmen said in his halting English while he drank water. "Pass through opening, we find good depths for ships. Then we move northwest and find new river. It takes us to large bay and see also marshes and many flowers. We follow along moving north. After many hours we turn back. Then they come."

"Who and how many?" Hudson asked.

Amplified with miming, the man told how there were two canoes full of savage warriors. They had paint on their faces, feathers in their strange hair crests, and clubs and bows in their hands. The two groups started with talking but it soon escalated to shouting, and then they were fighting. Though outnumbered, the ship's men had long pikes and muskets, and they used them for defense while they retreated by the same way they came.

"Who initiated the hostilities?" Hudson asked the man.

"They did, Master."

"You are sure?"

"Yes. The savages are skillful with bows. Two of us are struck with arrows. Then Meneer Colman stands to fire musket, and one arrow goes through neck. He falls and is bleeding. Soon, he lies still."

The Dutchman explained that the natives finally fell back, and the crew rowed with all their strength to escape.

Hudson asked, "Why didn't you return directly to the ship?"

"Can not fight strong flow coming from north through opening. So we drift until work back to ship. All night."

Juet, with his face deeply scarred by the pox, pressed forward and said to him, "You see. We durst not trust these savages. They are barbarous."

Hudson, who was prone to give the natives the benefit of the doubt, was now unsure. He was troubled by this account, and especially by the death of his friend. This left only three Englishmen on board: Hudson, his teenage son, and Juet, another official voyage chronicler. The dynamics and balance of the crew had changed.

That afternoon they carried Colman's body to shore for a proper burial. While they made the short trip, Hudson grappled with the loss and what had happened. Here he was at the entrance of the most promising location for a mid-continental passage, his primary goal. And that created a sense of wonder and excitement in him.

At the same time, the suspicions by Juet and others about

the natives were evidenced in the slain man wrapped in a soiled cloth at his feet. Colman was the first crew member in all the voyages he had captained to die.

As the boat carrying the man's remains nosed onto the shore's sandy beach, Hudson hoped that this would be the last of the calamities to befall them.

▶◀

Dancing Fish emerged from the trees at the rocky point. The sun was two fingers high, and the wind was fresh and strong from the water. He had left Kong back at the village—he liked to explore Kapsee by himself.

Kapsee Rocks, at the southern tip of the island where the Great River and the eastern waterway joined, was his favorite place. Standing on the shore and looking south, the Great Lake spread out before him. The hump of Pagganck islet rose closely by to his left, and in the distance were lands that were home to more tribes and bands. He saw these people when they came to trade around the point where the sun went to sleep.

Behind him rested the fullness of the island: Mannahatta— Island of Many Hills. It usually took two or three suns to walk its length, although he had once run it in four fingers on a dare.

"*Hè-yó!* Are you here to see me or to fish?"

He turned to find Owl standing no more than three bodies away. He had not seen or heard him approach; he had just appeared. Wearing only a hint of a man's apron covering, Owl was thin with ribs showing and with graying hair that hung like ropes to his waist.

"Both," Dancing Fish said, jumping across the rocks to join the old man.

He put his fishing gear down and handed Owl his gift: a small bowl of corn mush flavored with honey and dried berries. "Your favorite!"

25

Owl promptly jabbed his fingers into the mush and began licking them. "Mmmm. Sweet hominy is an excellent gift for a hungry Elder," he said, smiling and slurping at the same time.

Dancing Fish watched his friend and mentor eat the delicacy with delight. His skin was dark and wrinkled like a dried plum, but his eyes glittered like a child's. What was he: six tens of age? More?

Owl was a mystery. He was an outcast who lived as a hermit at Kapsee in the warm season and farther north when the cold winds blew. Dancing Fish knew only that he'd once been Holy Seer of the band, replaced by Long Pipe before Dancing Fish was born. There were rumors about his prophecies no longer coming true. A Seer who saw nothing, they said. So now he was avoided. No one visited him or asked for his counsel. Except Dancing Fish, who had struck up an immediate bond with the man. They had spent many hands of sun on the rocks or in his rundown hut talking about the riddles of life. Only his father in the stars had understood the ideas inside the head of Dancing Fish the way Owl did.

Owl handed the bowl back. "Thank you, young perch. But if you're going to fish, you need to go. No use standing here talking to an ancient man." He sniffed the briny air while he moved his head in an arc. "Yes, the Game Keeper for the fish will be good to you today. I foresee it. Go bring me something for my dinner before you leave."

▶◀

Dancing Fish treasured the changing colors, sounds, and tastes at Kapsee. This was water usually on the move. Sometimes waves rose up and crashed on the rocks with a roar. Other times, like now, it was calm and smooth. And with the tides, the water alternated from very salty to sweet. Kapsee Point was a good place to fish.

He sat on a flat rock for the blessing. Because fish were also creatures of the Great Spirit and no less so than any others, including himself, Dancing Fish spoke to his Manitto, the perch, and to the Keepers of the Game. He asked that the fish surrender themselves to him. He promised to take only the fish he needed and to give thanks for each one. And he would take no perch.

Seeing the tide high, he went to a shallow pool between two large rocks and the shore. He rolled out the long net he had designed with thin strips of elm in a special criss-cross pattern. After attaching each end of the net to stakes he drove into the sand on both sides of the pool entrance, he walked along the net to make sure its bottom was tight against the sand, using flat stones to hold it where there were gaps. When the tide fell and the fish wanted to leave, the largest ones would be trapped but the smallest could escape and grow. And because it took time for the water to drop, he could do other things.

Next came the lines. He hung three from the top of large boulders and baited them with clam. Each line ended with a straight piece of short bone—a gorge—tied at a groove cut around its center. He had improved on the traditional design with special hooked points on each end. When a hungry fish came to take the clam, it would swallow the gorge, and the tool would open and stick across its throat. The fish was then caught and only needed to be pulled in.

After net and lines were set and ready, it was time for him to enjoy the water.

Most of the band were afraid of these churning waters, just as he had been after the accident. At first, he could think only of how his parents had died in the dangerous currents at Monatun while he had not. They had disappeared, and he had found himself alone, huddled and shivering on top of a large rock. There remained only splinters of canoe bobbing around him, but there was no sign of his mother and father. They were now Sky Beings among the stars.

At first, he was terrified to be in the open water. He wouldn't go close to it for the whole season of planting. But he slowly forced himself to get in. He had always loved water, so he had to overcome this fear.

He started simply by wading in the stream that led from the pond. Just getting his legs wet. Then sitting with the water to his chest while the gentle current flowed around him. Then floating. Then swimming. And, when he was ready, diving down into the pond, and finally entering the wide waters at Kapsee. It had taken seven sun cycles, but he had done it.

Waiting for his fish, he swam away from the rocks and drifted on his back. He looked up at a blue sky speckled with white clouds like the back of a young fawn. But this image reminded him of his dream of the white bird, so he turned over to his stomach.

He let out his air and sank under the water. He watched the sun bounce its white ripples over the sand that sat in silent waves between the rocks. This was the dancing light for which he was named.

Multicolored perch soon appeared and darted back and forth in front of him. These were his Guardians, and he moved and mingled contentedly with them.

He played in the shallow waters until the sun was high and warm on his back. It was time to go.

Returning to the pool, he saw many fish thrashing against the net. He grabbed the largest ones, gave his thanks for each, and added them to the deerskin bag slung over his back. Then he loosened the net and let the others—and all the perch—escape, watching them wiggle away.

Dropping the shoulder bag, which was now heavy with fish, he moved to the hand lines and saw that two of them were taut and swinging wildly. These were good-sized fish.

He climbed to the top of the first boulder and pulled in the line, hand over hand. A large striped bass was struggling at the end of it. He spoke to it with respect and thanked it for its surrender. Then he smacked it against the hard rock and threw it onto the shore near the bag.

He jumped to the next boulder and was pulling in the line when he abruptly stopped. Off in the distance, just to the right of Pagganck, sat what looked like a white bird.

He froze. Was this the white bird of his dream?

The bird grew steadily larger as he watched, open-mouthed.

Then he dropped the line, ran to where his fish waited, and turned around for another look.

It's coming this way!

Six

"North by northeast, if you please," Hudson shouted to the helmsman stationed under the deck directly beneath his feet. The man, a Dutchman, stood at the whipstaff with only a small opening to see forward, so he relied on the captain's commands for turning the rudder.

The ship moved onto a reach, its sails set square to the south wind that blew warm and steady, whistling through the openings between the sails and the yards. The day before, they had passed the two headlands and the narrow passage Master Verrazzano had described 85 years prior. Now, in undiscovered territory, Hudson could see they were fully in an upper bay, more clearly defined than the shapeless lower one. And it was a bay such as he had never seen before.

"It's almost circular, like an amphitheatre," marveled his son, who stood by his side. "As beautiful as an open sea."

"And at 20 fathoms, almost as deep," Hudson added, unable to disguise his pleasure at what he was witnessing. "And smell the fresh sweetness of the air."

Hudson clapped John on the back while seabirds careened above. "It's a good day for discovering, wouldn't you say?" He felt giddy with enthusiasm.

Porpoises jumped on both sides of the ship as he spied the mouth of a vast river dead ahead. With the sun directly behind them, he could see a line of thick, green forest flanking both sides of the river, with hills climbing in the distance to meet the brilliant blue sky of midday.

"Remember this twelfth day of September, John," Hudson said to his son without turning from the sight. "I believe that history is about to change."

▶◀

Dancing Fish ran into the central meeting place, shouting.

"The white bird is coming!"

He was so frightened he had forgotten his fish and supplies, and even about Owl.

People came out of the longhouses, and soon his father, mother, and uncle circled him, telling him to calm down. Kong paid no attention and jumped up on him, happy to see his master. Thundercloud motioned for all to be quiet and listen. He signaled to Dancing Fish to speak just as Hard Stick limped her way to the front of the group.

"I was fishing at the Rocks and saw a white bird floating on the lake," he said, still catching his breath and pushing Kong down to quiet him.

All eyes were big and questioning. He caught Willow's worried look. Also Rock's. Even the arrogant High Limb seemed scared.

"The white bird was growing, and then I saw it was coming here."

The People were murmuring now.

"Is this the white bird of your dream?" Hard Stick asked, a look of amazement on her face.

"It could be." He was bewildered. "Yes, I think so." More murmurs, now louder.

Thundercloud said, "We'll send two runners to Kapsee to look." He pointed to two of the fastest and waved his hand at them. They ran off immediately.

He then turned to everyone. "We must be prepared for whatever news they bring. Go to your houses. Prepare your weapons and gather what you need to leave, if it comes to that. If this is nothing, then nothing is lost."

Before long, Dancing Fish heard the approaching footfalls. He ran out and saw the two runners breathing heavily, their hands on their knees. They were calling out to anyone who would listen.

"He is right!" one of the runners said, his eyes wide with alarm. "It's a great floating bird or a large floating house—from another world. And it's at the entrance of Mohicannituck and will surely float up it."

Mohicannituck was the Great River and Dancing Fish wanted to rush there to see, but Hard Stick spoke first. She raised her arms and then her voice to its loudest while everyone quieted.

"Real People of the rivers and the island," their Matron called out, her filmy eyes moving from person to person. "This may be a visit from Manitou, the Supreme Being. He is coming to favor us or to punish us. In either case, we must greet him correctly. We will go to our friends at Ishpatena where he'll shortly arrive. Prepare your best foods, put on your best skins and furs. Bring corn and tobacco for offerings.

"Hurry!"

▶◀

Ishpatena was a temporary settlement close to the Great River along a split and meandering stream known for its good-tasting trout. A small beach was set into a shallow cove there on the river. The narrow trail from Werpoes to Ishpatena ran between two hills, skirting the stream and the marshes on each side. That trail was now crowded with people, all talking and carrying their offerings for the visiting Manitou.

When Dancing Fish arrived at the beach, the sun was starting its downward journey. The singing and dancing had already begun, and corn and tobacco were stacked into several piles. Fires burned at intervals, and several dogs ran along the water's edge—Kong quickly joining them.

There must have been many tens of the People crowded onto the sandy beach. He saw Willow, who was with her family. She waved to him, but he noticed fear in her eyes.

Rock was with his family and High Limb with his. Both looked nervous. Then, at the far end of the beach, he spotted Owl, standing in the shadow of a tall pine. Of course, he would have seen the floating bird, too. And his curiosity would not allow him to stay away, although he would remain apart.

More runners came and spoke to Hard Stick and Thundercloud. Word soon spread that it was not a bird but more like a giant house or canoe. And it was filled with the strangest of beings.

Dancing Fish stood by his new mother and father and held their hands tightly in his. His father said to him, "These are the Visitors of the Prophecy. The time has come."

"Are they Spirits?" he asked.

"Whether Spirits or Spirit Men we shall see. But we'll soon know our fate."

At once, everything stopped when the giant came into view around the curve where the beach ended. Dancing Fish was astounded at the sight. It did look like a huge canoe, the size of several longhouses. There were large, white skins above and the color of wood below. He could see no paddles, yet the canoe still advanced slowly up the river.

And then he saw the Spirit Men. They had snow-like skin and thick hair on their faces. And their bodies were coated with strange coverings. They moved about like men, but they were like no men he had ever seen before. The Fire Prophecy was truly upon them.

The People were agitated. Some were singing, others chanting, some merely sitting with open mouths.

Thundercloud directed everyone to make a large semicircle. Then he shouted out to a few to join him and Hard Stick: his father, Long Pipe, and the minor leader from Ishpatena. Thundercloud then pointed to Dancing Fish and beckoned him with his hand.

He could not believe he was being selected. But Yellow Flower pushed him and he ran to the circle. As he did, he caught the nasty look on High Limb's face.

Thundercloud, who was dressed in his finest skins, leaned in and whispered to him, "You deserve to be here. You spotted them, and also for your dream. Now we will see the meaning of it all."

The Great Canoe stopped when it drew even with the beach. Then a smaller canoe appeared and was lowered onto the river. Several of the strange Spirit Men climbed into it. Finally, another appeared. He wore a coat colored as red as the leaves that blazed in the Dying Moon. And he was a very important Spirit Man for only he stood while the others took to their paddles.

The red-cloaked man yelled out something and the canoe started moving. Toward them.

Seven

In the days following Colman's burial, the naturals had come up to the ship several times, and there had been no troubles. The entire crew was on alert for any strange behaviors, and although the natives remained shy and skittish, the visits were peaceful. Hudson knew that communications between such different people were easily mistaken for a threat or an insult. Now, approaching the natives on the beach, he would have to be vigilant.

With a bright sun at his back, he stood at the stern of the small boat facing the rowers, all of whom had their muskets and pikes ready. These were the best fighters on the ship. He was taking no chances with this encounter, even though he desperately hoped there would be no conflict.

Klock was directly in front of him to starboard and Juet to port, both looking over their shoulders as they rowed slowly toward the beach. Klock was his insurance against the Dutch majority crew overpowering the others and sailing away with the ship. He had heard and read the stories about this very thing happening to unlucky captains.

And by bringing Juet he would be able to observe his actions, whether for good or ill. On the ship remained his son and other sailors capable of defending the vessel against—or attacking—the natives, whichever might be needed.

While the men splashed their oars, Hudson studied the

large group of Indians who waited onshore. They were well organized with several of them standing in the center of a half-circle. These were the leaders he would greet in this first stop on the expansive river that held the most promise of success.

▶◀

The boat hissed to a halt in the sand, and at Hudson's command the men disembarked. A cool, fall breeze followed them up the beach.

The order of procession was specific. Hudson led, followed by Juet and Klock alongside each other. After a short gap, three more men followed with their muskets, and the remaining two waited by the shallop with pikes ready.

Three large bonfires roared and smoked as the men walked slowly through the thick sand.

Without warning, they were entangled with three of the native dogs running between their legs and yipping. But Hudson saw their tails wagging and wasn't concerned. He squatted down and held out his right arm, well protected by a thick coat sleeve. Each dog approached and sniffed, satisfied. One of the waiting Indians yelled something at the dogs, and they ran back into the crowd.

Hudson stood up and laughed as he caught the eye of the native. The man responded with his own laugh, and soon the entire assemblage on the beach was laughing about the dogs. A good beginning.

The advance group of three Europeans came up to the six Indians—four men, a boy, and an old woman—and stopped at a distance from them. Hudson was struck by how tall the men were. Even the boy, who appeared no more than 15 or 16 years, was taller than any of his party.

He looked directly at the commanding native, who was also the most elaborately decorated, with many necklaces and bracelets hanging from him. His smooth head bore a single, stiff crest of hair embellished with a bright red crown. Clearly a chief or leader of this tribe.

Hudson held up both hands at chest level and then crossed them over his heart, all the while smiling. He said, "We come in peace to greet you." This was his standard welcome. He turned his head to see Klock and Juet repeating the hand motions but without speaking.

The old woman said something to the regal native, who nodded and then signaled two of the others to step forward with him. The leader, holding a large sheaf of golden tobacco leaves and speaking in a language both guttural and musical, offered the tobacco to Hudson.

He took the tobacco and handed it to Klock. Then he reached into his coat pocket and pulled out a steel knife. A shadow of concern crossed the face of the chief, but it soon passed as Hudson turned the knife around and offered it butt first.

The man caressed the knife as the other natives crowded around him, talking in their alien way and reaching out to touch the blade.

Other gifts were then exchanged. Klock handed his counterpart a small mirror, and the man became instantly engrossed with it after he gave Klock a large bunch of fat grapes.

Then it was Juet's turn with the boy. Hudson noticed that the boy's long hair was ruddier in color than the other natives, and that he had striking amber eyes, different from the almost-black eyes of the others.

Juet, who refused to smile and was clearly unhappy about having to deal with a boy, pulled a single glass button from his pocket and hurriedly handed it over. The boy seemed stupefied by the simple object and had to be nudged by the chief before he reciprocated. He handed Juet a woven basket with three oysters nestled inside. The boy didn't speak and Juet accepted the oysters without emotion.

At a sign from the old woman, the entire Indian aggregation began singing in their discordant manner. Then the six natives clustered together and sat on the sand. The tall leader signaled for his men to do the same.

The oldest native, probably the medicine man, picked up a copper pipe, already smoldering, from the ground. He repeatedly sucked on it to bring up its flame.

While Hudson eyed the copper, the old native said some words as if in prayer, blew a puff of smoke in each of four directions, and then passed the pipe to the others on their side who added their own strange words before smoking. The pipe ended up with the chief—who then extended the ritual to Hudson.

Hudson inspected the pipe, curious about the metal and where it came from. But now was not the time to ask.

He took a few pulls of the strong tobacco and gave the pipe to Klock. It then went to Juet and back to Hudson, who returned the pipe to the leader, closing the circle. The ceremonial greeting was completed.

The chief stood and the mass singing stopped. He then looked expectantly at Hudson, who had already made up his mind.

Eight

DANCING FISH'S HEAD WAS SWIRLING WHILE THEY PADDLED their canoe to the giant floating house. Hard Stick and the Ishpatena leader would stay behind to keep control if anything happened to them.

Thundercloud explained that the red-coated man—their leader, their Sachem—had invited them onto the Great Canoe, which sat quietly in the river. Dancing Fish had paid close attention to these peculiar men he knew could not be Spirits. They were men, but oh so different!

"Are we in danger from these visitors?" he asked his father as they followed the hairy men who moved so slowly that only one or two of his group needed to paddle to keep pace.

"I don't think so," he said. "They showed good signs of giving and receiving. They greeted us in a respectful way."

Dancing Fish thought back to the other men standing behind on the beach. "But did they not have weapons? Those spears and sticks that shined. Does the prophecy not warn about that?"

Thundercloud answered, "You're right to notice these things, and for the Fire Prophecy to be on your mind. But I didn't see the look of death or hatred on these men, especially their Sachem. About the weapons, I can't say. Yes, some had long spears, but this may be normal with their kind. The other objects they carried are unknown to me. Let's follow the second prophet's words: *If they are indeed brothers, let them prove it. Do not accept them in total trust.*"

The Seer and Two Winds voiced their approval of this suggestion.

Thundercloud looked back at Dancing Fish. "Tell us, what is the gift you received?"

He still held it in one hand, even as he paddled. He examined it again. "It's round, thin, and very hard. Like a river rock but clear in color. I can almost see through it."

"What else?"

"Something very odd. In the middle are four small holes, two and two. They make a perfect square in shape."

"This is important," Thundercloud said. "What do you take this to mean?"

"I think it's showing us the Fourth Fire. That we are at the point of prediction of the prophecy. The holes are empty, and now will be filled."

"Very good," the War Chief said. "And they gave it to you, the youngest of us. The one who has more of his life in front than behind. Again, I believe you've been chosen, Dancing Fish."

With these words the four paddled silently, each with his own thoughts. The sun was sinking in front of them as they moved into the shadow of the vast floating house of the strangers. Soon they would know more.

▶◀

Dancing Fish looked around him in awe. Never had he seen such a canoe, or habitation, or whatever it was. It was made of pieces of chopped wood, expertly fitted. There were many strands of rope going in all directions and making slapping sounds in the wind.

The floor rose in levels both in front and behind him. And

he counted three very large poles, like trimmed trees, coming through the floors and rising to the sky. Across these poles were others and from these hung the white skins he had seen, but now they were bundled tight. He didn't understand their purpose but thought they must be wings so the house could move across the water.

Now there were more of the men watching them. All with the same light skin and with much hair covering their faces. They wore loose animal skins, but when he looked and touched—which they allowed him to do—he discovered they weren't animal skins at all but something very different.

He noticed that the hair on their heads was thick and long, and they had few markings or paint on their skin as his own people had.

And then there was their smell. It was a powerful odor, not pleasant. In fact, it was difficult to stand near any one of them for too long before he felt the need to move away and breathe clean air. He was sure that Spirits would not smell this bad, so he felt certain that these men were not such beings.

The red-coated leader, who was short and sturdy with blue eyes the color of a starling's egg, took them on a tour of the Great Canoe, for that is what Dancing Fish now determined it to be.

All of a sudden, a strange creature crossed their path. It looked like a small black puma with large yellow eyes, and the four of them instinctively shrank back from it. But the white Sachem just laughed and picked it up by the neck for them to see.

"*Cat,*" he said, pointing to it. "*Cat.*" The strange, hairy men all laughed at this.

▶◀

With the tour finished and the shadows growing longer, the

red-coated leader told them to wait as he and the others moved away to hold a conference. The thin and bony man who had given him the gift on the beach was angry and speaking sternly to their leader. The man kept looking in his direction with an unhappy face when he was not speaking, so Dancing Fish named him "Sad Face."

Finally, the white Sachem came to them. He talked to each in turn with his curious tongue and a smile that flashed inside its cocoon of hair. When he came to Dancing Fish, he stopped. He spoke directly to Thundercloud, Two Winds, and Long Pipe and made signs with his hands.

Slowly, Dancing Fish understood what the man was saying, and he was astonished. The man wanted to keep him on the Great Canoe!

Two Winds immediately objected when he understood, but Thundercloud put his hand on his arm and told him to be quiet. "Let's hear them. This could benefit us."

Through a combination of words and much hand-signing, it became clear the visitors wanted Dancing Fish to stay with them while they traveled up the Great River. They would teach him their tongue, and he, theirs. They would learn about each other in friendship. Then Dancing Fish would return.

"For how long?" his father asked, signing to make the question understood.

Their leader held up seven fingers and then again. Fourteen suns or one-half of a moon cycle.

Two Winds sucked in a breath in surprise, then signed, "How come back?"

The leader pointed to their canoe tied below and made it clear that someone would be able to bring him back down the river.

"There's too much danger for Dancing Fish moving through other lands," Two Winds said to Thundercloud, shaking his head. "He's barely a man."

"Don't worry," Long Pipe said, trying to calm him. "I foresee they'll be coming back soon. They can take this Great Canoe only so far up the river, and the Mahicans—who will soon hear about these visitors and want to trade with them—are friendly to us in this time of peace."

From what Dancing Fish had learned, this was true. He could return with the visitors, or he could make his own way back. He was skilled at traveling alone and living off the land.

"But what of our winter stores?" his father asked. "The harvest is not over, and there is still much to do with all hands needed. Even the men, if not hunting or fishing."

"I realize this," Thundercloud said, "but there is plenty of time with a full moon before the first frost."

The War Chief looked at their group with a serious face. "There is something special happening at this moment. I have already said that Dancing Fish has been chosen, and now we see it's coming true. The prophecy of the Fourth Fire is giving us a strong sign. If Dancing Fish is the tool for the first prophet to show us the way to brotherhood with these men, then we should allow it."

The red-coated Sachem came forward carrying something. It was a large pot, but very different from theirs. It was black and hard.

The leader handed it to Two Winds, who almost dropped it. "Heavy," he said in their tongue. He felt around its surface and knocked it with his knuckles. "This pot is not made from earth but from something much stronger." Then the new father of Dancing Fish smiled. "This will make our cooking easier."

"He is offering this pot as a gift for the use of Dancing Fish," Thundercloud said. "He's suggesting an exchange."

Thundercloud now turned to speak to him. "Do you wish to do this, Dancing Fish? Do you want to stay with these visitors for some time and help them, and also learn from them? I feel it is a good way, but you and your father must decide."

Dancing Fish looked to his father, who was still admiring the pot but then turned to his adopted son.

"Now you have your chance to be different," Two Winds said, his face softening. "To be the first on this new path. What do you want to do?"

He didn't hesitate. His heart and his head spoke clearly.

"I will do it."

▶◀

The red-coated Sachem shouted a string of instructions, and the hairy men moved with purpose over the Great Canoe. Some climbed the tall poles and others pulled on the many ropes.

Suddenly, one of the giant wings unfolded, snapping and thundering as the cool wind filled it. The Great Canoe jolted and started to move.

Watching the shore, Dancing Fish saw they were floating up the river, which was crossed by shafts of dimming light and late-day shadows. He now understood how the strangers used the same principle as the People by sometimes holding up a skin in their canoes when traveling a great distance. But that could not compare to what he was now feeling. It was like an entire mountain moving under him.

Standing at the back of the mighty canoe, he could still see his friends and kin on the beach. A small group—those closest to him—were waving. Kong, his hide the color of burnt wood, stood at the water's edge barking, his tail down in disappointment. He searched for Owl, but he was gone.

Earlier, when he had paddled back to say his goodbyes, his new mother had cried, and he surprised himself by fighting back his own tears. She gave him extra furs for sleeping, along with a bag full of food and a smoking pipe.

Leaving beautiful Willow and his friend Rock had not been easy. But Dancing Fish was getting his wish to be different—to see another world, a world of people not like him, a world that stretched his imagination. He was starting on a new adventure, one he could never have envisioned. And he felt both the excitement of the present and the fear of the future flowing through him.

When those on the shore grew too small to see, he walked back to the middle of the Great Canoe. He passed near the man he called Sad Face, who was staring at him. Dancing Fish saw that the man's face, pocked with deep marks and framed by thin strands of dull gray hair, showed more than sadness. His eyes were narrow and his mouth turned down.

When Dancing Fish offered a smile that was not returned, a chill passed through him and he kept moving. He felt for the round gift with the four holes he had hidden in a pouch sewn into his apron. He touched it and remembered the words: *If they are indeed brothers, let them prove it. Do not accept them in total trust.*

Nine

THEY SPENT THE NEXT WEEK MOVING UP THE RIVER, WHICH bent left and right but, in general, kept a consistent line north. The mid-September days offered brisk mornings, pleasant afternoons, and colorful twilights as they sailed on.

From his high position on the quarterdeck, Hudson noticed abundant land for agriculture in the fields and meadows that ran down the hillsides, right to the water's edge. He wrote in his log: *The land is the finest for cultivation that I have ever in my life set upon.*

Good progress was made on some days. On others, there was little forward motion. With inland waterways, as Hudson knew well, the winds were erratic. Sometimes from the south, which billowed the sails and moved the ship many leagues up-river. Other times, when the wind was stiff from the north, they would have to anchor and wait.

But there was much more than wind involved, and Hudson was surprised at the complexity of the tidal influence on this generous river. He had discerned that the entire area was a tidal estuary, and he understood the dynamics at work. The lunar cycle had its effect on the ebb and flood of spring and neap tides, which could move the ship even in the face of contrary or still winds.

Hudson was accustomed to the workings of the Thames estuary, but that river had long been charted and studied. Here, they were in unfamiliar waters with seemingly unique characteristics. He would have to pay close attention to the moon, the points of high and low tides, the strength of the currents, and the depth soundings while they moved upriver.

And then there was the important issue of salinity. This was of particular interest to him—someone looking for a passage to another sea.

All rivers had a mixture of salt and fresh water near their mouths, but the salt percentage gradually declined as one progressed upriver. If this were only a river, Hudson knew that after a certain point—the salt front—the water would be fresh, fed by streams, rains, or melting snowpack.

Hudson spent each morning tasting the water for its saltiness. He used an empty bottle partially filled with small stones for weight, which he tied to a long rope and flung over the side. The presence of salt far up the river suggested he wasn't sailing on a river at all but, rather, on a fjord or strait, which to him could only mean one thing: this channel connected to a saltwater sea. The South Sea. The Orient.

So far, there was a fine taste of salt in his mouth in the mornings.

▶◀

Hudson tried to set aside time each day to converse with the native boy, who was a quick learner. Within a few days, they had mastered a basic vocabulary of signs and common words for parts of the ship and for distance and time: *leagues, fathoms, days, weeks, seasons*. The boy's name had something to do with fish, so that's what he called him—*Fish*. And he would be called *Master Hudson* in return.

They were at anchor this day and sat on the steps leading to the quarterdeck. A hint of light still held in the western sky. The air was cooler with each sunset as autumn approached, and the smell of wood smoke strayed in from unseen native fires on the land.

The boy wore his indecent breechcloth that barely covered his male parts. It was a single length of animal skin that passed between his thighs and over a thin belt, leaving square flaps hanging down both in front and back. To this, when the air chilled, he added skin leggings and a thin cloak of animal hide that hung over his broad shoulders.

The fading light made Fish's amber eyes glow. With his long hair—more reddish-brown than black—falling loosely onto his back, he was a handsome young man.

He had brought his copper-clad pipe as requested, and Hudson held it in his hands. "On the beach," he began, using signs while he spoke slowly, "we smoked from a copper pipe like this." He patted it with his finger.

The boy bobbed his head with what he hoped was comprehension.

"What is this metal? We call it *copper*. How do you say it?" He touched the copper again.

Fish looked puzzled, trying to repeat the words.

Hudson rubbed the copper and lifted his hands in a question. "What is it?"

Fish understood. *"Machasena,"* he said in his alien language as best Hudson could understand it.

The boy asked awkwardly, *"Cupper?"*

Hudson nodded and smiled. "And where did the copper come from?" he said and signed. He made a shoveling motion and pointed to the shore. He was constantly on the lookout for precious natural resources as he knew that knowledge would be well received, in spite of what the directors had said in Amsterdam. "Do you take it from the ground near here?"

Again, there was a doubtful look.

Hudson made more shoveling motions. The boy shook his head to say no. Then he signed with his hands to indicate trade or exchange.

"You trade for it?" Hudson asked, emphasizing the word.

"Yes," Fish said. *"Trade,"* he said slowly.

Hudson handed the pipe back. "Good," he said. He was now sure the copper was coming indirectly from the French in the far north. Whether other valuable metals and minerals could be found close by was still a question.

Fish was proving equally valuable during the times of trading with the Indians, which were many as the ship meandered north on the river. Because Hudson could not risk moving at night with the dangers of shoals and small islands, trading could only be done while the ship was anchored, at the end of each day, or when stopped by a contrary tide or winds.

His habit was to take a latitude reading with the cross staff at noon each day. This was done by Juet, an experienced seaman, who then entered the sun reading into his own log. If conditions were right, they would weigh anchor and start the next leg of the voyage.

The trading procedure was always the same. The natives paddled up and offered their goods from the water, holding them high above their heads. His crew then showed the few items they had for exchange. After both sides agreed, the trade items were handed up and down with a rope-tied basket.

There was no official Merchant or Supercargo assigned to oversee trade on this voyage, so they rotated the role between the officers and used Fish as interpreter. Although the goods were easy to see, the exchange requirements were sometimes complicated, and Fish could more easily communicate between the two sides. His knowledge of English and Dutch words grew rapidly. *Beaver, otter, hemp, corn, oyster, grapes, pumpkin,* and *tobacco* for the native goods being offered, with *knives, hatchets, mirrors,* and *beads* from their side.

Trading was not Hudson's goal, but it served important purposes. It led to good relations with the Indians. They were now numerous at every stage of the voyage, and he could not risk alienating them or causing more friction than necessary. And they were a valuable source of information—not only for their trade goods but also for knowledge of the river and any potential obstacles ahead.

And despite what his Dutch employers had said, he knew there was strong interest by merchants in the Dutch provinces—as well as in England, France, and even dreaded Spain—for the wonderful pelts of beaver, otter, mink, and fox that this land offered.

The height of fashion in Europe included the wearing of felt hats. And the best felt came from beaver peltries. The demand was insatiable. The French were taking full advantage of it in their territories to the north. If the Dutch weren't interested, then Hudson knew the French or English would be.

Ten

DANCING FISH HAD ESTABLISHED HIS PLACE AND A ROUTINE. His main activity was to help with the trading and to translate and teach words to Master Hudson, and to his son named *Jawn*, who had seen two or three winters more than him. He had offered to do the same with the lesser leaders named *Kluk* and *Joo-et*, the Sad Face, but they had shown little interest.

All of this he did with delight and excitement. These men were so different, their world so fascinating. He woke each day eager to see and learn more. Here was a place full of objects and creations that continually amazed him. There were ropes that looped around metal circles to help lift the heavy *sails*. Small floors they called *steps* to walk up or down easily. And a large *anchor* made of wood and heavy metal they released to the water to hold the ship from drifting at night.

He could imagine living among people like this and creating his own inventions that would not instantly be ridiculed or discounted.

He remembered when he had devised a better garden hoe handle and helped the women of the village use it. Breaking the ground with hoes for planting was hard work and exhausted even the strongest after time under the sun. He knew from his study and close inspection of nature that curved lines were stronger than straight. So after seeing it clearly in a dream, he spent four days carving a curved-handle hoe from a hickory branch. In secret. Attached to a stone blade with sinew, it worked well. But when his new father caught him in the fields hoeing, he was not happy.

"Our hoes are fine," he had said. "And this is women's work. Don't waste time on these silly things you make from your dreams."

But these strangers were surrounded by new ideas. He couldn't wait to see what more he would learn from them.

Each night, when it was dry, Dancing Fish slept on his fox-skins under the stars. When it rained, he slept next to the small-er canoe—they called it a *shallop*—under the deck of chopped wood. He ate when and what the men ate, trying to save the pemmican his mother had given him. Much of the food was unfamiliar, but most different was the drinking these men did. They drank no water—it was used only in the cooking.

With the meals, there was a juice they named *beer,* for which he had no word. At first, he could not drink it, but he soon developed a tolerable taste for the warm, brown liquid. But he could never match the quantities they drank. The beer gave him a good feeling, but he noticed how quarrelsome the men became afterward. He quickly learned to stay away from them then, and he usually fled to remote parts of the ship or even climbed a mast for more peace.

He was also getting used to the bad smell of these strange men. In fact, after one week, he recognized that he had acquired a similar smell. He tried jumping off the ship to bathe at each sunrise, as was his custom. But the men made fun of him and laughed so hard at this that he gave it up. He would be like them.

He even got used to the cat creature. It would prowl the ship in the night and sleep in the oddest places. This animal was so unlike a dog. His Kong would curl up next to him for sleep, but the black cat would hurry away.

Dancing Fish realized in the first days that there were no

women on the ship, but this made sense. With the Real People, hunting was only done by the men. So this was like a hunting group. But instead of stalking prey with bows, knives, and clubs, these men were searching for something with their great ship. What they were searching for was still unclear to him, but it had to be a very important beast or goal.

And he couldn't help wondering if these men also had women and families from where they came. Did they miss them like he missed Willow? Were they accustomed to being away from the ones they loved? Could he, if given the chance and with enough time?

But in all this thinking, he never forgot about the task he was assigned: learning the ways of the Visitors from the East. And watching to see if they were friends to the Manahate or not. The Fourth Fire had two prophets and two sides to the question. He knew he was in a unique position to see the truth of what was in the hearts of these strange, hairy-faced men.

▶◀

The sinking sun was at four fingers, and they were a small group from the ship: the Master, the man Kluk, two other men whose names he didn't know, and himself. With no wind to fill the sails and trading ended for the day, Master Hudson had decided to go to shore to do what he called *exploring*. Thankfully, the Sad Face Joo-et was left on the ship with the Master's son, Jawn.

Dancing Fish was so glad to be back on land and walking through the trees. The smell of the forest floor was strong as the men stepped on the layers of leaves of many winters passed. Birds sang out on all sides, and the dimming light was soft as it filtered through the top canopy.

The trees here were well formed and old. He pointed to the different ones and said their names to the Master as they passed: his Munsee words for hickory, elm, basswood, chestnut, many oaks, and his favorite, the tulip poplar.

The tulip grew straight and soaring with a bark of medium texture. The tree was used for making the canoes of the People. The leaf had an unusual shape with four points—it reminded him of a squatting man. He picked one from a young sapling to show the Master.

"This—tulip tree," he said, holding the leaf and then pointing to the largest one near them. "Good for canoe." He made a sign of paddling.

The Master nodded, took the leaf, sniffed it, and asked him, "What else do you see here?"

Once he understood the question, he stood taller. He felt honored. He was providing information to the visitors. He had knowledge they did not have.

He walked to a towering chestnut tree. Looking up, he spotted the spiky seed balls at the end of the branches. Most were now dry, some split wide open. He bent down and found several of the smooth, brown chestnut seeds. He picked them up. *Wáapiim,*" he said, holding them out to the Master. "Your word?"

One of the other men replied, "Chestnut."

"Chest-nut," Dancing Fish said slowly.

The Master took and turned them over in his hands. "Good for roasting and eating," he said. He mimed putting them to his mouth.

"Yes, for eat," Dancing Fish said. "Good." He made a grinding motion with his right hand over a cupped left one, then rubbed his fingertips together. *"Wchápihk,"* he said.

The Master frowned, so he repeated the motions.

Finally, the Master understood. Making the same motions, he said, "You grind them to make a powder or meal."

The Master recognizes it, Dancing Fish thought. Then he mimed adding water and mixing, followed by touching his hand to his arm and moving the hand in a circle.

Another man, who was carrying a bag tied around his waist, said, "A medicine salve. I have seen this."

The Master smiled in comprehension. "Medicine." He made a round motion on his stomach to show a good feeling.

Dancing Fish nodded. *Yes, he knows.* "*Me-di-cin,*" he said.

The Master instructed the man with the bag to gather the chestnuts on the ground. Then they heard another voice calling to them. "Have a look here!"

They couldn't see the man, but one of their group was missing. They walked toward his voice and found him down in a small gully. He was digging at something with his hands and soon climbed up to them and held out two pieces of flat, grayish rock—each the size of his head—and very happy about it. Dancing Fish knew the rock well, but the People just left it in the ground.

"Slate," the man said, rapping it with his closed fist. "Very high quality." He pointed down into the gully. "And right on the surface with surely more under." Then the man put the slate rocks next to the bag full of chestnuts, clearly satisfied with himself. Why, Dancing Fish could not comprehend.

A wind came then, and everyone looked up at the tall trees swaying and making the swishing sounds that trees make when obeying the Wind Spirit. No one spoke for many breaths.

"This good land," Dancing Fish said tentatively, opening his arms wide. He was starting to combine words, and he hoped he was right.

"Yes, Fish," the Master said, smiling broadly. "A good land indeed."

He watched as Master Hudson breathed in the air—Mother Earth's breath—and turned in a circle looking around him. The Master was pleased, and he started to speak to the men.

Dancing Fish listened closely to the words the Master said.

He did not understand them all, but he followed the meaning.

Here, there was wood in great abundance, many nuts to eat, medicines from nature, and great stores of slate rock for their houses. Also, animals of every type for food and skins, and fine land for growing the crops. This was a land that had everything a man could want.

He could only agree with these words coming from the white Sachem, for he knew it all to be true.

The Master then walked up to him and put a hand on his shoulder. "This is not only a good land; this is a wondrous land."

Eleven

HUDSON'S GOOD MOOD AT ONCE TURNED GLOOMY WHEN HE tasted the water on the morning of September 21. Freshening. This was a bad sign that only reinforced an earlier scouting trip Klock and several men had made in the shallop. They reported a narrowing channel, shoals, mudflats, and even small rapids. This was discouraging, but Hudson was not about to give up.

They had been anchored inside a bend in the river for two days due to contrary winds and the exuberant trading of the Indians. These naturals—Fish called them Mahicans, a different tribe—had obviously heard of their coming, and the word had spread. An endless stream of canoes approached the ship with furs, food, and hemp. Unfortunately, the supply of goods from the ship in return—knives, hatchets, beads—was close to running out. It was time for Hudson to take stock and fully analyze the situation.

"Let's prepare a meeting with the local leaders," Hudson said to both officers. Juet and Klock stood with him on the main deck watching the trading activity.

"Why?" Klock asked. "We can go no farther upriver. I think we must turn back."

Hudson had no desire for argument. "I want to talk to the leaders to make sure," he said. "They know this area better than we do. And with the boy, we can faithfully understand what they're saying."

Klock shrugged but Juet spoke up. "We cannot rest our future with this boy Fish. There can be more treachery, not less. I vote against this meeting."

"There is no voting here, Mr. Juet," Hudson said sharply, "and your mistrust of these people is tiring to me."

Juet shot back, "I think the death of Mr. Colman is good enough reason, do you not?"

"No, I do not," Hudson said, now angry. "I don't know what precipitated that terrible incident and neither do you. Apart from that, the natives have been kindly to us."

"They are kindly only to the point where they are not kindly," Juet said. "I do not trust them."

"Enough," Hudson said, slapping his hand on the rail to end the conversation. "I've made my decision."

He called for Fish, who was always nearby. "Tell the next group to go back and invite the local leaders to dine with me."

The boy appeared confused.

Hudson began again, speaking slowly and using the sign language they had developed between them. "A meeting with the local Sachem and one or two other leaders in the area. Here on the ship. They will be my invited guests. Tomorrow after the stars are out. Tell them to bring food of their choosing, for six or eight, and I will provide the drink." Hudson knew that anything the Indians brought would be far better than what they could offer. And he had a plan for the beverage portion of the meal.

The boy now understood. "Yes, Master Hudson," he said in very passable English. And he immediately started calling down to the traders in their canoes. The excited looks on the faces of the natives told Hudson the message was received.

▶◀

The sun was ending its curved sky journey when the call came for the game. The Mahicans had stopped their trading, and there was time before the arrival of the leaders that night.

The People loved to play their games with balls and sticks, so Dancing Fish was curious about this one the Master's son had invited him to join.

Jawn was not short like his father but taller and thin, like a twig. And with the same light brown hair on top. He was trying to grow the hair on his face like the others but only succeeded in looking like a baby bird with fuzzy patches and empty spots.

"What is game?" Dancing Fish asked Jawn as a group of the men crowded at one end of the ship's main deck. He instantly spotted the man Joo-et among them.

"It's a target practice," Jawn said in his small voice that was very different from his father's, which boomed when he spoke to the men. "We try to hit the target with our weapons."

Dancing Fish studied the items lined up on the deck at their feet. There was a knife made of the hard metal, a hatchet like the People used but also made of strong metal, and a spear they called a *short pike* like he saw on the beach at Ishpatena.

Then he looked at the target at the other end of the deck. It was a large yellow pumpkin traded from the Mahicans. It sat on a round basket with no holes, just wood pieces fitted tightly together. He knew these baskets were used for holding the beer. They were heavy and strong.

The basket was against the wall of the *forecastle*, another word he had learned. It was maybe three or four bodies distance from the pumpkin to the men. This was the target range for the game.

"We hit pumpkin?" he asked Jawn.

"Yes. Aim to hit it and try to smash it." He struck his open hand with a fist and laughed, showing his bad teeth. Dancing Fish had noticed that many of these men had poor or missing teeth.

"Smash it," Dancing Fish repeated, hitting his hands

together and looking around for Master Hudson. "Where is Master?" he asked. "He comes?"

"No, he's writing in his log," Jawn said. "You made a big impression on him during the exploration. He was delighted with what you showed him on the land."

Dancing Fish didn't understand all the words, but the meaning was clear enough.

"Stop talking and let's start!" one of the men said as he picked up the knife.

"Wait," said another. "What are the stakes?"

Joo-et answered, "Like we usually do. The winner with the best aim and most destruction can ask for one thing from any of the other players."

Jawn asked Dancing Fish, "Do you understand the stakes?" He signed and said, "Winner takes from others. Anything." He pulled at his cloak to show giving.

Dancing Fish understood immediately and nodded. He had played a similar game with his friends many times, and he was more often the winner than not. He looked at the others who would play, and he was excited and hopeful. He knew well how to handle and throw weapons like this. He wanted to win this game to show his ability. And maybe he could acquire something useful.

The man with the knife lifted and launched it at the pumpkin. It missed by a wide distance and fell to the ground, spinning. Everyone laughed at this and he joined in. This was a fun game.

Jawn was next and he tried the hatchet. It missed the pumpkin by only a hand width and stuck firmly into the wall behind.

Another man then tried the spear. Again, another miss.

"Your turn, Fish," Joo-et said with a strange smile.

Dancing Fish stepped forward and picked up the knife. He was an experienced bow-shooter and knife-thrower, sometimes bringing down rabbits in full flight. But this knife was different from his. He weighed it in his hand and felt its heft. He tapped the cool metal with his fingernail and made mental adjustments for these differences.

"Any time you're ready," Joo-et said loudly. The men all sniggered, then stepped back to give him room.

Holding the knife blade in his right hand, he turned his body, left foot forward, and stood firmly on the deck. He sighted the pumpkin and could see the knife's straight path from his hand. He pulled his arm back, breathed in through his nose, then flicked the knife forward with a strong throw. It struck the pumpkin at its center and pushed it back against the wall. The knife had sunk in up to its handle.

He smiled while the men cheered. No one would be able to match that.

"Now my turn," Joo-et said as he reached under a sail covering and pulled out one of the shining wood sticks Dancing Fish had seen on the beach.

"That's not fair!" Jawn said to Joo-et, reaching for the stick. "A musket is not allowed."

Joo-et shoved Jawn away, sending him sprawling to the wood deck. "No one said it had to be *only* those three weapons, now did they? And this is one of our weapons, too."

Jawn sat still on the deck, not speaking, not happy.

Dancing Fish watched closely while Joo-et went through an elaborate set of steps with a smoking rope, a bag of black powder, and a sparkling ball. He had no idea what this shining wood did, but he didn't have to wait long.

Joo-et pulled something with his finger, the smoking rope came down, and there was a flash of light with a loud bang like thunder. Smoke surrounded them, and when he peered through it he could see that the pumpkin was completely destroyed, lying in pieces around the basket. This *musket* was a powerful and accurate weapon.

"So, did I win?" Joo-et asked the men, obviously sure of

what he had done and taking delight in his trickery.

The men, with the exception of the Master's son who was still on the deck, blared their approval. Joo-et then stepped close to Dancing Fish and poked a finger to his chest.

"As the winner, and as is my right, I demand one of your fox sleeping skins. The best one you have." He made a hideous smile, showing his rotten teeth.

Joo-et turned to leave, saying over his back, "Whenever you have time, my little savage."

Twelve

Hudson had opened the cabin's window to air out the cramped room. Chairs of all descriptions were positioned around the map table, which was now cleaned off. An oil lamp hung above the table's center, casting a honey-warm light about the cabin. It would be a tight fit for the Indians and those from the ship, but they would make do.

The natives arrived in two canoes well after twilight had faded. And something must have been lost in translation because in addition to two elderly men—the leaders—came two old women and a younger maiden. The women were probably the men's wives, but the maiden was a mystery. She looked to be 16 or 17 years, and her appearance immediately sent a current of electricity through the crew. These hardened men had not had intimate contact with any women for months, and they strained to catch a glimpse of the savage girl. Hudson rushed the guests with their heavy bags to his cabin as quickly as he could.

The native men were old but lean and surprisingly well muscled. They wore the usual breechcloth aprons with leggings and animals skins as cloaks. The wives wore something like dresses over leggings and moccasins, all apparently made from deerskin. The girl was an adolescent version of the wives but thinner and with the healthy radiance of youth. None had a stitch of wool cloth or other fabric on them—something

Hudson had noticed consistently. Everything was made from animal hides.

After the obligatory exchange of gifts—knives to the men and ears of ripe corn in return—there was an embarrassing moment when Fish informed him that the People were used to sitting on the ground, not at a table. That was not possible in the narrow space, so Fish gave the visitors a short lesson in how to sit in a chair, which brought awkward smiles and titters from everyone.

Once they were settled, the women pulled wooden bowls of food from their bags and placed them on the table. There was dressed venison, a stew of corn and beans, and finally a large bowl of nuts and what had to be the last berries of the season. It looked and smelled wonderful.

While they ate, Hudson poured the ship's common beer into their cups. The natives sniffed and waited until the men of the ship were drinking steadily. Slowly, the old men began tasting the beer but only in small sips. Hudson could tell they didn't like it and were only drinking to be polite. The women did not drink and sat quietly. Hudson observed the maiden stealing glances at Fish.

At first, the conversation was stilted and difficult. Someone would say something and the boy would try his best to translate. There were long pauses, but Hudson had a plan for changing that.

When the food was finished and the friendship tobacco pipe passed around the table, Hudson brought out new drinking glasses and a bottle of aqua vitae. The strong Dutch brandy would soon loosen their tongues, Hudson thought, as he filled all the glasses.

He lifted his drink in the direction of his guests and announced, "To your health." Then he downed the liquid in one gulp. Klock and Juet followed suit.

The natives were very tentative when they smelled the drink.

The oldest leader finally tipped his glass and let the brandy cover his closed mouth. Setting the glass down, he licked his lips and made a pained face. Everyone at the table laughed. After a few moments, he lifted the glass again, put it to his mouth, and emptied it in one swallow.

Hudson watched carefully as the man suddenly lurched to his feet, grabbed his throat, and started breathing heavily. The other natives became distressed when the man spoke in a rasping voice between breaths.

The boy explained, "He says he is on fire from drink."

Hudson, now also standing, made slow downward movements with his hands and said in his most soothing voice, "Don't be afraid. The drink has only a happy effect. You will see."

The boy was at a loss to translate, but all watched as the man started wobbling and putting his arms out to his neighbors to steady himself. A few more moments passed before the man sat back down, still swaying. Then he pointed to his empty glass and smiled at Hudson, who refilled it promptly. The man drained the glass in an instant and soon, all the men were drinking and talking. Only Dancing Fish, who didn't like the taste of the brandy, abstained.

Hudson now needed to act fast. The food bowls were cleared from the table, and he laid a large map on the empty space, turning up the oil lamp to illuminate the parchment. Everyone stood to view the map better, although the natives were very unsteady on their feet.

"We are here," Hudson said, jabbing his finger on the map.

The leaders leaned over for a better look.

Hudson moved his finger to the large open area at the far left of the drawing. "We want to go here," he said, then turned his head to face the two leaders. "How do we get there?"

The boy translated.

The old men looked at each other and started speaking

rapidly. Hudson could hear the slurring in their voices.

The boy said to him, "Yes, canoes, but not ship. Too big."

Hudson, concerned, put his hand to his chin, then spoke. "Too big why? What is in the way?"

"Nunpeyihlele," said the boy instantly, if unclearly.

He shrugged his shoulders to show he didn't understand.

The boy reached up with his arms, extending them straight out, then wiggling his fingers while he moved his hands back. He repeated the motion and said again: *"nunpeyihlele."*

"Rapids," said Klock and Juet at the same time.

"Rapids," Hudson mumbled dejectedly to himself. Klock had been right about the river ahead. But he was not finished.

"Is there another river like this one farther up the coast?" he asked the old men. "Emptying into the Great Sea and deep enough for this ship?"

The boy struggled to translate and indicated the area east of where the Master had put his finger. Before replying, both men grabbed their glasses and extended them toward Hudson. Two crooked grins carved their faces.

Hudson swiftly refilled their drinks and repeated his question with more urgency: "Another river to the east?"

The men downed the brandy, looked at each other, and started laughing hysterically. Then the older man teetered and fell right onto the map, face down. He was passed out.

▶◀

Dancing Fish had caught the glances of the Mahican maiden but turned his head away. He knew why she was there. Master Hudson was the powerful leader of the visitors. The local leaders were smart enough to know that a liaison with such an important man, maybe even a Spirit Man as far as they knew, could mean shifting the balance of power between a village and its neighbors. Arranging strategic marriages was a common process. This, however, was not a common situation. Of that he was sure.

But the maiden brought a sweet and clear image to him— of Willow. He had rarely been this long away from her. And each day added to the weight of the reflection of her he held in his mind. The taste of her lips, the smell of her hair. And the memory of their touching and whispering together.

Their new courtship was known to all and jealously envied by High Limb. Dancing Fish remembered things as if they were just happening—the hidden messages, the love songs, and especially the night meetings under the furs when they explored each other's bodies.

He replayed these memories over and over while he battled with the inner conflict now storming inside of him. He wanted more than anything to see what was new and different in the vast world he now knew existed beyond what any of the Manahate could imagine. At the same time, his feelings for Willow were pulling him back like a fishing line.

No, he would pay no attention to this maiden. But the looks she was getting from the men of the ship troubled him.

▶◀

The Elder who was still standing spent time explaining another river to the east and the need for the ship to go back downriver and sail along the coast to find it. Dancing Fish watched the Master's eyes focus with intensity as they took in the meaning of the Elder's finger tracings on the map.

Then it was time for the People to go back to their villages. Master Hudson said the lifeless man would soon come back to normal. Even while he said it, the man started to wake up, but he was moaning and holding his head as if injured.

Leaving the women and the maiden to pack up the bowls and leftover food, of which there was almost none, Master

Hudson signaled to Dancing Fish and both started to lift the injured man. "And the rest of you help the others," the Master directed.

They carried the moaning man between them and put him on the main deck above where their canoe was tied. Soon, the other Elder, propped up by Kluk, was delivered to the same place.

Then they heard the screaming.

Dancing Fish didn't hesitate. He ran along the deck as fast as his legs would carry him, finally throwing open the cabin door.

A terrible sight greeted him. Several of the ship's men held the two older women in place with the maiden pinned in the corner of the room by Joo-et. He was trying to kiss her while she shrieked and battled him with her arms. Joo-et, who had taken much of the fire drink at the dinner, was yelling and slapping the maiden's face. The other men roared and encouraged him.

Dancing Fish reacted immediately and launched himself at Joo-et. He grabbed his left arm and spun him around.

"You!" Joo-et said, red eyes bulging with rage.

Joo-et reached for the knife at his waist, but Dancing Fish was faster. His sharp obsidian blade was out in an instant, and he pushed it against the soft skin under Joo-et's right eye while he held the man's knife arm tight with his other hand. The maiden wriggled free.

"No more," he said sharply to Joo-et. He pushed the knife harder until a thin line of blood ran down the man's cheek. The room froze in silence.

Master Hudson burst through the door with his son and two more men. "What is this?" he shouted while he and the others dragged the men away from the women and pried Dancing Fish and Joo-et apart.

"We're only having some fun," Joo-et said. "Harmless."

"No, not fun," Dancing Fish countered, pointing at Joo-et with his knife. "Not the way with women."

"It's finished," Master Hudson boomed. "Get these Indians off the ship. Now!"

They all helped move the natives to their canoes and watched them paddle away into the night.

Joo-et held a bloody cloth to his face when he passed Dancing Fish on the deck. "You will pay dearly for this, you foul savage," he said in a low voice.

Even without knowing what all the words meant, Dancing Fish could feel the menace in this evil man's voice. He grabbed Joo-et's arm and pulled him to a stop, his hand ready on his knife.

"No, you pay, evil Matantu," he said, leaning into Joo-et's stinking breath without fear. "One day, *you* pay."

Thirteen

HUDSON TOTTERED AROUND THE ROOM CURSING TO HIMSELF and drinking from the brandy bottle. He had banished both Juet and John from the cabin they shared, telling them to cool themselves on the deck along with the native boy. All night, if required.

Juet's actions were despicable. And undermining. Hudson had questioned bringing the man on this voyage, but he really had no choice. Juet was the best seaman he knew, and they had been together on voyages before. Hudson had always been able to count on the man. But he had not been so disagreeable as he was now. What had changed? Maybe Juet's true self was coming out with age?

Whatever the cause, he couldn't let Juet's hostility influence the others. Nor him. He had to keep the voyage composed and aligned. Within and without, all working for the common purpose. The ship. The crew. The natives. The river.

The blasted river! At its mouth, it was the greatest he had ever seen. Wide, deep, and without a steep grade. A perfect combination. And now? To start again and find another just as promising? Did he have the heart for it? Could he push on? More importantly, could he push the others on?

What choice was there?

None. Everything—and everyone—would have to be rallied. Hudson put the bottle down and lay in his bed, mentally rehearsing what he would say the next morning.

▶◀

The meeting was short. Master Hudson stood above them on the foredeck speaking while a strong west wind rattled the sails wound tightly against their yards. Everyone knew the ship would have to turn around and go back.

The Master spoke hopefully of another river to the east, but Dancing Fish could feel a sadness in his voice. And he felt it himself. So long as they traveled up the Great River, each day was a new adventure, a new possibility for him. Turning back was a kind of defeat.

And going back brought up the war Dancing Fish was having inside his own head. One side wanted this new life. The wind on his face while they drifted on the river through new lands. The sounds of the men's tongues that became less strange each day. The look on their faces as they gazed ahead. It was the same look that he felt—of wonder, of amazement.

The other side thought of the Manahate band. They were waiting for his return, depending on his watchfulness, on his understanding. And on his knowing what these strangers meant to them. He was the scout. Sent ahead to learn, to see, and to come back with the learning.

He was surprised by how much he missed his village. Small things. The smell of cooking stews over the longhouse fires. Teasing and laughing with his friends. The crying of children and the barking of dogs.

He missed the sweat lodges that purified his two Souls. Regular sweating was as normal as bathing for his people, but while it was possible to jump into the water, he could not build a sweat hut on a ship made of wood!

And the dancing. Dances with his clan were sacred and thrilling. A way to connect the People with the Spirits. The men of this ship never danced.

And then there was Willow. He pictured her each day. Tempting images. And with them came the longing that was strong between his legs. He had no control of that fire once it started, and he would find a quiet place on the ship to relieve it. His people taught that this drive was natural and must be released. If not with another, then by oneself. And he knew the white men had similar urges and relieved themselves the same way, some more open about it than others.

He paid close attention to his dreams, for they showed the way ahead. In some, he led Willow by the hand to a faraway place, sometimes running, sometimes flying in the air with the birds. They were free from everything. From people who had rigid thoughts. From evil people. Into a world of peace and happiness.

But in other dreams, he led Willow not up but down. Down into darkness. Into a world of conflict, fear, and suffering.

Which of his dreams divined the future?

▶◀

His mind back to the meeting, Dancing Fish watched the reaction of the others to Master Hudson's words from the foredeck. Some were grumbling, others quiet. He saw Joo-et staring at him without break. He stared back with equal intensity.

After the Master explained they would have to wait the day for the wind and tide to change, the men moved away in small groups. Some started fishing from the ship. The man Kluk pulled Dancing Fish aside. He wanted to talk.

They sat against the rail of the high deck while a hawk circled overhead on the gusting wind currents. The talking was not as easy as it was with the Master. The man spoke in a different tongue called *Dutch* with the other named *English*, which was what Master Hudson spoke. Between the two tongues the conversation moved slowly.

"Your people bring skins of beaver to the ship for trading," Kluk said using both words and signs. His head was naked and smooth on top, with what remained of his brown hair hanging down in tangles. "Are there many beavers on the land?"

"Yes. More beaver," Dancing Fish said. "Keepers of the Game have in the creeks. They give fur, meat, and—" he didn't know how to say it, so he pointed to his man apron. "We make medicine. Take away pain."

Kluk's head tilted. "You mean the balls?" He cupped his hands and made a squeezing sign with the fingers. "Beaver's balls? In the sac?" He moved his cupped hands down to where his legs joined.

Dancing Fish shook his head. "No. Inside beaver."

Kluk nodded, then asked, "And is not hard to catch these beavers?"

"Takes practice and"—he hunted through the new words he had learned—"*skill.*" He smiled at finding the good word. "Some hunters better than others. Some build traps. Others have bows. Or we go in beaver houses and catch them."

Kluk was listening carefully, his fingers scratching his hairy face. He asked, "Have you killed a beaver, Fish?"

"Yes. Many. Why?"

"Hats, Fish." He pointed to his head. "Hats."

Hats? What is Hats?

▶◀

It was soon after the sun reading by Joo-et when the canoe glided up to the ship. Dancing Fish saw that it held the Elder who was not injured in the night and one younger man.

The Elder signaled and asked to speak to the Master. Both men were helped aboard.

After a short gift exchange of corn for beads, Master

Hudson led them to the same spot where he had talked with Kluk. They sat on overturned boxes on the deck. The younger man from the canoe carried a large bag and sat a distance apart.

The Elder spoke in a rapid way, and Dancing Fish had to concentrate. He didn't know some of the Mahican words but could fill in by watching the man's expressions and by the sound of his voice.

"He is Sachem of village to south," he explained to Master Hudson. "Only one hand of sun from here on river." He held up his hand with fingers together to show the short distance in time.

Dancing Fish watched while the Elder signaled his younger companion over and pulled a band of wampum from the bag. It was a very fine one, almost as long as a man. With an intricate pattern that alternated the quahog shells of white and purple.

The Elder spoke while offering the wampum in the formal two-handed way to Master Hudson. The Master accepted the band with a look of puzzlement and turned to Dancing Fish for help. "What does he say?" the Master asked.

He suddenly realized Master Hudson did not recognize the sacred wampum. "He offers wampum for trust and friendship. Very important. And he invites you to his village in one day's night. They have feast for you. After sun sleeps."

"How far is the village in leagues?"

He had learned this word. "Two leagues. Not far."

After holding the wampum band awkwardly for some time, the Master turned to the Mahican Elder and held out his hand. They both shook. The Elder did it in the way of the Real People, right hand to hand, head to left, and left arm circling the other's back, pulling him close. Master Hudson seemed surprised by this and only succeeded after a second attempt.

Then the Elder released a smile with a lifted eyebrow and made a clear sign with his hand as he formed the words with his wrinkled mouth: "Fire drink?"

Fourteen

HENRY HUDSON SAT IN HIS CABIN THE NEXT MORNING STUDY-
ing the wampum belt, which smelled of the sea.

The belt was a band as wide as his fist with 12 single strings
perfectly aligned. Each string held a line of shell-bead cylinders
that were rounded and drilled to accept the string. He noticed
the beads were of only two colors: white and a dark purple that
was almost black. And they were so skillfully arranged that
when the belt was held at arm's length, a repeating pattern
could be seen: dark shapes of diamonds contrasting with the
white background.

Hudson had known from his reading of other voyages to
America that this wampum—what some called *sewant*—was
highly valued by the natives. The amount of labor alone would
make the wampum treasured. Hudson had sensed the ceremony of it when the elder native handed him the belt, but he had
not fully understood what was transpiring with this offering.
There was a seriousness in the act the boy had echoed in his
explanation, but he had missed the full intent, he now realized.

He filled his cup with more brandy while his thoughts went
back to the river and his judgment to turn around. He knew
himself and his ambition well, and he was not about to give up,
but he saw the window of opportunity slowly shutting. He was
running out of time for finding the elusive passage. The equinox
and Michaelmas would come in five days to signal the arrival of

autumn. This year's exploring season would soon close.

Then his attention went to the country through which they were sailing. Perhaps aided by his brandy haze, he could see snatches of what the future would bring to this ripe land. Industrious trading enterprises along the river. Rich farms, perhaps vast estates for agriculture and animal husbandry. Villages of busy settlers with spired churches for the devout and alehouses for the others, who, in most likelihood, would be more numerous.

It was all here for the taking. And simply too alluring, too full of promise to go unnoticed for long. There would certainly need to be some kind of reckoning between the opposing forces of savagery and civilization. But that would not concern him. Others would come and start that process. He was an explorer. A discoverer. He probed and searched. Others exploited those discoveries. "Before you can exploit, you have to explore," his father had told him long ago.

He was finishing his cup when he felt the morning air stirring in the cabin. The sterncastle window was cracked open, and he could hear the wind trying to squeeze through it. A breeze!

He slammed the cup on the table and ran up to the poop deck where Juet was already standing. "Is this the breeze we're wanting?" he asked his officer.

"Aye, Master, it is."

As if they were weathervanes, they both turned north to face into the wind. It was cool and steady. The river rippled with dark lines pushed on by the wind.

"God be praised!" Hudson exclaimed, loosening his mouth into a wide grin. "Take your sighting now, then we'll weigh anchor and be off. We've spent enough time here."

▶◀

They were making good speed down the river with the wind at

their backs when Hudson saw the natives crowded on the starboard shore ahead. There were dozens of them, all singing and dancing around bonfires that burned high.

A single canoe approached from the bank. In it were three natives dipping their paddles together. They intersected the ship's path and turned downriver to stay parallel with it. Juet immediately assumed the worst and was prepared to fire on them with muskets, but Hudson told him to stand down. He could see they had no weapons.

While two of the natives continued to paddle strenuously, the middle one cupped his hands and called out to him.

Hudson turned to the boy. "What's he saying?"

"He says the Sachem and village wait for you. Everything ready. A great feast to honor you and the men."

The ship was almost abreast of the crowd and Hudson had a decision to make. He had promised to make this visit, true. But he had finally caught a good wind after days of sitting still. He could not give it up after only two hours of sailing. It would be too frustrating to pause again so soon.

Anxious to continue, he reached his conclusion and turned to Fish. "Tell them that we have a fair wind now and cannot stop here. We are sorry."

The boy looked at him strangely without moving. Then he turned to the canoe and yelled down the message.

The paddlers stopped. Their faces showed incomprehension as the canoe fell off the pace of the ship. Then Hudson saw the crowd sag in quiet unison. He had snubbed them.

But the voyage was more important.

The crowd and the lone canoe were soon lost in the distance while the *Half Moon* kept up its steady progress down the broadening river. The future was unknown, but Hudson was racing toward it at full speed.

Fifteen

DANCING FISH TRIED HIS BEST TO UNDERSTAND WHY THE Master had shown such disrespect to the Sachem and the village. Accepting the wampum was accepting the invitation to the feast. It was wrong to keep the wampum but not follow through. He, himself, tried to ignore stupid traditions, but promises were to be kept, and honesty was sacred. This was the way of an honorable life.

He remembered his transition into manhood two sun cycles earlier. There were three others with him to take the initiation: Rock, High Limb, and a strange boy named Springs Softly. This boy had recently come to the village and made a habit of not telling the truth. His lies were usually small and of no consequence. That is, until the four boys were sent into the forest to shoot their first deer and embark on their personal vision hunt.

Each was told by the Elders to take a different direction and not come back until they had fasted and received the wisdom of their new Guardian Spirit. And with their first buck or doe.

His five days had been ones of high emotion, fear, and finally, revelation. He had fasted with only a small piece of smoked meat the size of a finger taken each day. His Manitto, the perch, was revealed to his Dreaming Soul on the last night. And he had stalked and shot a large buck with a single arrow. Then he proudly carried it home to Werpoes across his shoulders.

He was now a man.

The others had done the same or similar. Except for Springs Softly. During the village's celebration around the fire for all four boys-now-men—when the Turtle Clan tattoos were cut and scraped into the skin of their right arms—it became obvious to all that Springs Softly had not shot his deer in the honorable way. He had not spoken to the animal's Spirit correctly.

Instead, the Elders determined that the animal was already dead when Springs Softly came upon it and shot an arrow at close range into its cold body. And he had made up an elaborate story about tracking the deer for a full day, speaking to its Spirit, and finally shooting the fatal arrow with much skill. All of it a lie. And this time, it was a serious lie. His family was disgraced and shunned.

Then one day soon after Springs Softly was found hanging by his neck from a tree. Whether he had taken the action himself or had been helped along by someone else would not be known. But the contempt for honesty was not forgiven. The family of the dead boy quickly left the band, never to return.

Honesty and honor were not to be fooled with. And Dancing Fish was beginning to suspect the honor of these visitors. It was like a dark cloud forming behind his eyes when he looked in their direction. The hate and deceit from Joo-et, the questioning from Kluk, and the insensitivity of the Master—all this troubled him, and he wondered what more was being prophesied by it. He would pay attention to his dreams about this.

▶◀

It was the Balance of Days, when the light was equal to the dark. The time of the Full Corn Moon. Dancing Fish wondered how the corn was growing, whether the cobs were thick and the kernels fat. If the squash had shaded out the weeds. If the bean tendrils had twined high on the corn stalks. He would have been there, adding his hands to the others. Now, he was sailing back to them. But to a future he couldn't clearly see.

They had been moving south in starts and stops for five days. The river was wider and deeper now. The land was high around them, lifting to small peaks and cliffs, and with streams falling and rushing to join the river's water.

The ship was anchored while Dancing Fish watched an osprey search for its next meal. The bird flew low over the river then angled down sharply, its talons opening. It splashed heavily on water that soon boiled with the contest. Then the bird flapped its wet wings and struggled to rise with the added weight. Finally airborne, it flew away with its prey, the chosen fish twitching all the way as the bird disappeared over the trees of the forest. The sacred cycle of life and death continued.

The Mahicans soon came around in their canoes for trading. But Dancing Fish noticed a difference in their attitude—a subtle change he could see in their movements and in their eyes. They were guarded and hesitant. He wondered if word of the maiden or of the village humiliation had reached them.

He was at his position on the main deck when he observed one canoe with a single paddler staying near to the ship's stern. The man paddled closer and closer, which Kluk also noticed when he pointed to him. Soon, the man was hidden behind the ship, and Dancing Fish ran up to the high deck to see where he had gone.

When he looked down over the rail, he was surprised by what he saw. The man had somehow climbed up the ship and was standing on the part called the *tiller*. He had half his body through the small window that led into the cabin where the map meeting had taken place.

The man, wearing only an apron and with his hair greased to a high roach in warrior style, was pulling several items from the cabin when Dancing Fish shouted down to him in his Munsee tongue. "You! Don't do this. Are you crazy?"

The man stopped, and his head snapped up, anger spilling from his face, glinting in his eyes. "We're not the crazy ones. It's the hairy strangers who are." With his arms full, he looked sharply at Dancing Fish. "And you help them. You are no better. Are you their brother or ours?"

Loud noises from inside the cabin prompted the man to climb nimbly down with his stolen items, jump into his canoe, and paddle quickly away.

Dancing Fish heard a loud boom, glanced back to the deck, and saw Kluk holding a shining wood musket, smoke rising from it.

When he turned back to the canoe, Dancing Fish saw the man lying in it, his head and one arm hanging over the side. His body was still with blood streaming from it.

The other Mahicans cried out and paddled away, with some even jumping into the water and furiously swimming to the shore.

Then Dancing Fish saw Joo-et and the cook rowing the ship's boat—the shallop—toward the canoe. They pulled alongside and started retrieving the items the man had stolen. The man had not moved, and the bottom of the canoe was slick with his blood.

Suddenly, a Mahican appeared in the water and grabbed the side of the shallop in an effort to overturn it. Without warning, the cook raised a long, shining object Dancing Fish had learned was a *sword* and struck down on the man's arm, completely slicing through his wrist. The severed hand fell into the boat, and the shocked and shrieking man slid under the water and disappeared, a red stain swelling in his place.

Dancing Fish was stunned and horrified. In the time of a few breaths, two of the People had been killed. And for what? The theft of a few items?

Surely, the Master would not allow this to go unpunished. But when he ran back to the main deck, he saw him showing no signs of sadness or annoyance. The white Sachem said nothing to Joo-et or the cook when they climbed back onto the ship. He was accepting what had happened.

Dancing Fish caught Master Hudson's eye but saw no sorrow, no outrage. It was a cool eye. Not the eye of kindness or compassion. It was the eye of someone he did not know. Maybe would never know.

Heartbroken, Dancing Fish understood that the prophecy was being played out in front of him. What he thought was brotherhood had changed into something else. Was the second prophet right after all?

Sixteen

HUDSON TRIED TO REMOVE THE KILLINGS OF THE PREVIOUS day from his mind. It was a dastardly thing for Klock and Juet to do, but he couldn't risk any disfavor from them or any of the crew. He needed them now more than ever if he was going to succeed. They had one more chance, if even that, at sailing to the next river in hopes it would be the passage.

The fall equinox had arrived, and with it, the clear hint that time was running out. The days would be shorter, the nights longer. The air was cooling, and with that usually followed a man's cast of mind. The final quarter of the year was upon them.

Anchored in the lee of a mid-river island, their modest Michaelmas celebration had begun on the main deck. The Feast of the Archangels was a needed break, and he had decreed a night's interlude for emotions to ease.

The English crew anticipated the celebration, and although it was only observed by Anglicans, Catholics, and Lutherans, the Dutchmen—who were none of these—would never pass up a chance for extra food and drink. Not that there was much to spare for feasts, no matter how small.

Instead of the traditional goose and cakes, which no one of sane mind expected, Hudson distributed a bonus ration of salted pork and wormy biscuits from their dwindling supplies. And in addition to the ship's beer, he was obliged to give two fingers of aqua vitae to all, not just the senior officers. Most of the crew gulped it down before he could even loosen his hand from the cups.

While the sailors sang their bawdy songs and the night's gloom descended, he pulled his son aside and walked with him to the foredeck. He waited for one of the swabbies to pass after a trip to the beakhead for his bodily elimination.

"What do you think of the crew's disposition after what happened yesterday?" he asked John. The boy seemed to be thinning with each day of the voyage. His grimy clothes hung loosely from the lanky frame.

"Tempers are sour," John said in a slight voice that matched his mother's. "Many were hoping for the magical passage to the Indies and a promise of wealth beyond measure. Instead, they sit upon a river surrounded by penniless savages."

He couldn't disagree.

"Even a hint of gold or silver would have sufficed," John added, leaning against the foremast. "Instead, we have chestnuts and slate." The boy laughed at his own comparison.

Hudson asked, "But what of the bounty on the land? The beavers? Do the crew not know the value of the creatures back home?"

"Yes, maybe it's true. But the number of pelts we've gotten so far from trading our meager items would bring no fortune to these men. Maybe for others more prepared."

Again, he was right. "And what do you think of Fish? How he helps us?"

"Oh, he's a useful tool, to be sure," his son said. "But still, he is only an Indian, and a young one at that. What value does he really have to us? To you?"

Hudson took a long draw from the full bottle of brandy he had hidden in his greatcoat and considered this. The native boy's enthusiasm was ebbing. He could sense that. But Fish was still needed. Especially as they came close to the end. He could not afford to lose him now in the final days of the voyage.

Hudson offered the bottle to his son and impulsively clutched John's hand when he reached for it. "I'm glad you're with me, Son. Whatever happens, we'll be together. Whether only on this voyage or the next ones. Your mother would be proud of her boy."

John squeezed his hand. "Will you be joining the celebration now, Father?"

Hudson held up the bottle. "Oh yes," he said, smiling. "But it will continue in my quarters. The Master has to protect his drink from all enemies!"

He laughed as he walked unsteadily to his cabin.

Two days of sailing found Dancing Fish close to home. They had traveled a long distance after the terrible incident and were anchored off the high bulge they called The Wart for the way it jutted up and out into the river at his left. They were finally back to his island of Mannahatta. It was only another three leagues to Kapsee from here.

He had dreamed the same dream for two nights. He hovered over the masts looking down on the ship while hundreds of flying fish landed on the deck, flapping and jumping. These fish were magical and revered by the People and were always released back to the sea if they landed in a canoe. But the strangers in the dream knew nothing of this, and they moved over the deck like a horde of wolves, clubbing and hacking the fish to pieces with their weapons.

A dream repeating like this cannot be ignored, he thought when he stretched his arms and greeted the new morning.

A few trading canoes appeared but were quickly waved away by both Kluk and Joo-et, who stood near him on the main deck. Thick and low-hanging storm clouds rolled toward them from the west. There would be no trading today. And Master

Hudson was nowhere visible. Maybe in his cabin, where he spent more and more time.

Dancing Fish was studying the sky over the island when two canoes full of warriors with bows in hand and arrows nocked suddenly appeared, heading toward them. Both Kluk and Joo-et started yelling at the other men to grab what weapons they could.

The canoes had maneuvered behind the ship when a flight of arrows filled the sky and struck harmlessly against the stern. Dancing Fish understood immediately what this was—a symbolic act of protest by the Wiechquaesecks, as this band was called. They were showing their displeasure at the recent actions of the visitors. Clearly, word of the earlier incidents had reached here.

Joo-et was in full fury while he rushed with the other men to the high deck where they had a better view of the canoes. When Dancing Fish saw they all were carrying the shining muskets, he chased after them.

"Master Joo-et," he pleaded when he reached him, "do not use your death weapons. The People mean no harm. Only for show."

Joo-et pushed him roughly aside. "Out of my way, savage! We've been attacked, and now we will attack back." He ordered all the men standing with him to open fire on the two canoes.

There was a burst of smoke and noise, and it took a moment for the air to clear. But when it did, Dancing Fish had to blink several times to believe what he was witnessing.

The men in the canoes were crying out in alarm and confusion. Both canoes had holes in their sides, and several of the warriors were injured with bloody wounds. Three or more appeared to be dead. They lay in unnatural positions or floated face-down in the water.

He grabbed Joo-et by his stringy hair and pulled him close. "What you do?" he shouted at him. "You don't see you make death where not needed? Where is Master Hudson? He must stop this!"

Before Joo-et could speak, a rain of arrows fell around them. One of the ship's men dropped to his knees, an arrow stuck deep into the top of his head, his eyes wide with surprise as he collapsed forward. The others flew to the quarterdeck and scrambled down the narrow stairs.

Dancing Fish dove under a folded sail as more arrows hit the ship. There was a sudden screech, and the black cat bolted away in an instant.

He peeked out from his hiding position and saw a large group of Wiechquaeseck warriors massed on top of The Wart and unleashing their arrows down on them. They had seen what the muskets had done.

Then he saw Joo-et aiming one of the giant smoking pipes they called a *falcon*. This was a terrible weapon he had studied carefully when no one was around.

There was a loud bang and Dancing Fish followed Joo-et's gaze to the warriors on the hill. While he watched, the ball from the falcon struck one of the warriors and caused immediate panic in the others.

A sudden silence came, but it didn't last long. Another war canoe was heading toward them from the island's shore. The warriors in it shrieked and whooped as they approached the ship. This was a war party in full attack.

Joo-et yelled at Kluk, "Load the grapeshot!"

The canoe was closing rapidly.

Dancing Fish jumped up from his hiding spot and rushed to the two white men. Pushing down his rage, he appealed to them. "Please not use on the People. I can talk. I can stop it."

Joo-et turned and growled. "You can do nothing—you are one of them!" He turned to Kluk and screamed *"Now!"*

Kluk touched the burning rope to the falcon, and it exploded with a thunderous blast and a huge, smokey plume.

Dancing Fish cringed from the sound, then stood watching helplessly while a mass of grape-sized balls ripped into the advancing canoe, hitting some of the warriors and making most of the others jump out. Within moments the canoe sank, and all were swimming back toward the shore.

Joo-et whipped his head around and glared at him. "There, that's the way to talk to savages!"

With a crazed look on his face and holding out his metal knife, Joo-et, followed closely by a pike-wielding Kluk, advanced toward him.

Seventeen

HUDSON STEPPED RELUCTANTLY ONTO THE QUARTERDECK while daylight assaulted him. He shielded his eyes and shook his head in hopes of dispersing the effects of the borage-infused brandy. His skull ached and everything was spinning.

The sound of muskets and then cannon had pulled him out of his cabin and his stupor, and he now focused on the men crowded along the port rail below him. Something was very wrong.

"Make way!" he bellowed, pushing through the mob of men, the sharp smell of gunpowder wafting into his nostrils.

Juet and Fish grappled with each other like wrestlers, each punching and kicking as they hung over the rail. Others either urged them on with shouts or tried to join in.

"Stop this!" Hudson screamed, his head suddenly clear.

Just as he got close to the fighting, someone swung an oar that connected loudly with Fish's head. The force of the blow launched both fighters over the rail and into the water, where they landed with a great splash.

He groaned, then shouted the order: "Bring out the shallop!"

▶◀

What was happening here? Two of his most important crew members were trying to kill each other, and Hudson could see natives floating in the water and also wailing and chanting on the island shore. How could he have missed such a disaster?

His son was promptly at his side.

"What's happened?" he urgently asked John. "What's the cause of this turmoil?"

"We were attacked by the savages," John said, his eyes full of fear and confusion. "In canoes and coming from the island. There were many of them, coming from all directions."

"And Fish? What's his role?"

Klock suddenly appeared and answered, "Tried to stop us from defending ourselves, he did. We were attacked and had no choice. It was us or them."

"John, is this true?"

John moved his eyes from his father to Klock and back again. "Yes. But Fish offered to talk to them first. He wanted to stop the violence."

Hudson shot an exasperated look at Klock. "And you didn't let him try? You know our goal is to find the passage, yes? And to use the natives to help us do it." He stared hard at the man. "Not to murder them!"

Klock looked down at the deck without speaking.

"Fish is our bridge to these people!" Hudson raged. "Do you not grasp what a delicate situation we're in? Surrounded by them? We'll now have to leave here as soon as we can. And with Fish, if we can keep him. He understands the Indians and us like no one else."

Klock pretended not to comprehend and shifted his gaze to the water.

"Get to the boat and pull them out!" Hudson commanded.

Eighteen

HE SAW OYSTERS. CLUSTERED AND QUIET IN THE SHALLOWS. Light dancing over their barnacled backs. And quick perch darting between them over rippled sand.

He saw Willow. Her easy laugh when she turned and ran into the forest, daring him to follow her to the secret place where they met.

Then came the ugly face of Joo-et, and Dancing Fish woke from his vision. They were both under water, Joo-et above him. The man thrashed and lunged for him, bubbles blowing out of an open mouth. Dancing Fish's head throbbed, but he knew he was now in his element, and Joo-et was not.

He saw the glint of a metal knife and almost managed to block it, but it sliced his left arm above the elbow and also penetrated his right knee. He screamed in pain, but no sound came, only bubbles. Then his own stone blade was out of its sheath and striking back with a ferocity he barely recognized. This man had pushed him to his limits. He was the embodiment of the evil Matantu.

Hatred flowed through his veins as Dancing Fish thrust his knife deep into Joo-et's bony chest, only just missing his heart when Joo-et turned at the last moment. Frantic terror etched the man's face while he groped for the surface.

While Joo-et kicked and jerked, blood from both of them turned the green water brown. Dancing Fish, who had still not taken his first breath, was coming up next to Joo-et and saw his opportunity to finish him off. His knife was poised to end the life of this hateful man when someone landed on top of him, pushing him down again. With no breath left, he shoved himself away and pulled hard to go up.

Dancing Fish surged to the surface and sucked in the cool air. Kluk came up between him and Joo-et, who was crying out for help.

The ship's boat was there and men reached down to bring Joo-et on board. As they pulled him up, Dancing Fish could see he was bleeding badly and that his face had turned gray. Dancing Fish doubted he would survive, and he was glad. The killing of a man was a gravely serious act, but this one was justified.

Kluk made it to the boat, leaving Dancing Fish alone to tread water. The choice flickered in front of him. Would he rejoin these men on the ship? Could he continue to learn more from them? Or had he learned enough?

▶◀

He heard the Master's voice. "Swim to the boat, Fish."

Dancing Fish looked up and saw Master Hudson at the ship's rail. The others, including Jawn, were also there, staring at him.

"Come back to us," Hudson shouted down to him. "I know you were defending yourself. Don't judge us all by Joo-et. You are more like us than you realize. I'll forgive if you come back."

He saw the Master extend a hand and curl his fingers. An invitation. But he had decided.

"No!" he yelled out, holding his left arm tightly to help stop the bleeding. He kicked his legs in circles to keep his head and body up. "I came with you to learn your ways. To know your world. And to know the future. I do not like what I learn."

Hudson leaned down and extended his hand lower. "But our world *is* the future. Don't you see it, Fish?"

He stared into the questioning blue eyes of the Master. "I see only how you look to our land, to our animals, even to us. We are only for your using. This is not the way to be brothers in peace."

Hudson's face fell and his smile vanished at these words. "Grab him!" he shouted.

▶◀

Arms reached out and muskets appeared on all sides, and Dancing Fish didn't hesitate—he took a quick breath and dove.

He repeatedly pulled and kicked at the same time with all his strength, away from the ship. He prayed to his Guardian Spirit that he would swim low and long. Musket balls struck the water all around him, but he was deep enough. He could see the balls trailing white bubbles as they slowed and eventually dropped straight down, harmless.

He finally popped up when he felt the incline of the island's muddy bottom. Pulling his feet under him, he half stood and half stooped in the shallow water while his blood formed red ribbons around his legs.

Turning to the ship, he propped his hands on his knees to catch his breath, the salty taste of river and blood in his mouth. He was still within the range of the falcons, and he could see a man preparing one. But then he saw the short figure of Master Hudson approach, put a hand to him, and the man stopped.

The white Sachem shouted orders, and the men rushed over the ship. They were preparing to leave.

Dancing Fish straightened up and watched. Hudson stood at the ship's rail with hands on his hips, looking toward him, unmoving. Jawn soon stood next to him. Dancing Fish wished he could see the Master's face for its signs, but it was too far.

Sails swelled against a dark, threatening sky, and the Great White Bird began to move slowly down the river.

Both men stood still and looked at each other as the distance widened. Then Master Hudson raised one arm and waved his hand slowly.

Lightning suddenly flashed behind the ship, and he saw the two figures of the Master and his son outlined against it. While thunder cracked and growled, he wondered if he would ever see them again.

With a hollowing in his stomach and a sadness in his heart, Dancing Fish made a detached wave with his good arm as a cold rain began to fall. He stood rooted in the same spot until the ship grew smaller, then finally disappeared around the curve of the river.

He knew now that the Souls of both prophets of the Fourth Fire had been on the ship. Good and evil. Light and darkness. Hudson and Joo-et were the two sides of the prophecy. Hudson was curiosity and open-mindedness. Joo-et was anger and hatred. Both sides had competed with each other, and both had influenced Dancing Fish in their own ways.

His dream of the white bird eating his Manitto had started playing out on the ship. The dream had become real, as he feared it would. And while it was not yet clear in words, he now pieced together in his mind that if the two prophecies arrived together, difficult tests would surely face the Real People and their future.

"So, are you ready to come home?" came the familiar voice behind him.

He whirled to see Owl standing on the shore, eating with his fingers from a small pouch.

Nineteen

DANCING FISH SPENT TWO DAYS HEALING IN A CAVE STORMS had carved out of the beachside cliff just down from The Wart. A warm wind from the southeast had arrived and was a welcome break from the growing cold that warned of winter's approach. A low and hazy sun had replaced the rain.

The old man's medicines and poultices worked fast, and early on the third day they headed south on the long, slow walk home to Werpoes on the Mannahatta path. Dancing Fish's left arm was cradled in a sling of deerskin, and he walked with the help of a staff.

"How did you know I would be at this place on the island and in need of help?" he asked Owl while they walked.

"I still speak to the Sky People," the Elder said, "and they told me you would need my assistance. A dream then showed me The Wart, and here I am."

The path swerved close to the Great River, and they rested on a bank overlooking the vast stream. They ate Owl's parched corn and pemmican without speaking.

Dancing Fish closed his eyes and smelled the brackish water. He felt the sun of the false summer on his face and heard the wind whispering to him. He brought his thoughts both to recent events and to what lay ahead.

All this time, he had wanted to leave, and now, having done that, he could think of nothing better than to return home. Was this a passing feeling or something more?

He would pay more attention to the signs and to the signalers of the future that swirled around him. To Kishelemukong, the Creator of the Four Directions. To the Manetuwak Spirits who resided in all things. To his Manitto, the silvery perch, who would forever guide him. To his Star Parents, who he knew watched over him. And to his new parents, who were trying their best.

His friend Rock would always be his greatest supporter. Even High Limb, who had his own path to follow, had a role to play.

And what of Willow? What was her part? Was she a fixed point of navigation, or just a stop along the way in the crooked wanderings of his life? He only knew he could not wait to get back to her.

Dancing Fish pulled out the round gift from his apron and fingered it with his good hand. He felt its hardness and realized a small part of his heart had also turned hard. The four holes were starting to fill with grit, grime, and grease. Just as a space deep within him was filling. Was his strong need to break free—to belong somewhere else—also lessening?

"What do you have there?" Owl asked, squinting at what he held in his hand. "Let me see your bright stone."

He passed it over. "The hairy ones call it a *button*," he said. Another word he had learned on the ship. He explained its use.

"Very clever," Owl said after inspecting it and handing it back. "It is a fine button."

"Yes."

"We don't use these buttons like they do, do we?"

"No. But I predict that we soon will."

The ancient Seer chuckled. "Young Dream Makers predicting the future, Spirit Men arriving from another world . . . What kind of strange life is this becoming?"

Owl and Dancing Fish sat in stillness for some time,

watching the currents in the river.

"It's far from over, you know," his mentor finally said without looking at him, his tone serious.

"I know," he said. "It's just the beginning with the white strangers, isn't it?"

"Yes."

"And will I play a part?"

The old man turned to him.

"You will play the most important part of all."

Part Two

The Traders

1612–13

Twenty

October 30, 1612

CLAUDE BOUCHER WAITED BEHIND THE TREE, SHIVERING. His breath came out in clouds as night's gloom lifted to reveal the gray scene. A light drizzle fell with an occasional roll of thunder.

He desperately wanted to catch a beaver. Or two. After all, that was why he was here. But beavers were smarter than he had expected. "Clever brown devils," he muttered to himself in his native French while he blew warmth into his cupped hands.

He had found the beaver pond on the stream that emptied southeast from the big pool. The stream flowed peacefully until blocked by the animals' dam that spread its waters. The water emerged again at the base of the dam, and it was the freshest water he'd ever tasted. If only his luck with food were better. He was hungry, and a fat beaver could solve both his problems at once. But first, he had to get his hands on one. And he had only this last day to accomplish it.

Earlier, he had tried using his matchlock, but his aim was poor. He cursed himself for not having taken the shooting lessons with his brothers. Another failure in comparison with his siblings. But then he'd scored a hit on a skinny fox the week before. He was proud of that until he saw the destruction the musket ball had done to the hide. He would have to change tactics to do less damage to the precious pelts he was after.

He was admiring the pattern of newly fallen red and orange leaves layering the ground when he spotted movement in his peripheral vision. The beaver had emerged from his lodge, just upstream of the dam. The lodge was a ragged pile of sticks peeking above the waterline, and the beaver was swimming toward shore. In his direction!

Boucher clenched his quivering body and stood motionless as the wet beaver lumbered onto land. The creature headed for a stand of young maples that had partially been decimated by its strong teeth.

His plan was to hide behind the thickest trees nearby and surprise the big rodent with his sword. But now, he realized this animal was larger than he had originally thought. It weighed at least 75 livres, and while he studied the great orange incisors biting into one of the saplings, he started to get nervous. What if the beaver bit him? He could bleed to death in this lonely place.

His stomach growled. He knew it was now or never. With his eyes pinned to the beaver, he slowly reached to his sword's hilt and grasped it tightly in his right hand. He drew in a deep breath.

Boucher sprang out from his hiding place and ran toward the beaver with his sword raised, making his own version of a war cry: *"A-i-e-e-e-e-e!"*

The beaver, alarmed, sat back on its flat tail and squeaked, then took off, scrambling toward the water.

Boucher was gaining as the beaver crossed the muddy bank. He was just behind, slashing his sword up and down, looking for a head strike.

The beaver slid into the water and slapped its tail, making a loud *whack!* that echoed through the surrounding trees. Then it dove under.

The sharp sound startled Boucher, and he lost concentration. His feet slid, then slipped in the mud, and before he knew it, he hit the cold water of the pond that had already started to crust with ice along its edge.

But not before his own sword had opened a deep gash in his left thigh.

▶◀

Boucher had half-stumbled, half-crawled back to the empty hut that was his current shelter. He tore a strip from his toile shirt and worked it as a tourniquet above the wound. The bleeding had lessened, but blood still oozed.

It was already the tenth day, and the ship was due to pick him up. Sitting on the hard-packed dirt, he tried not to panic while he considered his options. He knew he needed to stop the hemorrhaging or he would die during the night. He was already getting dizzy. But he also needed to start a fire to warm up and dry out his soggy clothes—shirt, jerkin, capote coat, pantaloons, and boots—all of which were stiffening on him. The temperature was dropping, and he could imagine freezing to death even before his blood drained away.

And he was in no condition to walk back to the rude lean-tos at the island's point where his two shipmates were. He would never survive the hike with his injury and his frozen clothes.

"Merde, what have I done this time?" he said out loud. "Concentrate."

He tied the bandages around his leg, one by one, to help close the cut. Soon, he had encircled his left leg with blood-soaked cloths. He just hoped the edges of flesh would bind together.

While he rested from the exertion, he heard the other goal rumble through his insides. He was starving. Food would do a lot to help his body and his ability to think.

The inside of the musty hut would have been cave black if he hadn't earlier knocked away the flat stone covering the smoke hole in the roof. Daylight shafted down through the opening and gave him the barest of illumination. At least he had done that right.

Daydreaming about the pastries he used to eat in Liège, he heard a scuffling sound. He waited, then heard it again. Finally, he could make out the small gray form at the hut's round perimeter, the two eyes glistening with the dim light. It was a mouse. And a hefty one at that. It obviously knew how to find food. And now Boucher had found his.

Thinking hard about what he could use for bait, he noticed the cracked clay pot that lay near him on the ground. Picking it up, he felt wisps of powder with bits of seeds poking through. This was some kind of ground meal left by the previous inhabitants.

He reached forward and emptied the pot's contents onto the dirt floor halfway between his feet and the circular fire pit. He had to rest for a moment but was soon holding his musket. Luck was smiling on him when he saw the slow-match cord he had started before leaving for the pond still smoldering.

Gritting his teeth against the pain in his leg, he propped the musket on his knees with the barrel aiming at the small mound of what he hoped would be irresistible mouse food. Then he waited.

He was drifting in and out of sleep—or was it consciousness?—when he spotted the mouse tentatively approach the mound. Motionless, he felt the cold curve of the musket's trigger under his finger.

The mouse was nibbling in contentment when he fired. Because he was so close to the target, his poor marksmanship skills didn't matter this time. The ball rammed into the animal with such force the mouse skipped off the floor and thudded against the hut's far wall.

Boucher dragged himself across the space and found it. The musket ball had crushed and cratered the little body, but he didn't care. He needed the meat, not the pelt.

He sifted through the ashes of the ancient fire hoping for a hot ember, but it was cold and dead. Then he remembered his tinderbox. He pulled it out of his woolen capote pocket and opened the metal top. The three fire-making tools were there: flint, fire steel, and the scorched rag for tinder. But his heart sank when he felt the rag; it was still wet from his fall into the pond.

He cried out, *"Mon Dieu,* why are you so against me? Will I finally die from yet another failure?"

Challenging himself once more, he crawled and searched for tinder in the hut, but he was growing steadily weaker and more lightheaded. He sat still while the room spun around him. With little hope of accomplishment remaining, he stared at the inert mouse with its blood muddying the dirt floor.

As if reverting to some ancestral memory, Boucher lifted the mouse above his head and started to squeeze. While the still-warm blood dribbled into his mouth, he lay on his back. He was so tired. He just wanted to sleep.

He closed his eyes and was soon transported to his family's big house in Wallonia. Everyone was gathered at the dinner table. Father, mother, sisters, brothers. Cheerful lights sparkled, and the mouth-watering smells of roasted meat and potatoes filled the room.

"Eat more, my son," his mother encouraged. "Think of the poor wretches who have nothing. Eat."

Then he thought he heard two cannon shots. Even in his dream, he knew what that meant.

Twenty-one

DANCING FISH SAT CROSS-LEGGED NEAR THE FIRE AND TURNED the test model over in his hands, letting the light catch the angles and corners. The wood felt smooth from the long rock- and sand-rubbing. The two miniature disks turned easily around the narrow pin as he spun them. His grandmother would be pleased to have one of his inventions with her when both her Breathing and Dreaming Souls traveled to the Sky World.

They had been chanting and praying for three days and nights at Achqueehgenom, their winter village. Long Pipe had led them with his steady drum rhythms and hypnotic voice while the clan's Matron and Sakima lay near death on her sleeping platform nearby. The prayers for Hard Stick were for a swift journey to join the stars and the Sky People. The Dying Chant created the flow of energy that would soon carry her Souls through the clouds.

A pause was called and Dancing Fish watched the fire pop and snap, the sparks floating up toward the smoke hole of the longhouse. Yellow firelight hung in the sad eyes of his clan who would soon lose their leader. He wished Willow were sitting next to him so he could stroke her long hair, but she was in the women's house for her moon time.

It had rained most of the day with ranks of thunder rolling and banging. Two of the bangs had sounded oddly familiar to him, but he had paid no more attention. The burial was not far off, and he needed to finish his offering, which would rest with Hard Stick in her grave.

"*Hè-yó-hè*, Little Eel, what do you have there?"

The light from the fire abruptly darkened, and he looked up to see the speaker of the mocking voice he knew so well. High Limb stood between him and the fire, and his two young proteges flanked him like shadows on each side, ready to protect their towering leader. Their bodies were painted and smudged in black to honor the ending of a long life on Mother Earth.

"You know I am not called Little Eel now," Dancing Fish said, annoyed. "We were made men at the same time. We've both seen 18 winters. I don't use your baby name. Why do you use mine?"

High Limb bent his tall body down from the waist and a nasty grin spread across his blackened face. "Because you're still a baby in my eyes. A baby who always wants to go his own way. And a strange one at that." His shadows snickered. High Limb leaned in closer. "And who likes to spend time alone with that crazy Owl practicing sorcery or who knows what."

High Limb suddenly reached forward and grabbed the wooden model from his hands and stepped back with it.

Dancing Fish jumped to his feet. "Give it back! It's for the burial." He reached for it, but High Limb held it high over his head, taunting.

The giant finally lowered and examined the model. "Is this another one of your silly ideas? A toy to offer to the evil Matantu Spirit? Or just something to amuse women?" All three were now laughing at him.

Dancing Fish tightened his fists. "You're an ignorant fool, you know that? It's a model for making our drag-alongs easier. More useful. For all of us." He took a small step forward while keeping his eyes on the model. "Even someone as dull as you should understand how disks that turn are better than poles that drag in the dirt." He snorted with contempt.

"Dull, eh?" High Limb said. "Well, I'm no Dream Maker, like they say you are—" He held out the model toward him. "But then, I don't waste time." With a quick flip of his wrist, he tossed the wooden model into the hottest part of the fire.

Dancing Fish lunged forward, but High Limb was ready for him, wrapping his long arms around his chest and clasping him in a tight bear hold. Thinking fast, Dancing Fish lifted his foot and stomped down hard on High Limb's, and soon they were on the ground, wrestling in the dirt. The two shadows stood by, not moving.

High Limb suddenly screamed out and released his hold. His head had come too close to the fire, and the stink of singed hair was strong.

Older men soon pulled them apart.

"What's wrong with you two?" Thundercloud yelled before punching them both hard on the arm. "Our Matron is dying in the next area, and you fight like children? Show respect to the Turtle Clan and to yourselves." The War Chief pushed them away, and they took their places again around the fire.

Dancing Fish could do nothing but watch while hissing flames consumed the last of his tiny model. He glanced at High Limb, who was holding his head and moaning. The idiot deserved it. He could make a new model—the plan was in his head. If the Matron could hold on a little longer.

▶◀

The night's chanting completed, families stretched, yawned, and gathered their things.

"*Hè-yó*, Dream Maker!" shouted out Rock, who was still seated halfway around the fire circle. Dancing Fish's friend held a gourd bowl full of hominy between his fleshy knees and was fingering it into his mouth as fast as he could. He stopped to smile and make sure people were listening. "If you're so smart, why did you leave the fermenting turnips and cabbage on the island? They'll be mush when we return in the spring."

Rock's mother, now standing, nudged him. "Don't make him feel bad. He's already promised to go back to Werpoes at first light."

"And why don't you go with him?" Thundercloud said loudly, turning from Dancing Fish to Rock. "Two birdbrains can make one man and keep each other company."

Several around the fire laughed and Dancing Fish felt his face warming. "I admit my mistake. I'll make it up to everyone. How about some nice oysters? I know exactly where they're hiding."

"The water isn't too cold?" asked his mother, Yellow Flower.

"Not for me," he said. "I'll wait for the low tide. Besides, you know the saying—"

Everyone joined their voices after recognizing the verbal prompt: "Cold time is good time for oysters!"

Dancing Fish saw the many smiles—a welcome relief from the sadness and tension around the fire.

"But can you make the trip in a single sun?" his mother asked, a worried look on her face as she picked up their bowls. "We've already had frost, and Father Sun's journey is now short."

"Not with his fat friend he won't," High Limb blurted out, sneering at Rock and rubbing his head. "He'll stop to gather every acorn he sees on the way."

Dancing Fish glared but ignored the interruption. "Yes, mother. We both know the paths well." He looked at Rock, who nodded while he licked his fingers clean.

"We'll be back with light still in the sky. I promise."

▶◀

High Limb squatted at the edge of the outside fire, its glowing embers casting a weak light. His shadows sat facing him, waiting. The rain had stopped, but all three were wrapped against the cold in their fall skins.

"I want both of you to follow Dancing Fish to Werpoes tomorrow," he said, stirring the fire with a stick. "Stay out of sight but watch. Those two will get into some kind of trouble, I'm sure of it. And I want to know what."

The two figures—despite their real names he called them simply Big Shadow and Little Shadow—looked at each other with wrinkled brows.

He understood their concern. "Don't worry about being missed at the chanting. I'll say I sent you out to scout. I will soon be the Kit War Chief, so no one will question it."

"Will you give us more tobacco?" Big Shadow asked, lifting the empty pouch that hung from his neck.

He sighed. "You should be happy enough to be my assistants. And now you want gifts, too?"

Big Shadow, the taller of the two and a little slower in the head, looked troubled.

High Limb waved his hand with disdain. "Yes, yes, alright. More tobacco, if you want."

Both shadows smiled.

"So remember: stay out of sight but watch closely." He stared at each of them in turn. "Can you do this simple task?"

They both grunted.

He stood and they followed. "Don't disappoint me," he said as he threw the stick in the fire and walked off toward his longhouse.

Twenty-two

AT DAWN, A CHILLY WIND SAILED BETWEEN THE LONGHOUSES while wisps of blue smoke rose unsteadily from them. The snows would start early this year, Dancing Fish thought.

He and Rock were ready. They both wore their winter leggings, long hunting shirts, and beaver vests for added warmth, and all could be easily shed if they worked up a sweat.

He whistled to Kong, who was immediately at his side. A dog was always good on a hunt or a trip, and Kong, a wolf descendant, was a fine dog. More than once he had alerted his humans to the presence of deer, fox, beaver, or anything with a beating heart and a scent. And that included man. With Kong alongside, Dancing Fish had never been caught unaware when someone approached. Kong habitually froze and gave a low growl. The louder the growl, the higher the level of threat. Barking called for immediate action.

He placed a small pinch of tobacco at their feet. "For our safe return."

"Our safe return," repeated Rock.

The path led southwest and Kong trotted easily in front of the two friends as they walked side by side. The trees still burned with colors—yellow, orange, red—and the rising sun was at their backs, warming them.

"Teach me the words again," Rock said while they walked. Rock was heavy and breathed faster to keep up.

Dancing Fish had told him about the Visitors from the East soon after the disastrous voyage on Hudson's ship. And each time he did, Rock would shake his head with incomprehension. He wanted to learn the strange words, but he would soon forget, and eventually, he would ask the same questions all over. Dancing Fish would patiently say the words again, hoping they would stick in his friend's empty head.

Over the last three sun cycles there had been several ships of the white strangers passing by their summer camp on the island, but no sign of Master Hudson. The ships floated up the Great River and returned after harvest time, rarely stopping.

He could see that the bearded men were starting to visit their Lenapehoking lands more and more, either coming from the ships or walking from the east and north. They spoke mostly the tongue of the man Kluk and some of Hudson. Dancing Fish was often called in to translate, and every time he did, he learned more of their words.

These men never stayed long in one place; just long enough to catch the fur animals or trade for their skins. Then they would disappear. With each visit, the People were wary, but there was little trouble. The men never planted crops and rarely made a hateful move, and then only after drinking the water that flamed in the throat. The band called them "Alone Men" and left them that way. But these pale strangers were never far from Dancing Fish's thoughts.

Three fingers of sun later and they were at the waterway. They were careful to avoid Monatun, the Place of Dangerous Waters, where his parents had drowned and he had barely escaped the same fate. Instead of the wild currents that had swallowed many from the Manahate band over time, this was a calm and narrow section of water just to the north. It was only one bow shot over to Mannahatta, and once across to the island there was a clear and wide path south to Werpoes.

For as long as anyone could remember an old man with

long white hair had run a ferry service here to take people back and forth across the waterway. He asked for wampum or food in exchange for the short journey.

The man was snoring on a bed of reeds when they approached. Motioning for silence with a finger to his lips, Dancing Fish pulled out a single strand of the shell beads and dangled it above the man's open mouth. Rock giggled uncontrollably while he dropped the end of the strand into and out of the man's mouth in time with his breathing. Finally, Kong barked and the man jolted up.

"What's this?" he said, looking confused and spitting out the shells from his mouth.

Dancing Fish and Rock were both bent over with laughter while Kong barked excitedly.

The man was angry but soon calmed and pushed the wampum strand into his frayed apron. He motioned them to the canoe.

Three men and a big dog made a heavy load, and they were close to tipping a few times whenever the two friends laughed too hard, but the old man was an expert paddler and they landed safely on the other bank.

The two climbed a small hill with Kong in the lead and were soon on the trail. This was the Path to the Wading Place—the same one he had walked when he left the ship, and it led in a curving line down the island to Werpoes.

The sun was near its highest, and they made good time on the smooth pathway now layered with colored leaves they kicked while they walked.

In moments of silence between jokes and gossip Dancing Fish reflected, as he often did, on what had happened on Master Hudson's ship. The Fourth Fire Prophecy—questioning if the white strangers were good or bad—still hung over him and the band, and the appearance of the Alone Men was a sign. His dreams now included white men—some good, some evil.

The evil ones worried him.

▶◀

The sun hung low while the trio walked around the pond and went directly to the longhouse. Dancing Fish found the buried caches and was digging them up when he heard Kong barking. An alarm bark.

Kong stood rigid outside one of the smaller wigwams that made up the summer village. His neck fur pointed straight up. In between the barks and growls, Dancing Fish thought he heard moaning coming from inside.

"Kong, sit!" he commanded as he pulled back the door flap. He peered into the gloom and saw the man lying on the floor. Rock held the flap open while Dancing Fish entered slowly, his knife in his hand and ready.

The light was dim but he could see he was a white man, short and stout with dark hair that curled like winter's beech leaves. He was lying on his back, eyes closed, not moving, except he groaned from time to time. There was dried blood on his hairy face, and one of his legs was bandaged and also bloody. A dead mouse lay next to his head.

Dancing Fish crawled slowly up to the man and touched him on the arm. Nothing. He pushed on his unhurt thigh. Again, nothing. Then he poked the bandaged leg and the man stirred, turned his head and opened his blue eyes to look at him. He spoke a few words Dancing Fish didn't understand. It wasn't the tongue of Kluk. Or of Hudson. Something different. Yet he looked like them.

He called to Rock, who opened the flap to let in more light. Kong sat nearby, now calm but curious about what he had found.

The man was weak and shaking from cold. He spoke more strange words and made a sign for eating. He rolled over on his good side, propped himself on his elbow, and gave the sign for eating again, then extended his hand.

"Give me your pemmican," Dancing Fish said to his friend.

Rock handed over a small pouch with the traveling food.

Dancing Fish opened the pouch and shook some of the mixture of nuts, berries, and dried meat into the man's waiting hand, which went immediately to his mouth. He chewed and swallowed slowly and reached out for more. He was smiling now.

They soon had the man sitting and leaning against one of the wigwam's support posts. He looked better. He drank willow bark tea heated on a new fire Rock had made. This was for calming and for the pain.

While the man drank and warmed up, Dancing Fish touched his own extended tongue and asked, "Dutch? English?"

"French," the man responded. "But we can speak Dutch or English, if you like."

"Yes. English," Dancing Fish said. The tongue of Hudson was what he understood and spoke best.

Kneeling, he took time to open the man's bandages and study his leg wound. "The bleeding's stopped, but we must be careful with the poison," Dancing Fish said to Rock, who nodded in agreement. "He needs the poultice."

Rock pulled out another small pouch. It was filled with the salve of crushed nightshade, sassafras, tobacco, and dried beaver testicle, all blended with otter grease. Rock dipped his finger into the salve and smeared it gently on the wound. The man winced.

"This helps heal," Dancing Fish said to him.

The man let Rock continue applying the salve that soon coated his wound.

They all sat in silence for a while, staring at the fire. Dancing Fish asked, "What is name?" He pointed to himself and Rock, saying their names. Then he pointed to the man and raised his eyebrows. "You?"

"Boo-shay," the man said.

"Boo-shay," Dancing Fish repeated. Rock also said it but more awkwardly.

The man smiled.

"You know Master Hudson?"

Boo-shay cocked his head in surprise and looked at him. "Captain Henry Hudson? Of the *Half Moon*?"

Dancing Fish nodded with excitement. "Yes. Half Moon ship. Master Hudson."

Boo-shay faced back to the fire. "It's a long story."

Dancing Fish had decided. "We have time. We stay and sleep. Leave tomorrow."

The man gave a confused look. "Leave tomorrow for where?"

"Achqueehgenom. North on Aquehung river. Our winter home. You come."

"But the ship—"

"What ship?"

"The ship to pick me up. I think I heard the cannons yesterday. Two cannon shots, and they would wait at the point. For me and the others. But not for long."

Dancing Fish thought about the two odd thunderclaps the day before. They could have been ship cannons. He stood. "I go to Kapsee and look for ship. And for oysters. You rest now. Later tell story of Master Hudson."

He instructed Rock to clean up the man's blood with their water and replace it from the pond. And re-wrap the wounded leg with strips of deerskin they carried. He would be back soon.

Rock motioned to him and they met outside the wigwam. "Are you sure you want to bring this stranger to our home?" Rock asked in a hushed voice. "This is not normal. And dangerous, no?"

He looked into his friend's questioning eyes. "Normal is

changing. I feel this is the best way. Go back and watch over him."

Before he left, Dancing Fish opened the door flap and looked in at the man whose hairy face and eyes glowed in the fire's light. His dreams were coming alive again. And with another white stranger. Was his fate to be tied to them always?

Twenty-three

THERE WAS NO SHIP. AND NO ONE WAITING AT THE POINT.

The two young natives carried Boucher holding each end of the litter. It was made of saplings tied with weeds and vines and had taken them less than one hour to build. *These people are quite ingenious*, Boucher thought. They had bound his possessions—his musket and the bag he needed—to the litter's rails.

"We go fast," the one named Dancing Fish—and who was clearly the leader of the two—had said. "Oysters." He had opened a closed basket lined with black pitch and holding water and at least a dozen or more good-sized oysters. It was decided that Boucher would hold the oyster basket between his legs on the litter. Another smart decision by the young man he had a hard time calling a "savage." The native's mind was as keen as any European he had known, including himself at that age.

Dancing Fish guided them from the rear. The one in front, Rock, was thicker and bulkier, and seemed to be straining more. But Boucher noted how the leader would intentionally slow the pace from time to time in an obvious kindness to his partner. A large black dog led the group with occasional sprints off the path to chase a rabbit or a squirrel.

The trio and the dog moved with steady progress, stopping every hour or so to rest and to eat the surprisingly tasty and filling nut mix and drink the spring water they carried and replaced along the route.

At the first break, Boucher told them the sad story of Henry Hudson's end. How his ship had returned to London the previous autumn from another voyage of exploration—this time for the English—but without either Hudson or his son, John, aboard. It gradually came out that there had been a mutiny while the ship was high in the northwestern French latitudes, and the captain, his son, and several others had been set adrift in a small boat with neither supplies nor weapons. They had not been heard from since. And conveniently, none of the leaders of the mutiny, including Robert Juet and Cornelis Klock, had survived during the return voyage, and those who did claimed they were innocent like new babes. The ongoing depositions and an eventual trial would sort it out at some point.

"Master Hudson, son, Juet dead?" Dancing Fish asked him as he drank from the water pouch.

"Yes," he replied. He noticed the Indian got very quiet at this news and did not speak for a while.

"Why you here?" Dancing Fish asked him, the boy's striking amber eyes studying his.

He told them his story. How he was the middle son of the brother of Katherine Hudson, Henry's widow. How the family was from the French-speaking Walloon territory of the Low Countries. He kept to himself how he had tried various pursuits in life and had been unlucky in them all. And now, with a wife and young son and daughter to support—and nothing to inherit due to his being the second oldest of three boys—he made use of the only advantages he had: his family connection to the famous explorer and his natural way with words, whether in French, English, or Dutch.

Boucher had traveled to Amsterdam at the beginning of the year and approached the Van Tweehuysen merchant syndicate that was sending ships to the New World for trading. Beavers were growing scarce from the traditional sources in Russia, and everyone was talking about the unlimited supply of valuable pelts across the Atlantic.

With a letter of introduction from the famous explorer's widow—and some artful exaggeration of his trading skills—he was assigned to the next ship leaving for *Nieu Nederlandt* in the spring. It had arrived at the mouth of Hudson's North River in June, but they didn't stop. Instead, they continued up, deep into the land of the Mahican tribe. There they had spent the summer trading with the natives for peltries. The same pelts, he observed, these two young natives wore as jerkins against the cold.

With the end of the trading season closing in on them, the ship's captain, Adriaen Block, and the Supercargo—the trade master—had sent him and two others in an extra boat downriver to scout for last-minute trading opportunities. They would be picked up by the ship on its way down the river before heading for home.

"We'll be at the point of the island by the river's mouth in ten days time," the Dutch captain had told him. "Mark it carefully. We'll fire two cannon shots close together. No more. Shot is too precious if we meet freebooters on the crossing. We'll wait as long as we can for you. If the wind is fair and you don't appear, we leave without you." Then he gave him a sneering grin. "And you can spend the winter with the savages and greet us in the spring. By then, you'll be either a much wiser man—or very dead."

He had heard the cannons, alright. But there was nothing to do about it. Now he was stuck. And on his way to the home of these same savages.

▶◀

Dancing Fish stared ahead and tried to sort out his feelings while they carried Boo-shay north.

It had been three years—he now also used the white men's word for sun cycle—since he dove off Master Hudson's ship.

He was sorry to hear about Hudson. He felt he was a good man at heart. His son, Jawn, too. And he suspected Joo-et had something to do with their deaths. He was surprised the man had survived their struggle and stabbing, but he was not unhappy about him being dead at last. Joo-et was a dark Spirit who had threatened—even killed—the People.

The increasing visits by the Alone Men reminded him that the Fire Prophecy was not resolved. His Manahate band and the white strangers were dancing to their own rhythms around the fire of life. Others in the band said the visitors would move slowly out of their lives. Dancing Fish didn't believe this. Owl's words after he left the ship that day—and in his later dreams and waking visions—told him that their story with the Whites was not over. And whether they were good or bad for the People was a question still needing an answer.

Kong barked and bounded off the path after some animal.

As was his habit whenever his thoughts turned to the white visitors, he wanted to reach for the hard button that now hung from a loop of deer sinew around his neck, next to his tobacco pouch. He couldn't take his hands from the litter so he focused on the swinging and beating of the pendant against his chest. Remembering when he received it on the beach at Ishpatena from Hudson and his men, he kept it as a reminder of the prophecy, and that he should remain alert to the activities of the Visitors from the East. He thought about it now with Boo-shay lying in front of him. He had made the decision to help him, and he hoped it was the right one.

The Sakima had made him a new type of counselor on the subject of the Whites—the White Keeper. His thoughts and opinions of them were being listened to by others. Which was one reason he was bringing Boo-shay back to the village. This would be another opportunity to learn about these strange men. They were clearly not Spirits, but what they truly were remained a mystery.

Kong reappeared without a prize, but a happy tongue lolled from his open mouth when he retook his position at the head of the group on its slow pace north.

With his higher status in the band, Dancing Fish felt less pressure to discard his independent ideas. People were starting to appreciate his curiosity and his different way of looking at their world. He considered how he had created more tools that worked better than the traditional ones of the People. He had shown how to take a visitor's metal knife, soften it on the fire, then bend it to form a hook. It made a good hand tool for weeding in the fields.

His new leadership role gave him more confidence and, he hoped, made him more attractive to Willow. She would have to make up her mind soon. They had been preparing to unite their families when High Limb had stuck his dirty nose into their courtship and was now trying to steal her away for himself. It seemed High Limb's father, Sawgrass, had offered Willow's father more—and better—gifts at the last moment.

Willow had told him over and over she wanted to marry *him*, not High Limb—she despised him. But the tradition of the father and mother deciding what was best for their daughter was strong. He would have to do something special to win back Willow.

Twenty-four

HIGH LIMB WATCHED WILLOW FROM THE EDGE OF THE TREES. She was with the other girls preparing the harvest crops for the village. Some ground corn into meal, others cut squash into strips to hang and dry in the sun. Willow laughed and threw corn husks at the others. She was so beautiful. And so ripe. Long-legged with strong arms and hips growing wider for the children he wanted with her.

She had had her moon for at least two cycles and now retreated to the women's house with the others. He was surprised so many of the women went to the house at the same time, but there were many things he did not understand about women. Except that he wanted this one. And not just to show up Dancing Fish, although the thought also gave him great satisfaction.

It bothered him that Willow was already joining with Dancing Fish regularly, but it made him feel powerful knowing he could have her, too. And he felt confident he would end up with her. There was nothing the insane Dream Maker could do about it.

He caught her eye and motioned to her. She shook her head no. He motioned again with more force. Another no.

He marched across the open space and grabbed her hand. "Come with me. Now."

She shook her arm free and hurled a defiant look. "No. I

have work to do here."

All the others had frozen in place, watching.

High Limb would not be embarrassed like this. He looked down fiercely into her eyes. "You'll come with me now, or there'll be trouble for your family. Do you understand?" He grabbed her arm again, holding tight this time.

She narrowed her eyes and then dropped them to the ground. She nodded and let herself be led to the woods.

He pulled her down to the soft patch of moss he had found. He leaned across and kissed her, at the same time pushing her to the ground. He searched for her tongue but she kept pulling it away.

"Stop fighting me!" he shouted, trying to control his voice.

"I'll fight you as much as I want," she said, challenging him.

He quickly struck her with a loose fist on the cheek.

She cried out and pulled back from him, propping herself on her elbows.

He studied her face while she touched the growing bruise. "Then it will go badly for you. And for your whole family." He leaned away from her. "I am the son of Sawgrass, the future War Chief, and I am the Matron's grandnephew." He let that sink in. "And you—you and your family are nothing in comparison."

"Maybe so," she said boldly, "but don't forget Dancing Fish is the Matron's direct grandson, and he has been courting me much longer than you."

"That may be true. But where is he now? Off on one of his idiotic adventures, isn't he?" He shifted his body and attempted a smile. "He will always be different—an outsider. And I will always be strong and more importantly: here. I'm the one who can take care of you. Not him. He has his white, hairy strangers. And I have—"

He reached his hand under her short deerskin and found what he was seeking, sliding his finger in as far as it would go. He could see the muscles in her jaw bunching. But when he pushed her back onto the moss, she pulled up her dress and opened her legs to him.

▶◀

The small group had stopped to rest in a clearing next to the path. A stream gurgled nearby, and they sat on grass flattened and turned brown from the cold. All around them, colored leaves fell from the trees, knocking into others on their way down—whispering about the coming winter.

They had just started to drink and eat when Kong stood and growled. Then he plunged into the bushes.

"Wait here," Dancing Fish said in a hushed voice as he leapt to his feet. He motioned to Rock. "Get your knife and small spear ready." He nodded in Boo-shay's direction. "Protect this man." He sprinted to the opposite side of the clearing where Kong had disappeared.

Dancing Fish walked with silent steps and circled around the sound of growling and low voices. He soon saw the source.

Big and Little Shadow were crouched down, trying to calm Kong, who stood facing them with his teeth bared. They knew Kong, but the dog didn't like finding these two hiding so far from home.

"*Hè-yó!*" Dancing Fish approached the men's backs, his knife extended.

They jumped up, startled, and turned to face him. "We . . . We were just hunting," said Big Shadow, his voice trailing off.

"Yes, hunting," Little Shadow said after a moment of hesitation.

"Really?" Dancing Fish said while he made a hand signal to Kong, who immediately stopped his threatening noises to sit on his haunches.

He approached the two when he saw their knives sheathed. "Strange you would be hunting near the exact spot where we're

125

resting." He looked at the boys who were several winters younger than him and not yet initiated. "Don't you think?"

Big Shadow shrugged. "Not so strange. We all know the path."

Dancing Fish knew exactly what they were doing. Spying for High Limb, without doubt. "Well, come join us then."

▶◀

"Do you hunt beaver?" Boo-shay asked Dancing Fish while they took their final drinks and prepared to resume the trip. The white man was holding one of their beaver vests. They had built up a sweat walking with the added weight of the injured man and had removed them.

"Yes," he said. "Good skin. Keep us warm."

"And good meat," Rock added, showing off his new words while smiling and patting his stomach.

"And do you trade the skins with white men like me?" Boo-shay asked, now looking at both of them.

Dancing Fish suddenly remembered the conversation he had had with the man Kluk on Hudson's ship. Always more questions about the beaver. "Not many like you, but yes."

Rock started to laugh. He said to his friend in their tongue, "Why are the visitors so interested in these beavers? They're like rats to me."

Dancing Fish knew there was much more to beavers than that. Beside their meat and fur skins, the ponds they made were good for the land, helping with drainage, and as a water reserve in dry spells. Their inner testicles and the yellow secretions they made were used for medicines. But he also knew his People only took the beavers they needed. They never piled them up like these men did.

He asked Boo-shay, "Why you like beaver so much?"

Boo-shay took his time before speaking. "The furs of

126

beavers—and otter, fox, sable, and mink—have value to us back home. We make good clothing from them. They are much prized."

"For hats?" he said without thinking.

Boo-shay looked surprised. "Yes, exactly. For hats. And much more."

"Like what?" Dancing Fish asked, now more curious. And he noticed the two shadows paying close attention to this conversation. But they would understand nothing so long as he kept it in English.

Boo-shay lifted his eyes to think. "For many things: hats, gloves, overcoats, shoes, and trimmings for clothes."

Dancing Fish didn't know what all these words meant, but the message was clear: the Whites wanted the skins and furs of these animals.

"No beaver where you live?" he asked the man.

"Yes, but fewer. You have many, many more."

He watched Boo-shay's eyes light up when he said those words. Now he understood. These animals had become important, and the strangers had taken too many from their own lands. While he listened to Boo-shay, Dancing Fish focused his mind on something that was small during his days on Master Hudson's ship, but that was now growing. A realization.

These men knew little of what every Manahate—in fact, all the People—knew. That the Creator had made the earth and everything upon it. And there was a balance to all these creations. An animal was no less in the eyes of the Creator than a man. Or a tree. Or a flowing river. And if an animal was sacrificed for a human to survive, the human offered prayers and thanks. If the People took, they gave back. This was the right way. The great harmony of giving and taking.

Yet from what Dancing Fish had seen so far, these visitors did not believe in this balance. They took, but what did they give back? Only trinkets and tools. Some—like metal knives—were useful to the People. He could not deny this. But when they had enough knives, then what? What else were the Whites giving? Or were they only taking?

Then he remembered what Hard Stick had said about the second fire prophet: *Their hearts may be filled with greed for the riches of our land.* He still needed to learn more about what was in the minds and the hearts of strangers. And Boo-shay could show him.

As they got up to continue the journey, he said to the injured man, "We go hunt the beaver. Together. You see." *And so will I,* he thought.

Twenty-five

THE SUN WAS A MEMORY WHEN THEY FINALLY REACHED THE village and entered a cluster of rounded and oblong huts. But there was still enough light in the sky to see the crowd of natives that instantly surrounded them. Boucher suddenly felt nervous and vulnerable. At least two score of men, women, and children gathered around as the litter made its way forward. Some were pointing at him and talking. Others stood with inscrutable faces and their arms crossed.

His two carriers set him down gently in a wide clearing next to a central fire, its flames leaping high and shooting sparks skyward.

"Can you stand?" Dancing Fish asked.

"Yes, if you help me."

The two natives pulled him up, and he held onto them for support. His injured leg was stiff, but he noticed the pain had gone down significantly. The salve or the tea had done its work.

They were looking at the large crowd with their backs to the warming fire. Boucher saw that the Indians all sported furs of various descriptions, including cloaks, vests, and robes.

A man and woman stepped through the group. The man spoke sharply to Dancing Fish with a tone of rebuke.

"Father and mother angry with me for long journey," he told him. "And ask about you." The young man said something that seemed to calm his parents, then he handed the basket of oysters to his mother, who peered inside and smiled.

The mother quickly stepped aside when a tall, elegant native strode forward. His hair was tied back into a round bun with a copper skewer pushing through it. A thick line of white paint divided his face, and he wore a beautiful feather mantle tied at his throat and thrown over one shoulder. He was clearly a leader because when he held up his hand, the murmuring stopped immediately. He stood motionless, waiting.

Boucher leaned toward Dancing Fish's ear and asked if he could say something to the assembled group. "What you taught me, remember?" he whispered.

The young man smiled and nodded.

Still holding onto the two, Boucher pulled himself up as best he could and spoke slowly and carefully in their language, moving his head from the leader across the entire crowd, "I am thankful for your invitation to be with you."

There was an immediate reaction with low talking and faint smiles appearing on many of their faces. He asked Dancing Fish to translate the next part for him.

He touched his injured leg. "I won't be dancing with you tonight but hopefully soon." He looked into the eyes of the leader. "White strangers with hairy faces can dance very well!"

The leader laughed openly at this and approached. He grabbed him by both arms and said something to Dancing Fish, who translated: "For sad reasons, we are not dancing tonight, but you have a good heart and are welcome here."

Boucher thanked the leader and looked out at the mass of Indians who all studied him intently. One way or another, he would get to know these people. And learn what they could offer him. Which he hoped was more than he could offer them.

▶◀

A space was made for the man in the smoky longhouse where

his family lived. Dancing Fish watched while a curing woman started to work on Boo-shay's leg with her potions and chanting. His heart was heavy with the news Hard Stick would soon be joining the stars. New leaders had been chosen by the Sakima and the clan's other important women, including his mother, during the time he was gone. Thundercloud would be Sachem, and Sawgrass—High Limb's father—would be the new War Chief, replacing Thundercloud in that role. These were sensible decisions.

He had been summoned to meet the leaders in the Council House as soon as the white man was comfortable. Rock, who was endlessly fascinated by this man, would watch over him.

The Council House was the largest longhouse in Achqueehgenom village. Also the home of the Manahate band's Sachem or Sakima, it served many other purposes and was segmented into three sections, each divided by walls of reed matting. Dancing Fish entered the inner room, which was reserved for important meetings of the band. A fire blazed in the center, attended by the Sachem's children, who also served the food and drinks to guests.

Thundercloud, now the new Sachem, was already at his place on the stump covered by a thick bear hide. The stump was against the wall that led to a private chamber where Hard Stick was currently preparing for her final journey. Completing the circle around the fire were Sawgrass, Long Pipe—the holy leader—and the family bosses, mostly older women. All sat on folded skins and smoked from small personal pipes. Tea steamed in clay pots at their feet.

Thundercloud gestured to the floor, and Dancing Fish moved to the other side of the fire to sit on a skin.

"Tell us of your meeting this man and your decision to bring him here," the Sachem said evenly while he sipped his tea. "You saw how I welcomed him earlier, but now I want to know more."

He told the story of finding Boo-shay close to death at Werpoes, and how he thought it best to bring him to the village and see what they could learn from him. As a representative of the Salt People. This was one of their new names for the visitors who came on ships from the south and east, like the salt tide.

"You—on your own—bring an enemy into our midst?" Sawgrass suddenly bellowed, standing and throwing his tea into the fire. "You, who thinks he is different and knows better?"

"Enemy?" Dancing Fish said, ready to stand himself but thinking better of confronting the new War Chief.

"Yes," Sawgrass said, jabbing his thumb toward him. "Wasn't it you who saw these white men kill our people? You, yourself, have doubts about these Salt strangers, do you not?"

He looked into the man's eyes and recognized an older High Limb, and just as full of hostility. He responded cautiously, "We do have to be careful, true, but I think—"

"*You* think?" Sawgrass interrupted. "You, who have only seen 18 fallings of the leaves, will now impart to us your depth of wisdom? To us who have fought battles, who have hunted bear, who have created children." He laughed, shook his head, and sat back down.

Thundercloud rapped the Sachem's club on the ground. "Let's not throw stones so quickly. Dancing Fish was chosen as White Keeper because he has the most experience with these men. He dreams of them. His opinion counts." He stared at Sawgrass, who stared back.

Thundercloud then turned to look at Dancing Fish across the fire. "And you think there is no treachery in this man, or danger to us?"

"From this man, no," Dancing Fish said with conviction. "I know he seems a little helpless in the way of nature and our manner, but he is not stupid. You see how clever he can be when he speaks. If we are helpful to him, he can be helpful to us. We can learn more about these strangers if we keep him with us for the winter. I cannot speak about all these trading visitors, but I can about this man, who has a good heart. This is what I believe."

"And this is what I believe," Sawgrass said, standing again and capturing all eyes from around the fire. "I am now the War Chief, am I not?" Everyone murmured or nodded, including Thundercloud. "And the War Chief is responsible for the safety of this village, this band." More murmurs of assent.

Sawgrass faced the Sachem. "I do not trust the judgments of young Dancing Fish, and so I appoint my son, High Limb, to be both Kit War Chief and"—he paused and looked down, thinking—"*Enemy Keeper*. To share the role with Dancing Fish in watching over *all* these hairy-faced strangers who are coming more and more among us. This is the safest and best way." He made a grunting noise and sat down.

All eyes went to the new Sachem.

Thundercloud stared into the fire for some time before speaking. "We will keep this Boo-shay with us during the winter," he said in a firm voice to everyone assembled. "We'll learn from him what we can. Dancing Fish *and* High Limb will watch over him, each in his own way. This is both for our safety and his." He looked hard at Dancing Fish. "We cannot be surprised by anything this man might do. Is that clear to you?"

"Yes, Sachem," he said slowly. This was not what he expected.

"And you will learn more of his tongue every day and teach him ours," Thundercloud added. "This can only help us in understanding these Salt People."

"And you will help High Limb do the same," Sawgrass interjected.

Dancing Fish poked at the fire and watched it flare, pushing down his anger. "Yes, War Chief," he said without expression. He was not happy with this turn of events. He was now officially joined with the person he hated most.

▶◀

The debate was over and all stood to leave the council chamber. "Stay, Dancing Fish," the new Sachem said, motioning for him to come and sit near him.

"I know you are angry at Sawgrass and about High Limb," Thundercloud said, peering into the fire. "But it's for the best. There must be peace with the families and the clans." He made a fist and held it up. "There is strength when the Turtle, Wolf, and Turkey clans are together."

He turned to Dancing Fish. "You have your own mind, I know. But you must also try to think of the whole band. Can you do this? For all of us?"

Dancing Fish hesitated only a moment. He nodded his head.

"So," Thundercloud said, changing the tone of his voice and moving off the stump to sit on the ground at his level. "Did this man know your Master Hudson?"

He relaxed. "A good question, Uncle, with an interesting answer." He explained the family connection between Hudson and Boo-shay.

The new Sachem clasped his fingers together and bounced them against his chin in thought. "This is another sign," he said. "For you to find a white man connected to Hudson and to save his life. This is not a coincidence. You were led to Werpoes to discover this man—I am sure of it." He looked directly into Dancing Fish's eyes. "You continue to intertwine with the cord of the Fire Prophecy. I once said you were chosen, and I believe it more now."

Dancing Fish replied without thinking, "I hope I'm not hanging by that cord with just one finger."

"Then we're hanging with you," the new Sachem said.

Twenty-six

HIGH LIMB MET HIS SHADOWS BEHIND THE LONGHOUSE WITH the sun at three fingers above the trees. An area of brush had been cleared and three logs arranged for quiet smoking and talking. Each sat on a log and faced into a dead fire circle.

"Did you hear the news?" he asked his young followers.

They looked at him excitedly. Everyone knew there had been an important council meeting the night before.

"I am now the Kit War Chief," he announced with pride. He waited for a response but received only blank looks. "The War Chief's assistant," he continued, "who will one day *be* the War Chief."

Understanding finally showed on their faces. "Oh, good news," Big Shadow said, smiling widely.

"Yes, good," Little Shadow quickly followed in his quiet voice.

He frowned at his underlings. "From now on, do not use my nickname. I am Kit War Chief to you."

"Kit War Chief," they both said at the same time, glancing at each other.

"And"—he took his time to savor the moment—"I'm now also the Enemy Keeper!"

Silence.

"What does 'Enemy Keeper' mean?" Little Shadow finally asked, head tilting to one side.

He lifted his chest. "It means I will share watching over these Salt Men."

More glances between the assistants. "You will do this job with Dancing Fish?" one asked.

"Exactly. And I will also learn the tongue of these strangers." He was even prouder of his new positions after saying them out loud.

The shadows were clearly impressed, nodding and smiling. He was satisfied.

"So," he said, looking from one to the other, "what did you learn on your scouting trip to the island? What are these two up to?"

Big Shadow spoke for both. He explained how they could not follow the conversations in the strange tongue, but how they had later spoken to Rock, who could.

"And what did Rock say?" he asked impatiently. Why did he have such slow-witted followers?

"That the hairy man likes beavers and wants to trade for their skins."

Little Shadow jumped in. "And they will go on a beaver hunt soon. Together."

High Limb took in this information. This was good. He would get to know and help this man. And doing that would give him more power. Yes, this was good.

▶◀

Dust and fallen leaves, driven by a strong north wind, skipped along the packed dirt as Dancing Fish made his way to Willow's longhouse. It had been days, and he longed to see her. And he wanted to talk about his trip and of his irritations from the meeting.

The longhouses of the Turkey Clan were on the far side of the village, and when he came to the familiar wigwam he was disheartened to see Willow's father, Weetoq, squatting at a small fire he was working to rekindle. He was wrapped in a bearskin robe and muttering to himself. He glanced up at Dancing Fish's approach.

"Well, well," Weetoq started as he stood and pulled his cloak tight. "It's the wandering White Keeper." He motioned with his hand. "Join me."

He was hoping to avoid Willow's father, but it was not meant to be. He stepped closer to the man who was near his own height but with a growing stomach.

Weetoq was crafty. When hunting, he was usually the first to notice the footprints or other signs of the prey. But once he had spotted the deer or bear, he would save his energy and let others do the hard work of the chase.

Weetoq was of low birth but liked to act high-born, taking whatever advantage he could to help raise his position in the band—including using the beauty of his three daughters. He had the same wide-set eyes and flat nose of Willow, but the comparison ended there.

"So, I hear you're no longer alone in watching over the white strangers," Weetoq said, coaxing the fire back to life. "Including this new one you brought back." He snickered while he raised an eyebrow to Dancing Fish.

Word of the meeting had spread fast, as it usually did in the village. "I have a long history with these Salt Men," Dancing Fish said simply.

"But now High Limb has as much status as you, wouldn't you say?" Weetoq was baiting him, maneuvering.

"High Limb will never understand the visitors like I do," Dancing Fish said, watching the growing fire that popped from the wet wood.

"Maybe. Maybe not. But High Limb has a strong position for my eldest daughter. And his father has offered me respectful gifts and more wampum than your family." He stopped working the fire and inspected Dancing Fish from head to foot. "What do you have to offer that makes you a better choice for Willow?"

A combination of defeat and anger filled him. "How about the fact that Willow wants to be with me and not High Limb? Does that count for nothing?"

He could hear his voice growing louder, and he forced himself to remain calm. His overall goal was to start a new life with Willow, and to do that he needed to win over her father and her mother.

Weetoq gave Dancing Fish a doubtful look. "Are you really so naive? Do you think childish feelings are what matter most?" He scoffed openly. "When you can offer something of equal value to High Limb, I will consider it. Until then, go catch your dreams and make your inventions." He turned back to the fire.

Just then, Willow appeared. It was as though a wall of dark clouds had parted to reveal a shining sun.

"I'll leave you two alone," said Weetoq. He pulled close to Dancing Fish and whispered to him, "Remember what I said. No one gets something for nothing." He offered a false smile and crouched to enter the longhouse.

▶◀

Dancing Fish stood back and feasted on Willow's beauty. Her skin was the color of dark honey, and it glowed from the light greasing she had applied. "I'm glad to see you," he finally said with the only words he could manage. He noticed that her long, black hair was different; it fell loosely across her face.

She stepped closer and looked up at him with her dark eyes. "I hear you have some news."

On impulse, he grabbed her waist and pulled her to him. He kissed her deeply, finding her willing tongue, which danced with his until he had no more breath. He pointed to the log next to the fire. "Come."

"You met another white stranger," she said, moving close to him and watching the fire blaze. "You truly are the White Keeper. And Finder!" She giggled and turned to him.

"I think the Spirits like to reveal these hairy men to me," he said. "Maybe they're testing me—to see how much salt I can stand." They both laughed.

Willow's broad face turned serious. "Or, it's the Fire Prophecy working through you."

A sudden coldness chilled him. "Maybe so. But now I have to share my duties with you-know-who. He's also to be a Keeper, watching over these strangers."

She touched his hand. "I've heard that. What will you do?"

He was searching for the best response when he noticed something.

He reached up to Willow's hair and brushed it back from her face. She flinched and he saw a raised bruise on her cheek. "What's this?" he asked, a rage starting to pound in his ears.

She turned her head away. "It's nothing. An accident."

A bolt of fury shot through him. "Did he do this? High Limb?" He grabbed her arm. "Did he?"

Her eyes grew wet and she quickly wiped the tears away. "Yes. But it's not important. An accident, like I said."

"An *accident*? There are no accidents with that overgrown imbecile!" He was reeling. "Do you love him?"

She reached her arms across to his and looked deeply into his eyes. "No. Not at all. I love *you*."

He studied her face and focused on the swelling. "I'm going to kill him," he blurted out. "He can't do this!"

She squeezed his shoulders with a surprisingly hard grip. "Don't worry," she said. "I already have a plan to get back at him." One of her devious smiles erupted. "Let me show you something. Wait here."

She ducked through the longhouse opening, and he stood

fuming about what High Limb had done. And there could be much more to it, but he stopped his thoughts from going further. The image of Willow joining with High Limb was too hard to bear.

Willow reappeared holding a gourd bowl covered with a fine mesh of corn husk hairs. She wore hand moccasins and balanced the bowl on one of them. She stopped a few feet away before she carefully pulled back the cover and angled the bowl so he could see.

"What is it?" he asked, looking down at a mound of crushed leaves.

"Poison Vine," she declared.

He involuntarily stepped back and away from the plant that caused so much itching and pain in summer to anyone unlucky enough to touch its notched leaves.

"What are you planning to do with it?"

She winked at him. "You'll see."

Twenty-seven

DANCING FISH NEEDED TO CLEAR HIS MIND. HIS THOUGHTS were twisting and turning. The news from the meeting and now from Willow made his gut queasy. He had to get out of the village. He would visit Owl to talk things through and to understand his own thinking better.

The paddle from the point at Quinnahung across the water just east of Monatun was choppy but short. He welcomed the sharp taste of salt water that splashed his lips, and he felt the push of the crisp north wind at his back. Kong, who was as heavy as half a man, knew to lay down with his head on his paws to maintain the balance of the canoe.

The North Woods was a no-man's land. No band claimed it, which was why Owl made it his winter home. There were no real trails, and Dancing Fish and Kong picked their way through the trees whose limbs were slowly becoming skeletons as they shed their leaves.

Blue jays screeched a warning when he neared Owl's wigwam. Dancing Fish smiled when he saw the lonely figure standing in a clearing, smoking a rolled twist of tobacco leaves and watching him approach. Here was a man who had left the group to follow his own path, a man who no longer had to worry about rules and traditional roles or struggles for power and advantage. This was a man he admired.

"*Hè-yó,* young Perch," Owl called out. "Just in time to see my latest tobacco crop." He motioned to the plants lying on the ground around him.

"*Yó-hè-yó*, Elder," Dancing Fish said warmly, pulling the old man to him in a tight hug for more time than was needed for a greeting. Kong barked excitedly at this display, and Owl held out a hand for him to lick.

He stood back and studied his mentor. The tattoos marching across his forehead and on his cheeks had grown fainter. His hair seemed more white than gray, and it hung in ragged strands even longer than he remembered. And he noticed that he was getting shorter. Stooped. He was growing old.

"So let's see this tobacco," Dancing Fish said. He looked across the clearing. There were six rows of the herb, each row a body length apart from the next and maybe five bodies long. Although the full stalks of tobacco were already cut, he could clearly see that half the rows were different from the other. Three rows had darker and smaller leaves, the other three, lighter and larger.

Owl was at the end of the curing process, but he was doing it the old way. The stems with their heavy leaves lay on the ground to sweat and dry right where they grew. They were covered with brush and branches to help protect against the frost.

Dancing Fish shook his head and made an exaggerated frown. "This is the old way, my old friend. But it's not the best way."

"Why not?" Owl asked, reaching down to pull off a piece from a dark yellow leaf. "This is the ancient way of the People." He brought the dried leaf to his nose and sniffed. "Almost two moons and ready."

"Since when have you done anything by the ancient ways?" Dancing Fish said with a chortle. They both laughed at this since Owl was, after all, a hermit living by himself far away from anyone. "There are better ways that I've been thinking about," he said. "Making racks for drying and using heat for

142

curing. Lots of ideas swimming in my dreams." At these words, he saw the man's eyes sparkle like those of a child, something that hadn't changed at all.

"Oh, I'm sure you are thinking and swimming," his mentor said. "You're never lacking for ideas, are you Dream Maker?" He motioned with his hand. "Come inside and let's smoke together. You can tell me all about it." He revealed a sly grin. "And I can show you something new."

▶◀

They both sat close to the fire. Owl handed him a short pipe and reached to open a covered clay pot full of crumbled tobacco.

"Is this a new mixture?" Dancing Fish asked while he looked around the cramped wigwam that was barely large enough for a small fire and sleeping area. Kong sprawled in the only empty spot he could find and kept an eye on his human pack.

Everyone had his own way of combining tobacco with other herbs, but Owl's kinnikinnick mix was something Dancing Fish always looked forward to smoking. He knew it combined the two different tobaccos, but where the lighter one came from was still a mystery. And Owl also liked to experiment with other substances to add to his mix.

Owl handed him the pot. He took a pinch and deeply inhaled its distinctive aroma before pushing it into his pipe bowl. "I smell red willow bark. And your secret tobacco mix. But something else. What have you included?"

Owl gave him a playful look. "Let's see if you can guess."

After throwing a bit of tobacco into the embers as an offering, they both lit their clay pipes with sticks from the fire and puffed hard to bring the smoke into, and then out of, their mouths. Like usual, Owl's mixture was light and smooth. Not as bitter as the tobacco that everyone else grew and used. But there was a new taste that puzzled him.

"I give up. Tell me," he said after some time.

"Remember the stinkweed leaves you brought me on your last visit? What you found growing on the cleared land?"

Dancing Fish nodded as he began to notice a pleasant feeling of lightness enveloping him. A feathery sensation.

"I dried them and put a little in my kinnikinnick just to see what would happen."

"And?"

"And that is what you're smoking. Do you notice anything?"

The lightness had changed to one of floating. He felt himself lift off the ground slightly. "I do. But is it from the stinkweed or the two tobaccos? And where did that different tobacco come from? You've never explained."

"Ah, that is a good story." Owl leaned back on both elbows.

Dancing Fish felt as though he were hovering halfway between the packed dirt floor and the smoke hole. Wherever he looked, colored lights flashed and dimmed. A chorus of forest sounds grew louder and spun around him like a swarm of bees.

"It started with the traders from the north," Owl started. "Your Alone Men. Long before you were born . . ."

Dancing Fish was having trouble following Owl's story. The sacred smoke now filled the wigwam, and he saw himself circling the fire, soaring above it, just like a hawk that circles a cornfield looking for mice.

He focused on Owl's mouth while both smoke and words streamed from it in curious shapes.

"One in particular," Owl said. "His name was *Jacq* and he was a special man. He brought the tobacco seeds with him. Said they were from islands far to the south. *Spanish*, he called them. Strange lands with strange people."

What was Owl talking about? A man named Jacq and strange lands?

"He gave me some of the seeds, and that is the light-colored tobacco you see. And every year I put the crop's new seeds aside—both to grow, and because I knew that someday you would ask. And that day has come."

Owl's words faded as he looked to Kong, whose black body was starting to shimmer with a blue glow. The dog then suddenly turned into a fish—his Manitto, the perch; his namesake, his Guardian Spirit. It was odd to see a large, silvery fish sitting by the fire in a wigwam.

The perch then moved its tail and swam up to the smoke hole where he stopped and turned. "Are you coming or not?" the fish asked.

Dancing Fish hesitated. Then he flapped his tail fin to join his Manitto. And they both flew out of the wigwam.

▶◀

Dancing Fish woke when a patch of sunlight warmed his face. Both Kong and Owl were sitting, looking down at him.

"Did you have an interesting night?" Owl asked, grinning.

He sat up and pinched his nose between the eyes. His head ached.

Owl offered a gourd of water and another of pemmican. Dancing Fish ate and drank like a starving man, then leaned against a curved post to rest. "This new tobacco of yours is . . . is . . . different."

Owl chuckled. "Yes, it is. Let me explain." He shifted his body and crossed his legs. "We all know that smoking the tobacco is our connection from Mother Earth to the Sky World and to the Great Spirit. It opens the path to help see beyond. It helps with visions and dreams. To see things as they clearly are, not like we think them to be." Owl squinted at him with a serious face. "Did you see things as they are in the night?"

Unfortunately, Dancing Fish's vision was a confusion of fish, tobacco leaves, Willow, beaver skins, and all the white strangers he had known, including Hudson and Boo-shay. "I saw many things. But what they mean, I'm not sure."

Owl nodded thoughtfully. "Over time, the visions and dreams will make more sense to you. The formless will become formed. The unseen, seen.

"Here—" Owl held out two large bags. "One has the new mixture, but without the stinkweed." He grinned. "That I keep to myself. And the other bag has the special seeds of the Spanish tobacco."

"Are you sure? Do you have enough?"

He smiled a crooked smile. "Oh, I have much more, Little Perch. This is how I spend my lonely time." He paused and looked around the wigwam. "I'll be gone one day, and you will carry on. Take them. And make sure they don't get wet on your trip back."

Dancing Fish accepted the bags, which weighed little, and thanked Owl.

"You're here to discuss something with me," Owl said. "I saw it on your face when you came." He was silent. Waiting.

Dancing Fish tried to remember the reason for his visit. His head was still light. Then it came to him. "I discovered a new visitor from the east. His name is Boo-shay."

"Is he an Alone Man? A trader like the others?"

"A trader, yes. But from a ship. A Salt Man."

Owl put his hand to his chin. "You have a gift for attracting them, don't you?" He smiled. "Did I not tell you this?"

"You did. But this man has caused some changes in the band." He paused. He was now ready to say the words he had only been practicing in his mind.

"I am thinking that I want to be more like you. More independent. Maybe take Willow and leave. Make our own way. Like you have."

Owl's face instantly turned down as he uncurled his legs. "No!" he said with force, almost shouting. "That is not your destiny. That is not your path."

"But I can make my own path. I can make a new life. I'm strong—"

"No!" Owl almost screamed it. "You cannot be like me. You are talking like a selfish young man."

"But the band is trying to distance me. Push me down. Willow's father hates me. High Limb and many others hate me. I'm no good to the People."

Owl grabbed his knee and fixed his flaring eyes on his. "Listen to me carefully. You cannot leave the band."

"Why not?"

"Because I have seen it in my dreams and also in my waking visions. And you have, too. But you don't recognize it." He leaned closer. "The Manahate band needs you. All the Lenni Lenape need you. You do not see it clearly yet, but I do."

Owl leaned in more closely. "There are certain other secrets I know, but I'm holding them from you."

"What secrets? Why?"

"Because the time is not right. The Spirits tell me to wait. But the time will soon come." He straightened his body. "Listen to me. You must go back and give your good ideas to the band. Pay attention to this Boo-shay man. Be with your Willow. But stay with your people. Find a way."

It was like Dancing Fish had been kicked in the stomach. He was excited about his plan: taking Willow and just leaving the band. Starting a new life where he could do what he wanted. Create his inventions. Follow new dreams.

But now, Owl—the man he most admired—was telling him no. That he belonged with the Manahate band.

This was not what he wanted to hear.

Twenty-eight

DANCING FISH FELT NUMB AS HE WALKED INTO THE VILLAGE with Kong. Small, white flakes of snow fell from an ashen sky, but he barely noticed. His best adviser had just extinguished his new dream. Like throwing a pot of water onto a new fire, his head hissed and boiled with conflicting thoughts.

"Where've you been?" blurted Rock when he came around a corner and almost ran into him.

"With Owl. Why?"

"The time is close for Hard Stick. And she's asked to see you."

"See *me*?"

"Yes, you. Come with me. Quick."

They took off running to the Council House.

The room was dark and smoky. Long Pipe, the Holy Seer, was waving smoldering herbs over Hard Stick and puffing tobacco smoke into her face. She was lying on her back on layers of fur skins. Her eyes were closed, but he could see her chest slowly rising and falling.

After his eyes adjusted to the dim light, Dancing Fish saw others lining the walls of the room. Thundercloud. Sawgrass. Other leaders and family bosses.

"Come closer." It was Tanta, the most experienced curing woman, who knelt next to their Matron. "Her two Souls are pushing her skyward, but she is stubborn. And very weak from the Beast Fever."

"Beast Fever?" he asked, kneeling beside his grandmother, whose skin was covered by a rash of ugly red bumps. He had heard the stories of cruel fevers sweeping through villages and killing many in earlier times.

"It enters into the oldest and youngest first," Tanta said.

"There are others?" he asked.

"It's starting again. These fevers began with the coming of the Whites. From the east, the Salts; from the north, the Alone Men. The Spirit Powers of the Beasts are strong for a while and then go away. It has been some time, but I'm fearful they're coming back now. They are punishing us. And many will die."

"Will the fever come to all of us?"

Before Tanta could reply, he felt a bony hand touch his. Hard Stick's eyes opened slightly just then, and she spoke.

"Not you," she said softly." He felt her hand give a gentle squeeze. "You are different, Grandson."

"I know. My thoughts, my notions."

"No. More than that."

He leaned closer. "What do you mean?"

She coughed from deep inside, and Tanta rolled her onto her side to vomit into a gourd. Hard Stick rolled back, breathing harder, sweat glistening on her wrinkled face.

Her mouth, surrounded by the red rash, moved slowly, forming each word carefully. "You are different for another reason."

She was whispering now, and he strained to hear the faint words. "The Beast may visit you, but you will not be conquered by the fever."

"Why not?"

"Because your father wasn't. And because—" She stopped to suck in air in quick gulps. With her eyes barely open, she beckoned him closer with her trembling hand. "Because—" she coughed again, even more deeply, with a rattle from deep inside.

She tapped the edge of the skin she was lying on with a stiff finger dotted with red bumps and pointed to Tanta. Tanta leaned her head to the side without moving. Hard Stick tapped the skin again.

Tanta reached to the skin and lifted the edge. With a puzzled look on her face, she pulled something out. It was thin and flat, like a tiny reed mat but much finer. It reminded him of a corn husk leaf, but without veins or lumps. He saw that it was folded. Gray with a bluish tint. Not green, but like the color of a bluebird's underbelly.

"Give him," Hard Stick said, lifting her hand toward Dancing Fish.

Tanta handed the leaf to him. It weighed almost nothing. His fingertips brushed the surface. It was smooth, even more delicate than the finest corn hair mesh.

Hard Stick gasped several times, then spoke. "This will tell you."

Her body started to shake, and her breathing became rapid and shallow. He reached to calm her.

"No," Tanta said firmly, pushing his hand away. "Her time has come. Her Souls are ready. Do not touch her."

He rocked back on his heels.

The others moved in closer and formed a circle around the band's leader. Long Pipe had pulled away the smoking herbs. No one spoke.

Hard Stick suddenly opened her eyes wide and made a final sound—a low gurgling from the back of her throat that ended in silence. Her eyes remained fixed, looking upward.

"Her two Souls have left her," the Holy Seer said.

Dancing Fish stared at his grandmother for a long moment before his blurred eyes drifted down to the folded leaf. His tears dropped onto it one by one, darkening it. And when they did, he saw markings coming through from the other side. Marks made by a hand.

The sadness pressed on them like a stack of thick animal robes as they all walked back to the village from the burial ground. The women cried; the men silent in their thoughts.

And High Limb was already thinking.

He slowed to look up at a gray sky that was ready to drop more snow. The winter would be long and cold. Everyone was foreseeing it. And with the Matron gone, the powers within the band would be shifting. Thundercloud was now officially the Peace Sachem. His father, Sawgrass, was War Chief. The two were of equal importance. But the Matron and Thundercloud were from the same lineage of the Turtle Clan. He was also Turtle Clan, but one step removed by blood. All this was so complicated.

His best strategy for gaining more power—especially over Willow—was to get close to the new trader. Traders had objects of value—white traders above all.

He saw the pale stranger ahead, limping slowly and holding onto Dancing Fish. He increased his pace over the hard ground to catch up. They both stopped and turned when he reached them.

"He's recovering?" High Limb said to Dancing Fish while he smiled at the Boo-shay man and pointed to his injured leg.

"Yes," Dancing Fish said. "He's strong. He heals well."

High Limb continued speaking to his rival in their tongue. "I should also be watching over this man," he said with a raised eyebrow and an edge to his voice. "You know this."

"Of course," Dancing Fish said, showing no emotion. "Do you want to say something to him? It's good for him to rest a moment."

"Introduce me," he said. "The right way."

Dancing Fish pressed his lips together and shot him an annoyed glance but introduced the Salt Man to him in the correct manner, speaking the man's tongue and translating at the same time.

They both clasped hands and smiled. High Limb took a moment to focus on the man's astonishing blue eyes and to study the dark curly hair that covered not only his head but his broad face. Such a strange being, he thought. So short and ugly. But clearly someone of importance. Someone to get close to.

"Are you just going to stare, or do you want to ask him something?" Dancing Fish grumbled. "He needs to get back and rest his leg."

High Limb let the words settle for a moment. "Just tell him I look forward to hunting beaver with him soon." He glanced down at the man's bad leg. "And I hope Spirit Power and our cures help him recover quickly so we may do that."

Dancing Fish gave him a look of surprise. "How do you know we'll go beaver hunting?"

He cocked his head and smiled. "I know more than you think," he said, smirking. He clasped and shook the man's hand again. Then Dancing Fish turned Boo-shay, and they started walking away. The White Keeper looked back over his shoulder to scowl at High Limb before they blended into the crowd.

Then High Limb saw her. Willow was leaning against the shadowed side of the corn crib, peering at him. When she smiled, everything in his mind evaporated. Blind to anyone else, he headed straight for her.

The crib was a large box set on upright poles. It held their harvested ears of corn. It was mostly empty now. Much had been eaten, and what was left was being dried in hanging sacks in each longhouse or ground into meal and flour.

She looked up at him with seductive eyes. "I've been thinking about what you said earlier."

"About?" He felt his skin tingle and his manhood rising.

"About your courting me," she said, embarrassed, looking down. "I know that you spoke with my father. That you presented him with excellent gifts."

"Those gifts are only the start. There will be many more." He felt at once happy but also suspicious. Why the sudden change of heart? He wasn't sure he could trust her, but his eyes and his entire body could not question what was right in front of him. He wanted her now.

She must have read his mind because she grabbed his hand and led him around the corner to the back of the crib where no one could see.

He lifted her off the ground and started to kiss her.

"Mmmm," she purred. "What is that I feel?"

"What do you think?"

"Put me down and I'll show you what I think."

He lowered her and she reached into the pouch that hung from her neck by a long strap. Her hand came out covered in grease.

"What's that?" he asked.

"Bear grease. I want to use my hand." Without hesitating, she pulled his apron open with one hand and grasped his shaft firmly with the other. He could feel the grease slide as she tightened her grip on him.

He was breathing hard in rhythm with the hand strokes. He grabbed her by the hair and pulled it back so he could look into her eyes. The stroking grew more rapid until the spasm surged through him, and he let out a smothered cry.

He blinked several times before he focused on her. She was backing away. Smiling. Oddly. She took a piece of deerskin from her pouch and carefully wiped the grease—and some of him—from her hand. She seemed very thorough about it. Too thorough. Something wasn't right.

"I hear that acorn broth can help with the itching," she said, grinning.

"Itching?"

But she had already turned and run off, laughing.

Twenty-nine

THE MORNING ROSE CLEAR AND COLD WITH AN UNBROKEN blue sky, and anticipation buzzed among the hunters. They first had a light meal of pemmican and hot tea. After that came a short prayer with heads bowed and words Boucher couldn't understand. Then they each threw a bit of tobacco into the central fire and spoke more words in the strange language. He tried to mimic their ritual as best he could.

Boucher had been waiting more than a week for this. He had promised himself not only to kill a beaver but to see how the Indians hunted them. If anyone knew how to do it correctly, it would be them.

After his initial shock and despair at being stranded, Boucher was now glad to be with these natives. Missing the ship could work well to his advantage if he could keep his head straight and his ultimate goal in mind: beaver pelts.

They were four: himself, Dancing Fish, his friend Rock, and a boy they called Big Shadow, who, for some reason, was taking the place of High Limb. The natives all wore long hunting shirts and cloaks made of deerskin, plus full leggings that fell over their flexible moccasins. He wore his same wool capote on top of a borrowed deerskin shirt and leggings that he stuffed into his old boots, which he kept as a remembrance of home.

Once they were underway, the large wolf-dog, Kong, trotted ahead with a knowing excitement. Dancing Fish had to keep calling him back to stay with the group. "He knows where we're going," the native said, "and he loves beaver hunting."

They had a collection of weapons in hand—bows and arrows, knives, clubs, and hatchets. Boucher had left his musket in the longhouse but carried his own steel hatchet. He wanted to hunt like the Indians did.

He guessed that almost two weeks had passed since the injury, and his leg was healing. But he still favored it, limping, and he had to work hard to keep pace.

They were heading into the sun, due east. They followed a clear path and spoke little, breaths of vapor keeping time with their rapid steps.

When they reached an ice-covered pond, Kong could no longer be held back. Barking madly, he spotted two beavers gnawing at trees close to the pond's edge, and he charged ahead. The beavers, alerted by the dog, scampered across the frozen water to the plunge holes next to their lodge and disappeared.

Kong ran around the beaver lodge in circles, sliding on the ice and barking nonstop at the bramble of branches, twigs, and mud that stuck up at least three feet from the slick surface.

"Now we start," Dancing Fish said. He quickly explained the plan to Boucher.

They all walked slowly around the lodge, tapping their clubs on the ice. They were looking for enough thickness to support their weight but also for thin spots marking pockets of air. These were the places the beavers would go to breathe when they left the lodge. Using hatchets and clubs, the hunters broke through the ice to make holes in four of the spots. One of them stood by each hole.

"How do we get the beavers to leave the lodge?" Boucher asked across the ice.

Dancing Fish smiled at him. "Watch."

The three natives walked up to the lodge, bowed their heads, and spoke with the same prayer voices as before. Then, with a sudden fury, they attacked the lodge with their clubs and hatchets. They tore at the mound, battering the shrinking mass and throwing away the debris. Then, just as abruptly as they had started, they ran to their separate ice holes.

Boucher, who had yet to move, caught Dancing Fish's eye and opened his two hands in the universal sign for questioning.

"Wait, watch hole," came the simple reply.

He had no sooner heard those words when a beaver popped his head up from the hole at Boucher's feet.

"Now!" Dancing Fish screamed. "Hit him!"

With no conscious thought but somehow reacting to an instinct buried deep within himself, Boucher swung his hatchet at the beaver with all his might. To his surprise, the hatchet blade connected with the beaver's head and embedded in its skull.

Blood splattered over the ice while the beaver, with hatchet attached, began to disappear into the freezing water. But Dancing Fish had already slid to a stop over the hole and managed to grab the sinking beaver with his submerged arm.

The beaver was hauled out of the water and dropped onto the ice. The animal still moved. The native lifted his club high and smashed it into the beaver's head. The animal was lifeless, its red blood spreading over the hard, white surface.

Dancing Fish knelt over the dead animal, bowed his head again, and spoke softly. He appeared to be speaking *to* the animal. Then he looked up at Boucher with a face that was a combination of serenity and sadness. "This is how to take beaver."

They were interrupted as the same scene played out across the ice. Another bashing. And another prayer. Two dead beavers.

An idea started to take shape in Boucher's mind.

▶◀

That afternoon, Dancing Fish invited him to watch while the

beavers were skinned and prepared by the women.

Good, Boucher thought. He wanted to see how the skins went from animal to finished pelt. But he was curious why High Limb was not around and asked Dancing Fish about it. Although High Limb was taking to the language lessons, it was much easier to communicate with Dancing Fish, whose language skills were impressive.

"He has sickness," the native replied with an odd smile.

"A fever?"

"No. It is fine soon." Again, another curious smile.

The women worked on a large, flat stone next to the central fire, which kept the area surprisingly warm. The two beavers were on their backs, their fur a deep, glossy brown, offset by the darker tail, feet, and paws.

Boucher watched closely.

First, the front paws and rear feet were cut off with a stone knife. Then the tail. The tail was a delicacy and would be prepared for eating later, Dancing Fish explained.

The skin of the belly was slit in a straight line from top to bottom. The women then grasped the skin with its thick fur and pulled it away from the body with slow and steady movements. A special dull knife was used to separate the skin in tight areas.

The result was an oval pelt with fur on one side and pink skin on the other. The naked body was removed to be butchered by other women.

The inner side of the skin was then scraped clean of any flesh or fat with a sharp oyster shell. The women spent their time doing this. "Important to remove all flesh," Dancing Fish said, "or moths come and eat."

The inside of the skin was then roughened with a round stone, and a small pot of liquid was brought over from the fire.

"What's that?" he asked.

"Brain. The beaver's brain and water, mixed and warmed on

fire. Important. Makes skin soft."

Boucher watched while the women poured the brain mixture on the raw skin and rubbed it in by hand. They went over it again and again. When they were done, they weighed down the sides of the pelts with rocks.

"Leave skin to dry in night," Dancing Fish said. "And do again one, two days more. Then, stretch skin on hoop of branches and smoke on low fire. Skin finished."

Boucher asked, "Where do you store the skins?"

The young man gave him a questioning look. "Store skins?"

"Yes, keep them for trade."

"We not store. We use. Sew together to make robes, cloaks."

"But you trade these pelts with men like me, no?"

Dancing Fish nodded thoughtfully. "But only skins we not use. Keep in wigwams. Not trade many animal skins. All people, all bands have skins."

"What will you do with these?" he asked, pointing. The plan was solidifying in his mind.

"These two beavers help make new robe, and we are hungry for meat."

"Let's go in the longhouse," Boucher suggested. "We can eat and talk. I have something to discuss with you."

▶◀

Dancing Fish sat with Boo-shay near the low fire and ate steaming hominy from his gourd bowl. Others in the longhouse came and went—all staring at the white man—but none could speak the tongue of the visitor, so the conversation was private.

"Good?" Dancing Fish asked the trader, lifting the bowl.

The man licked his lips. "Very good. Like our gruel. But from corn."

Dancing Fish smiled. "We like corn."

More than one-half moon had passed, and Boo-shay's leg

was almost healed. He favored it when he walked, and it showed a raw scar, but his new coverings—old deerskin leggings and a hunting shirt—protected it.

After the food, they smoked the tobacco from Owl—the mixture of two tobaccos and red willow, but without the stinkweed. Too much of those leaves were dangerous and could kill.

Dancing Fish wanted to show Boo-shay the fine leaf from Hard Stick with the marks. He had carefully opened the leaf several times and examined the markings but could not find their meaning. The trader would know.

"This tobacco—" the man suddenly said, looking at the pipe and blowing out a cloud of smoke. "I have tasted nothing this sweet since I left home." He looked at Dancing Fish with curious eyes. "How did you come by this?"

"Different . . ." He knew no English word for what he was trying to say, so he made circles with both hands, fists closed, overlapping.

"Mixture," Boo-shay said. "A mix of different things."

"*Mix-ture,*" he said slowly, committing it to memory. "Two tobaccos. And willow bark."

"Interesting," the man said while he leaned back on his elbows and aimed another big puff upward.

"You like it?" Dancing Fish asked.

"Very much," the trader said.

He made a mental note of the man's reaction to the tobacco and started to pull out the folded leaf from a pocket in his deerskin cloak. "I have to show you. Want help."

The leaf was almost out when a noise interrupted. Suddenly, there stood a rigid High Limb, lips tight, anger shooting out from his body.

"I just heard of this meeting," he said, speaking their tongue and glaring at Dancing Fish. "You know I'm also responsible for this man and must be included in anything important. Have you forgotten?"

Dancing Fish had hurriedly returned the folded leaf to its pocket and now watched as High Limb pulled at his man apron. He reached inside to rearrange things, wincing and hissing through his teeth while he did so.

"I was only concerned about your . . . sickness," Dancing Fish said, trying to stifle a laugh but not succeeding.

"This isn't funny," his tall rival said as he eased himself down very slowly and gently onto a reed mat. He let out a breath once he had succeeded.

"Poison on me," High Limb said haltingly to Boo-shay, pointing to his crotch with his cheeks reddening. "Better now."

"I see," the man said, puzzled eyes flitting back and forth between a pained High Limb and a giggling Dancing Fish.

Thirty

"What is idea?" Dancing Fish asked Boo-shay after High Limb was settled and eating his hominy. He didn't like having to work with High Limb, but there was no way out of it. And he counted on being able to outsmart him when the time came.

The man looked to both of them. "What would you trade beaver skins for?"

"How many?" High Limb asked, taking the initiative after putting his bowl aside.

"As many as can be found. There is no limit."

There is no limit. Dancing Fish tried to picture what this meant. Did he mean all the beavers he could hunt? All the beavers on Mannahatta island? In all of Lenapehoking? What did this mean?

"Not for us decide," he said. "Skins belong to family and band." He had to translate some words for High Limb, who was slowly learning the white man's tongue.

Boo-shay asked, "And who is the trader for the family or the band?"

"No one person," Dancing Fish said. "Each family head. Or Sachem. But Sachem busy. He has other things to think."

"But if *you* were the person to trade?"—he nodded to Dancing Fish—"what would you trade for?"

Dancing Fish translated to High Limb but rushed to answer himself. "No beads, no mirrors. What your people call

161

trifles. Not good. We did before. Now want *practical* things." He smiled at his use of the new word he had recently learned.

"What kind of practical things?" Boo-shay pressed.

"Metal knives you call *steel*. Awls to pierce skins. Metal pots for cooking."

High Limb whispered to him.

"And hatchets," he added, translating the word back to High Limb. He detested conferring with High Limb like an equal, as though they were a team.

Dancing Fish stopped speaking and considered. He needed a good gift to give Willow's family if he were to succeed with her. Something special, of great value to Willow and her family. And now he knew what.

"I trade for steel awl from you," he announced. He hoped High Limb would not catch on. Willow had already talked about this. She was among the best in her family in sewing and decorating skins. She used the traditional bone awl for piercing, but an awl with a wooden handle and steel point would be better to work with and last much longer. He had held one in his hand on Hudson's ship and had immediately seen the benefits.

"And what would you trade for one awl?" Boo-shay asked. "In beaver skins."

He thought about what he had seen others trade when he was with Hudson. "Five skins," he said. He held up his hand with all fingers spread.

"Five skins," High Limb repeated, throwing an angry look at Dancing Fish and obviously trying to stay in the conversation.

Dancing Fish took back control. "Five beaver skins, one steel awl." He held up his other hand with one finger extended. It would not be hard to find extra skins in the village.

Boo-shay scratched his hairy face while he looked from one hand to the other. "Dried and smoked?" he asked.

Dancing Fish nodded.

Boo-shay smiled. "That sounds about right. Here is my

idea—wait a moment."

The man stood and went to the family's living area, reaching up for the bag they had brought from Werpoes. It hung from a high pole near the roof, which was the custom with special or important things.

Boo-shay returned and spilled out the contents from the bag onto the matted floor: one steel knife, a hatchet, an awl, and one hoe with its handle cut short to fit in the bag. Plus the usual trifles of beads and one mirror. The beads were made from the same material as his important button: *glass*, another word Dancing Fish had learned from Boo-shay.

High Limb leaned forward with eyes wide, and Dancing Fish couldn't help doing the same. He had not looked in the bag, thinking it contained worthless objects or something personal to Boo-shay.

Dancing Fish picked up the short awl and held it tightly in his hand. It was just like the one he had seen before, and it was beautiful—a rich wood handle and a shining metal shaft with a sharp point at the end. He touched the awl's barb to his finger and felt its sting. Pushing the beads and mirror to one side, he then picked up the other objects and studied each in turn. These were all white men's trade tools that could change the lives of his people. These were not trifles.

Boo-shay spoke first. "I am alone here all winter and cannot do trading with real goods. And I cannot trade away my samples because I have only one of each, like you see. But there will be more—much more—when the ships come in the spring. What if I give you what we call a credit for the trade?"

"What it means: *credit?*" Dancing Fish asked.

"It means I promise to pay you," Boo-shay said. "A pledge to repay. You give me the skins now, and I agree to give you the awl when the ships arrive. We shake hands on the understanding. And I can give you an accounting of what I owe for you to keep until the trade happens."

Dancing Fish was not unfamiliar with this idea of exchange and credit. The Manahate had always used it for small or simple things. Like when he played—and lost—the shell game and didn't have enough to pay the winner on that day. But the debt was usually paid quickly. Or if he was short by three oysters in a trade for corn, he would dive for three more oysters the next day. There was no *accounting* or delay. But he was intrigued.

Reluctantly, he turned to High Limb and explained the idea. A strange smile cracked the giant's face when he looked to Boo-shay's blue cloak, which the man seemed to wear everywhere. It was long, with a hood and a sash to close it in front. And it was made of a strange material with the English name *wool*. Several of the band's old women had felt it and marveled at its fineness. The man called it a *ka-pot*.

"I want this man's cloak, his ka-pot," he said plainly to Dancing Fish as he reached into his apron again, grimacing.

"What does he say?" Boo-shay asked, his eyes bouncing between the two of them.

Dancing Fish's mind worked fast and he said, "We now do new trade to see how it works." He pointed at Boo-shay's ka-pot. "High Limb will trade full beaver robe for your cloak." It was unexpected but seemed fair. He smiled at the man and waited.

Boo-shay looked intently from one to the other, then a wide grin opened on his face. "You two are clever young men, aren't you?" He looked down and held out his arms. "Very fine cloak, very warm." He showed off the hood, waist sash, and inside pockets. "Valuable in winter months." He asked, "How many skins in the beaver robe for trade?"

"Twelve beaver," Dancing Fish said. "You give us ka-pot now, and we promise you robe of 12 beavers when finished. This is credit, yes?" Without waiting for an answer, or even High Limb's consent, he extended his open hand to the trader.

The man hesitated a few moments, then he took the

outstretched hand and shook it vigorously. He shook High Limb's, too. "Yes, it is. We have a trade. On credit. On trust."

Boo-shay looked around the fire and grabbed a small, flat piece of kindling that was apart from the flames and not yet burned. He grabbed the knife from the floor and started cutting grooves into the wood. He made 12 straight cuts across the width and then a single circle below the cuts. He added two small circles to the larger one. "The ears," he said, laughing. He then made a square shape at the bottom. "The ka-pot."

Dancing Fish had an idea of what the man was doing, and he was happy to see some confusion in High Limb's face.

Then Boo-shay explained. "This is a tally stick. It shows what is owed to me from you—the 12 cuts and the symbol of the beaver. And the square box shows the cloak." He let Dancing Fish handle the stick, then retrieved it. "Now watch."

The man stood the end of the stick on the ground, placed his knife blade at the top, and used his other fist to strike down and split the stick along its length. He handed one of the two pieces to High Limb. "This is your accounting," he said. He pushed his half up against the other so they matched. "I have mine and you have yours. Both sides now have the same proof of the trade. When the trade is complete, both pieces are destroyed." He looked at Dancing Fish and High Limb with a satisfied grin. "Do you see?"

He translated to High Limb, who whispered back to him.

"Yes, understand. But where is ka-pot?" Dancing Fish asked, pointing to it and smiling.

Boo-shay let out a roar of laughter. "You are a strong negotiator!" he said as he started to take off the blue cloak.

Thirty-one

ALTHOUGH HIGH LIMB WAS EXCITED TO HAVE THE WHITE man's ka-pot—he had immediately put it on and was touching it over and over—Dancing Fish was not so sure about Boo-shay's idea. Part of him did not like killing more fur animals than needed. But another part saw the wisdom of trading something plentiful—the beaver—for something special and rare.

A steel awl would help with the stitching and decorating of their animal skins—both a task and a ritual that was an important part of their lives. And it could help win over Willow's family to approve a marriage match. He could see the advantage of this kind of trading.

Still, it bothered him. Deep down. Would the Animal Spirits be displeased? Would the lives of these animals be sacrificed for the right reasons? Was there balance to it? He liked new ideas—he thrived on them—but he also believed in a balance of Spirit Power. He needed to talk to the Sachem and the other leaders about this.

And just then, as if his thoughts were being heard, Thundercloud came into the longhouse where the three sat. "What is all the laughing I hear?" Thundercloud asked in their Munsee tongue as he approached the fire and held out his hands to warm them. He looked down at High Limb. "And what is this you wear?" he asked in surprise after seeing the white man's cloak on him.

"We make trade," High Limb said, standing up to model the ka-pot, turning around and showing its hood and how it opened with the sash.

"It's nice," said the Sachem but with little enthusiasm. Then he glanced at Boo-shay, sitting with only a shirt on, and to Dancing Fish. "But you have taken advantage of this man. What has he received?"

Dancing Fish wondered if he had done something he shouldn't have. He was the official guardian and companion of the white man, a role now shared with High Limb, but he was still a young member of the band. And he had made a decision without consulting an Elder or leader. Again.

"He receives a twelve-beaver robe," Dancing Fish said. "But in the future, when the robe is finished. We have only the first two beaver skins."

The Sachem's brows went up. "Hmmm . . . Have you been inventing again, Dancing Fish?"

He felt heat rising to his face. "He will have a temporary cloak from our family store. But this is a new idea from the Salt Man. Maybe he can explain it."

Thundercloud gave him a sharp look. "No, I want *you* to explain it. You and High Limb. To me and to the leaders. And to your father and mother." The Sachem made a sign with his finger. "Boo-shay stays. You two"—he pointed—"to the Council House. Now."

▶◀

Thundercloud was at his appointed place on the fur-covered stump and asked his youngest daughter to make tea for those who sat in a circle around the fire. Dancing Fish saw that all were there including Two Winds and Yellow Flower.

High Limb's new ka-pot cloak was drawing looks and whispers all around. His cousin was clearly pleased with his new treasure, while at the same time he grimaced and grunted from the itching under his male apron. Dancing Fish smiled inwardly at this.

Sparks flared up after another daughter threw a large log onto the flames. Thundercloud aimed his chin toward Dancing Fish and asked him to explain this new trading idea.

He put down his tea and spoke from his seated place. "Boo-shay wants to trade useful tools from his people to us and also to the other villages. He says there will be at least one, maybe more, ships coming to trade in the spring with the coming of the leaves."

"How does he know this?" Sawgrass asked, keeping his eyes on his squirming son and his new cloak.

"Because the Salt People want the skins of our beavers and other animals," Dancing Fish said. "The furs give them power because they make practical things from them. More furs, more power. He says that the ship captain and the trading leader promised to come back when the trees are newly green."

"You mean," his father jabbed, "like they promised to pick up this man when his ship left? Not a good sign to me."

"Let him continue," the Sachem said. "I agree with what he says about the ships. Where there is one mosquito, there are always more. This is the way with the ships, too. They will come."

Dancing Fish then handed Boo-shay's bag of trade tools, which the white man had offered for the meeting, to Thundercloud for inspection. The bag was passed around with everyone murmuring. He saw his mother with her sharp eye admiring the awl.

Dancing Fish added that the white man had only these samples of each trade tool, and then he explained the concept of credit and the tally sticks, and Boo-shay's wish to make the trades in advance.

"Boo-shay says the ships will be at Kapsee Rocks only a short time before they head north on the Great River," he said.

"Waiting until then to start trade talk would waste the time we have now when we do little else."

"Do little else?" his mother said, giving him a hard look. The only sound was the crackling of the fire. Yellow Flower didn't speak often, but when she did, everyone listened. The women had the true power with the People. They owned the houses and the fields. They picked the peace Sachems. And the clan lineage passed through the mother's line. Dancing Fish was of the Turtle Clan because of his mother's lineage. His father was Wolf Clan. His children would be in the clan of his wife—Turkey, if his longing for Willow came true.

"The time of cold and long nights is important for us," Yellow Flower continued, "and you know this. For stories, for repairing, for replenishing our Souls."

"Yes, Mother, I do know. But—"

"I think this is a good opportunity," High Limb interrupted. "Boo-shay says we can make better agreements with the other villages if we work in advance. Then we can gather the trade furs and have them waiting for the ships. If we can be the first to meet the ships with a large number of furs, then we can have the first pick of the trading compared to the other bands in the north."

Dancing Fish was impressed. High Limb had summarized the idea well and even come up with his own conclusions. Maybe he wasn't so stupid after all. And that worried him. He preferred a dumb High Limb to a smart one.

The Sachem asked, looking at Dancing Fish, "How will you do this exactly? What is your plan?"

"We will go together—Boo-shay, High Limb, and I—first to visit all nearby villages. The ones we know or are friendly. During these winter moons. We will show the sample trade tools from Boo-shay and make trade promises for the animal skins. We'll set down who is offering what for which tools in return." He handed the tally stick pieces to the Sachem, who

169

studied them at length before passing them around the circle.

He continued. "The people can spend the moons of snow and long nights capturing and preparing the animals for us. Then, we return before the coming of the leaves and collect the skins from each village. And we will give them a tally for each trade. He calls it *accounting*. When the trading ships arrive, we go with all the skins and make the trades."

He saw High Limb studying him. Dancing Fish had made up most of the details on the spot, but they sounded reasonable. The plan was logical, if unusual. But he could see holes in the thinking.

The Sachem could, too. He asked, "What if the People will not give you the skins without the awl or the knife at that moment? This is what they are used to."

"It will be up to us," Dancing Fish said, glancing at High Limb, "to convince them."

The Sachem gave a short laugh. "Well, you do not lack confidence, do you? But you are the one with the most contact with the Salt People, and everyone knows it. If anyone can do it, you—and now High Limb—can."

"But why do you do this?" Two Winds asked, showing his familiar negativity. "Is it only to be different and maybe to have an adventure?"

"No, Father," he said. "It's true that I want to see and do new things. I want to experience more, but—"

"*You* want to do this, and *you* want to do that," Two Winds spat out. "It seems that you think only of yourself. This is not the true way of the Manahate. We work together. We think first of the family and then the band. We think of more than ourselves."

"I understand this, Father. But I *am* thinking of the family and the band. I will bring more of the white man's tools back to us. These are for us, not for me. To help all of us."

As he heard himself say this, he questioned if it was true.

Was he thinking of the People, or was he thinking of himself? And of Willow?

The Holy Seer, Long Pipe, now spoke. "But what of the balance of the Spirits?" the old man asked, brushing back the long hair that indicated his dedication to a path of Spirit. "I fear it is not equal. There must be a harmony of giving and taking. Each side benefits. But only if the Spirit Powers are in agreement. This is the most important thing."

The old Seer squinted at everyone seated around the fire with his milky eyes. "Animals are sacrificed for our vital existence. For the most important essences in our short lives on Mother Earth: hunger, thirst, warmth, protection." He looked around the fire again. "And for connection to the many Spirits, including the Animal Spirits who provide the very animals. These Spirits smile on us when our Souls are in balance with them. When we are not . . ." He frowned and shook his head.

"I agree with our Holy Seer," his father said. "We have our ways, and they have worked for many lifetimes. We take the animals we need, and we do it carefully and with reverence. We do not change when a stranger comes into our midst."

Sawgrass thumped the floor with his war club. "And I take the other view. I like this plan coming from the white man. It will bring us useful things."

While Sawgrass droned on about Manahate power growing and gaining advantage over other bands and villages with this new trading idea, Dancing Fish reached up to feel for the glass button that hung from his neck. As soon as he felt its hardness, a vision began to form behind his eyes. Beavers—not just their skins but whole animals—were stacked in an enormous pile. The pile reached to the clouds and beyond.

The pile grew so large that it started wavering and soon toppled over, animals moving in the wind like dust. And the beavers grew smaller and smaller—so small that a giant school of perch appeared and started eating the beavers as they shrank in size. Eventually, the beavers were gone, all eaten. And then the perch started shrinking.

Dancing Fish suddenly stood, and the talking stopped. It was not usual for a young man to stand without invitation at an important meeting. But he already knew he was not a normal young man. And it was time to end the bickering and endless debate. He knew what he had to do.

Dancing Fish opened his hands. "If you like, High Limb can be with Boo-shay to trade the animal skins. And I will trade with something that keeps us in balance with the Spirits—and with these strangers."

"Like what?" Sawgrass shouted out. "What could you possibly offer in trade to them? Your silly inventions?" He laughed, and his son joined him.

"No." Dancing Fish held up his short pipe for everyone to see. "With this. Tobacco."

Thirty-two

HIGH LIMB SMOOTHED THE COLD DIRT OVER THE GRAVE OF his sister. The fevers had come upon them like a rainy downpour. One day, a few were sick. The next, it seemed like half the village was fighting the Beast and covered with the red boils. The young, the old, and those in between ... Many were already dead or dying.

His bare hands trembled, not only from the frozen clumps of soil, but also from the extreme sadness. There was no one left in the family except a cousin and his father, who knelt nearby, his head down and weeping. Mother, brother, two sisters, grandparents—all dead. Even Little Shadow was not strong enough to fight the Beast Fever. He was buried in his family's area, and Big Shadow seemed at a loss without his friend.

Winter's grip was tight on the village. They were coming to the Turning of the Days, and the nights were long and full of dark feelings.

Under a heavy gray sky that touched the tops of the trees, High Limb walked back to the longhouse next to his father. Their breaths plumed as they avoided frozen puddles and passed empty wigwams. No fires burned where the Fever's death had stalked and consumed entire families. Achqueehgenom, their winter village, normally bustling and busy, was as quiet as the deepest forest.

"When do you go with the white man?" Sawgrass asked,

wrapped and hunched inside his long bear-hide robe. A complete moon had passed since the plans for the trading trip were first discussed.

"Soon," he said, crossing the arms of the ka-pot, which he wore constantly. It wasn't as warm as a bearskin, but it had the hood and hidden openings inside. "Boo-shay is preparing his tally sticks and shining the trade tools. We only need to finish preparing our gifts, then we'll go with the Full Wolf Moon."

"And what of Willow? Have you spoken to her?"

He recoiled slightly when he thought of the terrible trick she had played on him. He still had lingering red skin in his most private places. Once he had her as his wife, he would make her pay for that insult. He was looking forward to that.

"Yes, Father, but I'm counting on you to continue influencing her family," he said, his hooded head down against a quickening wind.

"Don't worry. With my gifts, Weetoq still favors you. But Dancing Fish is making big promises of valuable tools from his future trade in tobacco. How foolish—trade in tobacco compared to trade in fine animal skins. Ridiculous."

He could hear his father struggling to laugh.

Sawgrass stopped walking and turned to him. "And how is working with Dancing Fish? I thought you were sworn enemies. Are you able to be with him?"

"As much as anyone can be with someone who is so peculiar. He's smart, I can say that. But his head is in a different world. He seems possessed of something."

His father straightened and pushed his finger against High Limb's chest, but without much strength. "You just make sure this trading with the white man works. We have to come out strong in this. For our ancestors, for the recently departed, and for our future. Our honor demands it." He pushed again to emphasize his point.

All High Limb could do was nod. And when they resumed

their cold walk through the village, he heard his father cough.

▶◀

The winter was frigid and full of snow after the solstice. Dancing Fish told Boucher it was the worst in memory. Luckily, he had a finished beaver coat to wear. When wrapped inside the thick pelts, the warmth the animal furs provided was unsurpassed. And the cold rain and snow just rolled off the thick hide. Better than his old capote, now traded to High Limb, which was made of Walloon wool that soaked up wetness and let off the distinctive smell of damp.

High Limb never stopped wearing the blue coat, even if it was not equal to the task of keeping its owner warm and dry when compared to natural furs. The native eventually discovered the trick of adding a mantle of skins over the capote, but when it was time to enter a new village, the mantle came off and the capote was the center of attention. It seemed that no Indian had ever seen wool before, and a crowd unfailingly formed around his trading partner, wanting to touch the blue cloth.

The people of the villages were always waiting with a warm reception. Word traveled quickly among them, what with itinerant storytellers and frequent family visits. Especially when it was news about visitors and trading.

They were surely a welcome relief from the devastation of disease Boucher was now noticing everywhere they went. The natives seemed even more stricken by pox than he remembered seeing among people in his homeland. To be sure, there had been many outbreaks of plague and epidemic in Liège and in Amsterdam, but the devastation here seemed worse. Particularly given the general health and vitality he saw among the Indians. Regularly, they came upon entire villages emptied of their inhabitants from the sickness. Only the dogs were left to forage for food and battle over every morsel.

Dancing Fish had decided that Kong would not come on the trip. Every village had their dogs, and it could cause too much conflict if Kong were to get into fights with them, which he said would surely happen. Boucher had watched Dancing Fish tie Kong to the longhouse when they departed, and had listened to Kong howl and howl until the pitiful sounds could no longer be heard.

Their trading routine at each village was well established. First came the ceremonial speeches of welcome and the ritual exchange of gifts with the village leaders—a small belt of wampum from their side, food from the natives.

Then, after eating and smoking with the leaders around a central fire in the council house, Boucher passed around the sample trade goods from his bag. At the same time, Dancing Fish pulled out the long skirt of deerskin his mother had beaded with wampum from careful awl work. The white beads glittered beautifully on the edges of the skirt. Some of the holes were left empty so the natives could see how well the awl worked. Next, the remaining women of the village were called in to see this exhibition, and they invariably fell in love with the idea of owning such a useful tool.

Then came the negotiations.

After Boucher—with Dancing Fish translating—explained the tally sticks and the concept of trading for the future, the two young men each took turns describing their separate propositions: prepared animal skins or harvested tobacco in exchange for trade items from the ships coming in the spring.

Apart from the obvious distinction between tobacco and pelts, the approaches of Dancing Fish and High Limb could not have been more different. Although Dancing Fish had, in Boucher's opinion, a weaker proposal—tobacco planting and harvesting for fewer or lower-quality trade goods—he had an innate ability for connecting with the villagers. He would hand over a small pouch of the special tobacco seeds and then explain the best way to plant them, cure the leaves, and ultimately coil the dried tobacco into the balls that would be needed for trade. And most significantly, he allowed them to take puffs from his prepared mixture, which always provoked many smiles and much head-nodding. He spoke—and handled himself—smoothly and gently.

High Limb, on the other hand, was more direct. He held up a trade good—a pot, for example—and simply stated "Ten beaver skins" with the fingers of his hands spread. Then he moved to the next item. When the Indians around the fire tried to negotiate—"Eight skins for the pot" was a common one—High Limb repeated his same statement: "Ten beaver skins." He didn't bend. Boucher could have interfered and accepted the lower number, but he had decided that these two young natives would know best and should handle their respective offerings. His interest was in getting the most he could from the trading, and he would benefit from a percentage of the trade value when the ships returned.

High Limb also had an air of superiority about him that was hard to mask. He was pompous and strident, while Dancing Fish was craftier in his down-to-earth manner. And Boucher could feel the tension between these two young men. He finally discerned that they were courting the same girl—Willow. That explained the dark and threatening looks between the two.

In the end, the negotiations went well, and the agreements were easy to conclude with Boucher finalizing the arrangements with marked tally sticks.

Every visit ended with a small feast, and the three traders were offered a place to sleep. That usually included a woman for each to lie with. He and High Limb frequently took advantage of this offer, but he noticed that Dancing Fish did not. "I have my woman," he would explain, saying it loudly for an irritated High Limb to hear.

Thirty-three

THE THREE SPENT THE WINTER MONTHS OF 1612 AND INTO 1613 traveling to the nearby bands and villages of the Indians in the area. Boucher recorded some of their strange-sounding tribe names: Sapokanikan, Rechgawawank, Marechkawieck, Maspeth, Canarsee. A couple of villages were on the island, but most natives had their winter homes in more-protected main-land areas to the east and north.

Boucher also learned that the Canarsee, with whom the Manahate sometimes warred, stated their own claim to the summer camp of Werpoes, where Dancing Fish had found him. The whole issue of who had jurisdiction over which land was something he had given up trying to understand. The natives had their own ideas of ownership that eluded his comprehension.

The winter traveling was not easy. When the snow was deep, they wore special shoes made from elm strips so they could walk on top of it. Other times, a storm would surprise them with severe cold and winds so strong that they had to take shelter in caves or inside thickets of mountain laurel. They would curl up and wait out the storm, eating their pemmican and talking.

They talked at every opportunity. Each day, Dancing Fish's languages improved measurably. English, French, and Dutch— he was a quick learner. High Limb learned, too, but at a slower pace. It was as though the new words took longer to reach his tall head.

"Tell me about ships coming," Dancing Fish asked Boucher one day while they hiked in single file along a narrow, twisting trail overhung by branches coated in ice.

"What is your question?"

"Who on ship speaks for the trading? The Master?"

"No. The Supercargo."

"*Super-cargo*," the native said slowly and repeated to make sure it was right.

"He is the man responsible for the ship's trading with your people."

"Not the Master?"

"No. Adriaen Block is responsible for the ship, the sailing, and the crew. But the Supercargo represents the merchants who pay for the voyage. He makes the trading decisions. And if it's the same ship with the same Supercargo that returns—with a man named Maarten Deen—this will be good for us.

"You speak for ship?" High Limb asked as he led the group and ducked under the low-hanging tree branches. "Make promises for trade?"

"Yes. I am officially the Supercargo's assistant. This is why I can speak for him and the ship."

Dancing Fish asked from behind, "What do you get from trading?"

"Like the Supercargo, I receive a share of the trade when the ship returns home. But a smaller part than the Supercargo."

"You get fur skins?" High Limb asked.

"No. Money. Guilders."

"*Money?*" High Limb stopped and turned, his brow pinched. "What is money?"

Boucher sighed. These natives seemed unable to understand the concept. They exchanged the shell beads—wampum—but it was more as an act of social ritual, friendship, or ceremony.

There seemed to be no clear idea of currency beyond bartering. He stood between two large roots crossing the path and looked into their curious faces. "It's complicated," was all he was willing to say. He would explain it more another day when they weren't tramping through the woods on an icy path.

"And this man," Dancing Fish asked, "the Supercargo—is he a good man?"

Boucher didn't answer right away when he thought about Maarten Deen. This is what troubled him most. Deen was greedy—and willing to do just about anything to increase his advantage. Boucher had seen it on the ship when Deen had tried to trick and cheat the natives whenever he could. Twelve beavers for two hatchets suddenly became fourteen beavers for one hatchet and one knife. He hoped there wouldn't be trouble when they finally met again.

Boucher turned his thoughts to the positive side. His being stranded in the land of these Indians was turning out to be the best thing that could have happened to him. With a plentiful trade in animal furs, he finally saw a way to be successful and to make a good life for his waiting family back home. But he'd have to be careful with his own people. Very careful.

▶◀

They had camped next to a small pond to bathe and spend a night between villages. It was a rare warm day, which made bathing and sweating the top priority. Thick, gray clouds hovered low and held in the heat coming from the earth.

Dancing Fish sat with Boo-shay in the sweat hut they had quickly built from branches and bark. Tiny shafts of light entering through the cracks added just enough light to see by. High Limb was taking his cold bath in the icy pond. Good time to talk in private with the white trader.

"You look more like us each day," Dancing Fish said with a

180

smile after they had removed their cloaks, shirts, and leggings, keeping on—for Dancing Fish—only his apron, and for Boo-shay, what he called his *trunk hose*. And the white man also kept on his treasured boots from when they found him.

Dancing Fish had been learning the tongues of the visitors steadily from Boo-shay, and they would sometimes have animated—although halting—conversations about all manner of things from animals to eating customs.

"And do I look thinner and more handsome?" Boo-shay joked.

"Maybe thinner." He laughed at his own attempt at the humor that came easy to this man.

Dancing Fish dribbled water from a gourd onto the red-hot stone pulled in from the fire outside. The stone sat in a shallow pit dug into the center of the tiny hut's dirt floor. It hissed as it released a steam cloud that filled the cramped room and enfolded the two men. He felt the heat soak into his body while sweat dripped from his nose and chin.

"Feels good to cleanse body, no?" Dancing Fish said.

"Mmmm, yes. This is a new habit I am getting used to."

"You do not sweat in your land?"

"We sweat, but not on purpose. Not like this. We try our best to avoid it."

"Is why your people smell bad," Dancing Fish said, laughing out loud.

The man joined in the laughter. "You may be right. I always thought smelling bad was normal, until I spent time with your people. In this way, I think your custom is superior to ours."

Dancing Fish liked this man with his quick humor and easy way. Then he took a more serious tone. "I want show you something." He reached to his deerskin and pulled out the folded leaf Hard Stick had given him on her deathbed. He opened it carefully and handed it to Boo-shay. "What is it?" he asked.

The trader's eyes widened when he saw the marks. "It's a

letter. In French. My language. Where did you find this?"

"*Letter*," he repeated while he watched Boo-shay's head move from side to side, his eyes passing over the marks.

"Writing, from one person to another," he said, lifting his head slowly to look into Dancing Fish's eyes. A sudden look of recognition. "You don't write, do you?"

"*Write?*"

Boo-shay cupped a hand to his mouth with a look of surprise. "Heavens, you have no written language! No way to communicate by hand."

Dancing Fish shook his head, thinking he understood but not completely sure. He remembered that Master Hudson had spent much time doing this in his cabin on the ship. It was something new to learn.

"Then I will teach you," the trader said, still looking surprised. He held up the leaf. "A letter from someone named Jacq. He is writing to his son." He paused a moment and added, "Talking, but using marks written with the hand."

Dancing Fish now understood the concept of the writing, but he was still confused. He remembered a Jacq from Owl explaining the man who had brought the tobacco seeds long ago.

"Let me read it to you," Boo-shay said. "I will translate."

The trader reached out and opened the hut's skin flap a crack so a streak of light could enter. He put the leaf between his legs and started to speak while his eyes looked at the marks:

To My Dear Son or Daughter,

If you are reading this, I am gone or dead. So let this be my only message to you.

I am a trader from across the great sea. And I have fallen in love not only with the beautiful land of Mannahatta, but also with the kind and gentle people of the island. And one especially: your mother, Smooth Twig. We love each other very much, but she is promised to another man. He does not know yet, but Smooth Twig

182

has a baby growing inside her. She believes I am the father.
Your father.

I am sure that you will be strong, smart, and proud.
Just like your mother. But because your father is white, you
will have many challenges. Remember that you are the
result of two worlds, and hopefully, the best of each. I wish
you a good and healthy life, my child.

Your father, Jacques

P.S. Please . . .

Boo-shay stopped and lifted his head to look at him.

Dancing Fish watched as Boo-shay's eyes carefully examined his hair, face, and eyes. "Why stop?" he asked.

Boo-shay held the leaf letter up and turned it around for him to see.

He now noticed that the letter was torn at the bottom, a tear cutting through the marks.

"There's no more," the white trader said. "The letter is not all here, the remaining words missing." He cocked his head and stared at Dancing Fish for an uncomfortable amount of time. "Do you know of this Jacq? Have you heard his name before?"

"No," Dancing Fish quickly answered, but he pulled his eyes away from the man and studied the stone that had lost its red glow. Slivers of memories flooded in . . . Owl talking about the man named Jacq who had stayed with the band only a short time. His grandmother telling him he was different. He, himself, *knowing* he was different.

Dancing Fish could hear his breath growing louder, his heart pounding, his thoughts spiraling. Was he . . . ? Could he be . . . ? He bent over and placed his hands on the dirt floor. Anything to steady himself.

Just then, the hut's flap opened all the way, and High Limb poked his head in, his eyes narrowed in suspicion, his wet hair dripping. "What are you two whispering about?"

Thirty-four

Sprouting Grass Moon

HIGH LIMB, BOO-SHAY, AND DANCING FISH WERE FINALLY back from the long trading trip. For three moons, they had been busy and distracted by their travels and the bargaining for the future trading. But now, instead of a joyful homecoming, they had found an ugly new reality.

High Limb sat on a flat rock close to the river path Achqueehgenom was named for and watched how the water rushed by, full of the last melting snow from an unexpected storm. He held a handful of cold, wet sand and tossed it, back and forth, between his fingers.

His thoughts were as jumbled as the clumps of sand. Part of him felt strong and confident—an excitement that matched the sounds and sights of the coming spring: birds singing, early flowers blooming, and worms wriggling out of the earth. Both the trading of furs and thoughts of Willow gave him a feeling of hope and promise.

But another side sensed only gloom and sadness. His father was now dead from the Beast Fever, along with many more from the village. There was a constant march of blackened faces to the burial ground. And sometimes, not all the ones who went came back. Weak and heartbroken, they simply chose to lie next to their family and die in the place of death.

Losing his father to the Sky World was a hard blow. A deep sorrow flooded High Limb, but even more, Sawgrass had been his link to influence Willow's father, Weetoq. And to make things worse, Weetoq was, himself, covered in awful red bumps and dying of the fever. He had no uncles left to speak for him to what remained of Willow's family.

Willow, herself, was still resisting the idea of being with him so long as Dancing Fish buzzed around her like a fly. But she was a smart girl, and he was sure she would change her mind once she saw the tools, wampum, and prestige he would have from trading the furs to the white men. The plan was good. Now they needed only to collect the skins and then meet the ship.

And he was now the recognized War Chief. Of a much smaller band, to be sure, and with only one assistant, the dim-witted Big Shadow. But he had power. And he would wield it to get his way. Now, more than ever.

▶◀

Dancing Fish was astonished that the band was half the size it had been when they left on the trading trip. The number of deaths overwhelmed his counting fingers many times. And even though he was not the natural child of Yellow Flower and Two Winds, their deaths from fever while he was gone shocked him. He had blackened his face and wept over their graves when he found out.

It was hard to stay encouraged about the trading prepara-tions, but he had to find the strength. There was much to do, and now, fewer people to do it.

They had moved back to the island, to Werpoes, with the spawning run of the fish. And now, the small group walked around the new section of land that was being burned and cleared of trees.

Kong, who had been so happy to see him again that he had knocked his wagging tail into anything and anyone for a full finger of sun, kept an eye out for rabbits fleeing the destruction and happily took off after them.

"This is where we build the trade storage huts," Thundercloud said, stopping and pointing to the middle of the scorched land.

Dancing Fish paused to look around the new area that had an unobstructed view of Xitkwe, the pond the village bordered, and also of the cliff that soared above it. It was a good place for the huts.

They would build two large wigwams, one for storing the animal skins and one for the tobacco. Each would have a small fire, but the fires had to be different. For the skins, the smoke from flat-needled fir would help with the drying. And they would have the extra benefit of making fine-tasting tea from the fresh needles.

For the tobacco, which would harvest before the Balance of Days, they needed more heat, not smoke, for the final curing. They would use aged black walnut for that. It burned hot, but with little smoke that could ruin the taste of the herb.

Spring was almost here. Higher leaves in the maples and beeches were already starting to come out; the oaks would need more time and warmer winds. The grasses were greening and the birds chittering. He had to throw off his sadness about the many fever deaths to move forward.

"When go back to villages for skins?" High Limb asked Boo-shay after they had walked a loop of the burned land.

"It must be soon," the trader said. "The ships will come in one month."

"*Month?*" High Limb asked.

"The filling of one moon," Dancing Fish explained, showing off his knowledge and grinning at High Limb. He had learned about the white man's years, months, weeks, and days from Hudson. It made some sense to him, although he thought using the moon, sun, and fingers was just as good.

"Our month of May," Boo-shay confirmed.

"Month of May," High Limb repeated awkwardly at the same time he shot Dancing Fish a nasty glance. He added, "And more months before tobacco comes." Now *he* was grinning.

▶◀

While others worked on the huts, Dancing Fish had something equally important in mind. They would need a drag-along to carry the quantities of skins they picked up from each village. And later, the tobacco. A drag was like a litter, held up at one end and dragged on the ground at the other if the weight was heavy. Boo-shay called it a *travois* when he explained it to him.

People frequently used their dogs for this, and Kong would normally be happy to have the task. But a mass of skins growing higher and higher when they traveled back to the villages would be too heavy for a dog to pull. It was time for another invention—and Dancing Fish already had the model for it in his head.

With the lengthening light of early spring, he set aside a hand of sun each day for the project. But he needed the Salt Man's tool. A steel hatchet would make for faster work.

First, he found a young tulip tree in the forest understory, and after saying a prayer for its sacrifice, stripped off the bark in a wide band all around. This started the death of the tree, which he helped along with hatchet chopping and cutting. He had been careful to pick a tree trunk that was straight and round. The circle was a sacred form in nature, and he would now put it to use.

Once the tree had fallen, he built two small fires on both sides of the trunk a short distance up from the base. The fires charred the wood and he chopped away with the hatchet to expose new areas for the flames. He repeated the procedure and moved the two fires closer as they ate away at the tree.

Both Rock and Kong sat and watched him work. Kong just cocked his head with intense curiosity, while Rock asked a never-ending stream of questions, sometimes lending a hand to tend the fires or cut the wood. High Limb stopped by several times to question their intelligence. "That dog is smarter than either of you two," he mocked before shaking his head and wandering off.

Eventually, he cut through the trunk in two places.

When he was done, Dancing Fish held up what looked like a short stump with two rough ends where the stripping, fires, and cutting had done their jobs. Then he went to work, slowly chopping down the remaining pieces with the hatchet until he had a round disk the width of one outstretched hand and with two flat sides.

He removed any remaining bark and took two more days shaving and fine-tuning the disk with a steel knife, including digging out a small hole in the center. Then he heated the disk on the fire to make it hard.

"Look what I made," he declared to Boo-shay in the central meeting place of the village the next day. He rolled the finished disk across the flat ground to him.

Boo-shay scooped it up and inspected. "It's a wheel," he announced to the puzzled onlookers. At once, his eyebrows shot up. "My God, I just realized . . . You don't use the wheel!" Boo-shay looked at him with an open mouth. "Well, you've just contrived it."

Dancing Fish nodded and smiled. "For the travois. Need one more for collecting trade."

Thirty-five

ONE MONTH HAD PASSED, AND BOUCHER STOOD ON THE NARrow strip of pebbly beach and watched the ship set its anchor. The three-masted *jaght* lay offshore a slight indentation in the coast near the island's point. This was only a shallow nook on the east side of an otherwise rocky shore, but it made for a natural anchorage.

It was indeed his ship—the *Fortuyn*. He saw the distinctive carving of a naked woman with full breasts jutting out from the beakhead. He could even spot the squat figure of Maarten Deen, shouting and waving his arms at someone for not doing his job or not moving fast enough for the Supercargo.

"They come for us now?" Dancing Fish asked.

He turned to the two young men on his left and nodded. Each had suffered personal tragedy from the plagues, but they had stuck firmly to their plans. They had their trade samples ready: a roll of three beaver pelts at High Limb's feet, and for Dancing Fish, a ball of last year's coiled tobacco covered in deerskin. Both had their eyes locked on the ship. The day was heating, but High Limb still wore the blue capote, now frayed and full of dirt.

Boucher swept his eyes past the natives and north toward the bulk of the island. A mild breeze rustled the newly green leaves in an endless wilderness of trees he knew was broken only here and there by streams, salt marshes, grassy meadows, wigwam clearings, and tiny garden plots. Birds sang with clear voices, and insects chirped and buzzed. Winter had finally fallen away, and he guessed they were passing through early to mid-May now. The Indian women were planting the corn, with beans and squash to follow. Small patches of tobacco, too. There was a seasonal rhythm to the simple lives of the naturals, and Boucher had become used to it.

But now he was leaving this lush country behind. He would soon rejoin the world of his own people and the family he sorely missed. Over the months, he had thought a great deal about how his future might continue to intersect with this strange but wonderful land. Maybe he would continue the Atlantic trade on another ship. Or even gather a group of investors to stake him with his own ship. The possibilities were boundless.

As he watched the men scuttling over the *Fortuyn* with their various duties, Dancing Fish turned to him and asked, "Why do your people call us *savages*? What it means?"

Boucher looked the young native square in the face. He was repeatedly struck by the curiosity and intelligence radiating from it. "It means not civilized. Wild." He saw an attentive High Limb also looking on, paying attention.

"What is *civilized*?" Dancing Fish asked.

He had to think for a moment. "It means to have a society or culture like ours. Like the Europeans."

"Euro-peens?"

Boucher sighed. A complex subject. He glanced at the ship, but no one was coming yet. They had time.

Dancing Fish continued. "So, it is good, civilized?"

"It can be good. But not always."

The native was quiet for some time, his face scrunched and serious. He finally asked, "Are white visitors good for our People, or bad?"

Boucher wasn't sure how to answer. He knew that most men like him coming to this new world thought only of exploiting it—or, if religious, converting the savages to their Christian faith. But no one seemed concerned about them as *real* people with traditions, feelings, and their own way of life. It was different from theirs, clearly. But was it inferior? He doubted that with each day he spent among them. Those he had met in the past months were, in the main, more honest, respectful, and generous than most of his own people. They spoke what they believed. Simply, effectively. Without complications. But he worried about this simplicity. Would it stand up to the contortions and intrigues of the people who would follow?

He studied his young partner while High Limb, standing close by, watched and listened intently. "Give me your hand," Boucher instructed. He clasped Dancing Fish's hand firmly and looked deeply into his gold-colored eyes. "I don't know if my people are good or bad for you." In fact, he thought he did know, but he would keep his dark opinions to himself.

Then he pulled the young man a little closer. "But I promise you this: I will do my best to honor you and the Manahate band." He looked at High Limb and nodded as a way to include him, too. "As far as I am concerned, we are equals. All the same." He smiled. "Especially now."

He turned and tipped his head to the ship and saw a launch being lowered. He released Dancing Fish's hand. Boucher felt the warm sun on his neck while he breathed in the island's sweet smell he had come to know well.

Now we will see.

◢◀

The two pale, hair-faced men strained at their long paddles, and the shallop moved easily over calm water toward the ship. The sound of the rhythmic splashing and of the gulls cawing overhead against a high sun brought back memories to Dancing Fish of paddling for the first time to the great floating canoe of Master Hudson. Oh, how awed he had been by it then! And by the strange Spirit Men who lived on it. How much had changed since those days almost three years past.

Now he knew these were not Spirit Men at all. Simply men. But in their own way, so different. Or were they? Maybe the better question was: was *he* truly different from them? Was he secretly more connected to the Whites than he dared to admit?

He remembered how, early on, he had wanted to be like them. He liked their independence, their way of thinking new thoughts. Just like him.

But he had also seen their hurtful side—their evil, their shocking cruelty, and their greed. Did that mean he had this living in him, too? Was this something he dreaded facing?

Dancing Fish fingered the glass button hanging at his chest. He could not forget the Fire Prophecy and his mission to find the answer of whether the visitors were good or bad for the People. A question now made more difficult by the words Boo-shay had spoken from the marks on the letter. And when he asked Boo-shay directly about their future with the Salt Men, he seemed to not know. If anything, the question burned even hotter and deeper inside him.

In less time than it took to start a fire, they were at the ship and being helped aboard. The vessel creaked and rolled with the gentle swells.

Gripping their samples tightly, they followed Boo-shay as he led them past men holding onto ropes or the ship's railing, all staring at them. The ship was almost identical to Hudson's, and the men, the same. The same oily clothes, hairy beards, white skin, and that distinctive and disagreeable smell from not bathing. It was a foul stench he had never forgotten. And now, here he was again, in the midst of more strange men from a faraway land.

A thin man with only wisps of hair on top of his head waited for them at the base of the foredeck. He had bug-like, protruding eyes and a large nose. He smoked a long clay pipe and wore a short coat that may have once been red but was now the color of wet dirt and full of stains. Master of the ship, Dancing Fish thought.

"I see you're not quite dead yet, are you?" the man bellowed in the Dutch tongue at Boo-shay.

"You predicted I'd be either very dead or very wise, Master Block," Boo-shay said with a strained smile. "I'm glad to report that it is the second condition."

"Well, we'll soon see the truth of those words," said the Master. Then he narrowed his eyes and focused on the two of them. "And what do we have here?"

Boo-shay introduced them. "Two trading representatives of the Manahate band that lives in this area: Dancing Fish and High Limb."

"Such strange names with these savages," the man muttered, shaking his head. "They're a bit young, no?" he said, staring at them and their bundles.

"They are. But they've been given the task of trading, and you'll find them more than up to it."

"Really?" he said, scratching his smooth head with his pipe stem. "Let's see what our Supercargo thinks of that. Follow me."

He turned and they started to climb the steps to reach the foredeck. This was where he and Joo-et had played the pumpkin game. Dancing Fish felt himself shudder at the thought of Joo-et, and he hoped the Underworld was making him miserable.

Waiting for them on the cramped deck was a fat man seated on an overturned box, his back against the foremast. The man looked almost a head shorter than Boo-shay, who was, himself, shorter than most. He seemed as wide as he was tall, like a toad.

Dancing Fish saw that his head was covered with odd

yellow hair the color of corn tassels. It gave the impression of choking itself with curls. His greasy beard of the same color was thick and long, and it covered his neck and most of his chest. He didn't stand but merely nodded his head first to the Master and then to Boo-shay.

"Meneer Deen," the Master said, "they're yours now. I have matters that await." He turned and climbed back down the steps.

The man Deen—the Supercargo—motioned with his right hand, and after Boo-shay's pointing, they all took their seats on other boxes crowding the foredeck and faced the Supercargo.

"I see you've been busy, assistant," the fat man said to Boo-shay in a high voice that matched the screeching of the gulls. But Dancing Fish noticed that his small, blue eyes never left the skins and the ball of tobacco.

"Oh yes, Meneer Deen, very busy. All winter, in fact. And ready to talk with you about trade."

"Very well. Let's get to the matter at hand," the man said, showing a mouth empty of most of his teeth, and those that remained, dark and stained. "What am I looking at?"

Boo-shay leaned back on his box. "Something very special."

Dancing Fish noticed that Boo-shay had changed the tone of his voice. It was like the first day he had entered their village. The voice was smooth and soothing. Like a warm stream flowing over a polished rock.

"I'll decide that," the Supercargo snapped. "Let me see the pelts." He pointed his pipe toward High Limb.

High Limb looked confused. His cousin had already pulled out a few strands of wampum from his apron and was preparing to offer them for his side of the ritual exchange. All important meetings began with an exchange of gifts, but something told Dancing Fish that this meeting—and this man—was going to be different.

"What are you doing?" the Supercargo screeched at High

Limb. "I don't need more sewant. I already have plenty of wampum from *Lange Eylandt*. We stopped and traded for it there with the Montaukett and Shinnecock before coming here. I will be giving the wampum, not receiving it."

Boo-shay jumped in quickly. "It's a gift," he said softly to the yellow-haired man. "A present from the Manahate to start the negotiations."

The man replied to Boo-shay, "I don't believe in this silly idea. A negotiation is a negotiation. That's all it needs to be." He tightened his eyes and looked hard at Boo-shay and his native coverings. "Are you turning into one of them now? Becoming Wilden yourself?"

Boo-shay stiffened. "No, Meneer Deen. But you don't understand their way of doing things."

"Nor do I need to," he snarled back. "I am the Supercargo. I control the manner of trade." He paused and glared at Boo-shay. "And I suggest you remember who you're working for—us, not them." He turned abruptly back to High Limb. "Let me see what you have."

A stunned High Limb untied the three skins and unrolled them into a flat pile. He picked up the top one—a rich beaver with fur as thick as his fist—and leaned to offer it to the short man with yellow hair.

When he sat back with the skin in his lap, the face of the Supercargo changed subtly. Everything seemed to soften and bend upward. "Oh my . . . " was all that came from his mouth. He motioned to see more, and soon he had the three skins balanced on his knees. The man's face reshaped itself to one of no expression. "These are satisfactory," he said in a flat voice. "Of course, there are flaws."

"Of course," Boo-shay said smoothly with a grin.

Ignoring him, the Supercargo directed a string of questions at High Limb: "These are all from midwinter? With the guard hairs removed? And brain-tanned and fully dried and stretched? With no mold?"

To his credit, High Limb, who had slowly improved his Dutch tongue, was able to follow the questions and give short *Yes* answers to them all.

"Good," the man said, letting the first real smile cross his face. "What do you desire in exchange?"

High Limb looked to Boo-shay, who flicked his hand and tipped his head. "Go on."

He saw High Limb take a quick breath before he spoke. "Want steel knives, hatchets, pots, awls." He paused. "And mirrors."

Dancing Fish smirked to himself. The oaf wants mirrors. Of course. To better see himself, no doubt.

Without a word, the Supercargo opened a sack at his feet and pulled out one of each: steel knife, steel-headed hatchet, awl, black metal pot, short-handled hoe, polished-metal mirror, and beads of many colors. "Here is what I have to trade," he said when everything was placed on the deck in front of him.

High Limb got down on his knees to inspect and hold each object. The Supercargo remained in his seat, looking down disdainfully.

"Four beavers for knife," his tall cousin suddenly announced with growing confidence.

"Five beavers," the man said in reply.

High Limb, kneeling, shook his head *No* and moved to the hatchet. "Seven beavers for hatchet."

"Ten," the man countered.

"Eight," High Limb countered back.

Dancing Fish marveled at how quickly his rival had overcome his hesitations and was now back to his usual aggressive self. He glanced at Boo-shay, who gave him a wink with one eye.

The back and forth between the Supercargo and High Limb went on until all the ship's trade tools were considered and agreements for each made. This included not only the trade objects but also the many hands of wampum High Limb would receive. It was an impressive list, and Boo-shay had marked it down on a special leaf. He made the Supercargo put a sign on it with his own hand.

"Very well," the Supercargo finally said. "When can you bring the skins to the ship?"

Boo-shay answered, "We were hoping to settle our understanding now but wait for what this young man has"—he pointed to Dancing Fish—"and bring everything at once on your return trip from the north, in the fall."

"No," Deen said firmly, shaking his head, his ample belly jiggling. "Do you want to trade or not?" He looked at each of them in turn. "I want the furs now. Yes or no?"

High Limb glanced at Dancing Fish with a triumphant smile before turning back to the Supercargo. "Yes. Now."

Thirty-six

DANCING FISH WAS NOW AT A DISADVANTAGE. HIGH LIMB would be getting the steel tools right away, but he would have to wait until the tobacco was harvested, collected, mixed, and balled. Willow's mother had already died from the fevers, and Weetoq was close to death and could be convinced to give his final approval of the marriage to High Limb.

Thundercloud would be on his side—and Willow, of course—but it might not be enough. He would have to make a strong impression on this Supercargo.

Boo-shay must have sensed his doubts. "We have one more dealing," he said to the man Deen, gesturing with his hand. "Dancing Fish?"

It was his turn. He untied the deerskin from the round ball of coiled and twisted tobacco leaves from the year before. It stood as high as a man's knee. He rolled to the Supercargo, who stopped it with his foot.

The man leaned over and touched it, frowning. "Tobacco. Nothing special. Savage tobacco is too bitter and rough for our taste."

"Wait," Dancing Fish said, ready. "Very special." He motioned to the man's pipe. "I show you?"

Deen looked puzzled.

"He wants to borrow your pipe," Boo-shay explained.

The Supercargo grunted and reluctantly handed his pipe to

Dancing Fish, who noticed it was made of wood, not clay.

Good.

Dancing Fish immediately stood up, walked to the deck's railing, and rapped the pipe on it with the bowl facing down. The old tobacco plug fell to the water where it made a little splash.

"Hey, what are you doing?!" the man shouted. "That's my best tobacco!"

Dancing Fish stepped back to his box, pulled out his tobacco pouch, and filled the empty pipe with Owl's mixture, tamping it down with his thumb. "No. *This* is best tobacco." He handed the pipe over. "You have fire?"

Deen, looking annoyed, pointed to a young boy, a ship hand. "Go bring a burning brand. Now!"

The boy was gone and back in an instant, holding a sliver of wood with a small flame at the end. "This better be worth the trouble," the Supercargo said as he moved the fire above the pipe bowl and sucked in the flame to light the tobacco. He was soon puffing and smoking.

The man's look of irritation suddenly changed to its opposite. His eyes were wide and his mouth turned up. He removed the pipe and looked at it, rolling one lip over the other. "What is this tobacco?" he asked Dancing Fish.

"Special mixture I make." He was lying, but he knew Owl wouldn't mind.

"Best tobacco I have yet to taste in this new world," he said, putting the pipe back in his mouth. He looked at him with a raised eyebrow while he touched the ball at his feet. "This has the mixture?"

"No. From last year. This harvest still grows. But in three months time, it is ready."

"Three months, you say." He puffed more and looked at Boo-shay. "Is this young savage to be trusted?"

"He is, indeed," Boo-shay said without pause. "I've smoked

the same, and, like you, find it superior to anything ever traded in *Nieu Nederlandt*."

"Well . . . ," the Supercargo said absently, thinking. He nodded to Dancing Fish, "Here is my offer: If you can have at least 25 of these balls—each wrapped in a skin like this for protection—ready for my return in September, we will make a good trade. Does this agree with you?"

Dancing Fish was pleased but he pressed on. "Yes. But we make accounting now." He had been learning about paper and writing and now understood its purpose. He grinned at Boo-shay, who smiled back and picked up his writing tools.

Deen snorted when he turned his head to Boo-shay. "You said these savages were capable, and you're not wrong."

While High Limb silently looked on, they spent the next two fingers of sun negotiating over how many tobacco balls for each trade object. And thinking of Willow, Dancing Fish put much more emphasis on awls. Tobacco was not as highly desired as furs by these white men, but he was happy with the arrangement. He would avoid killing more animals than needed, and he would receive the tools to help his people. And his hopes with Willow.

After full agreement was reached, Boo-shay handed the new account writing to the Supercargo, who again put his sign at the bottom.

"No tally sticks?" Dancing Fish asked.

"No need," Boo-shay said, handing the paper to him. "This does the same but better. It's called a *contract*. This is how we do it in our lands."

He nodded. He understood.

"And this tobacco ball?" Deen asked, looking at Dancing Fish and touching the ball with his foot.

"You keep," he said. "My gift to you." He stole a quick glance at Boo-shay, who gave a single nod with his head.

The Supercargo released a thin smile. "I will give it to the crew. They'll take anything offered." He rolled the tobacco ball to the same young boy and clapped his hands. "We are done."

The sinking sun glimmered on the water when they started down the steps to the main deck. Dancing Fish's hands were empty, and High Limb held two rolled skins, with one given to the Supercargo for his gift. "You see," Dancing Fish said proudly to his cousin in their Munsee tongue while they walked to the rail of the ship, "animal skins are not the only things to interest the Salt Men."

"Maybe not," High Limb responded teasingly, "but I'll soon have the white man's tools, and you have the whole summer to get through."

High Limb gave him a wicked smile. "And who knows what can happen with this tobacco of yours during a long summer."

▶◀

They delivered the skins the next morning under a clear sky. The tide was slack, and a light wind ruffled the water. Boo-shay and Dancing Fish helped with the loading of the heavy bundles into the shallop. High Limb, proudly wearing his blue ka-pot even though it was pulling apart in places, could see the disappointment in his cousin's eyes while the bundles moved from shore to ship. With each bundle, he was getting closer to Willow, and Dancing Fish knew it.

Boo-shay made marks on his leaf each time the white man's canoe paddled to the ship. They left Dancing Fish on shore, and the two stepped into the boat on its last trip.

"Good work," Boo-shay said to High Limb as the boat moved slowly to the ship on the wrinkled water.

"Good for both of us, yes?" he said, pleased with himself.

"Quite so," Boo-shay said. "We both benefit." The white man looked back to shore at the lone figure of Dancing Fish, standing in front of a wall of green trees. He pointed. "And he will also benefit later with his tobacco."

High Limb said nothing.

While different men carried the bundles of beaver, otter, marten, and mink skins into the bowels of the ship, High Limb stood on the main deck with Boo-shay and the yellow-haired man. This was the moment he had waited for: the exchange for trade.

"Here is what I have for you," the Supercargo said, handing him a large and heavy sack made of curious material somewhat like his ka-pot.

High Limb put the sack on the deck and curled down its edges. He crouched and pulled out each object one by one. There were the knives, hatchets, awls, mirrors, and a heavy pot. Many were dirty with no shining, but he would be able to fix that easily with sand rubbing.

He counted the tools and nodded to Boo-shay, who made his strange marks on the leaf. Then he put his hands back into the sack and searched again but found nothing more. Puzzled, he frowned at the yellow-haired man. "Where is wampum?" High Limb asked, standing back up and towering over both men. The wampum was important for giving to Willow's family. He had specifically asked for it.

The Supercargo smiled in an odd way and exposed his missing teeth. "Don't worry. You will get it on the return trip. We have to take it all to Castle Island upriver. Others want to see the quality of the sewant from the different villages and make a full count." He looked directly into his eyes. "You have my word."

Boo-shay, holding his leaf, spoke in a serious tone to the man. "But this was not the agreement. It was trade for trade." He gave the Supercargo a hard look. "All together."

The man made a dismissive motion with his hand and said, "Everything will be fine. This is how it must be."

High Limb was upset. He wanted the wampum. "Is it

good?" he asked Boo-shay.

Boo-shay hesitated then said, "Yes. We must trust this man. We have no choice." He pointed to the tools from the sack. "And you have these as agreed."

He wasn't sure he trusted any of these white men, but there seemed no other way. What could he do?

He grunted his approval to the man with yellow hair. "Wampum when ship return."

"Agreed," the man said, showing his awful smile while they both shook hands.

Boo-shay was first to start down the rope ladder to the boat. As High Limb climbed over the rail to the ladder, the Supercargo touched his hand.

"I'm always open to more trade," the man said with an unusual glint in his eye. "If you have more furs or anything else of value, let me know about it when I return in September." He motioned with his chin to the island a short distance away. "Anything at all of value."

Thirty-seven

Ripening Moon

THE SUMMER HAD PASSED QUICKLY, LIKE THE BLUR OF DEER running through the forest. Maybe because Dancing Fish was preoccupied with thoughts of his tobacco. Even when he hunted and fished, which all men were required to do, his mind was on the herb. And on Willow. Both matters were unsettled while he waited for the returning ship.

Following the custom, Willow was kept busy and away from her two suitors. She was always in the company of friends or relatives as they prepared food, cleaned fish, gathered berries, and tended to the corn, beans, squash, and tobacco in the small garden plots surrounding Werpoes. This was the usual work of the women, but there now was a new excitement in the village: the tobacco trade he had created.

Dancing Fish and Rock had made more than one trip back to the outlying villages—both on the island and off. Over the summer months, they first checked on tobacco growth and health, then finally collected the harvested leaves on the wheeled travois.

Most in the villages had followed his directions for cutting leaves from the bottom of the stalk as they ripened, and then hanging them to dry in their wigwams. Some leaves were too dry and smoke-filled. Some had rotted with plant disease. But most were in good condition. It was now time for the final processing before the ship returned. It was almost the Balance of Days, which he learned from Boo-shay was called *equinox*.

All the women and children of the Turtle Clan were recruited to help with the tobacco preparation. Most were excited to have something to take their minds off the earlier fever deaths, which thankfully had declined during the summer.

First, the leaves were sorted by type—traditional and Spanish—and banded into small bunches. These they hung close together by their stems from the extra roof poles crossing the special-built tobacco hut. The low but hot fire of seasoned black walnut burned continually to supply the heat needed to finish the drying process.

After the dry leaves were pulled down, each bunch was tightly twisted and rolled with added strands of red willow bark. These were then coiled and combined with other rolls to form the knee-high balls. The final step was wrapping the balls in old deerskins and tying them tightly with hemp rope.

All this work was done on spread skins and old furs to keep the leaves clean. When the weather was good, the workers moved outside where there was more room. When it rained, or at night, they moved the task back into the hut.

Dancing Fish supervised every aspect with a focused attention to detail. Boo-shay was also helpful with both his hands and his suggestions. Rock worked tirelessly when he wasn't fishing.

Willow had appeared once to lend a hand at the tobacco hut, but she was shouted away by the other women. Courting tradition had to be followed.

High Limb refused to help; it was beneath his status as a hunter and War Chief. But he made a point of stopping by often to watch and evaluate with a skeptical eye. Dancing Fish caught him more than once peering and studying the process with a hand to his chin.

High Limb had already given more trade gifts to Willow's family, what was left of it from the fevers, but it had been decided by Willow's aunt, Wawamis, and Thundercloud, that no decision about Willow's future would be made before the final tobacco trading with the white men was complete. This pleased Dancing Fish but angered High Limb.

The final goal was two tens and five balls of tobacco for the returning ship, which they expected any day. Dancing Fish was using his new skill in marking on paper to keep track of their progress.

One-half moon before the fall equinox, the tobacco balls were ready.

▶◀

Dancing Fish sat with Boo-shay on one of the boulders at the island's point. The last of the sun's coppery light fringed small waves that curled and broke on a tiny spit of sand below them. The tide was in retreat while an onshore wind blew steadily, and gulls, looking for a snack, cried out in flight overhead.

The trader had finally given up his cracked boots, and everything he now wore—cloak, shirt, leggings, moccasins—was made by the Manahate. His beard was longer, and his blue eyes sparkled with anticipation. He had told Dancing Fish that he would be leaving with the visitors to return to his home across the Great Sea. Dancing Fish was sad at this news, but he understood. Family always came first. Even to these strange men.

"So, are you ready with your tobacco?" Boo-shay asked him.

"Yes," he said. "Ready." He threw up a piece of deer jerky, and the gulls instantly converged in a screeching tangle until one flew off with it in victory.

There was nothing to do now but wait for the ship. It was a good time to talk to the white man, to settle his mind. Between thoughts of his tobacco and of Willow, Dancing Fish had noticed something over the summer. To the relief of all, the terrible fevers of the winter and spring had lessened. Not gone completely—Rock's father had also died—but the daily visits of death and fever misery had eased. And he wondered why.

"Do your people have the fevers, too?" he asked.

Boo-shay looked at him thoughtfully. "Yes, but not like I see here. It's frightening."

"Why it comes here so strong and kills so many?" Dancing Fish could not help but think of all the burials and wailing of death songs over the winter and early spring seasons.

Boo-shay's eyes moved to the lowering sun. "Our physicians and people who know of such things have different theories, different ideas. The science is not clear."

"Science?"

"Science is knowledge, learning. People with knowledge studying the world around them."

"Like our Curers or Healers?"

"A little, yes. But no angry Spirits. No punishments for rituals not followed."

"No Spirits? No punishments?" He was intrigued by this. He had repeatedly wondered if all their rituals were really necessary. He followed most of them, but still, he wondered.

"Oh, we have our rituals, too," Boo-shay said. "But with diseases, a new belief is that something is passing through the air. Or by being close and touching."

"You name the fevers *disease?*"

"Yes. Other names, too—plague, epidemic, pestilence, pox."

Dancing Fish thought about this while the last of the sun's disk slipped below the lowlands across the mouth of the Great River. The vast red-streaked sky reflected off the moving water.

This made sense to him. If what Boo-shay said was right, people who spent time close to each other were more likely to receive a visit from the Beast Fever. And during the time of high summer, when people were away from their wigwams most of the day, doing their work or hunting and fishing, there was less time for the dreaded fevers to pass from one person to the next.

Which meant that, with the weather cooling and people soon crowding into warm shelters, the fevers would likely return.

But a question remained. "Then why your people not have the fevers we do? Like the men on ships. They are always close, no?" He remembered how cramped the crew members had been on Hudson's ship, both eating and sleeping. But he didn't see these men suffering from the same fever.

Unusually, the wind had picked up with the sun now down, and Boo-shay pulled his deerskin cloak tighter around him against the cold. "This is a good question. And I am not sure of the answer. There must be a difference between your people and my people. Everyone on the ships has been sick at some time, but we live through it. I was sick, too, when I was your age and younger."

And what about me? Dancing Fish thought. He had been close to many who had already died. But he had not. And there was the strange thing Hard Stick had said to him on her deathbed. She told him he would not die from the fever. How could she know this? Unless . . .

"You remember the letter you read to me from the man Jacq?" Dancing Fish asked.

The trader nodded.

He now dared to ask the question that had been spinning behind his eyes ever since their last talk about this. He breathed in the strong smell of sea and stared into the white man's eyes. "Is it possible I am like you in more ways?"

Boo-shay held his stare but did not answer right away. Then he also took in a long breath and spoke. "I've been thinking about the same thing," he said. "Your eye color, your way of thinking, your—"

There was a shout from the treeline, then Rock suddenly vaulted onto the boulder next to theirs, breathless. "Come quick," he rasped, sucking in air, tears streaming over his cheeks. "A terrible thing has happened."

Dancing Fish felt his stomach turn over as he looked into the agonized face of his friend. "What?"

"Just come. Hurry!"

▶◀

By the time they reached Werpoes, running the whole way, the sky had changed from pale rose to deep purple, and the first stars were visible. Dancing Fish arrived to find a crowd gathered at the entrance of the storage hut. The murmuring group, illuminated by the central fire, fell away when he approached. And to the right of the door flap lay Kong on his side.

Panicked, Dancing Fish rushed to him and saw he wasn't breathing. *"Kong, Kong!"* he shouted while he knelt and put his hand on his dog's great chest. There was no movement.

Tears rolled from his eyes while he kept repeating: "Kong, wake up, wake up!"

Then he saw the foaming at his snout. Spittle and blood leaked from his muzzle and mixed in a small pool on the dirt. The eyes were open but sightless, and Dancing Fish could smell the strong odor—stinkweed.

"What happened?" he cried out as he circled his arms around Kong's cold neck. He looked up at the people crowded around, pleading. Willow stood nearby, crying.

"Who did this? Why?" His heart was bursting in his throat.

"There is more," Rock said gently in his ear, pulling on his arm. "Come inside the hut."

After closing Kong's eyes, Dancing Fish entered the dim interior, lit only by the embers of a low, smoldering fire. The instant shock overwhelmed him.

The hut was empty! All the tobacco balls were gone. Only the strong smell of ripe tobacco hung in the thick air.

Thirty-eight

"ALL STOLEN, YOU SAY?" CAPTAIN BLOCK QUESTIONED AS THEY picked their way along the rocky shore. The ship had arrived on the day of the autumnal equinox, and the small group was scouting for something to repair the mizzenmast. Boucher was told that a sudden squall had ripped the yard from the mast and tossed it into the river the day before. They would not be able to make the crossing without a replacement.

"Yes, stolen," Boucher said when they reached the edge of the forest. The boatwright and his assistant, both carrying their cutting tools, were pointing to different trees and chattering about the qualities of wood needed to be cut and shaped into a new yard. He turned back to see the ship floating peacefully in the small harbor nook. "The young native, Dancing Fish, is in despair over this. No one knows how it happened." He shot a quick glance at the Supercargo, who stood with them.

"Why do you look at me?" Deen said defensively. "I wasn't even here."

"Of course you weren't," Boucher said, still wondering. He felt badly for his young trading partner. Dancing Fish had worked so hard on the tobacco. Everything was ready. And now all of it stolen? Just at the moment before the ship returned to finish the trade? It seemed too strange somehow.

They reached the island's southern point and found the remains of the crudely built huts traders had slapped up over the years, and where he, himself, had spent some nights one year before. He laughed at the ignorance of the white hut-makers when compared to the natives, who could build a functional wigwam in a few hours.

With the others off cutting a young and straight chestnut tree, Boucher found himself alone with Deen and taking in the scene around them. They stood with their backs to the thick forest and looked out at the expansive southern view. Sunlight glinted off water that surged and moved on all sides of them: the North River to the right, the smaller eastern river at left, and ahead, the marvelous bay that held more islands and so many promises with its opening to the sea. Birds flew overhead and fish splashed here and there, and he was struck by the sublime beauty of the place.

"This spot is quite exceptional," Boucher said without taking his eyes off the scene in front of him.

"Tis, indeed," said Deen, who seemed equally awed. "And it's more than beautiful."

"How do you mean?"

Deen opened his arms wide. "Look at the location. It's ideal. And strategic."

"Explain."

The Supercargo waved his hand in front of him. "You have a great, protected bay a short distance from the sea with deep water for easy passage of the largest vessels." He pointed left to the anchored ship. "That's a natural shelter for anchoring. It could be improved, of course. Maybe some digging or a groyne built up for more protection against wind and waves."

Deen then lifted his chin in the same direction. "Another waterway that leads both around the island—and it is an island when the tides are right; both the captain and I have determined that—and to more bays and lands to the northeast."

He turned his head to face west. "And finally, the opening of a massive river that navigates far inland to where savages of

211

all varieties bring something to trade."

Deen turned to Boucher. "It will be a web of commerce and trade, and where we stand is where the fat spider will sit—in control of it all." He cackled and spun in a full circle, short arms spread wide. "I tell you, assistant, this will be an important place someday." Then he laughed. "Of course, that's only if our wise employers in Amsterdam can recognize the potential."

He looked at Boucher. "Do you comprehend? Or is your Walloon mind too small to follow what I'm saying?"

Boucher bristled at the last words. "Traders are traders, Supercargo," he said evenly, holding in his emotions. "Dutch, English, French, Spanish. And yes, even Walloon. We all speak the language of trade, do we not?"

"Yes, yes, we do. I see your point." Deen looked out at the broad bay and a nearby island while the onshore wind stiffened. "This savage boy of yours, Dancing Fish...I was quite taken by his ideas and the good tobacco he brought." He brushed a lock of greasy hair from his face. "Here is my thinking—I've lost no trade goods for the tobacco. If he's as clever as you think, maybe he can regain the situation."

The Supercargo glanced behind them in the direction of the sounds of wood being chopped. "Looks like we'll be here at least two or three days more for repairs. Have him come see me on the ship tomorrow."

▶◀

Dancing Fish knelt beside the shallow grave with morning's glow growing in the east. He started the death chant in a low, moaning voice and placed the gourd of water and the rabbit leg next to Kong. These would nourish him on his journey to the Sky World.

The full impact of both losses—Kong and the tobacco—had not yet found his heart, but he knew they would. He had learned this when his parents had drowned. First came the shock, confusion, and disbelief. Then the anger would rise, followed by the deep loss, and finally, the return to life. He was still in the first part. And when the anger came, he would know where to direct it.

Two voices joined his singing as he shoveled in the loose dirt with his hands. Rock knelt to his left and Willow, who had sneaked away to join him, to his right. In all this earthly world, these were now the closest to him, and he would need them.

Ending the song, he closed his eyes and allowed his conflicted notions to become fragments of light and wisps of visions. He no longer needed the help of special herbs for this. He could call on the Spirit Powers of all three realms—Sky World, Mother Earth, and Underworld—when he cleared his mind and entered the gaps between his breaths. This was the land of the Dreaming Soul. Thoughts were like chips of wood or strands of fiber. They could be pushed or blown aside to reveal what was unseen beneath them. Owl had shown him this.

But he was still new to noticing all that was hidden, and much of what he now saw was unformed and jumbled. But there were hints. Questions took on more solid shapes, like a lump of wet clay slowly being formed into a pot.

He released a slow breath and saw a hand that grabbed for everything in its reach. Leaves on a tree that shook and fell hard to the ground, smothering all that lay below. A tall water bird walking in shallow water, spying its fish prey but letting it swim to safety. A flower that blossomed with warmth, fragrance, and beauty. And finally, a painted face that emerged from the darkness. Two colors split the face from top to bottom. One half was red—the sign of war and turmoil—the other, white—the sign of peace. The white side showed first, but slowly, the face turned to reveal the red.

All these images, he realized, were his past, present, and future. They would be with him until either he or they were no more. Until the blurred fragments of vision were as clear and solid as the dirt in his hand or the tears in his eyes.

A gust of warm, southern wind bearing the smell of rain blew in his face, and Dancing Fish came back to the world of earth and graves. The low mound of soil was wet with their tears when the three stood over it, voices silent, arms wrapped around each other. One day, he would see Kong among the stars. They would be together again as Sky Beings. But now, he had something to do.

▶◀

Dancing Fish faced the Supercargo on the foredeck, sitting on the same boxes. The south wind had picked up strength, and the ship rolled gently with the sea. The high sun bounced off the man's odd yellow hair.

"I understand you've had misfortune with your tobacco," Deen said, showing little sadness or concern. He held the same pipe in his right hand, but it stayed unlit.

"It was taken," he said evenly, holding in every emotion that wanted to leap from his skin.

"Stolen, eh? I'm sorry to hear that. I imagine you had worked hard to prepare it for trade."

He could see that the Supercargo wasn't sorry at all. But he could hardly blame a man who wasn't even there at the time. Dancing Fish was ready with what he had practiced. "I ask you what we can save. I must make trade." He mentally reached into his store of words learned from Boo-shay. "I can have *delay*? Time to find more to trade?"

Deen snorted, the high sound coming from his nose. "Delay? Not possible." He pointed behind Dancing Fish, who turned around. "Do you see that crippled mast there? Once it's repaired, we leave." They faced each other again. "Then we won't be back until next year. Do you understand?"

He did. And now he was worried. With the theft of his

tobacco, he had lost an important lever for Willow. He needed the trade tools. "You give me credit?" he asked hopefully. "Tools now for future trade. I bring you what you like on next visit." He held up his hand and made a writing movement on it with his finger.

The Supercargo cocked his head and gave him a hard stare, an ugly smile forming on his face. "Credit, you say?" He shook his head and gave off a short laugh. "That's a fancy word coming from a savage." He chuckled, then turned hard and serious. "No credit," the man said, stamping his foot to help make the point. "Trade for trade. No delays. You have one—maybe two—days to make a trade with me before we go." He pointed his pipe stem at him and narrowed his eyes. "Am I clear?"

Dancing Fish nodded without speaking and looked over the man's head to the far-off sky with thick clouds advancing from the south. A storm would come soon, but his own had already arrived.

He paddled back to the island shattered. He wasn't sure what he had expected, but it wasn't this complete failure. He pulled the canoe out of the water just as the rain started. He needed advice. And quick.

▶◀

Boucher was busy writing a letter to his daughter, Marie, when Dancing Fish entered their longhouse section. Rain hummed on the bark above them, and small drips pattered the dirt floor in several places.

One of Boucher's best decisions was to bring his writing supplies—pen, ink, and paper—on the voyage in a small leather pouch he always had with him, carrying it belted around his waist. It had become his habit to write regularly to his family, already giving some letters in small bundles to other ships they had encountered for conveyance back home. It was one way to keep the memory of his family alive, and he would take these last letters with him on the ship.

"How was it with the Supercargo?" he asked while Dancing Fish hung his wet otter cloak on a wooden hook.

"No good," he said with a tense face as he pulled over a folded skin and sat near the fire. "I have little time."

Boucher placed a gourd under a new water drop from the roof and moved closer to him. "Tell me exactly what he said."

Dancing Fish picked up the water pouch and drank deeply from it. "He said I have one or two days more to make trade. Then he leaves."

"And I leave with him," he said gesturing to his open travel bag.

Dancing Fish raised his head in surprise. "I forget. You go with ship." He stared at the low fire and slowly shook his head. "I am so . . . What is word?" He looked at him with cheerless eyes.

"Sad?" Boucher offered.

"Yes. Sad," he said, slicking his wet hair back with his hand. "I lose so much. My family. My Kong. My tobacco. And now, my Willow if I have no trade."

Boucher could clearly see the anguish in the young Indian, and his heart went out to him. "What can I do to help?" he asked.

Dancing Fish looked up with tears filling his eyes. "Not your trouble. Mine. I fail."

Boucher reached over and grabbed the young man's arm, squeezing it hard. "Do not think like that! You are no failure. Far from it. You have achieved much. You have a strong mind and you must now use it. You have obstacles, certainly, but we all do. Our people, too." He paused. "Me, too. But we don't stop. We keep at it. We move forward. And you must do the same."

Dancing Fish wiped the tears from his eyes. "But what can I do?"

"Your losses of family and friends cannot be fixed. But you

can fix this trade problem. I am sure of it. Think deeply. What can you do to satisfy the Supercargo? Is there not something you can find to trade? Something missed before. Something unseen?"

"Something unseen," Dancing Fish said under his breath.

He saw the young native lean back and close his eyes before he let out a series of short, quiet breaths. Then he started swaying his body, slowly, back to front.

This went on for some time. Boucher didn't know what to do, so he returned to finishing the letter to his daughter.

Suddenly, Dancing Fish jumped to his feet, almost landing in the fire. "I have it!"

He rushed to grab his cloak and headed for the opening.

"But the storm?" Boucher shouted at the back of the disappearing native.

"The storm is nothing," he said over his shoulder. "This is everything."

And he was gone.

Thirty-nine

With a covering of thick clouds, and heavy rain washing from the sky, it took Dancing Fish deep into the night to reach Owl's summer home.

The point at Kapsee was too busy with activity for Owl now, and he had retreated up the island to the long-abandoned village of Shawkequa. It was around the Hook on the waterway that formed the eastern border of the island. The waterway was actually a tidal channel and not a river, as some thought, and it linked their winter and summer lands.

Owl had scavenged poles, bark, and cattail matting from the old village to make his lonely, oddly shaped house that he had set near a stream but above the flood line.

Embers from a small fire glowed as Dancing Fish shook the old man from his sleep. "Elder, wake up!"

Owl blinked his eyes open and slowly raised himself from his bed of skins. "Little Perch," he said with a sleepy smile, arching his back and cracking his old bones. "What brings you here before Father Sun even thinks of beginning his sky journey?"

With the sound of rain lessening, Dancing Fish blew on the fire's embers and piled on more kindling. It soon came back to life, and with it, more light to see by. He turned to his old mentor. "Remember that tobacco rope you smoked when I visited your winter home in the North Woods?"

Owl rubbed his chin. "You mean during the Beaver Moon?

When my plants were sweating on the ground, and you made fun of me and my old ways?" He crinkled his mouth in mock disapproval.

"Yes, Elder, and I'm sorry to tease you about your ancient habits."

Owl chuckled. "The young are always making fun of the old. Nothing changes. Then they learn and end up doing the same age-old things." He straightened up and reached for his water pouch. "What is it you need?"

"Do you have more of those tobacco ropes?"

"You mean *shíkaash*? The rope of twisted leaves?" He drank from the pouch and offered it to Dancing Fish, who shook his head no.

The old man focused his eyes somewhere near the roof and drifted to the past. "My grandfather used to smoke that way, from the twisted rope. Now, most use the pipe, although the rope is better for storing, for keeping away the mosquitoes, and—"

"I don't mean to interrupt, Elder," Dancing Fish said softly, trying not to be rude, "but I don't need the whole history. My question is, do you have more of these, and do they contain the same two tobacco leaves with the red willow bark?"

Owl continued to make his point as though he had not been interrupted. "Most now live only in the present. Make just enough of the tobacco herb for one sun cycle. No one has the time anymore. Everyone rushes here and there as if fleeing from a fire." He shook his head and grunted, then he looked at Dancing Fish and smiled. "To your question, Dream Maker: lonely old men like me have lots of time. In many ways, it's all we have." He raised his eyebrows. "For me, I make tobacco ropes. Store most, and just cut and crumble enough for a loose mixture when I need it."

"So you have some more?" he asked again, hoping.

"Some more?" the Elder said, chuckling while he slowly

219

rose to his feet. He walked the few steps to the edge of the oblong space and pulled back a pile of old worn skins. He reached and grabbed hold of a hard mesh screen made of woven saplings and lifted it, moving it to one side of a pit he had dug into the ground. "Come. Look."

Dancing Fish walked over, bent down, and peered into the deep pit just as the fire rose and popped, giving off a glow of light. He gasped. He saw what looked like an endless pile of rolled tobacco ropes, each the length of one spread hand, wrapped meticulously in corn husk. And all neatly stacked. He stood upright and looked at Owl in amazement. "How many are there?"

The ancient man gave him a sly smile. "How many do you want?"

▶◀

The eastern sky was only hinting at the start of a new day while High Limb watched from his hiding place among the oaks. Thankfully, the night's storm had moved quickly over the island. Rain would have been a disaster for his plan.

He saw the canoe nose its way into the salt marsh and stop. Three men jumped out and immediately started cursing in their strange tongue while they awkwardly splashed and pulled the canoe through the grassy stalks and pickleweed to higher and drier ground. These men were so inept when it came to the simplest things.

They were a short bow shot up from Kapsee Rocks and the ship. The island's eastern shore curved north and east from here to the Hook, before it bent back inward and then out again to follow the island's line between the waterway and the Great River.

Big Shadow appeared from out of the forest holding his nocked bow. "I checked all around. We're alone. It's safe."

High Limb nodded. He glanced over at the piled brush hiding the tobacco balls. If anyone had wandered by, he would have diverted their attention from the cache to talk about how they had just missed a fat buck after a hard chase. Everyone knew about the deer trail that bordered the marsh.

He stepped out from the screen of trees and made a sharp whistle. The bearded men all turned his way, and he motioned for them to come to him.

"Did you have to make it so difficult?" the short, yellow-haired man asked when he finally reached him. He was breathing hard from the effort. Even a small amount of walking seemed to tire these men. How they could travel long distances and make complicated trades was beyond High Limb.

"Diff-i-cult," High Limb mouthed, not understanding. His use of their tongue had improved greatly, but there were always new words to learn.

"No matter," the man said, examining the area with his eyes but not stopping in any one spot. "Do you have it?"

This trader was standing no more than three bodies from the tobacco, and he saw nothing! Why was anyone troubled about these visitors? They had no more sense than rocks lying in the dirt.

He walked the three men over to the brush pile and—with Big Shadow's help—started pulling the branches away. "Many balls of tobacco," he announced. "Ready for you."

An odd smile split the fat man's hairy face. "I won't ask you where you got these," he said in that strange voice that sounded like it came from a young woman.

"No matter," High Limb repeated. "You want?"

"Of course I want. That's why I'm here at such an unholy hour." He pointed to the canoe. "Let's load it up."

High Limb grabbed the man's arm. "Wait. Where are tools and wampum for me?" He had not forgotten the wampum owed from trading the animal skins, and now he was owed more for this tobacco.

"You needn't worry. You'll have it all. But first, let's get this tobacco to the ship before anyone sees us."

High Limb hesitated. He wanted the wampum to show Thundercloud. And more of the white man's tools in return for Dancing Fish's precious tobacco balls. He smiled inwardly at the idea of using his rival's own trade against him to gain advantage over Willow.

The man said, "Don't be concerned. I'll give you your wampum and more of the other trade for the tobacco. Here—" He pulled a steel knife from a small bag he carried and offered it, handle turned.

"Take this as proof. A promise of more to come."

High Limb took the knife and marveled at the smoothness of the cold blade. "Good knife," he said, finally sliding it into his apron next to his stone one. "Agreed. But I hold you to what you say. Yes?" He held out his right hand.

"Of course," the Supercargo said, shaking the hand, but without firmness. He looked with uncertainty to the waterway. "But let's hurry."

The Supercargo directed his men to start loading the tobacco balls into the canoe. Big Shadow helped them. Each man carried two balls, and they made a line of coming and going that soon emptied the pile.

While the last balls were being loaded, the man stepped close to High Limb and spoke in a quiet voice. "I will make you a bargain. Another exchange. I want more beaver pelts to take with me when we leave."

High Limb looked down at the short man. These white visitors never stopped thinking of ways to trade. They were like dogs that constantly sniffed for more food at eating times. "But you have the skins. There are no more."

The man gave him a curious look. "You know the man Boo-shay, who stays with you?"

"What of him?"

"He owns some of the skins you delivered to me."

"How he owns skins?"

The man looked away to the nearby water that smelled of frogs and decomposing marsh grasses. "You know how, if you catch many fish in your weir traps, you share the fish with the others in the village?"

"Yes," was all he could think to say. It was obvious.

"And so I share the value of the skins with the man Boo-shay." He stared directly into his eyes and raised one eyebrow slightly. "So if something were to happen to Boo-shay, the skins would all belong to me. No sharing."

He was beginning to see. "Something happens to Boo-shay?"

"I said *if* something happens to Boo-shay," he said, watching the men cover the tobacco balls with a large piece of sail from the ship.

High Limb studied the fat man with yellow hair. Physically, the Supercargo was weak. But his mind was not. He was presenting him with another opportunity in disguise. Hinting without directly saying it. This sort of scheming he understood. He felt both trust and doubt about the stranger's words. The man had power, and High Limb respected power, especially if it gave him an advantage with more tools or wampum. He would consider the words of this man and how they could help him.

The day after a storm always made Dancing Fish feel more hopeful and alive. The morning air was cool and his skin tingled with energy.

He paddled his canoe toward the ship under an immense blue sky held up by a low, blazing sun. In a small pouch tied around his waist were two sample tobacco ropes from Owl's pit. Everything now depended on them.

A large perch jumped clear of the water and splashed to his right. "Yes, Manitto," Dancing Fish said to it. "You are right to leap and prove your strength. Today is a new day for us both."

They were back on the foredeck, sitting on their boxes, with Dancing Fish facing the Supercargo, and he could sense the nervous energy around him. Master Block was shouting instructions, and men ran this way and that, with some climbing up and down the masts just as he had done with Hudson. They would leave soon.

"We've repaired the mizzen and are making our final preparations," the Supercargo explained, his eyes flitting around the ship. "We sail with the ebb at noon tomorrow if all holds well." He focused on Dancing Fish. "I don't have much time. What do you have for me? Did you find something to trade?"

He had already opened the pouch and pulled out the two *shìkáashak*. He handed one to the yellow-haired man.

"What is this?" he asked, rolling it between his fingers, then putting it to his nose to smell.

"The same tobacco you smoke in pipe."

The Supercargo held the tobacco rope at arm's length with a look of surprise. "Ah, so this is the famous *cigarro* the Spanish are in love with." He smelled it again. "Even the French prefer it to the pipe for some reason."

"Good for voyage," Dancing Fish said quickly, visualizing Owl's pit and all the tobacco ropes neatly stacked there. He had left them with Owl, not certain how this trading idea would go.

The man grunted. "Well, you are thinking. I give you credit for that." He snapped his fingers, and a boy was instantly at his side holding a slice of wood with a small flame dancing on its tip.

Putting the flame to the rope's end, he sucked until puffs of white clouds came from his mouth. Then he held the *shìkaash* out and studied it again, smiling. "This is as good as what I last smoked with you. Maybe even better."

Dancing Fish grinned. "We trade?"

The Supercargo puffed again and let the smoke stay in his mouth before slowly breathing it out. "I will offer the same trade goods we earlier agreed to," he said, watching the smoke drift on the wind. "But I want 200, just like this." He moved his eyes from the tobacco rope to him. "Yes or no?"

Dancing Fish had never counted so high. In his mind, he saw 10 fingers, and then 20 of those. This was the 200. He compared that to his mental tally of what he had seen in Owl's pit. "Yes," he finally said. "Two hundred." By all the Spirits, he hoped he was right.

"And I want them by tonight. Remember, we sail tomorrow." The Supercargo put the tobacco to his mouth again. "Can you do this?"

A vision appeared of a multi-hued perch jumping clear of the water, flapping and gleaming in the sun. He looked into the large, black eye of the fish. "I can do this," Dancing Fish said firmly, holding up his own tobacco rope and pointing to the boy's still-burning slice of wood.

Forty

FATHER SUN WAITED FOR NO ONE ON HIS SKY JOURNEY, BUT Dancing Fish had decided he must see Willow. If only for a few breaths, a few words. She was the reason he ached for this second chance from the man Deen.

He needed to get to Shawkequa to pick up the tobacco ropes and then back to the ship later that same day. He knew the best trails that bypassed the hills and forded the streams along the way. He had worked out in his head that from Werpoes, he could make it to Owl's house in three fingers of sun. One more finger to eat something and make the pack ready. Then four fingers back to Kapsee and onto the ship. He had enough time to see Willow.

He found her in the hunting and gathering territory of the Turkey Clan. It was the end of the picking time for fall-bearing raspberries, and luckily, their berry patch lay to the northeast of the village. Exactly in the direction he needed to go.

The young women were scattered in a small clearing between the chest-high bushes. Willow was with her sister, mockingly called Raspberry for her love of the berries, one of the few survivors of the fevers from the family. They both crouched next to a bush bursting with the dark red fruit. Sun-dried raspberries were always a welcome treat in the middle of winter.

Pushing aside his desire to rush to her—and taste some of the perfect berries—he stood and watched Willow from behind a dense thicket of laurel.

Her dark hair was tied in a long braid that hung down her back. Her teeth glistened whenever the two girls shared a laugh, which was often. A long dress of deerskin, decorated with shell beads in animal patterns, made a circle on the ground where she knelt. She whispered and chatted nonstop with her sister while her graceful hands expertly pulled at the ripe berries and guided them into one of the small bags that hung from her neck. Raspberries were delicate and easily squished under their own weight, so multiple, smaller bags were required.

She was so perfect there, picking her fruit and laughing with Raspberry. He could have watched and watched, but a quick peek at the sun's position reminded him of his purpose. *Psst!* he sounded from behind the thicket.

She looked up, and a broad smile spread across her face. Standing, she said something to her sister and glanced around at the other pickers. Everyone was busy with their work. She walked quickly to him, and he pulled her behind a big tulip tree. They embraced and kissed.

"What are you doing here?" she asked, breathing hard when the kiss ended. She reached into her bag, pulled out a few of the berries, and put them to his mouth.

He gobbled them, savoring the subtle flavor. "I don't have much time," he said, his eyes swimming in hers. "I'm on my way to see Owl and need to be back at the ship with the moonrise."

"Your new idea. Will it work?"

"I think so. The man liked the tobacco rope. Now, I just need to bring him the rest."

"And then?" she asked, a look of anticipation in her eyes.

"And then I'll have the tools and gifts I need to convince your aunt and Thundercloud that you should marry me, not High Limb."

She looked at the ground. "But High Limb has already given valuable tools from the visitors to my aunt. She is favoring him. And with the theft of your tobacco . . ." She looked up with tears forming in her eyes. "It may be too late."

He pulled her to him and let his nostrils fill with the scent of sweet fruit mixing with the light grease she used for the bugs and mosquitoes.

"I'll never give you up," he said. "We'll be together. I have seen it in my dreams."

"So there is nothing to worry about?"

His stomach turned over on itself. "No, there is much to worry about." He forced a smile. "But I'll take care of it. If one idea doesn't work, another will."

"Well, you are full of ideas, aren't you?" she said with a teasing smile.

He chuckled. "They don't call me Dream Maker without reason, do they?"

"No, they don't," she whispered before lifting her mouth to kiss him again.

"There is something else," he said, pulling away and lowering his voice.

She looked at him expectantly.

"It's about the fevers."

She slumped and let out a sigh. "What about them?"

"I think I know what causes them. Or at least what makes them worse."

"Don't speak like this. You know our Healers and Seers say it's the Spirits punishing us."

"And where are these Healers and Seers now?" he asked, sounding harsher than he wanted. "Tanta? Long Pipe? Even the Matron. They're dead. Just like all the others."

She backed away, scowling. "You think you know more than the Elders, Curers, and Healers? Now you sound just as arrogant as High Limb."

He had made her angry and had to be careful. "I don't know more, but I see things in different ways. I've learned much from the white visitors. And from my dreams and visions."

She cocked her head and studied him curiously. "And what is there to do about all this? What are you saying?"

He took in a long breath through his nose and held her hands in his. "I want you to come with me now to see Owl. To leave the village and the dangers of the fevers. They will descend on us again. I know it."

"You know only your own arrogance, Dancing Fish," she said, abruptly pulling her hands away. "You're asking me to leave my village, my clan, and whatever is left of my family?" Her eyes filled with tears again. "I've already lost my father and mother, and now . . ."

"And this is why I am asking you to leave. For your safety. That's all I care about."

"If you care about me, then don't push me with your mad thoughts. Sometimes you don't know when to stop being different. Right now," she said, looking back to her sister and the others who had stopped to stare at them, "I want to be the opposite of different. I want to be normal. I want to be with my people." She brushed tears away with the backs of her hands. "Can't you understand this?"

Dancing Fish felt worried, sad, and angry all at the same time. He saw and sensed the forces of danger and evil that she could not. But he couldn't force her. Forcing was what High Limb did. He pulled her to him and said, "I honor you. I love you. I won't force you." He tightened his arms around her. "Just remember what I've said. Think about it." He took a quick look at the sun. "I have to go."

He kissed her on the forehead, turned, and let the forest swallow him.

▶◀

High Limb had been on the ship several times, but he was

always amazed by the giant floating house. And by the hairy men who now scrambled all over it under the light of a waxing half moon.

But his wonderment was spoiled by the late arrival of Dancing Fish. He had heard about the offer and the task the Supercargo had given, and he had assumed the Dream Maker would fail. Yet here was his rival, aided by some strange Spirit Power, back with something new. Another one of his inventions.

A lamp of flickering light was brought close, and Dancing Fish opened his bulky pack on the floor of the main deck while men crowded around. Boo-shay helped the Supercargo count the mass of tobacco ropes that were stacked inside.

Tobacco ropes! High Limb could only stare. He had seen his grandfather smoke them when he was young. The clever Dancing Fish had just outwitted him.

"Two hundred," Boo-shay shouted out, and the yellow-haired man nodded.

"Well done," the Supercargo said, staring at the mound of twisted ropes. He seemed transfixed by them. Then he motioned to a man standing nearby. "Put them in an empty beer barrel," he ordered.

Dancing Fish, happy with his success, gave High Limb a victorious smile and turned to the Supercargo. "My trade payments?"

Instead of answering, the Supercargo pulled out one of their drinking bottles and announced, "We celebrate first, settle up in the morning. We're not leaving until noon on the ebb." He lifted the bottle over his head for all to see. "For this last night, I offer a special aqua vitae, brought from our home." A loud cheer went up from the other men, and small metal cups suddenly appeared, ready for filling.

Dancing Fish had a look of concern on his face that he directed first to Boo-shay, then to High Limb. All he could do was shrug his shoulders. He knew less of the customs of the strangers than Dancing Fish did. If this was their way to conclude the trading, then he would go along.

When he received his cup, High Limb sniffed the liquid and instantly jerked his head back. There was a sharp odor he couldn't place. Something like the leaves of water hemlock, which everyone feared. He looked around and saw all the men, including Boo-shay, drinking from their cups. He would try, too.

High Limb lifted the cup to his mouth and, following the others, swallowed the liquid in one gulp. At once, his insides burned. His whole body was on fire as he grabbed his throat and coughed with a bark. The men laughed and pointed at him.

"Don't worry," Boo-shay said when he came to him. "You'll feel different, but it will pass. Best not to drink any more right now. We still need to get back to shore."

"That's right," said the Master, who had joined them. He held up his hand to quiet everyone. "Let's get these savages back to their island." The Supercargo then tilted his head to Boo-shay. "And you, my friend . . . Go gather your things, say your goodbyes, and come back onboard tonight like we discussed. We can then arrange the trade goods."

Boo-shay nodded in agreement, and they all moved to the ship's railing.

In addition to his renewed dislike of Dancing Fish, a thick fog filled High Limb's head, and he wobbled unsteadily while he tried to walk. He felt like a fish must feel when caught and pulled out of the water, or when he had smoked five pipes of the strongest tobacco without eating.

The Supercargo was suddenly at his side offering to help him climb over the railing. "Remember," he said in his ear, his mouth reeking of a foul odor, "No sharing."

Forty-one

THE CELEBRATION IN THE VILLAGE HAD ALREADY STARTED while they were on the ship. Almost a full year had passed for Boucher, and even with all the deaths and grieving from disease, these people would send off their guest as best they could.

A couple dozen were gathered around the central fire that shot flames toward a black sky speckled with stars. The new corn hadn't been harvested yet, but there was enough food and drink to offer him on his last night. A hot stew of squash, pumpkin seeds, and roast rabbit was ladled into gourd bowls and passed around. There was mint tea, and when they were finished eating, their best tobacco was pressed into pipes of all sizes and smoked greedily.

Thundercloud was the first to rise. He seemed markedly gaunt and less grand than Boucher remembered from their first meeting so many months ago. As he spoke, Dancing Fish translated for him.

"We welcomed this strange man to our band and to our island before the lengthening of the days of the last sun." Thundercloud looked at Boucher and shook his head in an exaggerated manner. "He was in bad shape, this one. A fish flapping out of the water, a mouse clinging to a branch in a swollen river. Beyond all hope." He smiled widely, and others laughed or nodded their heads.

"But he opened his heart to us, and he became one of us."

Thundercloud spread his arms to him. "And you will always be welcome here with the Manahate."

Everyone yelled out together: *"Wülu-wülu!"* Which he took as a sign of group agreement.

Others Boucher had come to know rose in turn to offer their goodbyes, even the ever-chubby Rock. But he noticed that High Limb, sitting with his eyes cast down, said nothing.

Dancing Fish was the last to speak, and he did it in their tongue with a rolling translation for his benefit. He talked of their friendship and of Boucher's willingness to share his views of life and of his people. "They call us *savages*," Dancing Fish said, turning in a full circle to catch all eyes, "yet they are the ones who look and smell bad!" Everyone erupted in loud laughter at this, and even Boucher joined in on the joke.

With the moon descending and the people tired, the celebration finally broke up. As he walked with Dancing Fish to their longhouse, a soft sound came from the shadows. Peering, he saw that it was Willow, motioning with her hand.

Dancing Fish turned to him. "Can I leave you now?"

Boucher laughed, then gave him a wink. "Of course. We'll see each other on the ship tomorrow. I know my way there."

Dancing Fish nodded and rushed to Willow.

Boucher watched while the two embraced and then disappeared into the night. "Young love," he murmured, smiling and ducking to enter the longhouse.

Sitting next to a small fire, he gathered his few possessions, including the stack of letters he had written to his family—each one carefully folded and sealed with melted beeswax. These he bound with a short hemp rope and placed with the gifts and mementos he had collected into a deerskin sack.

As the fire sputtered and crackled, Boucher looked around the longhouse slowly, taking in all its details for the last time. The woven reed mats, sleeping platforms, and folded skins. The stacked bowls and baskets. The nets and sacks full of dry food hanging from roof poles.

Boucher couldn't deny that he'd grown attached to the island, the village, and especially the people. He yearned deeply to see his family again, but his heart now had an added place carved into it for his Manahate friends.

His daydreaming ended when the door flap opened and High Limb entered. "I come take you to ship," he said with a warm smile.

"It's not necessary. I know my way."

High Limb sat next to him. "Safer if I go. Bear, wolf . . ." He pantomimed grasping claws with his hands. They both laughed.

"Alright. Why not?" He stood and picked up his sack. "I'm ready."

After passing a few people with their smiles, handshakes, and backslaps, the two left the village on the path heading south to Kapsee. The partial moon shone with a surprising luminance that cast dark shadows from trees lining the well-worn trail. The air was chilled, and the scent of wood fires lingered far from the village.

The hoot of an owl stood out from the sounds of night insects and the soft tread of their moccasins. Up ahead, Boucher could see a break in the trees where the moonlight reflected off the water surrounding Kapsee Rocks.

They turned left off the main trail and headed to the shoreline where the ship was anchored. As he approached the edge of the trees, Boucher suddenly realized he was alone. High Limb had vanished.

Strange, he thought. Then he heard a rustling behind him. He turned, and in the gloom of tree shadows, saw what appeared to be two men. "Who's there?" he asked, the hair on his arms prickling.

Saying nothing, the men approached rapidly, and Boucher noticed one lifting something. In the next instant, he saw the heavy club coming. He tried to duck, but he was too slow.

The blow struck the side of his head with a loud *crack*, and for a moment, Boucher was suspended in the air. There was no pain, just an odd feeling of floating. He noted the luminous moon and smelled the strong scent of the sea. And then, black.

▶◀

Dancing Fish stuck his head out of the longhouse to greet a bright morning. A chilly breeze brushed his face. The wind had shifted to the north during the night while he had slept, dreaming of Willow and rainbow-colored fish.

He played over in his head the conversation he had had with Willow during the long night of coupling and talking. The recent deaths of her mother and father to the Beast Fever had her considering his idea of going to stay with Owl. At least until the Turning of the Days in deep winter.

He was relieving himself behind the bushes when a sudden realization shook him. "The ship!" he shouted to the trees and two puzzled squirrels.

He immediately started running down the path to the Point. It wasn't long before High Limb, with his long strides, had caught up to him.

"Are you thinking the same thoughts I am?" High Limb asked between breaths while they both flew down the trail like frightened rabbits before a hunter.

"Let's hope not," he said when both careened off the main path at full speed toward the ship that waited offshore.

Except the ship was gone.

"By all the Worlds and Spirits!" High Limb screamed. He picked up a rock the size of a man's head and threw it with a mighty heave to where the ship should have been. "Where is the ship?" he cried out while the rock splashed and sank.

The only things on the empty water they faced—besides the glare of a blazing sun off its surface—were the ripples and waves pushed by the wind. Rotating his head slowly and studying every detail, Dancing Fish first saw the far shoreline where the Marechkawieck lived. The island of Pagganck came next. And then the great bay where a lone log slowly rose and fell while it drifted with the current. But no ship.

"What's happened?" High Limb spat. His eyes were slits of rage. "My wampum . . . the trade tools owed me by that yellow-haired weasel Deen . . ." He punched the air with his knotted fists. "I could kill him!"

Dancing Fish may not have been outwardly as mad, but he was equally unhappy. The ship had simply left without them. And with the ship went his dreams of trade objects to influence Willow's aunt and Thundercloud. All that work of organizing the tobacco trade. And not just once! Now, what did he have to show for it? Only two steel tools. He had believed the Supercargo, but was tricked by him in the end. Did these white men have no honor?

He turned his head into the wind in order to feel the touch of anything normal when a shape caught his eye. It was a stone's toss away at the water's edge. "Look!" he shouted and pointed with his right arm.

High Limb turned and joined his gaze. Without waiting, Dancing Fish bounded down the rocks until he reached the smaller pebbles and dark sand that met the waterway.

It was Boo-shay. He lay face up in the shallow water with his arms and legs spread. Flies buzzed around his open eyes, and his body shifted backward and forward with each small wave that sloshed onto the beach. Floating next to him were his letters with their distinct writings, tinged red with his blood.

With shocked numbness overwhelming his body, Dancing Fish turned and looked up at High Limb, now standing behind him. The expression on the giant's face was not what he expected. The rage was gone, now replaced with a strangely hollow look. He saw no surprise in his eyes.

Forty-two

HIGH LIMB WAS BACK AT THE BURIAL SITE WITH BOTH A heavy heart and a seething gut. Another cousin—the last of his family—lay in the ground on his side, his body curled, his favorite things placed around him. At least he was finally at peace. His Souls would soon head to the Sky World, while High Limb was still here trying to make sense of his confused life.

He was a fool for not anticipating the deception of the white Supercargo. The signs had been there: delays and promises. He knew these tactics all too well, and he had fallen for them!

A black beetle crawled across the loose earth of the grave. He pulled out the steel knife and bent down to spear it. He inspected the wriggling beetle and then the knife the thieving man had given him. It only reminded him of the loss of what he was owed.

High Limb looked down at the faded blue ka-pot he wore that was once his pride. Now, it was no more than a dirty, moth-eaten expression of the cleverness of the white visitors. Too clever.

He pulled the ka-pot over his head and threw it to the ground. Then he knelt and slashed into it with the keen blade, tearing it to pieces, bit by bit. He stared at the pile he'd made and thought of Boo-shay, who had given it to him. He felt bad for the man. Had even liked him. But helping Deen get him out of the way was supposed to help his cause. And he hadn't really done anything except take Boo-shay to the shore. He wasn't responsible.

And now, after all that, he is tricked by the Supercargo? He should have seen this coming. He had been spoiled by the decency of Boo-shay only to be deceived by another white man.

He finished mounding the dirt over his cousin when two old women came to do the same service for one of their family members. The two women sat close by, a brisk breeze carrying their voices to his ears.

"Owl is to blame," he heard one remark. "They say he is causing all this misfortune. His Spirit Power walks through the village at night, scheming and conjuring curses on us. He brings bad luck."

"But not on all," the other said.

"No. You can see he favors Dancing Fish. You notice how the young Dream Maker is never sick with fever or anything else? Some say Owl has cast a protective spell over him to help with his desire to marry Willow. That High Limb is doomed to fail."

He concentrated on the words.

"I've also heard this, and Willow has just left to visit Owl. Why, I cannot imagine, but shhh . . . Don't you see him there? He might hear us."

"I don't care if he does," the other said in a voice even louder. "He needs to know."

High Limb had heard enough. If Owl was involved . . .

He looked closely again at the gleaming knife blade.

▶◀

The dropping sun warmed High Limb's back, and a burning hatred heated the rest of him as he followed the main path north, and then the smaller trails east to Shawkequa. He found the Seer smoking fish over a low fire in a small clearing.

"Old man," he said without any formal greeting when he walked out from the trees. He stopped at the fire and remained standing. "I have something to discuss with you."

"And hello to you, young War Chief," Owl said in a mocking tone. He pushed another fish head down onto a walnut spear and bent it over the fire. "Come sit. Would you like some striped bass?"

Even as he took in the tantalizing smell of cooking fish, High Limb didn't like the insolent sound in the Elder's voice. "No. I want to know something from you." He was about to say more when his eyes caught movement coming from a run-down hut at the clearing's edge. It was Willow!

He took a step back and almost stumbled. "What are you doing here?" he asked, his suspicions confirmed.

She walked up to the fire and handed Owl a basket. She stood and stared at him for a moment with a neutral expression. "I can ask the same of you." She sat on a folded skin next to Owl and motioned with her hand.

Obediently, High Limb stooped and sat, crossing his legs on the fire-heated earth.

"You want to know something?" Owl said, eyeing him curiously while the fire spat and flamed from the fish drippings. "About what?"

High Limb moved his eyes from Owl to Willow and back again. "They say you're conjuring. Casting spells."

Owl laughed. "Casting spells? Who says this?"

"It doesn't matter who. Are you?"

"Don't be stupid," Owl said, paying attention to the fish.

High Limb moved his right hand so it touched the handle of the knife tucked into his apron. "I said, are you scheming against me?" He looked and nodded toward Willow. "In favor of Dancing Fish? A spell perhaps?"

Owl stood up with the speed of a younger man. "A spell? Do not speak of things you know nothing about."

High Limb jumped to his feet and tensed the muscles in his arms. Willow now also stood. "What am I to think?" he sputtered. "You are a guide to Dancing Fish, and now Willow sits with you in this"—he glanced around—"shabby place. He looked at her. "The woman I will marry."

"Only in your dreamings, High Limb," Willow said, her voice rising. "I will not marry you." She moved closer to Owl.

He clenched his fists. "I will have you, and this old fool is not going to help you or stop me with his plotting." He took a step toward them.

Owl was fast with his stone knife, and he held it out with one hand while he pulled Willow to him with the other. "Leave this place now," the old Seer ordered. "She doesn't want you and neither do I. Go!"

Enough of this! He jumped the fire in one bound and easily deflected the old man's knife swing as he sent Willow—screaming and clawing—sprawling away with a hard push of his open fist. He was soon on top of Owl, straddling him with his legs and holding the steel point to his throat. "I suggest you stay still, old man," he said, enjoying the power rushing through him. "We'll get to the truth now."

Willow suddenly appeared at Owl's head, kneeling. "Please don't hurt him. He's only protecting me."

High Limb didn't take his eyes off Owl and pushed the steel point harder against his throat until he saw a thin trickle of blood. "Protecting you? From what?"

"From the fevers . . . and from you."

High Limb tilted his head up to look at her. "I don't know about the fevers, but you are *mine*. You know it." He heard himself pleading and immediately regretted it. He looked deeply into her wide eyes. "Say you will be with me, and I will let this crazed old man go." He waited. "Say it."

Owl suddenly moved and let out a sigh. High Limb looked down and saw the steel blade sticking halfway into the Seer's neck. Blood spurted when he pulled the blade back out.

Owl was smiling as his head lowered and the blood flowed freely.

Willow instantly reached out and pressed her fingers to the man's neck. "What have you done?!" she shrieked, looking at him through cold, raging eyes.

He leaned back and struggled to his feet. "I . . . I didn't do it," he stammered. "He lifted his head and pushed into the knife. You saw it. I didn't stab him!"

"Give me your hand," she shouted. "Now!"

High Limb reached forward and she put his thumb over the pulsing, bloody hole. "Push. And hold it there. I'll find something."

He pushed, and she jumped to her feet, sprinting toward the hut.

He looked down at Owl. The old man's eyelids fluttered, and then another smile appeared. He reached up and put his hand on High Limb's arm. The smile crept wider. "Now you will never have her," he said. "You've just cast your own spell."

Forty-three

Dancing Fish raced along the trails and paths. The scattering of animals to all sides matched the jumbled thoughts bouncing inside his head. It was only after he questioned the old women and discovered both Willow and High Limb missing that he knew where they would be. Willow had finally taken his advice to at least visit Owl and listen to his thoughts about the Beast Fever and the white visitors. She must still be there, and it was easy to imagine that High Limb was, too. Nothing would surprise him about High Limb now.

The sun had already disappeared behind him, but orange-tinged clouds gave enough light to see when he broke free of the trees and entered the clearing. He smelled the fire before he saw it, small and twirling a single ribbon of smoke skyward. Then he saw Owl lying beside it. Alone.

His mentor was on his back, his long shirt covered with blood. Satisfied to see his chest slowly rising and falling, Dancing Fish studied the tight bandage around Owl's neck. It was a strip of deerskin, and he could smell the poultice pressed against what must be a deep wound. The bandage was expertly prepared, but the blood still seeped. And looking at the man's body and the wet ground around it, it was obvious a lot of blood had already been lost. Too much blood.

Owl opened his eyes part way and cracked his mouth. "Come close," he said in a raspy voice almost too quiet to hear.

"Don't move. Don't speak. You'll regain your strength only by being still."

"No," he said softly. "I'm dying. Closer."

Dancing Fish knelt next to his beloved guide and took hold of his hand, which was limp and cool. He turned his head to listen.

The wheezing sounds came out between shallow breaths. "Willow . . . High Limb . . . gone."

"Gone where?"

Owl closed his eyes and shook his head. He motioned with his hand for him to come still closer. "The seeds," he murmured. "Remember the seeds?"

"Tobacco seeds?"

He squeezed his hand. "Jacq," he said.

"Jacq was the man who gave you the seeds."

He squeezed again.

"I know of this man, Jacq," Dancing Fish said. "Boo-shay told me. He spoke of the marks on the man's leaf. Words to his son."

Owl squeezed and said, "But did he tell you all?" His breathing was more ragged, coming in short puffs and pants.

His stomach lurched. "No. Something was missing from the leaf."

Owl nodded imperceptibly. "I will tell you what's missing."

Tears flooded his eyes as he bent closer to listen.

"This man Jacq was your grandfather. I knew him. Good man." He coughed and his body shook.

Dancing Fish looked down at his old friend in confusion. "But the letter spoke of a 'Smooth Twig.' How could this—"

He squeezed. "Smooth Twig was his pet name for Hard Stick." He convulsed and wheezed. "Hard Stick was mother to your father."

He couldn't believe what he was hearing. "But . . . But . . . This means that . . ."

"Yes," Owl said faintly. "Your father and mother were half brother and sister. Same mother, different fathers." He coughed again. "Do you understand?"

He couldn't move. He was as frozen as a hailstone. *He was part white!*

Owl's eyes suddenly opened wide. "I see him now. Jacq. He is warning me . . ." His mouth was gaping; short breaths coming from it.

"Warning about what?"

"About his people." He paused and took two shallow breaths. "*They will destroy you*, he said to me." He blinked and stared at Dancing Fish. "His people will destroy *us*." He bored deep into his eyes. "You must fight them, Dancing Fish. You are the one."

He cradled the old man in his arms and pulled him close, sobbing. Listening.

"High Limb is not your enemy," he whispered, panting between each word. "The Salt People are the enemy. This is what Jacq told me." His eyelids shivered. "And now I tell you."

Dancing Fish buried his head in the old man's white hair and wept.

"And now I tell you," Owl repeated in the weakest of voices. Then he let out a long exhalation. And he was still.

▶◀

Dancing Fish found them on the southern side of the island's hook, at Nechtanc. He surveyed the hunting camp of the Turtle Clan from the treeline. Willow, sitting near High Limb, had her hands bound and tied high to a vertical stake. Her hair hung in a loose mess with dirt and leaves flecking it. One eye was bruised and swollen. She looked miserable.

Holding in a fire of anger, Dancing Fish strode with purpose into the clearing. "It's the Balance of Days," he shouted out to High Limb, who jumped to his feet. And this is how you choose to honor it? By killing Boo-shay and Owl, and now taking Willow with force?" He kept advancing.

High Limb held his steel knife in one hand as he moved slowly to Willow's side, towering over her. "I didn't kill Boo-shay or Owl, and Willow is now with me. Where she belongs." He pulled her head up by her hair. "And she came willingly. It was her choice."

"Liar!" she yelled, now on her feet and trying to separate from High Limb. "He took me!"

"Enough!" High Limb said, pulling harder on her hair, which led to a scream.

Dancing Fish took this moment to charge. With no thought to extracting a weapon, he raced across the clearing and dove head-first over the fire. He twisted his body in mid-air and landed against the giant's legs, immediately upending him.

High Limb kicked furiously with his feet and pushed Dancing Fish toward the flames.

Dancing Fish felt the heat against his cheek at the same time he saw the small metal pot—from the white traders—sitting atop the burning embers. He didn't know what the pot held, but he instinctively reached for it with his right hand.

His skin sizzled with instant pain but he didn't let go. Instead, he hurled the pot at High Limb, who was scrambling to his feet.

The pot struck the giant on the chest, splashing its boiling contents up to his face.

High Limb howled in agony and reflexively pounced on Dancing Fish, beating him with one fist and trying to drive his steel blade home with the other.

Curled into a ball, Dancing Fish was kicking and deflecting the blows while trying to get in his own. But the tall rival was strong, and a swipe of steel finally met his right arm and slashed it open to the bone.

The knife strike and the punches were having their effect as Dancing Fish started to lose his senses. His vision turned gray, his nose and ears started to numb.

The attack suddenly stopped when he felt—more than heard—a crack. Then High Limb's dead weight slumped on top of him.

Unable to move his body, Dancing Fish shifted his head and saw Willow. She stood over both of them with a wild look in her eyes and her hair jutting out in all directions. She held the stake—now broken—in both hands, which were still bound to it with straps of sinew. She had somehow managed to rip the stake from the ground and swing it like an axe at just the right moment. He gaped at her and rolled the motionless High Limb off him.

"He still lives," came the deep voice from behind them. It was Thundercloud, who stood with Big Shadow and one of the healing women. "I knew I would find trouble with the three of you."

The woman bent to study Dancing Fish's arm wound and opened her healing bag. Big Shadow knelt next to High Limb, who was now groaning loudly.

"What did you see?" Dancing Fish asked Thundercloud.

"I saw—and heard—more than enough," the Sachem said. "Owl and Boo-shay, too." He knelt on the ground after he had untied Willow's bindings. "This has to stop between you and High Limb," he said, shaking his head slowly. "We have many other things to worry about."

Thinking about what Owl had told him, Dancing Fish knew this was true. There would be more ships. More Boo-shays. More Deens.

And it would be up to him to do something about it.

Forty-four

DANCING FISH SAT NEXT TO THE FIRE AND HELD THE GLASS button in his hand. It had been rubbed smooth by the constant wearing and touching. Its edges gleamed, but the four holes remained dark, partially filled with soil and old grease. The Fire Prophecy was still alive, but the question of whether the visitors were good or bad for the People was now pointing more in one direction, like smoke slanting in the wind.

"Are you coming, or are you going to miss your own marriage ceremony?" Rock grinned from several paces away and motioned for Dancing Fish to join him.

He stood up, looped the button and its thong around his neck, and tucked it—along with his mix of thoughts—inside his shirt. They both left the longhouse together.

It was decided that the marriage would be held at the same time as the Green Corn Ceremony, when the corn stood ripe on the stalk. It was the white man's month of October, and the Balance of Days had passed. The leaves were starting to turn and the days were becoming colder with them. It would be a good omen to combine the two ceremonies before they left Werpoes for their winter camp. So many had died from the Beast Fever that a renewal was needed. A time not only for thanks but for strength, for restoring balance, and for rebuilding.

The central fire had been swept clean. Nothing remained but the smell of burned wood and a round shadow of the season's ashes. All other fires throughout the village had also been extinguished, awaiting rekindling from the main fire.

The sun had started its downward journey when the couple's two clans—Turtle and Turkey—came into the open meeting place to sit and complete the inner circle around the cold fire pit. The rest made a looser outer circle. High Limb, who had been publicly reprimanded by the council for his behavior, was forced to the outer circle. He was shamed, but he was needed. And Willow's aunt, Wawamis, at first reluctant, had finally agreed with Thundercloud to the marriage.

Dancing Fish and Willow sat inside the smaller circle on a short log, looking out, the ash shadow at their backs. They faced east, toward the newness of each day. By custom, they both looked straight ahead and not at each other. But he had already memorized everything about how beautiful Willow looked. From her braided hair to her shoulder mantle made of heron feathers to her long deerskin dress sparkling with tassels of wampum.

He wore his best beaver cloak over a deerskin shirt and full leggings, also fringed with shell beads. Willow had spent days making a new pair of moccasins that he now proudly wore. His long hair was up in a pom pierced with a gleaming copper skewer. And both of them were lightly greased with the finest blend of sunflower and bear-fat oils.

Dancing Fish was the luckiest man on Mannahatta island this day and possibly on all of Mother Earth. "Are you happy?" he whispered without moving his eyes. He nudged his arm to touch hers.

"Of course," she whispered back. "This is the day I've been dreaming of." She poked him with her elbow.

He smiled and felt a tingling of heat shoot through his body.

Thundercloud rose and walked to where they sat. He stood in front of them and turned in a slow circle to address everyone.

"To the Spirits and to my friends and relatives of the Manahate band—" he started, his deep voice soaring over the last buzzing of the people. "The Turtle, the Turkey, and the Wolf clans—indeed all the Lenni Lenape people—have suffered greatly during the last moons."

There were nods and murmurs from all sides.

"We have lost many to the fevers. Fathers and mothers, brothers and sisters . . ." There was soft crying at these words.

"And our precious children, too."

Loud sobs could now be heard.

Thundercloud raised his arms for quiet. "But let us think to the time ahead and not to the sad past. As the sun rises each day, so will we. As the new fire will burn here"—he pointed to the empty fire pit—"so will it burn in each of our home hearths. And in our beating hearts."

He walked behind the couple and put his hands on their heads. "Here we have our future: Dancing Fish and Willow. A mingling of earthly bodies and the Souls of our ancestors. A succession of the lines of the Turtle and Turkey clans that extends from Creation to the end of the Seven Fires Prophecy."

Dancing Fish internally winced at the thought of the clan lines now blurred with what he had learned of his father from Owl.

Thundercloud continued. "They sit here in their finest clothes, both looking to the east, looking to the new warmth of each sun. And we all know that Father Sun will always rise to light Mother Earth and to guide our way."

A hum of assent moved through the people at these words.

"And now for the marriage ceremony." He nodded to the new Holy Seer, an old man who had somehow survived the fevers, then took his seat in the inner circle.

The Elder entered the circle with the sacred, long-stemmed pipe, painted white for peace. A thin lace of smoke climbed from the bowl as he stopped in front of the couple and held the pipe aloft with his thin, wrinkled arms.

"To Kishelemukong, Creator of the Four Directions," the holy man said solemnly while he swept the pipe to the North, to the East, to the South, and finally to the West.

"To Kishelemukong," repeated the two to be married and then the entire assemblage.

The Holy Seer took two short pulls from the pipe, spoke a prayer to the sky, then handed it to Dancing Fish.

He sucked deeply and slowly before giving the pipe to Willow, who did the same before handing it back to the ancient man.

The old Seer moved slowly to the inner circle and offered the pipe to Thundercloud. He silently puffed and handed the pipe reverently to the next person on his right, who took his turn. The pipe was passed around the circle in this manner until it returned to Thundercloud, who stood again.

"I now proclaim Dancing Fish and Willow to be married," Thundercloud announced, raising both arms above his head and smiling at the couple.

Everyone stamped their feet, raised their arms, and cried out in unison: *Hó-hó!*

"Let us relight the central fire and start the dances and the feast!"

▶◀

The fire flared and grew higher when more wood was added. Dancing Fish held Willow's hand tightly while the Step Dance began with the sun sinking behind the trees, sending sloping shafts of coppered light through Werpoes village. High clouds—puffing and rippling like wet reed matting—turned from white to pink.

The old Seer led the first dance, calling out the ancient words and receiving the response from the other dancers who followed in a flowing line around the fire. Behind him came Thundercloud and then Rock's mother, who kept the rhythm with shell shakers tied to her legs. Rock followed as the male rhythm keeper. Then came Dancing Fish and Willow, both timing their steps to the pattern of the calls and rattles. It would be a long night of dancing.

Rock turned and did his rattling and shaking backward so he could face them. "On top of winning this beautiful woman"—he nodded to Dancing Fish—"I hear you're now officially the Kit Seer." He danced a full circle to make sure he was still in the line.

"Who would have thought," Rock continued. "A moon-struck adventurer who wanted nothing more than to escape the group, now training to be a spirit leader for the whole Manahate band." He turned his head to find the old man slow-shuffling at the head of the line and pointed to him. "And you probably won't have long to wait."

All three of them laughed at that, stepping in time to the rhythm.

Dancing Fish was as surprised by the changes the last seasons had brought as his friend. First, being enchanted by the ways of the white strangers. Then wanting to live alone with Willow away from everyone and everything. To now, being an essential part of the three clans. He had finally found the wisdom of Owl's demands that he belonged with the band.

He touched Rock on the shoulder. "And you've been made a Master Fisherman, I hear."

Rock spun around while continuing to shake the rattles on his legs. "I realized that fishermen don't have to run as much as hunters. They stay in one place. Much more to my liking." He grinned and patted his ample paunch.

They all laughed again.

At a break between dances, Dancing Fish grabbed Willow's arm and pulled her away from the crowd. He led her to his longhouse, and they slipped behind it.

"Soon, I'll be living with you in *your* house," he said, holding both her hands in his. "At least, you have plenty of room."

She dropped her head, and he instantly realized what a mindless thing he had just said. The only reason her longhouse had more room was because so many in her family had died. The new husband usually moved in with the wife's family, but this only reminded her of her loss.

"I'm sorry," he said, pulling her to him and squeezing gently. "I shouldn't have said that."

She took a step back, and instead of tears, she smiled. "It's alright. An innocent mistake." Then her smile turned into something different at the same time she raised one eyebrow. "And besides," she said, putting his right hand to her belly, "we'll need the room."

For a moment, he didn't understand her words. Then, like a thunder burst, it hit him. "You carry a child?" He couldn't breathe and felt his feet pinned to the earth.

She chuckled and grabbed him around the neck, whispering in his ear. "Yes. Your child."

▶◀

Dancing Fish and Willow came around the longhouse and almost ran into High Limb.

"The wedded couple," he said without smiling, stepping back. "I suppose I should congratulate you both."

"Not if you don't believe it," Willow snapped back.

"Let's not argue," the giant said. He inclined his head to Dancing Fish. "You got what you wanted: a wife and the sole trading role with the Whites."

"And so did you," Dancing Fish replied, looking at the heavy breastplate that shone brightly against his cousin's chest. It was the one worn by his father, Sawgrass, and now the symbol of a

War Chief who would deal only with outside threats. He knew that in normal times, High Limb would have been severely punished for all he had done. But these were not normal times. Every able man was needed.

"A truce between us?" Dancing Fish offered, feeling like their conflict had gone on long enough. He was tired of it. He put out his hand.

High Limb studied the extended hand but didn't move. "How do I know you'll even be around? Not off traveling with strangers to who knows where?"

Dancing Fish glanced at Willow and shared a smile with her. "Oh, I'll be around. You needn't worry about that."

"And if I shake hands with you," High Limb said, "what will we forget? What can we leave behind in the past?"

"Everything," he said without hesitation. "Willow. Boo-shay. Owl."

"Tobacco?"

Dancing Fish had always known High Limb had stolen the tobacco balls but could never prove it. "That, too."

"But I'll never forget the deception of the smelly, hairy whites on the ship," High Limb said. "Against both of us," he added.

"Neither will I," Dancing Fish said.

High Limb brought his brows together. "You know that I can never truly be your friend," he said.

Dancing Fish sighed and looked up into the War Chief's eyes. "We don't need to be friends. But we do need to be allies. My dreams and visions tell me that more danger awaits us."

"Ah, your famous dreams and visions," High Limb said, releasing the first hint of a smile. "Well, I'm not unfamiliar with danger."

Dancing Fish realized this was probably the best he would get from the man he had loathed most of his life. He extended his hand farther, nodding to it.

This time High Limb shook it, and with a crushing grip. "Agreed. And we'll see what the future brings, won't we, Dream Maker?"

"We will," he said simply but thinking of the revelation of his own whiteness, and whatever that could mean for the days ahead.

They walked back to the celebration and joined in the feasting with Rock and their few remaining friends. Most had finished their food and were either smoking or drinking tea. Talk about the upcoming corn harvest and the move back to Achqueehgenom drifted through the air like welcomed warm breezes in the dead of winter.

Dancing Fish looked around. In this moment, life felt almost ordinary. As it always had been.

Then suddenly, there was a commotion, a tension rippling through the crowd.

Big Shadow, breathing hard, ran up to High Limb. "Another Salt Man is here!" he announced, eyes wide with urgency. He turned to point.

The people had parted to allow an open space to form between their small group and a single person at the far side of the clearing. It was a white stranger with a pale face full of brown hair and a startled look in his eyes. And holding a musket that pointed down.

The only sound was the roar of the central fire.

High Limb, his eyes sharpened to points, looked directly at Dancing Fish. "So, White Keeper . . . Ally . . . " He cocked his head and half-smiled, half-sneered. "What do you suggest now?"

Dancing Fish shifted his gaze to the white visitor and felt the old glass button pressing against his chest, searching for his heart.

Part Three

The Settlers

1625–26

Forty-five

MARIE BOUCHER—SHE REFUSED TO USE HER HUSBAND'S name—stopped weeding around the oat stalks that reached to her waist and stood, a hand to a very sore back. She adjusted her dirty coif, and summer sweat dripped off her nose in a stream.

"Where is that bastard?" she said aloud in her native French to the green stems bending and moving with the wind on all sides. The oats that filled one of their garden plots would soon need cutting and then threshing, hulling, winnowing, and all the rest. It was hard work by hand. And now with a baby coming. Where was that lazy wastrel of a man? What was he thinking, leaving her here to do all this in her condition?

He wasn't thinking. Certainly not of her. Only of himself and his schemes. Always trying to get something over on the other person. The easy path of the gambler. The cheat. That was Jacob de Witt.

But at least he had done one thing right: marry her so they could make the crossing and leave Amsterdam behind. This New Netherland was strange and wild, but it was a fresh start. Something she—and the others—needed. Her father had been right in his letters: this was a land of opportunity. It wouldn't be easy. Of that she was already convinced. But the chance for a new beginning—and a place for a baby's future—was all around.

Leaning against the hoe, Marie suddenly heard her belly gurgle, and then all her insides shifted. There was an immediate lightening; a weight lifted, a space made. And she could breathe again. No more of the tight chest and short breaths. It was the baby dropping, just like Mother had told her.

More water leaked, running down her legs to muddy the red dirt. She reached and brought a wet hand to her nose. Odorless. With that and the bloody show that had popped out like a cork yesterday, the time was short now. The baby, already a strong kicker, would arrive soon with the full labor.

A spike of fear shot through her as she looked around at their small clearing and the surrounding forest. She was utterly alone. The only sounds were the rustling of the grain heads and the constant drone from unseen insects. If the baby came now, what would she do so far from the other settlers? In this condition, she was at least a half-day's walk from the island's tip, if not more.

One thing she needed was to relieve herself. The urge was immediate and strong. But not here. Not near the important oat crop the animals and the Company needed.

Marie hiked up her thick duffel skirt and petticoat, grabbed the hoe, and started a determined walk toward the rude hut they called home. Bastard husband or no, she would have to make do.

▶◀

Dancing Fish watched Meekak and Sunshell romp through the strawberries, alternating between picking and kicking them. Giggling and laughing all the while, they certainly ate more than they put in their tiny shoulder bags. His two girls were so full of life, he would sometimes just stand and watch them play and tease each other.

They threw strawberries at each other, then grabbed and pulled on their long braids and deerskin skirts. The skirts went up only to their waists, and nothing but a light coating of protective grease covered their bare chests and backs, which he knew irritated the white Europeans, especially the women.

"Father, there are more over here!" Meekak shouted as she and her younger sister skipped their way up the hill to a spot full of the low-lying fruit.

They were on a sloped field just north of Werpoes, their summer village. This was the gathering territory of Willow's family lineage, and although the strawberry peak had already passed, there was still plenty to be harvested for drying and storing.

He glanced at the sun, which had started its downward journey. It was the month of July, but he wasn't sure which week. He was using more of their words for time, and he sometimes mixed them with the People's system of moons, seasons, and special days.

They were now beyond the Turning of the Days—*Solstice*, they called it—and the heat and heaviness in the air had started. A time to be careful with hard effort.

"Come little squirrels," he said, using his favorite nickname for them after he caught up and sat down on a broad, smooth rock. "Bring your berries, and we'll look at the clouds."

The two girls, ages 12 and 10, their faces smeared with strawberry juice, lay down on each side of him, arms and skinny legs straight, eyes up to a perfect blue sky spotted with bulky clouds that hinted of coming rain.

"You see that cloud there?" he said, pointing. "What does it look like?"

"A bear!" shouted Sunshell.

"And have you seen a bear?"

"In the dances. I've seen them."

"But those aren't real bears. The real bears are in the woods."

"Where?" she asked, immediately sitting up and looking around, worried.

"Over there," he said, pointing to a dense stand of oaks and poplars. "But don't worry. The bear won't come here when he sees me. He knows I'm strong."

He laughed and pulled his younger daughter back down. "Keep looking."

"I see a beaver!" Meekak said finally.

The cloud did look like a beaver.

Meekak said in her small voice, "Father, why are there not many beavers? I remember more when I was like Sunshell."

He hesitated. This was an important question from such a young girl. With a difficult and far-reaching answer.

"The beavers around here, around the island, have been hunted too much."

"But why do we hunt them too much? Can't we leave some?"

"Well, you know the beaver robes and vests we have—that help keep us warm in winter?"

"But we already have our robes and vests. Why do we need more?"

He sighed. A child had hit on the key question. One of many such questions involving the visitors that everyone—even the wisest—was struggling with.

"It's partly our fault, but it's also because there are now more and more of these people."

He sat up and the girls mimicked him. He looked into both of their sticky, questioning faces and explained, "The Salt People—the white strangers—also like the fur of the beavers. Just like us." He saw confusion in Meekak's eyes.

"But what happens when all the beavers are gone?" she asked, working things out in her head. "What if there are no more beavers?"

Again, she hit the target. "Then, I'm not sure." It was time to change the subject.

He pointed to the next field on the other side of the dry creek. "I see many more strawberries over there. Should we go get them?"

Meekak lit up. "Is that our gathering land? Can we go?" Little Sunshell added, "Are those our strawberries, too? Forever and ever?"

He smiled and looked at both of them in turn. "They're not *our* strawberries. They're from the Creator, Kishelemukong. For all of us to share." He pointed again. "Of course we can go there. That's the hunting and gathering land of Uncle Rock's family. He can come here, and we can go there."

Dancing Fish stood and they followed him up. "See how many you can pick over on that spot. Go!"

At once, the girls started running toward the field, laughing and pushing each other, their moccasined feet flying over the land.

As he watched them and started a slow walk to Rock's field, his mind was full of troubling thoughts. Most involved the new batch of visitors—they called themselves *settlers*—who had recently arrived on the ship. There were so many. At least five hands, maybe more.

Most were concentrated at Kapsee Point, the island's southern tip, but a few had started to move inland, claiming vacant farms and garden plots. Land that was deserted because of the terrible fevers. Fevers that always struck the People more harshly than the visitors.

There had been few problems over the last years between the People and the white visitors, who would normally come and go. After the disaster with Master Block and Supercargo Deen, they had learned how to manage the trading and the negotiations for good exchange. But these new people were different. They were more than traders. And it was only a question of time before something unexpected happened again.

Dancing Fish slowly shook his head while he crossed the streambed and looked up to an endless number of red dots and to his two little squirrels dancing on top of them.

Only a question of time.

High Limb pulled the bowstring taut, the arrow aiming true to the big buck that grazed on summer grass nine body lengths away. Hidden in the shadows of the trees that lined the meadow, he had already given his words of thanks to the Game Keepers. It was now time for the sacrifice.

Suddenly, the sound of voices came to his ears. The buck jerked up his head, gave a loud snort, and vaulted before High Limb could release the arrow. In an instant, tasty food for several stomachs and a good hide for coverings was crashing through the trees and out of sight.

"By all the Spirits!" he shouted, throwing down his bow and looking in the direction of the sounds. "Who is this?"

He didn't bother to walk silently through the trees but stamped toward the voices, adding his own grunts of annoyance.

He came to the edge of the clearing he knew well. It was the intersection of two main trails south of Werpoes, and its guardian was the giant white oak they affectionately called Old Bark. It was said to be as old as five Elder lives strung end to end. Its canopy was massive, with lower branches reaching far out, parallel to the ground. And under those branches sat the white man named *Jay-kub* and two of his own warriors, all laughing and shouting.

He walked purposely toward them until the thin, white man finally looked up.

"Ah, another player," Jay-kub said in the Dutch tongue, flashing a wide smile that was smothered in a dense, brown beard.

The two warriors instantly jumped to their feet and turned to face their leader. "War Chief," sputtered Big Shadow, his trusted assistant. With his head down he took a step forward in greeting.

"Stop there!" he commanded, raising a straight right arm

with his finger pointed.

Big Shadow, thin and muscular, stared at High Limb and was quickly joined by the other warrior—one of the younger ones, Green Leaf—who was now shaking in place.

"You're so busy you didn't even hear or see me?" He was disgusted. "What if I were a Canarsee raider? What has you so entranced?"

Neither warrior said a word, and High Limb looked down at the spot in front of Jay-kub, who remained seated, disrespectfully. It was the game of knucklebones.

"It's only a game," Jay-kub said, still smiling. "We call it *Hazard*. Want to play?"

He frowned and shook his head no. Jay-kub, who was the husband of the pregnant settler woman, had another part to his name, but it was too hard to say, so they simply called him Jay-kub in their Munsee tongue.

High Limb walked over and spotted some items in a pile next to the white man. In addition to several empty bottles of the burning drink, there were small strings of wampum, a feather, and two moccasins. Moccasins?

He turned and studied the younger warrior and noticed he was standing with bare feet. He couldn't believe it. "You're gambling with your own moccasins? Have your senses left you?"

The young warrior was clearly shamed, his head down almost to his chest. He suddenly ran back and started to grab his moccasins.

"Hold on there!" Jay-kub challenged, tugging at the moccasins at the same time Green Leaf was pulling.

High Limb stepped forward and rapped Jay-kub's arm with his bow, causing him to release the moccasins and grab his arm in pain.

"What are you doing?" the visitor yelped. "I won these fairly. I—"

High Limb squatted down directly in front of Jay-kub and

looked deeply into his gray eyes. He could smell the drink on his breath. "You play games with *your* people," he said, holding in his anger. "Not mine."

He scooped up the two knucklebones, tightened his fist around them, and held the fist up to Jay-kub's hairy face. "You understand?"

Jay-kub was still, then silently nodded his head.

"Good." High Limb stood back up and looked down at the white man. "Go home to wife with baby." Then he threw the knucklebones and empty bottles into the trees.

Forty-six

Marie sat next to the hut's opening and read the letter again. Maybe for the hundredth time. It talked about the island, the animals, the rivers, and, of course, the Indians her father had clearly taken a liking to. Especially one that he mentioned over and over: Dancing Fish.

She rubbed the gray-blue paper between her fingers and softly stroked her thumb over his neat writing. *Where are you, Father?*

She so wanted to find where he was buried. *If* he was buried. The only thing she knew was that he had died on this island, and no body was brought back on the ship. The statements given by Maarten Deen and Captain Block had lacked detail. Something was missing. Exactly what, she was determined to find out.

A loud snore from Jacob broke her attention, and she turned from the small opening to peer into the gloom where he slept. They had thought of expanding or demolishing the native wigwam and building a proper house with walls and a floor of some type, but they had had no time for such improvements since arriving in March. It was hard enough to do the spring planting and clear away the debris and tall weeds from what was obviously an abandoned farm, even such a small one.

She had no idea why the previous inhabitants had gone. Only that Director Verhulst had told them to move in and start farming as best they could. And he had given them some basic tools, seeds, and four hogs to do it.

It seemed they were one of the lucky ones. Others were stuck in more crowded conditions at the island's point.

She studied Jacob, lying on his back. His mouth was open, and she could still smell the alcohol that lingered around him and permeated the hut. As usual, he had stayed up late drinking his oat spirits. He had it stored in green bottles and tin-glazed pots and jars around the inside of the hut. Different jars had the seeds in different stages of sprouting, fermenting, and eventually, drinking.

She didn't mind the occasional sip herself, but he had taken too many of their precious oat seeds and used them for making his drink, and not for planting. She hoped to God they would have more seeds from the harvest in August to replenish these lost ones. They were running out of the food the Company had supplied and were counting on an oat crop for eating or bartering for something else to put in their stomachs. Including the new stomach coming.

She pushed on Jacob's foot, but he just mumbled and turned away, still sound asleep. Just then, she felt a series of kicks in her belly. Not the typical baby kicks she was now used to as a welcome sign of life, but something more demanding. Like the baby was struggling inside her. Was this normal?

"Jacob!" she cried out in Dutch. "Wake up!"

He grunted.

Another series of strong, urgent kicks.

She pulled hard on his foot with all her strength, at the same time knocking over two of his oat pots.

"What—" he grumbled while he turned to face her. "What is it? Why do you wake me?"

"There's something wrong." The kicks came again, but with more force. "The kicking. It's not—"

"Kicking is normal," he said, yawning and rising up on his

elbows. He spotted the overturned pots. "My oats! What did you do?"

"Forget your cursed pots!" A pain in her belly added to the thumping. "This kicking is *not* normal, I tell you!" She was breathing hard now, trying to control her fear. "Not normal."

"So what do we do?" he asked, probably more concerned about his sprout jars than her.

"Run for help!"

She gulped and belched while more strong kicks came in rapid succession, like someone punching her from the inside. "Go get help!" she screamed. *"Now!"*

He fumbled with his clothes. "But where? What help?"

"To the closest natives, you fool. To the village by the big pond. To Dancing Fish. Hurry!"

▶◀

Dancing Fish walked with Willow along the rows of corn, inspecting them. A solid layer of gray clouds hung low from the sky, softening the light from Father Sun.

He pulled off a big, green worm from a cornstalk and spoke to it while it twisted in his hand. "I know you've been created for a purpose. But our survival depends on your life ending." He dropped the wiggling worm to the ground and stepped on it, pressing and moving his foot left and right. "It never ends with these worms, does it?" he said.

"And why should it?" Willow responded. She smiled one of her captivating smiles at the same time she slapped away a bee. "Every creature has its place. And what would we do with our time if there were no corn worms?"

She laughed. The same laugh he had fallen in love with so many years before.

The Werpoes corn was now up to their chests. The flower tassels reached skyward, and he could see the small ears starting to grow. It looked like they would have a good crop, and he was thankful to the Plant Spirits. And the squash and beans that twisted and mingled with the corn looked healthy, too. The family would not go hungry this fall and winter.

"Where are the girls?" he asked.

"Helping my sister and aunt clean fish at the creek. They'll be here soon."

"I hope they wash their hands first," he said, spotting another worm.

They—" She looked toward the longhouses. "Ah, here they come."

The two girls were skipping together, arms entwined. They wore matching skirts fringed with wampum. Each had a long braid flecked with the same white flowers.

He envied their carefree lives. They were ignorant of the dangerous forces he knew swirled around them. Wolves. Enemy raiders. And now, the new settlers. There was much to teach them.

"We cleaned this many fish!" Sunshell said proudly, holding up all 10 of her little fingers.

"Let me smell," Dancing Fish said, putting his nose against her hands and sniffing loudly. He jumped back with surprise. "It's the perch! You've killed my Manitto!" He exaggerated his shock by staggering backward and opening his eyes as wide as he could. "You've hurt my Guardian Spirit."

"No we didn't!" Sunshell and Meekak both said earnestly, shaking their heads at the same time. "No perch. We don't hurt the perch—you told us."

Their eyes suddenly widened and shifted at the same time to a point over his shoulder. "Who's that?"

Dancing Fish spun around and saw a white man half-running and half-stumbling toward them on the narrow path. He wore the distinctive *clothes*—another of the many new words he had learned—of the newcomers who lived away from the Point:

a shirt and leggings made from their thick, woolen duffel cloth, hard and stiff boots, and a broad hat that covered the top of his head and shaded his full brown beard. His small eyes flitted between them and took in their garden plot in sharp movements.

"Are you Dancing Fish?" the man asked in the Dutch tongue while he tried to catch his breath. He had a wild look about him, like something between a curious opossum and a frightened deer. Clearly, there was a problem.

"Yes. Is there trouble?"

"It's my wife. You know her."

Did he? These white strangers all looked the same to him, men or women. Then he remembered. "You are the one named Jay-kub and live in the place two fingers walk to the northeast from here, yes? Your woman, called Mar-ee, will have baby soon."

He nodded his bearded head, looking carefully at Willow, and then at the two girls who hid behind her. Dancing Fish had already heard stories and rumors about this man. Not much of it was good.

Willow stepped forward. "What is trouble with woman?"

Jay-kub seemed to relax at Willow's words. "Something's wrong with the baby coming. She needs help."

Willow instantly turned to him and the girls. "You three go find my sister. Tell Raspberry to come to the old place where the paths split. And to hurry." Then she looked into his eyes with a calm confidence. "I will go with this man now. You stay with Meekak and Sunshell."

"But—"

"I'll be fine. And there's nothing you can do. This is for women only."

She ran past the white man, grabbing his arm when she did. "We go!"

Concern rose as Dancing Fish watched the two running together down the path. But he also knew that Willow could take care of herself in any situation.

Meekak said, "Who is that man, Father? And why is Mother going with him?"

He studied the little faces full of curiosity. Then he spoke with a voice he kept intentionally emotionless. "He is one of the new strangers. One of the settlers. Someone we'll be seeing more of."

Dancing Fish took one last look at Willow and Jay-kub before they disappeared around a curve in the path. The image lingered in his mind: a stranger with—their word for them—a "savage." Running toward an uncertain future.

He turned to the girls. "Now let's go find Aunt Raspberry."

▶◀

They had her standing, leaning against a young tree, legs spread wide over a high pile of leaves and grasses.

"Are you sure this is the way?" Marie said in gasps between the convulsive pains of her labor. She had never heard of standing to give birth, but she was in no condition to argue. All she could do was clutch the tree with both hands and scream when the contractions came. And push.

Jacob had wanted to wait in the nearby hut, but he was sternly sent away by the two native women. No man could be close, they warned, or it would anger their "spirits" and bring bad luck.

She felt the first drops of rain on her arms when the contractions started again, stronger and longer. She gripped the tree even harder and closed her eyes, howling in pain.

"Push more now!" Willow urged from below. Willow's sister stood next to her, holding her, encouraging her.

"Push, push," the sister said in her ear. "Time soon."

"It hurts! I can't. Make it stop!"

A thankful pause, and then it started again. She was crying

now, her legs quivering with fatigue. The pain was unbearable.

"I see it!" Willow shouted. "Baby comes!"

Another contraction and instructions for a final—"*Push!*"

There came an intense burning between her legs, one final contraction, and the strongest push she could manage, all the while screaming at the top of her lungs.

Then a sudden feeling of relief and the sound of the baby landing in the leaves.

"Well?" She asked, gasping for air, not ready to give up her grip around the tree.

Nothing.

"Well? How is it? How's my baby?"

She could wait no longer. She turned and collapsed next to the leaves, her eyes level with her purple baby. Something was wrong.

"*What's happened?*" she shrieked, moving to her knees.

Willow was busy with the cord, holding it in one hand and cutting it with a stone edge. Raspberry was slapping the baby's back and squeezing its tiny hands.

Marie reached for the baby to feel it. The skin was like jelly and started to slip where she touched it. Exhausted and terrified, she looked into Willow's eyes. "*Please!* Please do something."

Willow and Raspberry kept working on the baby, slapping, squeezing, and breathing into its little mouth.

Nothing was working and Marie started to sob. Deeply and violently. A wave of heartache and anguish pulsed through her.

Willow finally sat on the ground, her face wet with sweat and from the rain that fell steadily now. "Rope come first," she said, her concern filling the space between them. "Then baby come. But rope around neck. Not living."

Marie, still on her knees, was swaying rhythmically, back and forth. Her eyes were closed, and she was trying to make sense of what had just happened. She felt dead inside.

She burst out sobbing again.

She grabbed the stillborn baby boy and pulled him tight to her chest, hoping to squeeze forth his first breath. A deep feeling of love battled that of despair—until despair finally won out.

Drained and bone-weary, she put her baby down on the leaves and tilted her head back as far as it would go. Then she let out a throbbing wail of anger and hopelessness that reached all the way to the heavy rain clouds above them.

Forty-seven

THE LOWERING SUN WAS A WHITE DISK SHINING THROUGH the last wisps of the storm. The rain had brought out the bass, and they all laughed at Rock's jokes while they walked back from the fishing trip.

"Why does the raccoon not eat the striped bass?"

Both girls giggled and asked at the same time, "Why, Uncle Rock?"

"Because he already has his stripes!"

The girls just looked at each other, and Dancing Fish punched his friend's shoulder playfully. "That's a terrible joke!"

Rock, the band's Master Fisherman, had taken them to one of his secret places on the eastern waterway good for catching the bass heading back to open water after spawning. They had carefully given their thanks and sprinkled tobacco on the water, and the Game Keepers had rewarded them well. Each carried a bag weighed down with fish.

Dancing Fish was looking forward to the smell of sizzling bass over the family's fire. He could already taste the flaky white flesh being pulled from the bones.

As soon as the path cleared the forest, he knew something was wrong. He spotted Willow running around the cornfield, frantically waving their long hoe and shouting at something he couldn't see.

They all started running and were soon at the field to

understand the problem. Four of animals of the settlers were destroying their crops!

These were the animals the visitors called *pigs*. They were like dogs but thicker and heavier with strange upturned noses and thin, curly tails. They were making loud grunting noises while they dug their snouts through the roots of their precious plants, eating whatever they came upon.

Whenever Willow started to hit one with her hoe, it would squeal and flee to a new spot in the corn rows. Then it would resume digging and eating.

They dropped their fish bags and were soon in a wild hunt across the field, chasing the stocky animals and using whatever they could to beat them away. Dancing Fish wielded the short pike he carried with him to pummel the beasts on the head and back.

The entire field was in ruins. Not only were the corn stalks tossed and toppled to the ground, but the beans and squashes were also ravaged. Plants were broken, crushed, or eaten. And no matter how hard they chased and struck the pigs, they came back again and again, looking for a new place to dig and destroy.

Everyone—including the girls—was running around and yelling at the pigs when one of them suddenly fell over, squealing and kicking for a moment before it lay still—a familiar arrow stuck deep into its neck.

Dancing Fish looked up to see High Limb bounding over the field toward them with his bow drawn. And as he ran, he aimed and struck two more of the animals. The final one saw what was happening and took off, weaving and snorting, trying to make its escape. High Limb stopped, calmly nocked another arrow, drew back, and let the arrow fly.

The shaft found its mark and dug deep into the pig's backside, bringing the horrible animal to a quick halt; collapsing it to the ground, shaking.

A towering High Limb casually walked up to the jerking

animal and drove his steel knife deep into its flesh, just where the heart was. It stopped moving.

"Ugly, awful animals," he said, wiping his bloody blade against the pig's skin. "They had already been at my field, and I followed them here."

"Thank the Spirits you did," Willow said, hands on her knees to catch her breath. "What do we do with them now?"

High Limb pushed the end of his bow against the dead pig. "We do what they do."

He looked at them, smiling. "We eat them."

▶◀

Gatherings at the Council House were smaller now. The shrinking of the band meant fewer families and fewer leaders. Many had succumbed to the fevers of the past years, but others had simply moved away, leaving their houses and fields empty. Dancing Fish guessed that the total number of Manahates was no more than 65 now—half as many as in the time of Hudson's arrival.

A fire blazed in the center of the room, and sparks floated up to the open smoke hole that was black with night. Three young girls, the same ages as Meekak and Sunshell, were busy handing bowls of stew to everyone in the circle or attending to the fire.

Thundercloud sat on the Sachem's fur-covered stump and holding the ceremonial staff topped with eagle feathers. Their leader was getting old, but he still had authority in his wrinkled face. He pointed to High Limb while lowering his bowl. "I hear we have you to thank for this meal."

The stew smelled wonderful and tasted even better. Dancing Fish had heard about this food named *pork* from different Europeans over the years, but this was his first taste of it. The texture was more like fish than the other land animals, but it had a flavor of its own.

"Yes," High Limb said. He chewed while he turned his head to catch the eye of each person seated around the fire. "When an animal shows no respect and destroys our fields—especially our sacred Three Sisters crops—they deserve no respect from us. Then they are killed. And eaten as their payment."

Dancing Fish signaled to speak. "We thank High Limb for his swift action." He nodded to him and received a quick head dip in return. "We've lost most of our summer's crop. We'll need to rely on others in the family and clan for corn and beans. And I will offer more deer and fish, or tobacco, in return."

There were nods of agreement all around. His tobacco blend was the most prized, and his trade in it with other villages was still strong.

The Holy Seer, pulling on a carved hickory cane, slowly stood for attention. Amazingly, this old man was still living on Mother Earth after so many seasons. He was the one who had presided over the marriage of Dancing Fish to Willow, and who now guided Dancing Fish as Kit Seer—the assistant—using his dreams and visions to help tell the future.

"Killing the animals of the Salt People requires a payment from us in return," the old Seer said. "We must restore balance with the Animal Spirits." He looked sternly at High Limb. "Eating them is not payment."

Thundercloud asked, "What sort of payment? Food? Wampum?"

High Limb jumped to his feet. "I'll tell you what kind of payment." He pulled out his knife and hurled it toward the fire where it stuck hard into a waiting log. "I would like to smash these visitors now before it's too late. They destroy our crops, confuse our warriors, and kill our fur animals."

He walked to his knife and pulled it from the log. "I say we pay them back by defeating them and driving them away." He glanced at the Holy Seer. "Then balance will be restored."

"Let's not get worked up," Thundercloud said firmly, glaring at High Limb and then turning to Dancing Fish. "Dream Maker, you are the White Keeper, the White Seer. What do your dreams tell you?"

Dancing Fish moved his eyes from Thundercloud to High Limb and took his time before he spoke. "I appreciate our War Chief's concern. His responsibility is to keep us safe from outside threats."

High Limb nodded his approval.

He continued. "But let's be clear about two things." He lifted the long finger of his right hand. "We take as many of the fur animals as they do, maybe more. And certainly more than is needed." He heard murmurs both agreeing with him and not. "We want their gifts and tools too much. So we kill animals for them." He looked around the fire. "We are all guilty of this."

Dancing Fish knew there were few beavers to hunt now on the island. That the taking of the animals for trade in their skins and furs—many times without the proper rituals—had been a mistake. There was now a scarcity of female beavers to mate in the coming winter and then give birth to the next litter.

There had been a frenzied response to the prospect of the Whites tools, with everyone flooding into the forest, finding any animal with fur and killing it without further thought or respect for the Animal Spirits. Their connection to the animals and with the Game Keepers was breaking apart.

Dancing Fish put down his food bowl and added a second finger. "The visitors are now many. Almost one-half of us. And they keep coming. You saw how many came on that one ship in spring. And that will not be the last ship. They have the tools and weapons to defend themselves—their muskets, their swords, their long pikes."

He looked directly at High Limb. "You and I have both seen what these weapons can do."

"But they are not smart," High Limb countered. "They

don't understand the forest, the soil, the water, or the air. They are like children. And children need to be punished from time to time."

"But these are dangerous children," Dancing Fish said. "Their ways are unlike ours, and they have much power. We've all seen it. If anything, they will try to punish us for these pigs we eat."

"Let them try!" High Limb boomed to muttering around the fire.

Thundercloud struck the Sachem's staff on the ground. "So, what do you suggest, Dancing Fish?"

"I think we should study them even more carefully now. Get close to them and watch. Something has changed with the arrival of these new ones. They're not like the traders we've known before. They hunger for something different."

Rock spoke up, "Especially this new Sachem of theirs. From my fishing near Kapsee, I've watched him."

"Yes, he's a nasty one," Thundercloud said. "And he'll want something of high value in exchange for the pigs and for any other injuries we cause them in the future." He looked around the fire at the leaders. "Here's what I say: we'll follow the advice of Dancing Fish and watch them closely. All of us. Then we'll decide."

Thundercloud took in the reactions from the leaders and thumped his staff on the ground. "So be it. Now, let's finish this pig."

▶◀

Willow was waiting when Dancing Fish emerged from the Council House. A bright moon and glittering stars looked down on them from the Sky World.

"That was a long council," she said, grabbing his hand to walk the short distance through the village to their longhouse.

"Long and troubling."

"You talked about the pigs?"

"The pigs and what will happen when the visitors find out."

"Are you sure they are from the woman Mar-ee and her man Jay-kub?"

"I'm certain of it," he said. "I've seen four of those pig animals in an enclosure there. It must be the same four."

"And they will know we've killed them?"

"They won't know for sure once we bury the bones, but they will guess. Especially the man. He acts like a fool, but he's smarter than everyone thinks."

He handed her a small gourd holding some of the pork flesh. "Try it."

"Mmmm," she said after tasting the meat. "This is good."

They walked by the central fire that was now down to its glowing embers. A small boy stirred them, making them spit and smoke.

"*Hè-yó*, young fire tender," Dancing Fish called out to him.

"*Yó-hè-yó*, Leader," the boy responded, bowing his head slightly.

Willow squeezed his hand when they were past the fire. "You like being called 'Leader,' don't you?"

"It's better than being laughed at, like I once was." He chuckled at the memories of so many discounting him and his ideas as a boy and a young man.

"No one is laughing now, are they?"

"No," he said. "It's the opposite, it seems. We're facing serious threats, and there is much confusion and concern. The Fire Prophecy always hovers above us."

"Like the moon?"

He looked up to it. "But the moon is neither good or bad. It just follows its path in the sky. Our future with the white visitors is not so simple."

She stopped and turned to him with a serious expression.

"What does your white blood tell you about our future?"

He thought about his mixed heritage and what it could mean. "My white blood tells me the same thing your blood tells you. That our children—and their children—will someday have less and less of my grandfather's blood flowing through them. And no matter the color of the blood, the future will eventually come to all."

"But what did the first prophet say?"

He repeated it from memory. *"You will know the future of our people by the Visitors from the East."*

"And your button? What does it tell you?"

He stopped, pulled it out of his apron, and held it up to the moon's light. Its round surface was smooth from years of touching and handling. And the four holes in the center were almost filled. Filled with dreams and visions, come and gone. And of events. Of the coming of the visitors and the many losses since then. Loss of lives. Loss of animals. And mostly, he now thought, a loss of peace and harmony.

He sighed. "Life was simpler before I was given this button by them, don't you think?"

"It's what *you* think that's important," she said. "You're the Dream Maker and the White Keeper. You have the Spirit Power. You're the one who knows."

I am the one who knows, he repeated in his mind as they started to walk again. If only that were true.

Forty-eight

MARIE WAS SURE SHE COULD STILL FEEL THE KICKING IN HER belly. She knew it wasn't possible, but what a cruel reminder of her recent loss.

The stillbirth was taking its toll. She stayed in the small hut, weeping, with no energy for the simplest tasks. Which meant they weren't getting done. Weeding the oats, fetching water from the creek, cooking the porridge they ate most days—nothing was happening.

Jacob put up a show of being helpful, but he took every opportunity to be busy either with his oat spirits or with the native visitors who were constantly dropping by their little clearing to smoke, gamble, or drink the liquor. By the end of each visit, Jacob would have more trade items than he started out with. And he was usually drunk, as well.

And now the four hogs had disappeared. What was next?

"Sounds like we have visitors," Jacob said, slurring his words. "Better put these away."

He was placing furs and duffel blankets over the oat pots when she heard the noises outside the hut. Then the distinctive, rasping voice of their director, Willem Verhulst. "Jacob and Marie! We've come to see how you're doing."

Soon, the head of the director poked in and looked around the interior. He was short, fat, and overdressed for this heat. An ill-fitting wig covered his head. "Well, there's certainly not enough room in here. Come outside and let's talk. It's a beauti-ful, if hot, day."

The bright light from a scorching sun momentarily blinded Marie, and she had to put her hands to her eyes. This was the first time she'd been out in days, and she had to steady herself against the hut.

The director's wife, Phaebae, came up to her and pulled her hands down. "Dear Marie," she said in her nasally voice that pretended to be of high rank. "We've all heard about your misfortune. And that you were attended by the savage women? How horrible for you."

Phaebae was a large woman, but her dress was even larger. It was a full-length tangle of silk and expensive lace, which was absurd in this heat and in such a desolate place. Her clothes and fancy hairdo were fit for a queen, but her manners were those of a milkmaid—which, in fact, was what she had been when first seduced by the director, as the story was told.

"The *savages* did not cause the problem," Marie said firmly, looking the obnoxious woman directly in the eye. "If anything, they helped me."

"Well, if you say so, my dear. But let's not dwell on that." She took a step back and swung her arm grandly to the side. "Look what we've brought you as a gift."

There stood one of the wagons from the ship with a horse tethered to it. It was a simple wagon, more of a cart really, with four short sides and a leather harness leading to the horse. And that horse, gray and so skinny its ribs clearly showed, was one of the oldest she had ever seen. She doubted it could pull much in the wagon and was surprised it had made its way from the island's point to their farm. A young boy had ridden atop the horse, with the director and Phaebae following in their private cabriolet pulled by a more handsome—and healthier—animal.

To say it was a gift was absurd. They had repeatedly asked for more proper tools to help with the farming, but they never had enough in bribes to entice the devious Verhulst.

Every one of the settlers had been told their purpose, and then promised the farming implements needed to start a colony on the island. But it seemed that only those with money or other favors received what was meant for all. In his own way, Verhulst was very much like Jacob: always looking out for himself. Or for his ludicrous wife.

"Thank you" was all she could manage. There was no point in arguing about this.

Verhulst spoke to Jacob. "We will have a meeting with the savages soon. As you know, I have instructions from the Company to purchase their land and gain their alliance."

"And what about my hogs?" Jacob asked. He was having trouble standing up, so he went to lean on the wagon. "Those savages stole my pigs, and I demand compensation."

"Do you have proof of this?"

"No." He burped. "But I'm sure of it. And that ugly, tall one—"

"High Limb?"

"Yes, I think that's his name. I would put nothing past that one to do us damage. I'm sure he's involved."

Verhulst gave Jacob a dubious look. "In any case," the director said, "Seeing that you're on my Council of Five, you'll need to be present for the meeting. I'll send a runner when the day and time are set."

Marie jumped into the conversation. "And what about me? I also want to be in that meeting."

Phaebae chuckled and Verhulst's eyes widened. "You? You're a woman, and there are only men on the council." He looked at Jacob. "Jacob represents you."

At that moment, Jacob sank to the ground and vomited on one of the cart's wheels. The old horse turned back his head and neighed.

Marie was having none of this. With a sudden burst of

strength and courage that came from some unknown place inside her, she walked right past Phaebae to Verhulst, looking straight into his close-set, blinking eyes.

She sank her finger into his flabby chest. "Director Verhulst, my father, Claude Boucher, one of the first Christians on this land, died here." She pointed south. "Right at the end of the island. He is one of the reasons we're all here. You know very well it was his letters that helped cause the Company to send us."

She stepped away from them and balled her fists. "I am coming to this meeting!" She hoped the tone of her voice left no room for debate.

Verhulst shared a glance with Phaebae and then stared at Jacob, who was now sprawled on the ground in his own vomit next to the wagon.

"Very well," Verhulst said with resignation. "In memory of your father, you may also attend. But only as an observer."

They turned to leave, and Marie felt her energy returning. She had her strength back.

▶◀

High Limb and Big Shadow sat at the base of a tall oak and watched. They didn't bother to hide. The Whites were so unaware, they both could have waved their arms, and few would have noticed.

The small collection of old wigwams and makeshift huts spread out before them along the southeast edge of the Point at Kapsee. The sun, sinking behind their bare backs, cast a warm glow on the houses and on the ripples of the eastern waterway and the bluffs just beyond. Seagulls squawked, and the summer air was like sap—thick and sticky.

Right in front of them, a section of trees had been cut and small stakes driven into the ground in the pattern of a square.

"What do you think that shape is for?" Big Shadow asked,

swatting at the mosquitoes now assembling for their daily ritual. The layer of grease that covered them would keep most away, but there were always missed spots or adventurous mosquitoes looking for a meal.

"I have no idea, but those sacred trees are now gone. So it must be important."

Just then, sounds arrived from the left, and a strange sight came into view from the main trail. One of their enormous beasts—they were like giant dogs—came running and pulling a large wheeled travois. And inside were two of the visitors. When they rolled past them, High Limb saw a young boy sitting on the back of the animal, his short legs kicking at its sides.

At their first sight of the beasts, the People thought they were huge, uncontrollable monsters, but they quickly realized that a person could ride atop one and direct it. It was something out of dreams they were only now getting used to.

The wheeled travois entered the area of the huts and finally stopped between the largest one and an enclosure where more of the giant dogs stood. The two visitors—High Limb could now see that it was their leader and his fat wife—climbed down and entered the hut that was once used by the hermit Owl. The boy helped a man untie the beast and lead it into the enclosure, which, he saw, was some sort of weir or pen for keeping the animals from running away.

High Limb was fascinated. "Let's go see what we can learn."

"Are you sure?" Big Shadow asked, not moving. "We're supposed to just watch. What if—"

He gave his assistant a hard stare. "I am War Chief of the Manahate Band. I don't sit and watch. I take action. Come with me."

They both stood and swung their shoulder bags to their backs. They started walking and High Limb whispered to Big Shadow, "Make no aggressive movements. Keep your bow unnocked and your knife sheathed, but be ready. These people can be so unpredictable."

They slowly strolled past the strange shape on the ground and then came to the first huts. As they walked, High Limb's eyes took in every detail: the number of dwellings, the distance between them, which building materials were used, and how much cut wood was stacked.

When he spotted the same thing on three huts in a row, he stopped. Affixed near the opening of each house was a small object. It was the size of an outstretched hand, and it was in the shape of a clam, but with no center. It was like a ring with the bottom edge cut out.

"What do you think that is?" Big Shadow asked. His assistant was simple-minded, but even High Limb wasn't sure what this was.

"A charm to keep out Evil Spirits, no doubt," he said finally. "An important protector. They have different Great Spirits than we do."

They resumed their walking, moving closer to the man who had handled the beast.

Several of the visitors were standing by their huts, and they stopped what they were doing to look at them while they walked past. No one spoke or showed any sign of welcome, nor of hostility, either. High Limb nodded deeply to each of them—a gesture that was returned by most.

They neared the man, who was busy slapping at mosquitoes. He was fully dressed in heavy duffel coverings, and his bearded face was covered with sweat. A long sword hung at his side. The strong smell of excrement filled High Limb's nose, and he could see piles of it near the strange animals.

The man reached for the musket that rested against the pen holding the huge beasts. "What do you want?" he asked.

He held his musket in both hands, and High Limb could see he was young and obviously nervous about this encounter.

"We are friends," he responded in the Dutch tongue, hoping

to put the man at ease. He smiled and offered his hand, like he had seen them do many times. The man didn't know how to manage both hands and the musket, so he placed the musket back down against the pen surrounding the beasts.

If this is a guard, how stupid can he be? High Limb thought, inwardly clucking and shaking his head. "I am from Werpoes," he said in his warmest tone, gripping the man's jittering hand. No point alarming him with the fact that he was an important War Chief. Better to keep him dumb and happy. "We come to greet and welcome you. And make trade."

The mention of trade always calmed the waters with these visitors, and it seemed to be working here as well. "My friend"— he nudged Big Shadow—"likes the beasts." He nodded to the enclosure holding the animals. "You can show him?"

High Limb pushed Big Shadow toward the pen and scooped his arm in a sign to get the young man to join his assistant in evaluating the animals. He had already spotted the pile of protector charms stacked near one of the posts of the enclosure.

Watching Big Shadow and the man talking about the giant animals, he moved slowly toward the pile. When he saw no one looking, he bent down and grabbed three of the heavy objects and dropped them into his bag.

Forty-nine

IT WAS A DOUBLE INSULT TO THE SPIRITS. NOT ONLY HAD A stand of sacred trees been cut near the water at the Point for no apparent reason—leaving a big hole to the sky—but they were sitting almost on top of Boo-shay's grave! Dancing Fish would have to explain this to the Mar-ee woman when he could. She would certainly not have allowed this if she knew.

There were eight Manahate leaders in the group for the gathering, and they sat on one side of the split circle, with the visitors on the other. The sound of small waves mixed with the cries of the gulls that wheeled and hovered above them. The sun was rising to its peak, and the strength of the heat followed it. If only the south wind would blow harder.

Dancing Fish spotted Mar-ee seated in the line next to her man Jay-kub and nodded to her. She smiled back. She was short and thin, with the same pale blue eyes of her father. Her hair was curled like a pile of wood shavings and tucked under a white hood.

He had heard from Willow about what had happened with her baby and was sad for the woman. Oddly, she showed no sign of mourning on her skin or clothes, but these people had strange customs. He would try to get her attention later.

The pipe had been passed and the gifts already exchanged—grapes, pumpkins, and a large bag of last season's tobacco from their side; a steel knife and several mirrors from the Whites—and it was time to find out what the purpose of the meeting was.

Their leader—a man with a name sounding like *Furhoost*—stood up from the center of their half circle to address them. Dancing Fish, who sat between Thundercloud and High Limb, would give a live translation for those who didn't know the Dutch tongue.

The leader wore the heavy clothes of the visitors, which made no sense in this summer heat. Dancing Fish studied his own people and they were, without exception, almost naked. He had been around these Europeans for many years now, and it continued to surprise him how much they stuck to their odd manners, even when shown better ways of doing things.

"We welcome you to our village," Furhoost announced to them, turning and swinging his arm toward the odd collection of rundown wigwams and crude huts dug halfway into the ground.

High Limb leaned over to whisper, "They call this a village? It looks more like a bunch of abandoned nests for blind skunks."

"Shhh," whispered Thundercloud. "Let him speak."

Furhoost—the visitors also called him *Director*—stepped past the gifts and handed one of their papers to Thundercloud and went back to stand at his place.

The Sachem looked at the paper with a bewildered expression and handed it to Dancing Fish, who had learned their way of reading and writing from Mar-ee's father.

Before Dancing Fish could finish reading the paper, Furhoost held up another in his hand and started to speak in a loud, grating voice that sounded like two oyster shells scraping against each other. "With this contract, and in the name of the West India Company, and of the States-General of the United Provinces of the Netherlands, I make a claim of purchase of this island land you call Mannahatta."

"What does he say?" Thundercloud asked Dancing Fish, clearly confused.

He hurriedly finished reading the paper and turned to the Sachem. "I think he wants them all to live on this land."

"*All live on this land?* What does it mean?"

"I'm not sure. Let me ask."

Dancing Fish stood and faced the Director. "We do not understand. What do you want?"

Furhoost took a step forward and held the paper high in his right hand and made a large circle with it. "I offer to buy the land we stand on—in fact, the whole of this island—to make our headquarters." He grinned in an odd way. "And for a very fair price."

Dancing Fish, who had learned how to negotiate from Boo-shay and was well practiced in it from years of tobacco trading, turned and crouched to face Thundercloud. "May I continue speaking directly with this man? I'll get more quickly to the full meaning."

Thundercloud nodded. "Of course. You're more skilled in these matters." He turned to High Limb. "War Chief, do you agree?"

High Limb nodded. "My ally will not lose his temper as fast as I will, so yes."

Dancing Fish now took control of the conversation. He stood and faced Furhoost again. The two were less than two body lengths apart.

"I am named Dancing Fish, and our Sachem"—he indicated Thundercloud—"asks me to talk with you. I have many dealings with your people for years. It pleases you?"

The man shifted his ample weight from one foot to the other and cocked his head to the side. "We know who you are. Whether it is pleasing, we shall see. But yes, let us talk."

Dancing Fish glanced at the paper in his hand. "You want to make a *claim of purchase* of this land."

"That is correct."

"You mean a kind of trade."

"Exactly. I buy, you sell."

"*Sell?*"

Furhoost looked annoyed. "To give up. Trade."

Dancing Fish directed his gaze to the trees beyond the man and let an idea form. "But land—our Mother Earth—cannot be traded like a pumpkin or an ear of corn."

He walked over and picked up one of the yellow pumpkins that had been brought as a gift. He tossed it from one hand to the other. "This pumpkin can be grown from seed, tended, cut from the vine, and finally, eaten. Or, it can be traded." Dancing Fish suddenly lobbed the pumpkin to the man, who fumbled trying to catch it, letting it fall to the ground with a thud.

Embarrassment covered the man's face while chuckling erupted from both sides of the circle.

Dancing Fish looked up to the sky that was now a deep blue and streaked with high clouds. "Shall we trade the sky to you? Or the clouds?" He heard the deep laugh of High Limb behind him. Others from their side joined in the amusement.

Dancing Fish then pointed to the shimmering water that moved and swirled past the rocks on its way out with the ebb. "Can the water be purchased, possessed, or traded?"

The man's cheeks puffed in and out. "What does this—"

Dancing Fish stamped his foot on the ground. "And what of the land?" He bent down and grabbed a handful of dirt and sand, raised his hand high, and let the dust fall and catch the moving breeze. "This is our Mother Earth. She provides for everyone." He stared at the man. "Even for you."

More laughter came from behind him.

Furhoost's face had turned a deep red. He was angry now. "You are making a joke, but we are serious. We wish to acquire your land. And in a peaceful way."

"And that is the point," Dancing Fish said, looking hard at

291

the man. "It is not *our* land. It is land of the Creator, and we share in the bounty while we live on it. We take care of the land, and the land takes care of us."

He looked down the line of visitors trying to catch each of their eyes. "The land is here for all to share. It cannot be traded or possessed. The land simply *is*."

▶◀

Marie was enjoying Dancing Fish's cleverness in the meeting. He had a way of making his case with both intelligence and humor. He looked to be about thirty, with hair longer and not as black as the others—more ruddy in color—and eyes that seemed almost yellow. His odd appearance and dazzling smile gave off a hint of mischief as well as confidence.

Marie felt an odd connection to this native her father had respected. She wanted to talk to him more, especially about her father's fate on the island.

With both sides still facing each other at the island's tip, the sun was now directly overhead, and it was unbearably hot. Insects buzzed incessantly and sweat gleamed on Marie's arms. Her mouth was parched, and she would have given anything for a drink, but, of course, they had not thought of bringing any water with them. Dancing Fish's people, on the other hand, took frequent sips of something from their odd-shaped containers.

Pieter Minuit now stood to speak to the Indians. He was a thin, small man with speckled gray hair and a trimmed beard that came to a point. He had been on the ship with them, another Walloon like herself, but his role was still unclear to her. All she knew was that he worked directly for the Company, and he appeared to have the ear of the director, who still stood, agitated, like a pot of boiling water ready to spill over.

"We know that you have certain territories of land under your authority," Minuit said to Dancing Fish in a calm, controlled voice. "You—the Manahate—are here on this island, but over there," he pointed to the eastern river, "are the Maspeth. And the Canarsee. And others. You hunt, fish, and plant here, and they do the same there. Am I not correct?"

"What you say is true," Dancing Fish said, "Meneer . . ."

"Minuit. Pieter Minuit." He pronounced it in their French way: *Min-wee.*

"Minwee," Dancing Fish repeated carefully, drawing out the word. "It has a nice sound. Almost like the name for a savage." He smiled and raised an eyebrow.

Minuit smiled back and chuckled. The two seemed to be on equal footing.

Dancing Fish now addressed himself to Minuit and not Director Verhulst. "But the Canarsee do not *possess* their land, and we do not possess ours. We are both caretakers of the Earth. And we have agreed to watch over different parts of it." Dancing Fish fixed his eyes on Minuit. "Now, if you wish to go to another place . . ."

"We do not wish that," Minuit said firmly. "This is the place we want to be."

Verhulst grunted his confirmation.

"And why is that?" Dancing Fish asked with understandable curiosity.

Minuit looked over at Verhulst then turned back to Dancing Fish and continued. "As Director Verhulst has said, we need a place for our base of operations. To establish our colony."

Dancing Fish cocked his head with a puzzled look. "*Colony?*"

"A place for us to live, work, and trade," Minuit responded quickly and quietly.

Marie realized that this was not the full extent of what the West India Company meant by the word "colony." She had seen the official instructions to the director and had guessed at an even deeper meaning between the lines.

Verhulst, having had time to calm himself, now spoke to

Dancing Fish. "And as you can see, we have already begun to advance things here. You and your people hardly use this land." He waved his arms around. "You make no improvements. You build no permanent houses. You only come to the island in the warm months and then leave again. You make no profit from the land."

Dancing Fish looked hard at their director, who now had large sweat stains under his arms.

"Profit?" Dancing Fish said. "You mean, do we take benefit of the land?" He laughed in a way that showed disbelief. "Of course we do. We plant crops, and we take animals needed to feed and cover us. We scoop the water from the creeks to drink. All this we do."

Dancing Fish now turned to point to the outline of the fort the director and the engineer, Cryn Fredericks, had started staking. "And you call this improvement? Cutting down sacred trees that have been here for generations? And for what?" He looked at Verhulst. "Tell me, Director, what is improved? What is better than before?"

Marie felt movement next to her and Jacob suddenly jumped to his feet. "Enough of this circular talking!" he shouted. In horror, she watched him stride toward the tall native, High Limb, his arm pointing. "You stole our property—our pigs—and there must be compensation."

"Jacob!" she cried out, trying to stop him, but High Limb and several other natives had immediately leapt to their feet and were pulling out their knives and moving forward.

At the same time, three of their soldiers with muskets had stepped behind Jacob.

She saw Dancing Fish instantly move to a position between the two advancing groups. He turned and held up a hand to each side and yelled *Stop!* while he swiveled his head back and forth. "Do not be fools," he said in a firm voice.

No one moved.

Then she saw the native's leader, the Sachem, also on his feet, give Dancing Fish a hand signal.

Dancing Fish nodded and turned to face Verhulst. "We return to Werpoes to discuss what is said here." He held up the contract. "We study this more, then give our thoughts. Good?"

Verhulst looked at Minuit, who nodded.

"Stand down, men," the director ordered Jacob and the soldiers. He glared at Dancing Fish. "Do not take too long in discussion."

Then he raised his voice so everyone could hear and kicked the dirt at his feet. "And keep this in mind while you do: *This* is where we want to be."

Fifty

THEY WERE BACK IN THE VILLAGE AND SEATED AROUND THE central fire. Stars filled the sky, and so did the mosquitoes. Gourds of succotash and charred bodies of fish on sticks were passed and hungrily consumed.

The families of the leaders had joined the group. People praised the food and moved on to drinking tea and smoking their favorite tobacco mixtures. Smells of food, fire, and tobacco smoke carried through the open gathering space.

The thought suddenly hit Dancing Fish.

On the walk back from the Point, shards of a broken vision had crowded his head. Empty longhouses tangled with vines, cooking fires burning with no one watching, corn rotting in the fields.

"I know what they want," Dancing Fish said.

The talking stopped, and the area went quiet except for the crackling of the fire. Even the crickets and frogs took a pause. All eyes were on him.

"They want the land. They want the island. They want it all."

"What do you mean?" Thundercloud asked, putting down his pipe. "We all heard you explain to them how it's not our land to give. And it was well said."

Murmurs of agreement came from all sides of the fire.

"No. I saw hints of the future in my visions on the walk

296

back. And you have seen them, too."

"Explain," Thundercloud said.

He used an example everyone would understand. "You know how the honeysuckle vine chokes and strangles the poke-berry bush?"

All heads were nodding. Everyone knew this, but he continued as if they didn't. And because he had a specific point to make.

"The vine starts at the bottom and pushes its green shoots up, seeking the sun. Over several seasons, it intertwines with the bush. And both live together for a time, don't they?"

He scanned their faces to make sure they were paying attention.

"But in the end, the vine takes over the bush. It covers it so no sun can get through. And at last, the bush dies."

He let that sink in while he looked at the different families of the band. "And that is what these new visitors will do."

He stood to make his final point. "This island—he stamped his foot—is the bush, and they—the strangers, the Salt People, Europeans, visitors, settlers, whatever you want to name them—they are the choking vine."

The silence was absolute. No person spoke, no mosquito buzzed, no fire flame popped.

"He is right," came the voice of a woman speaking in their tongue.

Everyone turned to see the white woman, Mar-ee, standing beyond the fire's light under a tall hickory tree. Her eyes were wide with an emotion that was hard to decipher.

Surprised, Dancing Fish called to her, "Come join us." She had apparently learned enough words in Munsee to understand.

She slowly walked to the fire, and Thundercloud pulled a folded skin up next to him and gestured for her to sit.

Everyone silently stared at her until Willow finally broke the tension by walking over and offering her a water pouch.

Mar-ee took it and drank deeply. "Thank you."

Willow handed her a fish stick, and Dancing Fish said he would translate both sides of the conversation.

He asked her in the Dutch tongue, "Why do you come? And where is your Jay-kub?"

She swallowed a piece of fish and explained that after they had returned home from the gathering, Jay-kub had immediately started drinking his oat spirits. "He's drunk," she said, shaking her head. "I won't be missed."

Dancing Fish translated to sounds of snickering.

She looked at the people around the fire with a solemn face. "I am here to explain more to you." She fixed her eyes on the leaping fire. "And to warn you."

Dancing Fish asked the question on everyone's mind. "But why? You are one of them."

She turned her head to him. "Because my father, the man you simply call 'Boo-shay,' liked and respected you, Dancing Fish." She stared directly into his eyes. "And he loved this island."

She took another sip of water. "I want to tell you more about why we are here. I feel I owe it to you. And to my father." She looked down at the ground. "And I want to know what happened to him."

There was a momentary silence, then Thundercloud asked, "Why do they—you—want the land, as Dancing Fish says?"

She put the water pouch down and straightened her back. "For many reasons. Some are easily seen, but others may not be."

She told them about needing to clear the trees both for trade in logs for ship masts, and for making tar and pitch. But also to have more room for them to build houses and create more farms.

"And what of this strange shape we see on the ground at Kapsee Point?" High Limb asked.

"That is to be a fort."

"*Fort?*"

"Fortification. A large building with high walls. For people and soldiers to protect the area."

"Protect against what? Us? Our enemies?"

"That, but more. To keep the English and Spanish away."

High Limb smiled and nodded his head. "A defensive alliance against enemies."

"Yes," she said. "That is part of it."

Dancing Fish sensed that she was still holding something back. Suddenly, the Holy Seer—who rarely spoke—cleared his throat and added in his old man's voice, "But all the land at the end of the island is sacred to us. Our shared memories live there." His eyes were starting to tear. "It is sacred ground that breathes with Spirit."

"I'm sorry," she said, her eyes downcast, "but our people do not see the land as sacred. What we call sacred is different."

"Yes, your strange Gods," the Holy Seer said, frowning and shaking his head.

"They are not strange to us. It is our religion."

Dancing Fish realized this was the right time to tell her and sat back down.

"Mar-ee Boo-shay," he started. "There is more that is sacred at the Point where you want your fort." He looked directly into her blue eyes. "We also believe burial grounds are sacred. They hold the bones, ashes, and Soul Traces of the ancestors."

"You have burial sites at the southern end of the island?" she asked, her eyes widening.

"No. *You* do."

She blinked and her mouth opened silently.

"The area for your fort also holds the bones of your father." Mar-ee gasped. "What?"

"That is where your father is buried."

He watched the white face of Mar-ee become even whiter.

Her lips trembled as she tried to speak.

"Will you take me there?" she said in the faintest of voices.

"I will," he said firmly.

After a long silence, Thundercloud used his staff to pull himself up. The look on his face combined worry and turmoil. "So this is real plan of the visitors?" he asked her.

Mar-ee looked first to the Sachem and then around the fire until her gaze stopped at Dancing Fish. "Yes."

She took a deep breath through her nose. "Because we are not *visitors*. We are not leaving this island."

Fifty-one

Hunter's Moon

HIGH LIMB WAITED WITH BIG SHADOW BEHIND A LAUREL thicket. The smoke was so heavy it made Father Sun, climbing the sky, appear only as a faint glow. They each wore masks of fine doeskin cut with tiny knife slits to keep the stinging smoke out of their lungs.

The others had started the fire near the Great River earlier in the day. Using pouches of water and beating specially made sticks—and the west wind doing its job—they were driving the deer right toward them. The fire would consume the old brush and some of the youngest saplings, but the older trees would survive, and the land would be easier to travel through.

This was the northern edge of their territory above the island's hook, and the main group of hunters was stationed on both sides of the creek that emptied into the eastern waterway. The deer, fleeing the fire, would funnel through the narrow opening between the two hills and right into the arrows and spears of the waiting men.

High Limb always enjoyed this tradition that fell while the days cooled after the Balance of Days but before the Turning of the Leaves. It was a way for him to gauge the shooting and spearing skills of the younger warriors, and they would have enough meat and deerskin to help them pass through the winter.

Big Shadow asked, "You're not angry that Dancing Fish is not helping us with the hunt?"

"No. He has his tobacco harvest to prepare and, in truth, I tire of his predictions and always wanting to give his advice."

"And still nothing about the land agreement with the Whites?"

"No," High Limb said. "There is much arguing in the council about this. I say we can trade again and again for the same land, but Dancing Fish has convinced Thundercloud to wait and see. So we wait."

Big Shadow, his lopsided grin spreading across a face painted with red stripes, chuckled. "He's already acting like a Sachem, isn't he?"

"Well, he isn't one. And I'm not sure he's destined to be the Holy Seer, either. He doesn't seem to fit anywhere."

"Don't you want to be the Sachem?" his longtime assistant asked him.

"Oh no. War Chief is best for me. I have warriors on my side. And with warriors, I have the true power." He cast a sidelong glance at him. "And I can fight against the Whites."

"But he's the White Keeper."

"And let him be that. I'm not interested in helping the Whites." He smiled and raised his eyebrows. "I'm more interested in hurting them. Or taking what I can from them." He winked at his assistant who grinned back.

High Limb could hear the start of the rumbling. The deer were getting closer.

"What do we do if we take more deer than needed today?" asked Big Shadow in his slow-minded way while he peered through the smoke. "There are fewer of us now."

"I've been thinking about that," he said, nocking his bow and checking the quiver of arrows hanging from his neck. "We should visit the village of the Whites at Kapsee again. They always seem to be hungry, and we can trade deer meat for something useful."

High Limb laughed. "And maybe we can find something

more to steal. I enjoy taking from the Whites almost as much as I enjoy hunting!"

The rumbling suddenly became a thundering. Hooves beat the ground, bushes tore, and the loud snorts of the bucks filled the air.

"Get ready," he whispered to Big Shadow at the same time he signaled the others with his raised arm.

The first of the herd emerged through the trees in full stride. In the lead were the big bucks. He could see their large eyes blinking and darting from side to side. They were tightly packed and running with all their strength, bouncing on their thin legs with tails high in alarm.

"*Now!*" High Limb shouted, and he and Big Shadow jumped out from behind the thicket.

Two of the leading animals looked up, snorted, and swerved in an attempt to run past them. But they both released their arrows at the same time, and the bucks crashed to the ground within a body length of them. Before they fell, two more arrows were nocked and found their targets.

The small group of warriors now stood close together and unleashed arrow after arrow at the charging and surprised herd coming directly at them.

One after another of the frightened beasts fell on all sides. Some were already dead when they hit the ground, but others struggled to rise and continue their flight, stumbling and bellowing.

Carefully avoiding the thrashing hooves that could slice a man in half, the younger warriors now descended on the animals, spearing or cutting their throats and letting the blood flow freely over the marshy ground.

Finally, after the last of the deer had either escaped or were lying in the great pile around them, High Limb gathered his warriors, covered in blood and sweat, to speak.

"Friends and clan members of the Manahate band," he said,

looking into each of their painted faces. "You have been brave and strong today. What we do here is honorable, and it shows respect to the Game Keepers and to the other Spirits."

He raised his hand to stop their murmuring. "Let us each bow our heads and say our thanks to these animals who give themselves for our benefit."

He watched to make sure each warrior had his head bent, then he did the same, saying the sacred words:

> *Oh Great Creator.*
> *We thank you for this blessing.*
> *And we thank our animal brothers in their sacrifice.*
> *Life is a privilege, and you give yours for ours.*
> *Your Souls are leaving, but your bodies remain to*
> *become a part of us.*

When he was finished, he looked up and saw the first flames of the approaching fire in the distance. They had less than one finger of time.

"Let's hurry. Gut the deer now and load up the litters. We need to head back before we're cooked along with the meat!"

▶◀

Dancing Fish could smell the lingering smoke from the hunt while he walked along the narrow path, early sunlight slipping through the gaps in the forest canopy.

Days like this—with a clear sky and cool, dry air—always gave him extra energy, especially before the leaves burned with color. He felt so alert and alive around the time of both equinoxes.

He often caught himself thinking and using the words of the settlers. He wasn't sure if it was because of the diluted white blood flowing through his veins, or if the word *equinox* just sounded better to him. In any case, it was shorter than *Balance of Days*, so he liked to use it. At least to himself.

The path widened and opened to a clearing surrounded by tall oaks, hickories, and poplars. He noticed two garden plots. One held thin brown stems cut just below the knee. The other was empty except for weeds. In fact, the weeds dominated.

Walking past the gardens, he spotted the huge, gray beast named *horse* that was tied to a tree. Even though he was now used to seeing these giant animals, they still surprised him with their massive size and big heads.

He stood for a moment to study the horse and then the wheeled travois they called a *cart*, or sometimes *wagon*. It was like his original idea for making the travois more effective with two wheels, but he had never thought of giving it four wheels and using an animal to pull it. It was a striking solution, and he immediately saw its utility for carrying both supplies and people.

Not seeing anyone, he walked toward the old wigwam and spoke out in the Dutch tongue, "Hello!"

He heard movement, and Jay-kub emerged from the hut's small opening and stood. "What do you want?" he said in a challenging way. He was thin like a reed, and his clothes hung on him as if from another man.

"I want talk to you and Mar-ee. She is here?"

A head popped out of the opening, and as soon as she saw him, she offered a warm smile. "Hello, Dancing Fish. Is Willow with you?"

"No, she works with other women to dry crops and smoke meat. I come alone."

They were soon sitting on two facing logs between the wigwam and the gardens, and Dancing Fish opened the top of his shoulder bag. He pulled out two tobacco ropes—many now called them *cigarros*—and handed one each to Mar-ee and to Jay-kub.

"My own mixture. We smoke together?" he suggested.

"Here's a better idea," Jay-kub said, reaching into his shirt and pulling out a small green bottle of liquid. He took a deep sip and offered it to Dancing Fish.

He shook his head. "No. Not for me." He didn't like the bitter taste of the strong drink and what it did to him and his thoughts.

Jay-kub shrugged and took another sip.

Dancing Fish noticed that he didn't offer the bottle to Mar-ee, whose hair was even curlier without a hood covering it.

"How can we help you?" she asked, a kind and open expression on her face.

He was amazed she was offering to help him when he could think of many ways he could help her.

He turned and looked at the garden plots. "I see you have one plot for growing your . . ." He tried to remember the word. "Oats," he finally said. "But the other is empty."

Mar-ee turned down her mouth and shot a hard glance at Jay-kub. "We were supposed to plant our winter crop, but most of the seed is going to his drink."

Jay-kub paid no attention while he titled the bottle for another sip.

"I have idea for you," Dancing Fish said, lifting a cigarro to his nose and breathing in the distinctive smell. "This tobacco is good for trade. The Salt People—your people—always want more of it."

Mar-ee mimicked him and smelled the cigarro she held.

He explained, "I give you seeds for sowing or small plants for planting in your new year," he said. He looked around at the neglected state of their surroundings and at their skinny bodies and thin faces. "Then, I trade you for any food you like. Even trade in advance. On credit."

Mar-ee was about to speak, but Jay-kub cut her off. "If we're going to plant anything, it will be oats!" he said a little too loudly, at the same time swinging the bottle around his head. "The Company wants oats." He grinned and added, "I want oats." He took another drink and saw the bottle was now empty. Cursing, he threw it at the horse, which rose up and tried to run but only tangled itself around the tree.

Jay-kub laughed, his mouth half open and his eyes half-closed. "What was all the smoke we saw and smelled?" he asked Dancing Fish.

"From hunting fire. To drive deer. And also to burn brush and old bushes and leaves. For clearing."

"Hmmm . . ." Jay-kub started while his head slowly sank to his chest. Soon, he was snoring.

Dancing Fish looked at Mar-ee with concern. She had only recently lost a baby, and here she was struggling with a man who was clearly not a good partner. "I can help you," he said softly to her. "I want to help you."

Mar-ee looked down at her hands. "Can you show me where my father is buried?"

He saw small tears running down her cheeks. "Yes. And you tell me more about what you said in the council? About not leaving?"

Jay-kub suddenly jerked his head up and growled. "No more talk." He eyed Dancing Fish with wariness. "Did the savage bring any food to eat with him?"

Marie shoved a grumbling Jacob through the hut's opening and rolled him to the sleeping area.

"Why are you pushing me?" he slurred as he tried to sit up.

"You're an embarrassment, that's what you are," she said, propping him against one of the support poles, then sitting next to the small fire that was down to its embers and twirling a thin ribbon of smoke. "This man comes to offer help, and you insult and argue with him?"

"He's not a man," he said, shaking his head in his manner of regaining it. "He's a savage." He squinted at her. "And don't think I didn't notice how he looked at you."

"How? As someone who's married to a lazy drunk? With a husband who can't even stand long enough to weed the garden? Who wastes our seeds on gristing and fermenting spirits?"

She tried mightily to hold in her anger while she added two wood pieces to the fire in the middle of the hut. Each day was chillier now, and she worried about staying warm during the coming winter.

She watched as the flames caught and the smoke spiraled up to the smoke hole. "We need more wood to burn," she said, looking at him with contempt. "Can you at least do that? Or do you want us to freeze to death in our first winter here?"

"I can do that and much more, woman," he said in a defiant tone.

She stared at him, and he stared back. They both seemed to realize at the same time that there was no point in arguing further. They had been through this before. So many times.

"Maybe we should follow his advice and plant some tobacco," she suggested in the most neutral and calm voice she could gather. "Everyone praises it, and it's another thing we can trade."

"To have tobacco, we need to clear more land," he said with more conviction and a clearer voice.

"That or prepare the empty plot we have," she said, hoping to keep a constructive conversation going. "The Company wants us to trade in furs, timber, and grain, but I reckon that tobacco could be added to the list."

"That plot is for oats," he said firmly. "Once the director buys the land from the savages, we'll be free to do more clearing for whatever we like. Oats *and* tobacco."

"The natives don't seem interested in the idea of selling their land."

"Oh, they'll sell it, alright. Then we can plant whatever we want—even tulips!" he said, cackling.

She looked into the handsome face she wished had not attracted her in Amsterdam when she was pregnant with another man's child. "But we still have to make the effort. We're obligated for six years of service to them. Then we can be freeholders with our own land and work for ourselves."

She knew she shouldn't, but she couldn't help saying another mean thing to this careless man. "Not that I see any future in working with you."

"Nor I, you, woman," he said, his body stiffening and his eyes narrowing. "You've already lost one baby—at least it wasn't mine. I want children who'll have my name, and who I can put to labor."

A dreadful smile came across Jacob's face. "And I suggest we start with the next child now."

She groaned. "Now?"

"Now," he said firmly, crawling to her and lifting her dress.

Fifty-two

High Limb sat with Big Shadow on a log in front of the trademaster's hut. It was early, with the sun only starting to rise above the low hills across the waterway. So he wasn't surprised that no one other than the same guard he had met more than a moon ago—the Whites called their warriors *soldiers*—greeted them.

He didn't know the soldier's name, but this hut was next to the largest one in the little village, the one he had seen Furhoost enter before. The same one Owl had used for his home, although now expanded with more saplings and bark. The workmanship on the building was extremely crude, almost childlike.

The village—if he could even call it that—looked the same as before: a strange collection of huts and wigwams facing in different directions along the Point's rocky eastern bank. He could see one of the People's tall shell mounds beyond the last hut. And now that he thought about it, he couldn't remember ever seeing the visitors picking or even eating the vast quantities of oysters, mussels, crabs, and even lobsters that he knew were waiting for them beyond Kapsee's shoreline. Could they possibly be that ignorant?

While they waited, High Limb checked the meat. They had hung the gutted deer to bleed after they returned from the hunt, then quartered and cut them up the night before, placing the mesh-wrapped pieces off the ground on platforms for cooling and to the keep scavengers away. By this time in the season, the night air was cold enough and the danger of meat spoiling was low. Even with the skin on, the meat was good, and the Whites would be able to use their salt or cook it.

He saw the smoke rising from the top of the wigwam and heard talking inside. Finally, a man emerged from the hut.

"Are you here to trade?" the man asked in the Dutch tongue. He looked like all the other strangers with a face full of hair, blue eyes, and wearing their heavy coverings made of the duffel cloth.

High Limb stood and prompted Big Shadow to do the same. "Yes." His Dutch had improved greatly over the past years, and while he was no match for Dancing Fish in the use of different tongues, he could make himself understood. And could usually make sense of what the Whites were saying, even if only in main outline since they often spoke too fast for him to catch every word.

The two had brought the deer meat on a pole litter that now lay on the sandy ground. The man squatted next to it and unwrapped a thick rump piece. He poked his finger in as deep as he could, then pulled it out to smell before licking his finger.

"Good," he said simply, with no expression. He used his other fingers to count the number of pieces. "What do you want in trade?"

High Limb was about to answer when Furhoost suddenly appeared from his hut. He was rubbing his eyes and yawning.

The Director walked over to them and nodded to him, ignoring Big Shadow. He stepped in front of the trademaster, pushing him aside with his elbow. "You want to do some trading, do you?"

Why else would I be here? "What do you offer for this?" High Limb asked, waving his hand over the deer meat.

Furhoost scanned the meat pieces. "We have many fine kettles, knives, hatchets—"

High Limb suddenly spotted a group of men walking toward the trees. They were carrying different tools, and one immediately caught his eye. "What is it he has?" he said, pointing. "The man with yellow hair."

Furhoost turned to look and yelled out, "You men! Come back over here."

The men were young, and when they drew closer, High Limb could see that they held tools for cutting and clearing the land.

"That one," High Limb said, pointing to what the man in front carried. It had a long handle and two opposing metal blades at the fat end. One was in the shape of a hatchet, but much bigger. The other side was also flat but turned a quarter circle. It looked like the blade of a hoe.

"It's called a *mattock*," Furhoost explained. "Good for chopping and digging."

High Limb saw it first as a weapon. And a good one. He held out his hand to show he wanted to hold it.

"Oh no," Furhoost said, shaking his head. "We only have a few of these. They are very valuable. Too valuable to trade for meat." He stepped toward High Limb and looked up at him. "Unless . . ."

High Limb cocked his head. "Unless what?" He knew what was coming.

"Unless you can help me with getting that land contract signed." He attempted a smile that only emphasized his crooked teeth.

High Limb, feeling Big Shadow's eyes on him, decided to play the slow-witted one. "What contract?" he said, trying to act as his assistant might.

Furhoost narrowed his eyes and frowned. "You know very well what contract. The land purchase agreement. I've been waiting almost a month for a decision by your leaders. How long will it take? We're soon coming to winter, and I want the agreement signed and sealed."

High Limb waited to let the question linger before he answered, "I am leader also."

Furhoost leaned back in a way of digesting these words. "So you are."

High Limb sprang the trap. "You give me mattock, and I give you good decision on land contract."

Furhoost grabbed the mattock from the man's hands and balanced it on his shoulders. "Let me get this correct," he said, staring at High Limb with his small eyes. "If I give you this mattock, you will convince your leaders—including you—to sign the land purchase agreement. Is that right?"

"That is right," High Limb said with confidence after a suitable pause.

"You promise me this?"

He thought about the promises the Supercargo Deen had made—and broken—so many years ago and smiled inwardly. "I promise."

▶◀

Dancing Fish watched Willow pounding the round berries on the hard stone that was worn down into a shallow bowl. Both girls helped by separating the holly tree's red berries into two piles, one for drying and making the powder for purging, the other for eating whole to cure stomach pain. Another pile of the spiny leaves awaited bagging and hanging for future use in preparing tea.

"Here," she said, handing him a bundle of branches. "Be useful and pull off the leaves." She grinned. "Don't stick yourself."

They sat on the ground in front of their longhouse. The wind was shifting to the north, the air cooling. Not like the bitter cold that would come, but a sure sign of it. The blue sky was full of clouds with dark undersides, and a slim crescent of moon was rising above the treeline beyond Xitkwe, the deep pond.

They could have done this work in the warmth of the long-house, but Willow always preferred to be outside in nature. He couldn't blame her; that was his preference, too.

"How's the tobacco?" she asked, stopping to stretch her back.

"The fire curing is only beginning, but it looks like a good mixture this season for the cigarros." He picked up a handful of berries. "Maybe I should add these to the mix," he said, letting the berries drop in a line from his hand.

"Only if you want people to throw up their food after they smoke!" She laughed and he joined her. Little Sunshell and Meekak laughed with them.

"Does the Mar-ee woman want to plant tobacco for you?" she asked.

"I think she does, but her man is always contrary. And he likes his oat plants more."

"And what he makes from them," she said, clucking her disapproval.

"What is he always drinking?" Meekak asked. "He smells funny."

"And sometimes he can't walk and falls down," Sunshell added in her small voice.

Both girls started giggling.

"Don't make fun of the visitors," Willow said. "And prom-ise me you won't drink any of that water he has in his green bottles." She gave Dancing Fish a knowing glance.

"Your mother is right," he said. "It's best to stay away from that man.

"But why?" both girls said at the same time, eyes questioning.

"Because we know what's best for you," he said in his fa-therly voice.

Willow changed the subject. "Have you made a decision about the land contract? What do the leaders say?"

"Each has a different opinion. Some, like High Limb, say we can trade the land over and over—it means nothing. Others don't want to give any more power to the Whites, no matter how unimportant it seems."

"And what do *you* say, dear husband?" Willow asked, staring at him. "What do your visions and dreams tell you? You are the one people listen to."

He was quiet for a moment. "My visions tell me to be very careful with this idea of trading the land. To not hurry. To wait and see."

"Wait for what?" she asked, a serious look on her face.

"I'm not sure. But waiting is sometimes the best plan."

Suddenly, Dancing Fish saw the girls raise their heads in unison and sniff the air. Then he smelled it.

He stood and looked to the northeast. He saw it and pointed. "*Smoke!*"

Great waves of it—gray and black—were swelling up to the sky, now filled with more clouds.

Willow was standing. "Isn't it from the hunting?"

"No. That's over." He squinted his eyes and studied the dark mass rising above the treeline. "This is new."

He stepped away from them to get a better view. Just then Rock emerged from his longhouse, also sniffing and looking at the smoke.

"Something's wrong," Rock said. "There should be no fire there. Where is that?"

Dancing Fish knew instantly. "It's Mar-ee and Jay-kub." He said to Rock, "Run and get as many men as you can from the village, then meet me there." Rock immediately turned to sprint away.

He looked at Willow and the girls and pointed to the ground for them to stay.

"And tell everyone to bring fire tools!" he shouted out to Rock's disappearing back.

The heat scorched his skin the closer Dancing Fish got. Even the mask and the deerskin mantle he'd brought weren't doing much against it. His eyes watered and his lungs burned from the smoke of the fire.

He rounded a large elm tree, and animals of all kinds and sizes ran past him going the other direction. Rabbits, turkeys, raccoons, deer, and even a big black bear had only one goal: escape.

Dancing Fish started to ford a shallow creek, stopped, and dropped down into it on his back, splashing water over himself with both hands. The relief was welcome as the water cooled his coverings and his skin.

Back on his feet, he ran forward and took shelter behind an outcropping of rock that reached over his head. He pressed his back against the rock while he watched thick smoke and flaming embers swirling past him, pushed on by a steady northeast wind.

As he coughed and tried to rub his eyes clear, he realized that the wind was aiming the fire in a direct line to their village—to Werpoes. Where their entire corn crop waited for harvesting. A fire could wipe it out in less than a finger of time!

He quickly developed a strategy to survey the situation. Putting down the hoe he carried, he took in a breath and peeked around the rock for as long as he could against the fire's blast, then retreated back to his hiding spot. After bending low with his head down to breathe cleaner air, he repeated the action.

In those moments, he could see entire pine trees bursting into flares of light when their sap ignited. Bright flames of yellow and red flashed upward wherever he looked. Everything took on a strange orange glow, and the smoke was so thick, that the sun was completely obscured. It seemed like night had overtaken the day. And the fire was getting closer. It had to be stopped somehow. But how?

He was concentrating when he saw movement through the waves of heat that flowed around and over his temporary refuge. It was the men of the village coming.

Rock was the first to reach him, and the others took shelter behind the outcropping. They each held different metal tools they had acquired from the visitors, including hoes, hatchets, and even a couple of shovels.

"What do we need to do?" Rock yelled into Dancing Fish's ear to be heard over the whooshing and popping of the fire.

"We need to clear a line to stop it." He pointed left and right behind them. "There hasn't been a fire here for many seasons. Too much old brush and dead wood. That's what the fire's eating."

He grabbed Rock's shoulders. "Tell the men to use whatever they have to dig, chop, and clear the land in a line all along this side of the creek. Go!"

Suddenly, there was giant High Limb, wearing a long fur robe, emerging from the smoke and walking toward him. He carried a long, heavy tool that Dancing Fish had never seen before. It was like a hoe but with two opposing blades turned at angles to each other.

"I think you need my help," High Limb said, shouting above the roar of the fire.

Dancing Fish pointed. "What's that?"

High Limb held it out for him to hold. It was so heavy he almost dropped it.

"It's for digging and chopping, High Limb said. "And killing when needed." He laughed. "Show me where to use it."

Dancing Fish pointed and watched as High Limb ran to a spot full of rotten tree limbs and trunks. He attacked them with his new tool and was soon clearing more than four men with their smaller tools. He carried the dead wood by the armful and dumped it on the other side of the creek.

Dancing Fish grabbed his hoe and joined in the clearing.

Two fingers of time passed, and the men stood in a line looking at the approaching fire with their feet in the creek. They were soaked in sweat, coughing and exhausted. Piles of old branches, brush, and dead pine saplings were heaped behind them.

The fire had advanced in pieces, moving and changing course several times, but it was now at the edge of the empty space they had cleared. Flames rose up left and right from trees and bushes, almost like an enemy who throws taunts and insults at its opponent. Would the cleared area hold?

Dancing Fish saw the fire stop at the far side of their clearing line, and shouts and cheers came from the men standing in the creek.

But then, they watched in horror while tiny sparks were thrown by the wind across the creek to land in the woods behind them.

Without need of instruction, everyone ran frantically to where sparks were igniting more blazes, hitting or stamping them out with their feet.

But they were losing the fight. The fire was jumping the line they had cleared in more and more places. This was a relentless adversary, and it was starting to look hopeless to Dancing Fish.

Then he felt it. A drop of rain. Then another. Soon, it was a downpour.

The fire that confronted them first started to hiss and offer resistance. But the rain continued, and the bright flames grew smaller and sputtered. Eventually, all they could see were fingers of white smoke that signaled the end. The fire was beaten.

As they gathered to start the walk home, Dancing Fish heard voices. Speaking in the Dutch tongue.

He turned around, and there were Mar-ee and Jay-kub, standing at the edge of the cleared area and arguing. Their skin was black with smoke, and their clothes were almost burned off. They looked like two rats that had been roasted over a fire. Except these rats were screaming at each other.

"But why? Why did you think this was a good idea?"

"I told you: to clear more land."

She waved her arms. "And you couldn't use the axes and saws we have for that purpose?"

"I thought this would be faster. The savages use fire—"

"The savages know *how* to use fire," she said, turning away from him. "You obviously don't!"

High Limb, muttering angrily, splashed through the stream and strode up to the white couple. He stopped just short of Jay-kub and towered over him. "*You* start this fire? You?!"

Jay-kub cowered and started to back away. But not fast enough.

High Limb drove a fist into his face and knocked him down to the charred ground. "You stupid white man. You almost destroy us all!"

Jay-kub held his bloody nose with one hand and propped himself up with the other. He spit out blood and sneered. "I'll get back at you, savage," he said.

High Limb leaned forward and pulled his fist back to launch another blow. "I will kill you now and save trouble."

But Dancing Fish was already there to grab and stop the giant's arm. "Trouble is over now," he said in his strongest voice.

He pulled High Limb away and toward the creek. "Let's give thanks the fire is out."

"Yes, let's do that," Mar-ee said, nodding to Dancing Fish and mouthing a silent *thank you.*

Fifty-three

MARIE LIKED WALKING ALONE, ESPECIALLY ON AN EARLY October morning like this: crisp and dry, the sky a brilliant blue without a cloud in sight. So different from Amsterdam and Liège with their overcast skies and the always pressing humidity.

She had left Jacob sleeping it off after a long night of drinking to ease the pain of his broken nose. She was going to visit the natives to apologize and thank them, and she wanted to do it by herself. It had taken a full day to wash the smoke off her skin and out of her clothes, and she was now wearing a clean duffel dress over two linen shifts.

She had traveled well through the devastation of the fire, and she hummed a childhood song while she walked south along the dirt path. She had taken to wearing the native moccasins for shoes, and she loved the comfort and the way her feet could feel the ground under her. She had also left behind her white coif. Why shouldn't she adopt the more practical ways of the Indians?

A low sun cast striped shadows across the trail as she adjusted the shoulder bag that held the gift she hoped they'd like. Birds sang out to her, and the constant noise of insects had almost disappeared.

Marie reached a split in the path and could see the water on her left, sparkling in the sun. She took the right fork and soon came to a rise that overlooked the enormous pond that was framed by large hills and a steep cliff. The village's longhouses nestled along the southern side.

She smelled the smoke of their fires, and as she approached, the dogs of the village sounded the alarm and swarmed around her, barking and begging. She tossed a small piece of cooked rabbit into the trees, and the dogs took off in a shot.

Willow and her two girls were waiting for her when she reached their longhouse. Word of her arrival must have spread quickly.

The girls ran right up to her, chattering in their strange language.

"What are their names?" she asked Willow, who spoke some Dutch.

"Meekak," Willow said, pointing to the oldest. "And little Sunshell."

The girls started whispering to each other.

"What are they saying?" Marie asked.

Willow pointed to her bag. "What is in? Their father brings gift in bags. They hope you are same."

"Well, let's see," Marie said teasingly. She put the bag down, and the girls immediately came close.

Willow said something harsh to them.

"Oh, it's alright. Let's look to see what's inside."

She pulled out the piece of gray linen she had brought with her on the ship. It was three ells long, and she was hoping to make something special for the baby with it, but this seemed to qualify just as much.

She let the girls touch it, then handed it to Willow, who couldn't stop running her hands and fingers over it.

"Linen," Marie said. "It's linen cloth."

"*Lin-en*," Willow repeated, her eyes never leaving the fabric.

"For you," Marie said with a smile, scooping both hands to show that it was a gift. "To thank you and Dancing Fish for all you have done for us."

On cue, Dancing Fish emerged from the longhouse and spoke to Willow, translating for her. He was lean and well muscled, something she could easily see with his scant clothing. He wore only the breechcloth around his middle and a sleeveless vest of animal skin. The tattoo of a turtle covered his right shoulder.

He turned to Marie, his eyes smiling. "You did not need to bring such fine cloth gift."

"I know, but you both have done so much for us—for me. The linen was for the baby, but now . . ." She slumped and felt tears forming. It was still bitter for her.

"Come," Dancing Fish said, guiding her to logs surrounding a small fire, where they all sat.

They spent at least an hour talking. The girls joined with their giggling and laughing, and Willow showed her bright smile at every opportunity.

The warmth of the fire and the cheerful conversation made her feel happy—for a change. Dancing Fish was a good host, offering her hot tea and the odd mixture of meat and nuts she found so filling.

She felt comfortable with these people. The idea that they were "savages" was the opposite of what she was experiencing and feeling.

They talked about her life before Jacob, the long voyage over, and the disastrous fire they all had barely escaped—for which she apologized again.

She tried to stay away from discussing Verhulst's proposal to acquire land. There was an inherent conflict within her about that. She could see how important the land was to the natives, yet she also saw the need for it by the Company and her own people. They were there to build a colony. So both sides needed the land. How to satisfy the two was something she couldn't see clearly, so she avoided the subject.

She also didn't want to talk about the baby, but when the conversation came around to her father, a flood of tears spilled from her eyes. Soon, she was sobbing and Willow was at her side with her arm around her.

After Marie wiped her tears away, she looked up at Dancing Fish and asked with a voice that wavered and cracked with emotion, "When can you take me to see my father?"

He came over and sat next to her. "We go tomorrow. See your father." He sighed. "Your father"—he put his hand over his heart—"was my friend."

Dancing Fish waited atop one of the boulders at the very end of the Point. He had fished from it so many times over the years that he knew every crack and crease on its wind-worn surface.

He listened to the rhythmic surge of waves washing around the rocks that poked up beyond the narrowing tip of land, and he smelled the distinct combination of sea and seaweed that made this part of the island so special for him. The air was still cool and dry, the sky veiled with the thin, wispy clouds that always came two days after the rain passed.

Rock and High Limb had both wanted to come, but he knew there would be more chance of conflict, so he said no. He wanted to be alone with his memories. And with helping Booshay's daughter.

When he looked over the edge of the boulder, he saw several of his Manitto perch swimming and darting over the rippled sand. *Ah, Manitto, so much time has passed, and still, here we are.* He threw a pebble into the water and watched the silvery fish scatter. *But this world is changing around us, isn't it?* He waited for a reply or a sign, but none came.

With his back to the Great Lake and looking up the island, he studied the curious four-sided shape on the sandy ground in front of him. The Whites had not made much progress on their fort, but he noticed that in the time of the two moons since the last gathering here, more trees had been cleared, and a few more huts built.

The whole tip of the island was starting to look very different. He even had a hard time remembering how it was when only trees and a few paths came up to the shoreline. Maybe Mar-ee was right after all. Maybe these were not visitors at all.

He let these thoughts float in his mind, and he was enjoying the smells and sounds of the water when he spotted them coming down the trail. Jay-kub stood in the cart and directed the gray horse in front with straps he held in his hand. But Mar-ee, who he expected to be standing next to him in the cart, was, instead, walking alongside it. He wondered what this meant.

Dancing Fish watched the large wheels of the cart turn until they came to a stop to the right of the fort markings. He bounded off his boulder and walked to where they waited.

He smiled at Mar-ee and nodded to Jay-kub, who stood motionless, glaring. "Your nose is better?" he asked him.

He grunted. The nose was swollen and bent, with a deep cut that was starting to heal. Two black eyes were already forming. He was lucky that High Limb had not done more damage. The War Chief could easily have crushed Jay-kub's entire head.

Ending the awkward greeting, Dancing Fish walked to the burial place, and they followed. The grave of Boo-shay was directly under a rope that hung between two short poles. This was how the fort was shaped: ropes between poles.

They were on the east side of the fort, and he remembered that they had buried him in a small clearing surrounded by tall oaks and hickories. Now, those trees were all gone and the ground was bare of even the stumps. Only the weeds that would soon sleep over winter were visible.

He had no trouble spotting the slight rise in the ground and the small triangle of shells they had put at the grave's head.

It pointed west, where all Souls went to wait before ascending to the Sky World. During the burial, he and High Limb had no idea if Boo-shay's religion was the same, but it would certainly do no harm to follow their own spirit customs.

"Here lies your father's body," he said, pointing to the shells and moving his hand above the grave.

Mar-ee sucked in a short breath and immediately knelt to the ground where she reached out to touch the shells. He saw her body shaking, so he stepped back to leave her with her thoughts. He also noticed that Jay-kub did nothing. He neither moved to be closer to her nor did he step away. And the man had a look of impatience, like he didn't want to spend more time here, either with Mar-ee or her father.

After a few moments, Dancing Fish heard footsteps and turned to see the fat Furhoost approaching in his white stockings and three-cornered hat. He was flanked by two of the soldiers.

"So, have you decided about the land?" Furhoost asked, out of breath, when he reached them, tipping his head to Jay-kub and Mar-ee. "Did you bring the signed contract?"

There was still no decision. "No. We must think more at our winter home. We go there soon."

Furhoost bristled. "And when you come back in the spring, there will be a massive fort here with masonry walls topped with cannon."

"That's right," Jay-kub added. "And with it, you will know how serious we are."

Furhoost ignored Jay-kub, then stared at Dancing Fish. His eyebrows furrowed over his narrowed eyes, his mouth turned down. "Then what are you doing here?"

Dancing Fish stepped back and nodded to Mar-ee. "This is burial ground of Boo-shay, her father," he said quietly.

"What? Boo-shay, the trader? Here?"

"Yes. It is near place where he died," he said, pitching his chin in the direction of the beach where they had found him.

Furhoost cocked his head. "Did you murder him?" he asked harshly.

Dancing Fish saw Mar-ee look up from her place on the ground, her eyes filled with tears.

"Of course not," he said firmly. "No one knows how he dies."

Furhoost snorted. "So you say."

Dancing Fish sucked in a deep breath and took a step toward the short, ugly man, as the two soldiers put their hands to the hilts of their swords. "I do say," he said calmly.

Mar-ee jumped up and directed an angry finger at their leader. "This is my father here." She pointed with a trembling arm. "Show respect, please."

"Well," Furhoost stuttered, "the grave . . . the body . . . will have to be moved. Obviously. The fort—"

"My father's body will not be touched!" she screamed at Furhoost, walking right up to him and stopping her nose only a hand's width away from his. "He loved this place. He will stay. Your fort will have to move."

"My fort—move?" He laughed. "Don't be ridiculous. I can't move my fort."

Without saying a word, Dancing Fish stepped around the grave and grabbed the rope that hung over it. He pulled hard on it so that both poles on each side came out of the ground. Then he walked to the poles and replanted them in the soft soil.

"There," he said, looking directly at Furhoost. "Fort moved. Sacred bones stay."

Fifty-four

IT WAS UNUSUAL TO HAVE A SPECIAL COUNCIL IN THE MIDDLE of winter. And so soon after celebrating the Turning of the Days, or Solstice as Dancing Fish now called it. Winter was for being with family and friends inside longhouses warmed by crackling fires. For repairing bows, threading wampum, sharing visions, and dancing long into the night.

But times are different now, Dancing Fish thought while he shuffled through the deep snow toward the Council House, his fur robe pulled tightly around him, breath pluming from his mouth.

He was glad to be away from the visitors and all the tensions surrounding them. But they were never far from his thoughts. And now there were rumors of more of them moving into neighboring territories, with more conflicts between the People and the new settlers.

The band had returned to Achqueehgenom, their winter home, after the corn had been harvested and the meat smoked and dried. An island exposed to harsh, cold winds from three sides was best left behind for more protected locations to wait for the return of spring.

It had been decided to make council with the top leaders of the island's neighboring bands, the Rechgawawanks and the Wiechquaesecks, to discuss and debate the new Whites and the land contract proposal from their leader, Furhoost.

The Rechgawawanks, proficient in fire hunting, occupied an area on the island to the north and had burned vast plains across the island up at the widest part before its outline narrowed and continued northward. And above them, at the far tip where the island started, were the Wiechquaesecks, who were fine basket-makers and creators of colorful body paints.

While they were all divided among the same three clans—Turkey, Wolf, and Turtle—these other two bands had their own customs. And their own ideas, which he wanted to hear.

Dancing Fish entered the main council meeting chamber and immediately shed his robe to the warmth of the fire and the many bodies. Familiar smells of roasting meat, root tea, and tobacco filled his nose as he surveyed the room. The central fire burned high and bright, and everyone sat around it in a circle, talking vigorously and eating, drinking, or smoking. He was happy to see that many were smoking his cigarros with their distinctive wrapping style.

The visiting leaders and lesser leaders were seated on furs at the top of the circle surrounding Thundercloud. They were distinctive in their face paintings and tattoos, and in the particular ways their deerskin mantles and leggings were trimmed with shells and beads specific to their bands.

"You're late!" Rock shouted from his seated position, handing him a gourd cup of steaming tea.

Dancing Fish sat on a folded skin next to his good friend. "Willow. You know." Willow was with child again, and there was always something she needed help with.

Rock smiled, his eyes gleaming in the firelight. "Soon you'll have three, one ahead of me."

"I didn't know it was a contest for the most children." He nudged his friend with his elbow, and they both spilled tea on their leggings.

Thankfully, Dancing Fish had already missed the long-winded welcomes and speeches that always started off any council. He had come at just the right time.

Thundercloud, looking frail and even older than Dancing Fish remembered, and seated again on his fur-covered Sachem's stump, started the main conversation. "You have seen the new settlers in your territories?" he asked, looking at the two visiting Sachems.

"Not many, but yes," said the leader of the Rechgawawanks, whose winter home was to the northeast of Achqueehgenom. He was short and stocky with an immense chest and long, muscled arms. "They are taking more animals and even clearing land without asking us! They offer nice gifts and tools of knives and kettles, but we are still concerned about these changes."

"We are the same," said the Wiechquaeseck's Sachem, Stands Tall, a very big man with long hair and faded tattoos covering his forehead, cheek, and neck. "When we returned from the island to our winter village, there were two new strangers living close by. They either move into an abandoned place where our people have died from the fevers, or they attempt to build their own wigwams." He laughed. "Only they do it so poorly, we usually have to show them how!"

There were whoops of laughter around the fire at this. Everyone seemed to enjoy joking about the lack of ability of settlers in so many things.

Thundercloud, who was listening intently, thumped his staff on the ground. It was time to reach the heart of the matter.

"The reason we have invited our good friends on the island to be with us," he said in his still-strong voice, "is this: we—the Manahate—are the ones who are closest to where the leaders and Sachem of the visitors stay. We see them more often, and they have been in direct contact with us about something important."

Thundercloud looked at Dancing Fish and signaled with his head. "I will now let Dancing Fish, who you all know as our White Keeper and who has much experience with these people, explain the situation and the reason for this council."

Dancing Fish felt all eyes turn to him and he stood. He found that standing helped him organize his thoughts when he spoke before a gathering.

"I welcome the leaders of the Rechgawawank and the Wiechquaeseck bands." He made eye contact with each of them in turn and nodded. And each returned his greeting.

He looked into the fire. "I know that we all love the Island of Many Hills and its land that holds the bones of our ancestors."

There were murmurings of assent from around the fire.

He reached into the sewn pocket inside his shoulder mantle and pulled out the contract. He held it up high for all to see, then handed it to Rock to pass to the visiting leaders. Each leader looked and puzzled over the paper, turning it over in his hands, before passing it on.

"What is this thing?" the Wiechquaeseck leader asked, holding it up.

"It's called a *contract*. An agreement. Not unlike our wampum belts for special occasions. To affirm or recognize an understanding."

Stands Tall asked, "And what is this understanding?"

"That is the main question," Dancing Fish said. He then went into length explaining what he thought Furhoost wanted, and what he also thought the consequences were to accept the agreement.

The Rechgawawank leader spoke up first. "So what you are saying is that if we—all the bands with territory on the island— agree with this"—he grabbed the paper and waved it—"this agreement, this . . ." He paused and frowned.

"They name it *purchase*," Dancing Fish said. "They want ownership or possession over the land that includes the island—Mannahatta."

"But don't they know the land cannot be possessed?" the leader said. "That we all share the island?"

"Yes. We've already gone over this with them. But they see things differently."

High Limb now stood, his copper breastplate—indicating his status of being War Chief—shining in the fire's light. "If they want to 'purchase' the land—whatever that means—I say we let them. Nothing will really change, and we'll have fine tools and gifts from them."

"I agree with the War Chief," said the Rechgawawank leader. "What harm is it to let these simple-minded people live on the land as we do? They can even help us in other ways."

"Help us how?" Thundercloud asked.

The leader smiled and nodded to High Limb. "I'm sure your War Chief has already thought of this, but we can share the land with these foolish Salt People in exchange for a defensive alliance with them. To help us against any of our warring enemies."

High Limb saw the opportunity. "The esteemed leader of the Rechgawawanks makes a good point about defending against the Iroquois, Mahican, Pequots, Susquehannocks . . ." He paused. "Even those troublesome Canarsees to the south who are always meddling with us."

Titters and cackles filled the chamber. The Canarsee had always been a thorn in their sides.

"But there have been no wars with these others for some time now," Dancing Fish said, trying to bolster his view that no agreement should be made over the land. He knew with his deepest Souls that it was a mistake. "I'm not sure a defensive alliance is really needed. Especially at the price of bargaining with our sacred land." He paused and then added, "Even without an agreement, they are already changing the land at Kapsee."

"They are?" asked one of the lower Rechgawawank leaders.

"Yes. They have cleared more trees and are building what they're calling a village."

There was more muttering at this.

The two visiting Sachems whispered to each other for a moment, and then Stands Tall spoke. "To better understand, we both want to see for ourselves what these strangers are doing with the land at the Point."

The leader faced Dancing Fish. "We plan to send hunting parties to the south soon. We have blood ties through marriage with the Sassians there. Maybe you can organize something?"

Before letting him answer, the Sachem added, "If you can take time out from your dream-making and inventing."

Laughter filled the chamber. His reputation for having his own mind had traveled far.

"Sachem," Dancing Fish said, making sure to show no anger and waiting for everyone to quiet, "I will be happy to lead a small group—including anyone you choose—to see what the strangers are doing at Kapsee." He smiled, then straightened his mouth and moved his eyes slowly around the circle. "But we may not be laughing in the future, depending on what we finally decide."

Fifty-five

THEY HAD WORKED THEIR WAY DOWN THE EASTERN LANDS IN
two days. As a War Chief, High Limb would not normally have
been on such an expedition. It was supposedly only a hunting party looking for small fur animals and hibernating bears,
but the other purpose was to check on any new activity by
the Whites. And, he wanted to keep a close eye on Dancing
Fish and the minor leaders from the Rechgawawank and
Wiechquaeseck bands.

The small group had passed through the lands of the
Maspeth and the Marechkawieck without incident, not really
seeing anyone, but smelling the smoke from fires that burned
inside longhouses where people sheltered against the bitter
cold. The only sounds were the cracking of tree limbs under
the heavy weight of snow and the muted gurgling of streams
covered in thick layers of ice.

Even the birds were conserving energy and venturing out
only to find the last seeds that the squirrels or other birds had
already not eaten. The monotonous views of white and gray
were occasionally interrupted by red flashes of a male cardinal
singing out to a female with his *teeooo, teeeooo, whoit whoit whoit*
song.

They were like a column of ants, breaking a path through
the knee-high snow, wrapped in their thick skins and heavy fur
robes. High Limb had long ago replaced his cloth ka-pot from

Boo-shay with a beaver cloak that covered an otter-fur vest. He was sweating and would need to remove one covering soon.

They stopped where the trail split, one path going south to the Sassian inlet, the other going west toward Red Hook and Pagganck Island.

"We separate here," Dancing Fish said to the group.

High Limb noticed that his old rival had the famous glass button from Hudson on a thong around his neck. Maybe a sign of good luck? Or the opposite? For his part, he fingered the heavy protector charm he had stolen from the Whites and now carried in the inner pocket of his cloak.

The real hunters headed south toward the inlet, and the rest—including himself, Dancing Fish, Big Shadow, and two sub-leaders from the other bands—started walking west.

After another finger of time moving around the base of a large hill, High Limb spotted something and held up his arm. They all stopped.

"Hunters," he said, squatting and examining a pear-shaped sac lying in the snow a body length away from a patch of blood.

He pushed on the sac with his hand and felt the liquid sloshing. "Piss sac," he said. "From a buck or a doe. Gutted here. And not fully cold."

"Sassians?" Big Shadow asked, touching the sac with his bow end.

High Limb stood back up. "No. Canarsee. I've seen their way before. They always leave this." He looked at the small group around him. "Keep your eyes and ears open. And if we run into anyone, remember that we're hunting. Only hunting."

They finally emerged from the snow-coated trees at a spot where the salt marsh touched the waters of the Great Lake. Directly in front of them: the small island of Pagganck, and to the right, the southern tip of Mannahatta. And just as Dancing Fish had predicted, the water in the shallow channel separating the small island from the eastern shore was frozen solid.

It would be a quick walk on the ice to the Island of Nuts that would serve for their spying station.

The gray sky was turning a strange rose color with the approaching night while they stepped and slid across the hard surface to Pagganck. Once there, they made their way through the forest of bare nut trees and were soon on a snow-crusted sandy beach and hiding behind two large boulders with a perfect view of Kapsee Point. Mannahatta was only five bow shots across the deeper water that was not frozen but filled with chunks of ice, some as tall as a man.

Dancing Fish pulled the two sub-leaders to his side. "Look carefully. You see the changes?"

The two men, each with a hairstyle and tattoos that denoted their band affiliation and their leadership rank, studied the opposite shore.

"Many trees are gone," said one.

"And homes built," said the other.

"Do the visitors look like they're staying or going?" Dancing Fish asked them.

The two looked at each other and then at Dancing Fish. "Staying," they both said at the same time.

High Limb moved closer to them. "On that, we can now agree," he said, looking across the water at Kapsee. "So the question is: what can we gain from them? In a way, they've already taken some possession of the land. But we can still trade for our benefit."

He urged, "Let them think what they like about the land. The ground does not change. What is above does, but it always comes back. Trees grow again, houses can be torn down and rebuilt."

High Limb looked into the strange yellow eyes of Dancing Fish and chuckled. "I say, let's take what we can from them. Even if they want to have a ferry from the Point to here, what do we care?" He laughed at his own absurd idea. "We can let them *purchase* the water between here and there, too!"

They all laughed at the ridiculous thought. Everyone except Dancing Fish, who raised one eyebrow and said, "Some day, there *will* be a ferry from here to Kapsee. And, I believe, much more than that."

▶◀

The hunters had been lucky, taking several snow hare and three fat otters. After the two groups found each other, they all passed the night sleeping under the branches of a laurel thicket, furs spread under and skins over them. Not wanting to make a fire that could alert anyone in the area to their presence, they huddled together for warmth.

Dancing Fish's eyes opened to another gray and cold day, and they were soon on the move, following their worn path through the snow, marching back north, toward home. The wind had stiffened, hissing and sighing as it wrapped around the dark tree trunks and left trails of white dust hanging in the air.

Dancing Fish was holding and rubbing his glass button, thinking about what they had seen at Kapsee and what lay ahead for the band, when High Limb joined him at his side.

"What is your button prophesying about our future?" the War Chief asked, intentionally shortening his long stride to keep the same pace.

"The button is a reminder to be careful with these strangers," Dancing Fish said, "and my visions tell me not to agree to this land contract."

"And if others disagree?"

"If it's the wish of all leaders to sign the contract, then I will, too. But until then, I will wait for more signs."

"The signs are clear to me, and I predict they'll be clear to you, too," High Limb said.

Maybe, he thought. *Maybe.*

Dancing Fish and the others were rounding a curve in the trail when they saw them. They would be hard to miss, standing in the middle of the path, waiting, their hands either holding a weapon or ready to grab one. They were also covered in furs and skins, but their face tattoos and the type of feathers in their hair crests made it certain: they were Canarsee warriors.

Dancing Fish and High Limb, who were in the lead, stopped three body lengths from them, the two groups facing each other in the snow, clouds of warm breath rising silently in the air. For several moments, no one spoke, choosing instead to study the others.

Dancing Fish took a half-step forward. "Greetings. We are hunters traveling back to our homes."

One from the Canarsee group stepped forward. "Hunters, you say?" he scoffed, turning back to his companions, who were openly smirking. "I think there is more to it." The man, obviously a leader, was short, and even under his hides and furs, his powerful strength was visible from his bunched shoulders and muscled forearms.

Dancing Fish then saw the leader focus on his glass button, which he had forgotten to hide under his vest.

"You're the Dream Maker, the Inventor, are you not?" the man said, smacking his war club into his palm.

The subterfuge was spoiled. "Yes," he admitted. He gave the formal greeting: "I am Dancing Fish of the Manahate. Son of Yellow Flower and grandson of Hard Stick of the Turtle Clan."

"Ah," the man said. "The White Seer we've heard so much about. The one who supposedly knows more about the strangers than anyone."

Dancing Fish waited.

"I am Gowanie, War Chief of the Canarsee band. Perhaps you have heard of us?" His entire group started chuckling and shaking with laughter. He continued. "But what I don't know is

337

what you're doing here."

Gowanie swept his gaze across their group again, studying each man in turn. "And such an interesting mix. I see hunters, but others, too." He nodded at High Limb. "By his symbols and bearing, I suppose a War Chief?"

High Limb snorted.

Gowanie continued his game. "And not only Manahates." His wide-set eyes, hooded by thick eyebrows, squinted. "Do I see signs of the Wiechquaeseck and the Rechgawawank?"

The sub-leaders in their group grunted.

"I thought so. All islanders." He grinned. "You know, we also visit the Island of Many Hills.

The tension was thick when High Limb took one of his long steps forward and said, "We know you visit Mannahatta. You claim use of many lands, including this one of the Maspeth. But who invites you?"

The Canarsee leader measured the imposing figure of High Limb, who towered taller than anyone. "And who invites *you*, War Chief?" he said, challenging. "This is not your hunting territory, is it?" He stared at the gutted otters and hares slung over Big Shadow's back. "It seems you have hunted our fur animals."

"They are not *your* fur animals," High Limb countered. "This is also not *your* hunting area, is it?" he provoked. "We have an invitation from the Sassians. And you?"

Gowanie grinned. "But are we not all welcome on Mother Earth?"

The two War Chiefs studied each other silently while the opposing groups leaned forward, ready to spring into battle.

Dancing Fish stepped in front of High Limb. "Let's not have an argument with each other. Let us, instead, talk of the Salt People and these new settlers."

Gowanie smiled and held up both arms to hold back his group. "An excellent idea." He looked at Dancing Fish. "So, tell me, White Seer, I hear you have the power to make inventions and to know the future." He lowered his war club. "What is the future with these white strangers? What do your dreams and visions tell you about them and us? Should we be afraid, or should we just laugh at them?" He cocked his head and smiled. "As I laugh at you right now." He chuckled and his entire group joined him.

Dancing Fish sensed High Limb's forward movement but placed a hand on his arm to stop him. "I cannot know the complete future, but we've been watching the Whites carefully. We are asking the same questions."

"And we watch, too," Gowanie said. "Especially their Holy Dogs. They are impressive."

High Limb suddenly pulled out his charm from the horses, tossed it in the air, and caught it on its way down. "This is one of their shoes."

"From the Holy Dogs? You have these creatures?" Gowanie was clearly surprised.

"Not only Holy Dogs, as you call them," High Limb said, "but many new weapons from the Whites. Powerful weapons that make yours seem like toys."

He was boasting. And not helping the situation. Dancing Fish pulled High Limb back and stepped past him to within a body length of Gowanie. He held up his left hand and reached very slowly into his cloak with his right, pulling out two strands of wampum.

He extended the wampum to Gowanie. "Let's part on good terms. We head back home, and you go your way. We leave as friends."

Gowanie studied him and the wampum. Then he smiled and stepped forward to take the offering. Moving back, he nodded to Dancing Fish. "You are a good leader, Dream Maker. You keep the peace." He looked at High Limb. "Peace is not always the best solution or even possible. But in this case, it's the correct way."

Gowanie stepped to the side of the snowy path, and his group followed his lead. He swung his arm until it pointed north. "Travel home safely."

Dancing Fish nodded to him when they walked past. "Until we meet again."

"Until we meet again," Gowanie said, dipping his head deeply in a hollow sign of respect.

▶◀

Dancing Fish let the heat of the fire and the steam of the water soak in. With his stomach empty, his senses were focused on the touch of sweat, the smell of red cedar shavings, and the sound of hissing water as he dripped it onto the hot stones in front of him.

It was the night of the first new moon after the Solstice, and his duty was to go inside himself while the others debated in the council. Thundercloud's death during their scouting trip had been a shock. But the role of Sachem had to be filled. Someone in the band had to balance High Limb. Raw and emotional action had to be steadied with reasonable and level-headed thinking.

The confined space of the dark sweat hut helped his mind explode into countless vision fragments, each a sliver of light that represented a part of his life—past, present and, undoubtedly, future. Beavers turned into dogs, perch into people. Fields of grain changed to flowing rivers. Stands of corn and tobacco burned inside searing fires that melted steel knives and kettles.

Now he was an eagle flying over the island. He dove down to find a perch. But the closer he came, the farther away the island seemed. He kept trying to land, but the island was always out of his reach. He was struggling, fighting, battling.

His eyes snapped open. His fasting stomach rumbled, and

he had to hold out his hands to keep from toppling over from his seat. The fire was down to muted embers. Cold from the outside leaked into the hut. He had sweated most of the day, and he finally felt his connection to Spirit and to his Souls fading.

The leadership meeting would soon be ending with a decision. His future with the band was now in their hands. They would finally accept him for what he was. Or . . . He wasn't sure what the *or* was.

Was he now truly one of them? He had a wife. He had two children and another coming. But he was still different. He felt it every day with each rising sun. He had white blood flowing through him. He created inventions. He had an independent mind in the middle of those that clung to ancient traditions.

He had always been between two worlds. Not fully of the People, and not one of the Whites. Would he always be a stranger to everyone and everything around him?

It could not go on like this. No one could stand in two earthly realms at once. And he wasn't yet ready for either the Sky World nor the Underworld. So what would he be? What future waited for him?

The door flap suddenly moved, bringing in a current of chilled night air with it. He could just make out the face of his friend Rock in the small opening.

"It's decided," Rock said, his voice and face indicating no emotion, no hint one way or the other. He paused for a long moment. Then he grinned broadly.

"You are the new Sachem of the Manahate band!"

Fifty-six

May 1626

MARIE AND JACOB ARRIVED LATE. AS USUAL, JACOB HAD BEEN drinking the night before, and it took longer than expected for Marie to get him clear-headed and looking presentable for the special council meeting. Pieter Minuit, just returned from months in Amsterdam, had called for it within a day of the ship's anchoring.

The winter had been hard on them. Heavy snows had been frequent and food was scarce. They were constantly hungry and probably would have died of starvation had it not been for the Indians, who traded them fresh meat and stored food for whatever duffel cloth, metal pots, and other tools they could part with. They had traded away most of their things just to stay alive. The horse had perished, and they ended up eating what was left of his emaciated body. They had to walk to the meeting.

But it was now spring, and nature's reawakening had overwhelmed and rejuvenated Marie. Everywhere she looked, shades of green flooded her eyes with a vibrancy that was hard to describe. And with the colors and new growth came the promise of hope, both for them and for their tiny outpost in this new land.

They were gathered between the unbuilt fort and the village at the end of the island, near where they had met the natives in the fall. Small waves crashed on the rocks with a measured rumble, and gulls soared and screeched all around them.

The sky was a deep blue, and the warm breeze brought a strong smell of the sea.

The council was seated on logs around an ashen fire pit, native style. There was still no structure big enough to have a real meeting with more than three people. One had been planned, but, typically, Verhulst had never organized the effort.

They were now six on the council: Verhulst, Minuit, another settler named Tonis Verbruggen, the Englishman Jan Lampo, who had the title *Fiscal-Schout* and was a kind of sheriff, and the two of them, her being added at her insistence. A lively debate was raging as they took their seats.

"You've made no progress on the fort at all?" a startled Minuit asked, glaring at the director.

"We've been busy," Verhulst said unconvincingly.

"Busy with what?" Minuit retorted, looking around at the tiny village of shabby huts.

"You question my authority?"

"I most certainly do," said Minuit. "The Amsterdam Chamber is upset by the lack of progress here." He held up a piece of paper. "We discussed this enterprise—and you specifically—at length over the winter while I was there. There are major discrepancies in the accounts of the colony, and they have assigned me the task of doing whatever is required to right the matter."

Minuit was a slight man, but he was full of fire now. "And what of the land purchase? Why haven't you at least accomplished that?"

Verhulst, his tiny eyes blinking rapidly, was at a loss for words. He finally sputtered, "It's not so easy dealing with these savages. Their ideas about the land are very different from ours. They—"

"I don't care what they think!" Minuit shouted, his face uncharacteristically distorted, his voice rising high. "Your duty was to take possession of this land, and you have failed."

343

"How dare you speak to my husband that way," the fat Phaebae bleated from the edge of the group. She was not an official member of the council, but that didn't keep her from pushing her nose into anything of importance. "He is the director of this entire colony. He is in charge."

"Is he now?" Minuit shot back. "Then why does he do nothing about the disaster in the north where the commander of our Fort Orange was killed and eaten by the savages?" He moved his eyes to Verhulst. "And why has he not brought all the settlers safely to this island, which has been chosen for the center of our activities?" He stared. "Why?"

Verhulst looked at the ground and stammered, his cheeks blowing in and out. "It ... it ... has not been an easy assignment. There are many vagaries."

"Vagaries?" Minuit repeated in a manner of disgust. "Well, *this* is not a vagary." He looked at the paper in his hand and read from it. "I have here an order from the Chamber to put this issue of leadership to a vote by the council."

Phaebae jumped forward, almost falling over her husband. "This is outrageous. We"—she pointed to her husband—"I mean, *he* is in charge here, not you. Willem, do something!"

"Please," Minuit said sternly to her, "you are not on the council. Be quiet and seat yourself." He looked at all of them one by one. "We will now vote."

He read from the paper. "All those in favor of removing Meneer Willem Verhulst from his position of directorship of this colony of New Netherland, say aye." He raised his hand. "Aye from me."

They looked at each other. Then Lampo said forcefully, "Aye!"

Verbruggen quickly followed. "Aye."

Verhulst and his wife shouted together, "No!"

Minuit frowned and looked directly into Marie's eyes and nodded imperceptibly.

"Aye," she said, then nudged Jacob with her elbow.

"Uh, aye," said Jacob, as if being wakened from a deep sleep.

"We are agreed, then," Minuit said, smiling. "To the next point of concern." He glanced at the paper again. "All those in favor of installing me, Pieter Minuit, representative of the Amsterdam Chamber of the West India Company, to be the new director-general of this colony of New Netherland, voice your approval by saying aye."

"No!" Phaebae screamed. "A thousand times, no!" Her face was a blotch of red.

Verhulst joined in, boiling with anger. "This is scurrilous," he fumed. He grabbed his poor-fitting wig and threw it to the ground, showing a completely bald, sweaty head. "I'll return someday as the head of an army and take this land back!"

Paying no attention, Minuit rose from his seat. "With the other ayes from before, the matter is now settled," he said in a controlled voice. "This council is concluded." He turned and walked away.

Marie was stunned. What had just happened?

▶◀

The two Sachems waded close together in the waterway that reached to just below their short aprons. They had removed their shirts and leggings, and the shallow water was pleasantly warm on their skin.

Looking down to the silty bottom, they searched for the smooth and brightly colored river stones that accented the pottery of the Wiechquaesecks and made it so distinctive. The sun was lowering behind the western highlands, and deep shadows crossed the newly green reeds of salt marsh that spread on both sides of the water.

It had been a long journey for Dancing Fish, but it was now nearing its end. His last stop was the summer home of the

Wiechquaesecks, who occupied three villages at the far northern tip of Mannahatta. There they hunted, fished, and planted crops up to the Wading Place that designated the island's starting point. It was an area marked by both high hills and bluffs and also marshy land that held the curving and wandering stream of water that created the island's northern boundary.

The waterway was shallow enough to wade across at the ebb tide of both the Great River and the eastern waters that it connected, but with the flood, it became a true water channel that could only be crossed by canoe or raft. A ferry service was ready to take anyone across at high tides.

After celebrating his becoming Sachem with the clans of the band at Werpoes, Dancing Fish had spent the past two moons traveling to the other bands and villages on the island to formally make the announcement and to receive their blessings. And to share news. It was the accepted way, and he wanted more than anything to do what was expected.

He finally felt that he belonged. That it was time to give up his thoughts of independence and, instead, help the People find solutions to their problems. He was now the Peace Sachem of the Manahate band, and he wanted to implement the best ways of keeping that peace.

He traveled in the company of two young men from the other clans. One was a hunter apprentice while the other was being groomed for a life of Spirit. The real hunters and Holy Men—what was left of them—were needed to tend to the stomachs and to the Breathing Souls of the shrinking band at Werpoes. These two, only recently initiated into manhood, were the most expendable.

Each man in the trio pulled a wheeled travois, two of them loaded with various gifts for the villages being visited. Another was filling with the gifts they were receiving in return.

In addition to the tobacco seedlings Dancing Fish gave away at each stop—root balls wrapped in pieces of duffel cloth from the Whites—he had special gifts for the two other bands on the island.

For the Rechgawawanks, he had brought several examples of his improved invention, the spear-thrower, to aid in their hunting. The tool, a short piece of ash wood, used leverage to increase the speed and distance of a thrown spear. He had seen himself using it in a dream and fashioned one that same morning. They, in return, had offered him deerskins and several fine bows and quivers of perfectly straight arrows.

The Wiechquaesecks, well known for their fine baskets and pottery, received bags filled with Kapsee oyster shells, considered the best for making the lime that helped strengthen their pots. In exchange, Dancing Fish was given five intricately woven baskets, each one smaller so they all fit inside the other with no wasted space.

A large black dog suddenly ran toward them, splashing, yelping, and biting the water. It abruptly stopped in front of the Sachem, Stands Tall, its pink tongue hanging out of its mouth to pant. The dog reminded Dancing Fish of his Kong, who had been poisoned so many years before, and he stopped to admire the animal. "What's his name?" he asked.

"Runs-and-Runs," the Sachem said, rubbing the dog's wet head. "He's a trustworthy one. Protective and loyal." He looked at Dancing Fish. "You seem touched by him."

The truth was that Dancing Fish had never been able to replace Kong in his heart. Rather than immediately finding another dog—something everyone had advised—he had preferred to just let the whole gang of village dogs divide his attention.

"It's a long story," he finally said, picking up a floating stick and throwing it as far as he could. True to his name, Runs-and-Runs happily sprinted after it.

The sun suddenly dipped behind the rim of the high bluff, and rays of yellow and orange filled the clear sky. "Let's go back to my longhouse and talk," Stands Tall suggested. "You have a long day ahead of you traveling back. We'll rest and eat."

Shorakapkock was their largest village, lying in a pocket of hills that faced the meandering waterway and the open salt marshes that separated the island from the soaring bluffs of the mainland to the north. It was still early for mosquitoes, so they sat outside, next to the central fire. Dancing Fish's young companions grouped themselves next to the travois, chatting with others their own age from the village.

As the two Sachems spooned their succotash and ate strips of sizzling fish, they talked about the changes taking place. "The younger men now spend all their time hunting fur animals," Stands Tall said, "not seeking the deer that can better fill our stomachs."

"Because of the trade with the Whites?" Dancing Fish asked.

"Yes. But there are so few beavers and otters now, it's pointless. And this also means fingers of time not spent in the fields clearing more land or doing other important tasks." The Sachem shook his head in frustration.

"It's the same everywhere," Dancing Fish said. "Too many hunters looking for too few fur animals."

"Exactly. And no time spent making arrows or helping with the tanning of hides. Why do it the hard way when you can trade for a steel knife or a length of duffel cloth?" He let out a long sigh. "We're losing our ways to these strangers. You must see it too, being so close to them at Werpoes."

"Everything you say is true. And the Rechgawawanks say the same."

Stands Tall tapped a stick on the edge of their metal kettle. "We're becoming too reliant on them. We are forgetting our own history. And now there's something else." He threw a piece of fish to Runs-and-Runs, who gobbled it in an instant. "Payment for different wrongs our people have committed against the Whites.

348

"Like what?"

"Stealing and killing their animals. People are hungry."

"And let me guess: building up gambling debts and buying fire drinks on credit."

"Exactly so," the Sachem said.

The two didn't speak for a few moments, listening only to the popping of the fire's flames. Then Dancing Fish pulled out two of his cigarros, handed one to Stands Tall, and lit them with a burning brand. They both puffed and blew the sweet-smelling smoke up to a sky that was starting to sparkle with stars.

"I remember you were undecided earlier about the land trade," Dancing Fish said. "Have you formed an opinion?"

The Sachem sucked slowly on the tobacco, his worn tattoos dancing on his skin with the flickering light. "I can say that I have a mixed mind about it."

"How so?"

Stands Tall explained that while he hated relying on the tools and gifts from the Whites, he recognized their value, and that the changes and movement to the new ways were unstoppable.

"It's like this," he said, leaning back on his elbows and stretching out his long legs. "Say you have three fish and five oysters to trade. The other person has only three ears of corn. You hate oysters but really need the corn. But you don't tell him that. Instead, you say no to the trade and start to walk away. Then you mention at the last moment that if there could be three more ears of corn, you might consider trading the oysters that he loves. You lead him along, playing on his desire for oysters, which you really care little about. He works hard to find more corn, and you finally make the trade. Both sides are happy. Do you see?"

Dancing Fish nodded.

Stands Tall continued. "Let the land be your oysters. There

will always be more oysters, so use the other's lust for them to get what you want. There is plenty of land. Trade it again and again, if you want. And get as much as you can in trade each time."

Dancing Fish studied the older Sachem. "You want me to sign the white man's paper, don't you?" he said. "Even if it involves the whole island and your band?"

"I say you should make the best deal you can. And share with us the gifts and tools that are exchanged." Stands Tall looked over at him, eyes bright in the firelight. "I trust you will come to a good conclusion."

Dancing Fish watched the chest of Runs-and-Runs rising and falling while he lay napping near the Sachem's feet. "I still feel it's wrong to trade the land, but I will consider everything you've said. And I appreciate your trusting in me."

The Sachem turned himself on his folded skin so a young girl at his back could braid the long hair that signified his age and status. "If I cannot trust the White Seer who makes his dreams become real, then who can I trust?" He smiled, crinkling his tattoos. "You will make the right decision."

Fifty-seven

HIGH LIMB WAS BOTH HONORED AND WARY OF THE INVITAtion to meet alone with the new white Sachem, Minwee. The man wanted something, but High Limb would see what he could gain from it. His family was growing, and new tools and gifts were always welcome.

A light rain fell steadily on the roof of the crude dwelling, and they sat next to an unlit fire with the hut's opening letting in enough light to see by. He had never been inside one of these huts before, so he took his time to study its interior while Minwee searched for something in a large sack at his feet.

The hut was built over a shallow pit dug into the ground. The sides and bottom of the pit were covered in bark and reeds, and over the hole was a box frame made of tree limbs interlaced with more reeds. The roof was flat and covered with large pieces of grass cut from the land.

It was the poorest construction High Limb had ever seen. Only a short man could stand without hitting his head, and they had not even thought to have a hole for letting the soot and smoke of the fire escape! And because this was the home of the Sachem, it was surely the grandest of all the huts in the village. He couldn't imagine what the others were like.

The small man with the intelligent face who had probably seen at least 40 winters found what he was looking for. "Here," Minwee said, offering him a small bottle before lifting his own to his lips to take a drink.

High Limb had learned to sip the strong drink slowly with these people, or even better, to not drink it at all. He had watched far too many of the band walk unevenly and even fall to the ground after gulping this water that burned the throat, made the mind spin, and turned men foolish.

"Let's discuss how we can help each other," the new leader said, smiling. His voice was controlled but full of power. This man was much smarter than the fat Furhoost, who had been banished to another hut with his ugly wife and obviously not invited to this meeting.

"How can you help me, and how can I help you?" the man said in the straightforward way these people had of speaking. There was little ceremony or formality. Just get to the point.

"Your biggest wish is to trade the land, yes?" High Limb asked, already knowing the answer.

"Indeed it is," Minwee said. "Is this something you can help me with?"

High Limb was ready. "You give me something of value"—he looked at the man and raised his eyebrows—"and I help you with the land trade."

Minwee took another drink and studied him before speaking. "You can do this?"

"Yes. I am War Chief."

"But Dancing Fish is now Sachem."

"We have equal power," said High Limb. "He for peace, me for war." He sipped the tiniest bit of the bitter drink to show courtesy.

Minwee nodded thoughtfully. "And what do you want?"

"One musket," he said without hesitation, offering his kindliest smile.

Minwee opened both eyes as wide as they would go. He shook his head vigorously. "Oh no. Not possible. No, no. No muskets for Indians."

High Limb thought he heard the man start to slightly slur his words in the way he had come to recognize with the drink. "Why not?"

"It's forbidden," he said with conviction. "Not possible at all. Something else?"

He was ready for this, too. "A sword."

"A sword? What would you do with a sword?"

"Good for cutting vines and reeds," he said innocently. And enemies, he thought but did not say.

Minwee stared at him, obviously thinking. He stroked his bearded chin.

"You will have the land contract," High Limb added with confidence, filling the silence.

Minwee thought a moment more without moving or saying anything. Then he stood, reflexively stooping, and walked over to a large basket in the corner of the hut. He opened the lid and pulled something out.

Back at his seat, Minwee started unwrapping a bundle of the white man's duffel cloth. The bright blade of steel was soon visible, and the man finally held it up by its grip, raising it as high as he could in the small space. The blade was the length of High Limb's arm below the elbow. It had two cutting edges, and even though the light was dim in the hut, the steel gleamed.

"It is short," was all High Limb could think to say.

"Because it's called a *short sword*—for thrusting and jabbing." He cocked his head and grinned. "And for cutting vines, of course."

Minwee took in a deep breath through his delicate nose. "It is forbidden for us to give you dangerous weapons. However, I'm prepared to offer you this sword." He started to extend it to High Limb's waiting hand but immediately pulled it back. "But only if you assure me you'll help deliver the land contract I seek from your people." He leaned forward, eyes fixed on his. "Do you assure me of this?"

High Limb didn't blink or hesitate. "You have my word," he said carefully, imitating the sounds he had heard from the white strangers more than once before. *My word to you is as good as yours is to me*, he thought, smiling and reaching for the weapon with its cold, steel blade.

▶◀

Dancing Fish hid behind the line of trees bordering their cornfield. Watching and smiling.

Willow was hard at work planting the corn. With her big belly holding their next child, she moved slowly from mound to mound, carefully kneeling and putting four seed kernels from the year before into the mound and then covering it. It would be another one-half moon before the beans could be added to the mounds, and the squash just before.

Dancing Fish moved his eyes to the two girls. They were pretending to help with the corn kernels and mound building with small hand hoes, but behind Willow's back, they were teasing each other and playing with some colorful bits of cloth. They even had some tied in their long hair.

A fresh breeze from the south greeted him when he finally emerged from the trees pulling the loaded travois. The girls saw him first and instantly started running to him, screaming "Father, Father!" He saw Willow stop and smile. She would wait in the cornfield for him.

Meekak and Sunshell already looked older in the short time he had been away. Or maybe it was the strips of cloth they wore, not only in their hair, but circled around their necks and arms like bracelets.

He grabbed each of the girls and swung them around and around before lowering them back down.

"What do I see that's different about you two?" he asked slyly. "What is it, I wonder?"

Both girls started giggling and then laughing.

"What could it be?" he said, pretending to not see the obvious.

Sunshell finally blurted out, *"We have ribbons!"* The girls started dancing around him, letting the red and yellow strips bounce with every movement.

"Well, I don't know what a ribbon is, but you certainly do have them, and they make you look even prettier than you already are." He pulled them both to his side and squeezed. "Let's go see what your mother is doing, and then I have a surprise for you."

"A surprise!" they both yelled at the same time and then started helping him pull the travois toward Willow.

After they had hugged and kissed, he stood back and admired his wife. She wore a thin mantle to cover her shoulders, and her belly extended over the skirt that fell to her moccasins.

"It won't be long now, will it?" he said, beaming, as he put his hand on the smooth, stretched skin of her belly.

"One more moon," she said, rubbing it.

Nodding, he stepped to the travois, stopped, and turned to face them. "I have a surprise for all of you. And especially you two little squirrels," he said, pointing at his daughters.

He reached to the special basket, untied the rope, and pulled out the tiny puppy that whimpered and yipped at his first attempts to bark.

"A puppy!" both girls screamed at the top of their voices before they rushed toward their father.

He gently put the puppy on the ground, and the girls were immediately down next to it, touching and talking to it. "His name is Run-Run."

He glanced up and caught Willow's look. "I know. I said never again. But look—"

They both watched while the girls took turns holding and smothering the black, male Run-Run with their kisses.

With the girls running ahead toward the longhouse, he was able to pull the travois and walk slowly next to Willow, filling her in on all that had happened. He explained how the Rechgawawanks and the Wiechquaesecks had reacted to the news—both to his being named Sachem and also their views on the new white settlers becoming more and more numerous.

"The Sachems gave me their assessments but left the negotiating to me."

"A wise decision," Willow said, her eyes on the squealing girls ahead.

"We'll see," he replied. "They seem to not care about the Whites living on the island. Maybe I'm more worried than I should be."

"If your visions and dreams tell you to worry, then you need to pay attention. You're now a Sachem and the White Seer. Others may have their opinions, but it's yours that count most."

He let her words sink in while they continued to walk, his forehead starting to sweat in the warming spring air. "And now you," he said, wanting to change the subject. "Tell me what I've missed."

He suddenly stopped. He had not seen that Willow had woven a bright red ribbon into the end of her long hair. "And what are these ribbons?"

Willow explained how Mar-ee had visited more than once and brought gifts of the ribbons and more. There were mirrors for the girls and a nice length of cloth for her.

"I like this woman," Willow said, pulling her hair around to feel the ribbon. "And so do the girls. She understands us more than we think. But that husband of hers will always be trouble, I predict. How could such a nice woman be with such a horrible man?"

She shook her head and sighed. "And they do need more land. Especially if they're to grow tobacco. I gave her the seedlings like you suggested. She was very pleased. Now she has to get that man to help her clear more land to plant them."

"Yes," he said, his eyes drifting up to the blue sky and seeing not one cloud. "Everything seems to be about the land now, doesn't it?"

"Maybe so. And I almost forgot: their new leader, the man Minwee, has asked for a meeting with you and the others. He wants to welcome you as our Sachem."

"And talk about selling the land, no doubt," he said.

"That, too," said Willow. "Mar-ee warned me about it."

"Well, we're not selling anything."

Fifty-eight

Although the stated purpose of the gathering was to introduce the two new Sachems to each other, Dancing Fish knew that land was the real focus. And he had picked the meeting spot carefully. The settlers had requested that it take place at their new village at Kapsee. But he countered by suggesting the same clearing under Old Bark, the tall white oak halfway between them and Werpoes. Acting as a go-between, the man named Lampo, who seemed an important person, returned with Minwee's approval. Dancing Fish had won his first point of negotiation.

They were now in June by the European calendar, and coming to summer's Turning of the Days by theirs. The falling sun was a round glow in a hazy sky that announced heavy air and hot days to come. Gray clouds could be seen moving toward them from the southwest. Bird calls battled with insect droning from the surrounding forest, and the smell of the fire's burning wood mingled with the bad odors of the Whites, depending on the wind direction.

They were again arranged in a split circle around a low fire pit. Dancing Fish had ordered the two young men he had traveled with to sweep the ground of sticks and stones, and they all fit under the wide canopy of the oak, sitting either on logs or on folded skins and cloths.

This was a meeting only for leaders, and Dancing Fish

counted six Whites, including Mar-ee and the ever-unhappy Jay-kub. They had arrived in two carts pulled by horses, now tied to trees and flicking their tails against the flies.

His group was eight, including High Limb, Rock, Big Shadow, a matron from each clan lineage, and a new Holy Seer. The old one had passed to the Sky World, and Dancing Fish had given up his quest for the position when named Sachem, although some still looked on him as the White Seer.

After the ritual exchange of gifts and pipe smoking, it was time for the introductions and speeches.

Minwee, dressed in his best duffel and linen clothes and wearing a three-cornered hat, spent a great deal of time explaining how hard they had worked to establish themselves on the island and about their good and peaceful intentions regarding the land, the animals, and the People. Most of the words were incomprehensible on their side, so Dancing Fish did his best to translate, although even he lost interest after a finger of time.

When it was finally his turn to speak, Dancing Fish—proud to be wearing his finest apron covering decorated with purple wampum and a cloak made from red woodpecker scalps and white eagle-tail feathers—held onto his Sachem's staff and delivered a shorter welcome speech, first in the Dutch tongue, then in Munsee.

The ultimate purpose of the gathering became clear when Minwee stood, waved his right arm across their side of the circle, and started to speak in a voice surprisingly deep for a man of such small stature.

"I come to you, the proud band of the Manahates," he said, "to complete the land purchase agreement that has been waiting between us."

Minwee unrolled a piece of paper handed to him by Lampo. He seemed to cast a quick, curious glance at High Limb while he started to read the familiar words that Furhoost had spoken before—the same words about land claims and possession.

Dancing Fish was expecting more. "There is nothing new here," he said, noticing the dark clouds that now filled the sky above them. The wind had also grown in strength. He continued. "There is no mention of price. Your other leader, Furhoost, spoke of a *fair price*, but"—he looked down at the ground around the feet of Minwee, moving his head in an exaggerated way of pretending to be searching for something—"I still see nothing being offered for trade. Am I blind?"

Those who could understand the tongue of the Whites smirked and chuckled.

Minwee smiled at Dancing Fish and signaled behind him. Immediately, two men, including Lampo, carried two sides of a large bundle of cloth and set it at the man's feet.

Minwee leaned down and let the sides of the bundle fall away.

A loud gasp came from the mouths of those sitting on their side of the circle. Everyone could see the good gifts and tools showing on the cloth. There were steel knives, hatchets, axes, drilling awls, hoes, kettles, and many colored beads in long strings. The People had tired of the beads long ago, but the other trade goods were highly sought.

Minwee looked to Dancing Fish. "This is what we are prepared to pay for the land. It is a fair price."

Dancing Fish, well versed in trading strategy after years of practicing it, remained silent. He had learned long ago to never rush speaking during a trade. The silence hung in the air and mixed with the sounds of forest animals and the wind that breathed through the trees. The skies continued to darken.

"Do you want to see the contract?" Minwee finally said, breaking the silence.

Dancing Fish smiled. "It can be helpful." He didn't move from his position, requiring Minwee to send Lampo across the circle to hand it to him.

Dancing Fish read over the paper. Then he read it again. He took his time, remembering what Stands Tall had said about using the land as oysters.

"Well?" Minwee said, the impatience clear in his voice.

Dancing Fish kept silent and decided to read the paper one more time. When the murmuring from both sides had built up, he was ready to speak.

"Honorable Sachem of the white visitors," he said slowly, emphasizing the word *visitors* and smiling broadly at the man. "What you offer is a good start, but . . ." He nodded first to Mar-ee, then to Minwee. "There are many questions still unanswered before this can be"—he searched for the right word—"considered."

Minwee scowled. "Like what, Sachem?" he asked stiffly.

Dancing Fish made a show of putting his finger to a spot on the paper. "You mention the entire island of Mannahatta, but there are three bands who make use of it in the good seasons." He already had the approval of both the Rechgawawanks and the Wiechquaesecks, but he would use this as a bargaining point. "I cannot speak for the others."

Minwee frowned, then spoke quietly to his group, with Mar-ee adding some words he couldn't hear. He turned back. "Leave this for now. What else do you want?" he asked, obviously frustrated, and looking again at High Limb, who turned his head away, releasing a thin smile that Dancing Fish recognized whenever his tall rival knew he had taken advantage of someone.

Dancing Fish looked down again at the paper. "You list *compensation for grievances and damages.* What does this mean?"

"You killed my pigs!" Jay-kub suddenly shouted from his seat. "And more animals since then."

Dancing Fish smiled at Jay-kub like he would a child. "Pigs? You are concerned about pigs?" He stared hard at the man. "Do we also talk of the fire you started? Or the trees you cut?" He focused his eyes on the repulsive man. "And the men you make crazy with your oat drink?"

Jay-kub stood and balled his fists. "I don't have to listen to a savage questioning me."

High Limb jumped to his feet, and it looked like another fight would erupt.

Dancing Fish and Minwee both stepped to the middle of the circle to stop the escalation. Minwee looked at Dancing Fish. "We will not talk of these compensations just now. Agreed?"

Dancing Fish nodded and took hold of High Limb's arm, guiding him to sit back down. Minwee did the same with Jay-kub.

After the tension had eased, Dancing Fish pointed again to the paper. "And where is mention of defensive alliance?" He still wasn't convinced such an alliance was good for them or even needed, but many others had spoken of it, so it was worth throwing into the negotiating pot. Always better to ask for more when bargaining.

"I was not sure you wanted this," Minwee said.

"If we are to live on the land together, then we are allies. And allies come to defense of others. No?"

Minwee eyed Lampo. "It could be so, and it is something to consider, but let us be clear about one thing."

Dancing Fish looked at the small man with his close beard that was starting to gray. "And what is that?"

"We are asking you to sell us the land—the island." He paused, then added, "In a manner that is satisfying to you in all ways." The man looked uncomfortable, as though he did not believe what he was saying.

"We don't *sell* the land!" Dancing Fish almost shouted, showing his annoyance for everyone to see. "Were you not there when we talked of this with Furhoost? When we said it is not our land to give away or trade? And we will never leave the land that is our summer home for generations and holds the bones of our ancestors?" He pointed a finger. "Do you not remember this?"

Not waiting for an answer, Dancing Fish walked over, bent down, and picked up one of the knives in the cloth bundle. He quickly spun around and hurled the knife at the closest tree where it stuck, blade-first, and vibrated with a ringing sound.

"For trinkets and trifles?" he said, looking into Minwee's blue eyes. He displayed anger and disgust. He knew the trade goods were valuable but did not want to reveal that.

Minwee appeared shocked. His voice cracked slightly when he said, "We are not forcing you. We . . . we are asking what it would take to satisfy you so we may acquire this land." He raised both hands in the air in a way of easing things. "All of this is a discussion. I am sure we can find a solution to satisfy us both." He looked at him with a concerned face.

At that moment, Dancing Fish knew he had won the upper hand. But he also knew that for all his talking skills and clever thinking in the ways of the Whites, these settlers were not going anywhere. He had seen it in the eyes of Mar-ee and now again in Minwee. They had already shown their resilience, and with more of them constantly coming, the People were at a disadvantage that would only grow larger.

He realized now that he was a rabbit bargaining with a wolf. He could hold them off for a time, but his stomach—and his two Souls—saw many more dark clouds ahead. And to emphasize the point, he looked up at the blackening sky and felt the first drops of rain. This was a good place to end it.

"The talking is over," he stated simply to Minwee and threw the paper roll back to him. "We must meet again."

Receiving no acknowledgment from the man, Dancing Fish turned and signaled for the others to stand and follow him back to Werpoes. He was sure he could gain a better outcome in sharing the land. But there would be no *selling*.

The solid mass of clouds had turned such a deep gray that it seemed almost blue. Thunder rumbled after streaks of lightning flashed across the sky. The south wind bent the trees with a howl that chased the eight of them up the trail toward their village. Dancing Fish ran alongside High Limb, turning to look back for stragglers as large raindrops pelted them.

"Don't worry about the others," High Limb yelled to him above the roar of the storm. "I need to get this out of the rain." He had pulled the shiny weapon from his leggings, and he was holding it high in his right arm while they ran.

"I wondered why you were wearing full leggings on such a warm day," Dancing Fish shouted, remembering the looks Minwee had given the War Chief. "Don't tell me you—"

"That's right, Little Eel," he said, using his baby name. He laughed as he swung the sword back and forth, trying to slice the fat raindrops in half. "I promised him I would persuade you to sell the land in exchange for this beautiful weapon. Another victory for the War Chief!"

Laughing so hard at this they had to stop. High Limb grabbed his arm with his free hand. "And the way you stuck that knife in the tree over your disgust with those *trinkets and trifles*. A beautiful bit of trading strategy."

The others soon caught up and joined in the unplanned celebration. They were all soaked to the skin by now, so it made no difference how fast or slowly they moved to the village. Standing in the middle of the muddy path that now flowed with water, they took a moment to relive the high points of the meeting and talk about how they would use all the gifts they would receive from the Whites.

Dancing Fish knew it was only a temporary victory, and he took a step back to observe his friends while they splashed and opened their mouths to the falling rain. These were the leaders of the island band with a very uncertain future in the midst of a lighthearted moment. They might as well enjoy it. How many more times like this would there be?

High Limb caught his eye and cried out to him, "Old rival, could it be that we are starting to be friends *and* allies?"

"You said it would never happen, remember?"

"I do. But times change, and men change with them." He suddenly jumped onto a fallen tree trunk and raised his sword again. "To us—to the Manahate!" he called out at the top of his lungs.

Just then, a ragged shaft of lightning arced down from the black sky and struck the raised sword. A ball of light encircled High Limb just before a loud bang exploded around him.

High Limb fell to the ground, face down in the ooze, and everyone rushed to him, with Dancing Fish reaching him first. After a moment of stillness, the giant War Chief rolled himself over and smiled at Dancing Fish through his mud-covered face. "Another victory for the Manahate."

Everyone, including Dancing Fish, fell to the mud around High Limb, laughing.

▶◀

Marie had no sooner crawled into the hut, soaked from the rain, when Jacob's fist slammed into the side of her head, knocking her flat.

"How dare you embarrass me like that at the meeting!" he screamed.

Her head pounded with pain, and she pulled herself up to sit against the wall. "What are you talking about?" she croaked through a mouth that ached and was swelling by the second.

"You're nothing but a savage lover, aren't you?" he said, snapping out the words, uncontrolled anger sparking in his eyes. "I saw how that savage leader, Dancing Fish, smiled and nodded at you." Jacob spit onto the ground next to her. "And then Minuit chooses to get advice from you and not me?" He was fuming. "I am your husband. Or have you forgotten that?"

He lurched forward and struck her again on the same side, this time with an open hand. But the pain was just as intense.

"Stop it!" she screamed, covering her face with both arms. "Calm down."

She peeked out from between her arms and saw that he had slumped to the floor on the other side of the hut. He had found one of his hidden liquor bottles and was guzzling from it.

"Spending too much time with savages . . ." he muttered to himself, finishing the bottle and throwing it at her. It barely missed her head.

She knew she had only minutes before he would either be unconscious or fighting her again. She grimaced while she tried to speak softly. Her mouth was swollen and each word hurt. "Please, I'm doing what I can to make peace with these natives. The Willow woman can help us. She already has by giving me important information. And those two girls, they are bright and strong. And Dancing Fish—"

"Don't mention that man's name to me!" Jacob slurred. "He's their new leader, and he is close to that evil High Limb." He put his hands over his eyes, trying to stop the spinning that he was surely experiencing. "That giant attacked me, and if he's not careful, I'll strike back in a way he'll never forget."

She tasted blood in her mouth and tried to speak without anger. "Look, whether we like it or not, we have to live with these people. This is *their* island, after all. They were here first."

"But not for long, if I have my way," he said, trying to keep his body upright.

"Well, whatever happens, we have to weed the new corn and the oats. And plant those tobacco seedlings from Dancing—"

He jumped to his feet. "I told you not to mention his name!"

Not knowing how he had the strength to remain standing,

she watched in disbelief when Jacob staggered to the tobacco plants—graciously given to them by Dancing Fish as a way to expand their farming and livelihood—and started trampling on them with his boots.

"Oh no," was all she could manage while her drunk husband crushed and crunched every last one of the tiny tobacco seedlings into the dirt floor.

Fifty-nine

HIGH LIMB NUZZLED IN THE ARMS OF TWO BUDS. THIS WAS his favorite time of the day, the early morning hours before the sun was up. Except for the gentle breathing of his wife and the occasional snoring of his nearby children, all was quiet in the longhouse and also outside. The insects had not started, and the birds—

The birds! Where he would normally be hearing the distinctive sounds of the chickadees, there was, instead, complete silence. Something was wrong.

He slipped out from under the sleeping skins and silently pulled on his moccasins and hunting shirt. He crawled to the longhouse opening and lifted the flap just a crack to peek outside. As his eyes adjusted to the dim grayness of the morning fog, rolling close to the ground, he saw them.

He counted two hands of them, crouched low to take advantage of the fog. They were moving in from the forest and across the cornfields. The perimeter scout, whose job it was to alert them to any enemies, was either asleep or already dead.

"What is it?" asked a sleepy Two Buds.

"Shhh," he whispered, putting a finger to her lips. "Gather the children, go into the corner, and cover yourself with skins and furs." He handed her the short sword from Minwee. "Hold this firmly with both hands," he instructed her. "If an enemy comes in, jab it into him with all your strength. And keep jabbing." She nodded, her eyes wide with alarm.

He reached for his bow and quiver, then grabbed the heavy mattock. He would now find out if this settler tool would also make a good weapon. As a last thought, he wedged one of the horse charms into the top of his apron. Its heavy steel could come in handy.

Staying low and crawling on all fours to the other longhouses, he first woke Big Shadow, then Rock, and finally Dancing Fish, quickly explaining the threat.

Gaining two more warriors, they formed a silent line between the edge of the cornfields and the longhouses. The corn was barely to their waists, but with them squatting down, it made a screen in the fog that only seemed to thicken. And there was still a finger of time before the sun rose.

High Limb, an arrow nocked in his bow, watched carefully while the moving shapes approached. Then one of the raiders suddenly stood upright. He immediately recognized the short, muscular form of Gowanie. The Canarsees!

"Now!" the enemy leader shouted, and all the raiders stood and started running toward them and screaming out a war cry.

The War Chief moved his open hands rapidly downward as he looked to both sides and mouthed the silent words to his fighters: *wait for my signal.*

When the fastest of the enemy was no more than five body lengths away, High Limb sprang to his feet, pulled his bowstring, and released his arrow. It struck the man running toward him square in the chest and dropped him like a stone. At the same time, High Limb shouted, "Kill the raiders!"

From either side of him, his men unleashed their own arrows, and three more of the enemy fell to the ground.

Within moments, the warriors from both bands were on top of each other, locked in hand-to-hand battle. High Limb was trying to reach Gowanie, but another Canarsee, his face painted red and black, swung his war club at High Limb's head.

He ducked the blow and set upon the man with a fury. Rolling over corn stalks, they punched and battered each other with their hardened fists.

With the man finally under him and a knee to his chest, High Limb pulled out his horse charm, raised it high over his head, and drove it deep into the man's skull, splitting it open.

Pushing the body aside and catching his breath, High Limb watched as Gowanie stood over a kneeling Big Shadow, who had blood pouring from a deep gash across his face. The invader raised his long knife, ready to strike, but instead, he stopped to look over at High Limb.

They were only a couple of body lengths apart, so he could hear Gowanie's words clearly. "We have weapons, too," he said, smirking. "And they're not toys."

He was laughing when he turned back and slit Big Shadow's throat from ear to ear, then pushed his dying body to the ground with his foot.

Roaring with anger, High Limb picked up the mattock and rushed toward Gowanie. But the leader was instantly surrounded by three of his warriors, clubs and knives raised, ready to defend him—so they didn't see the attack from both sides by Rock and Dancing Fish.

Using this distraction, High Limb wasted no time swinging his new weapon with all his strength at the raider closest to him. The steel blade struck hard and chopped the man nearly into two pieces at the waist.

The battle was tough and long, with clubs, knives, fists, and teeth all used in a fight to the death. Bones cracked, voices shrieked, and blood flowed freely over the carefully weeded planting rows.

When it was over, High Limb looked over at a bleeding but alive Dancing Fish and nodded. Three others from the band were also moving. The new Sachem signaled back. "Did we get them all?"

"Not quite all," High Limb said, indicating with his head.

The sun had just crested the eastern hills at the Hook and was outlining the running and limping forms of three of the invaders escaping toward the trees. They could see the squat Gowanie in the lead, carrying something over his back.

"Should we chase them?" Dancing Fish asked.

"Yes, but let's first survey our dead and damaged first. That'll spur us on."

Dancing Fish nodded, and they quickly checked over each other's bloody and sore bodies. They next walked the battleground and were shocked to see that, in addition to Big Shadow, Rock had also perished in the fight, his face smashed in by a club.

Both he and Dancing Fish spent a moment mourning their closest friends. These were their childhood companions. Even if they hadn't always liked each other—they had split into different factions early on—they were trusted allies and important members of the band. And, sadly, both men left behind wives and children. It was a shock to see them lying broken and lifeless in the dirt.

How many of the raiders do you count here?" asked Dancing Fish, looking at the enemy bodies.

"Six."

"Ten minus six is four," Dancing Fish said.

High Limb's throat tightened. "One's missing." He started running and yelled: "Check the longhouses. Hurry!"

High Limb burst into their living chamber and was relieved to see Two Buds and the children alive in the corner. His wife was frozen in position holding out the bloodied sword. On the floor in front of them lay the unmoving body of the missing Canarsee raider.

"You managed it well," he said, seeing the multiple stab wounds on the man.

"You said keep jabbing, and that's exactly what I did," she

said, a tense smile on her face.

He could only grin and cry at the same time as he hugged them all.

"And now Dancing Fish and I will hunt down the surviving dogs who did this."

▶◀

Dancing Fish sprinted along the paths consumed with rage and revenge. He had found Willow injured in the longhouse, her right arm cut deeply and bleeding, but alive. Her sister, Raspberry, had helped protect her, and no harm had come to the baby that he could see. The poor puppy was dead, its head crushed.

But the real horror was that the girls were gone.

"They took them!" Willow had howled before she collapsed in a heap of sobbing. "Go find them!" she bellowed while her sister tended to her.

Ignoring the cuts and stab wounds to his own arms and chest, Dancing Fish ran with a single focus: finding and bringing back Meekak and Sunshell. Glimpses of them being violated, beaten, or even sold as slaves flashed in front of his eyes, but he pushed the images away and ran even harder.

He had left High Limb so each could follow a different trail of the injured raiders, who had split up to confound them. He cursed the War Chief for saying the words that probably caused Gowanie to plan the attack—taunting him about horses and powerful weapons from the settlers—but at this point, it didn't matter who was to blame or why. He had only one consuming goal: find the girls.

Dancing Fish was running so fast he almost missed it—a piece of red that caught his eye when he sped past. He went back to the bush and reached for it. It was a bit of red ribbon with its ends frayed.

The girls were alive! And leaving him tracking signs. He had taught them how to track rabbits and turkeys, and now they were leaving him a trail to follow.

Hope filled his chest as he grabbed the piece of ribbon and studied the clear sky and the position of the sun. It was midday, and the fog had lifted. And he was traveling northeast. The invaders were heading to the waterway where they must have left their canoes for crossing over. They would have landed up the island near Shawkequa to avoid being spotted on their way to Werpoes.

He didn't have much time. Once back on Maspeth land, it would be harder to follow them. Or to catch them.

Holding tightly to the ribbon with one hand, he broke back into a full run, feeling neither fatigue nor injury. Nothing would stop him.

He quickly found more pieces of ribbon on the trail, both red and yellow. More clues! He was close.

Smelling the marsh and water first, he rounded a curve and saw them. The two raiders were struggling to hold onto the girls while at the same time trying to launch a canoe. The girls kicked and screamed with everything they had. Finally, one of the warriors punched both girls hard in the stomach, instantly bending them over and disabling them.

While one man steadied the canoe and tossed in the paddles, the other started dragging the girls, coughing and fighting for breath, to it.

This was his chance. With both men's backs to him, Dancing Fish rushed forward, crashing through the reeds. The men heard him at the same time and whirled around. The girls screamed out *"Father!"* and started to kick and claw at the warriors.

Dancing Fish splashed through the thigh-deep water and launched himself at the closest man, his right hand holding his longest steel knife. The man had pulled out his own knife, and soon they were swinging, punching, and grappling in the churning water.

He finally got behind the man and stabbed him repeatedly in the back. Then he slammed his enemy's head against the edge of the canoe. To finish him off, Dancing Fish turned the warrior around and drove his long blade deep into his stomach, pulling it up hard toward the heart. The man's eyes went wide and he coughed blood directly into Dancing Fish's face. He was soon dead.

Dancing Fish looked up to see the other man knock both girls unconscious and throw them into the canoe, which he was now desperately trying to get into, to paddle away.

Dancing Fish dove head-first into the shallow water in pursuit, swimming with all his power and experience. He caught up with the canoe and grasped its back edge—but just then, the warrior lifted his war club skyward.

"No!" Dancing Fish screamed before the man brought the club down hard on top of Meekak's head, shattering it and exposing the red and gray brain inside. Meekak let out a gurgling sigh as her body collapsed.

Then the man lifted the club again.

Dancing Fish jerked and screamed while he tried to tip the canoe with both hands. But it was too late. Sunshell's chest caved inward when the heavy club met it, her small breastbone and ribs crunching under the club's weight.

Crazed with fury, Dancing Fish flipped the canoe and catapulted the man into the water. Then he attacked him.

The warrior was strong, but he was no match for Dancing Fish, who was uncontrollable with wild, desperate energy. He was able to encircle the man with both his arms and legs, then roll him over to submerge him underwater. The man thrashed and struggled mightily, but Dancing Fish had spent his whole life in and under water, and he simply held on until the man stopped moving and was still.

As a final act of madness, Dancing Fish released the man, grabbed a reed from the water's surface, and rammed it with all his remaining strength into the dead man's eye, pushing it in so hard that it almost came out the opposite side of this skull.

In complete shock, Dancing Fish could only stare at the inert bodies of his two girls, floating face-down and beside each other in the undulating water. He stood immobile, his feet sinking in the mud, his mind frozen. Two of the most precious things in his life—his two little squirrels—had just been ripped from his heart.

▶◀

Dancing Fish carried the girls over his shoulder in an old woven sack the raiders had left in the canoe. It was somehow comforting to feel their limp bodies rubbing against his back. But he knew that the reality of what had just happened had not yet taken hold. They had a term for it: "Floating Over the Earth." Not being aware of the ground. Being separate from it and everything around you in the aftermath of great loss. Numb to the world.

And that's what he was as he walked slowly back to Werpoes. To face Willow with this dreadful turn of events.

When he approached a turn in the trail, he heard the familiar whistle enter his foggy mind. It was the safety signal of the Manahate band.

High Limb emerged from the trees and came up to him, his eyes on the sack.

"Is it—?" he started.

"Yes," said Dancing Fish, carefully putting the sack down and sitting next to it, sobbing. He started to reach out to touch it but pulled his hand away. He couldn't face the truth of what had happened. The two shining lights in his eyes had been extinguished, their bodies now crumpled together in a piece of cloth. He needed to get his mind off of it.

"Did you catch Gowanie?" he asked High Limb, not even caring about the answer.

"No. The little Matantu Spirit escaped. But someday I will see him again. And then . . ."

He nodded absently, not paying attention. He briefly thought of lashing out at High Limb and blaming him for the raid, but he had no energy for it.

"I think we should press them on the defensive alliance in the land negotiations," High Limb said from some far-off place. "When do you think . . ."

High Limb's words evaporated from his hearing, like snow-flakes falling on a fire. Dancing Fish had no ability to think about this now. He needed to get back to Willow—to give her the news that would surely destroy her.

Sixty

MARIE'S HEAD WAS SPINNING. THE CANARSEE RAID HAD shocked everyone. And to think that if she had been at their farm when they had come through, plundering and burning much of it, she would have suffered terribly at their hands. It was only luck that she was at the village and that Jacob had wandered off in a drunken stupor in search of firewood.

But the raid had served one useful purpose: to move both sides to complete the land agreement on this Sunday of the summer solstice, June 21.

Although still morning, the heat and humidity could not have been more oppressive. The sky was gray with it. Even the insects seemed too overcome to hum at full strength. And the dreadful mosquitoes were simply waiting somewhere in the shade for a later opportunity.

It was turning into a real spectacle. More Indians than Marie had ever seen at once were converging on the meeting place under the same tall oak that marked where the two trails met.

Paying little attention to the heat, the natives were clothed in their finest feathers, skins, and dresses, most decorated with elaborate patterns of shells and beads. Some wore shiny gorgets at their throats or dangling copper from their ears. Many had their faces painted with strange stripes and spots in white, black, yellow, and blue.

The settlers were also dressed in their best doublets, breeches, linens, and dresses, but they looked dull in comparison to the colorful natives.

The fire pit and the dirt around it had been swept clean; there was no need for a fire today. Shade was what everyone sought. The long branches of the giant oak provided it for the main party of leaders, but the other witnesses were on their own to find a cool spot for sitting or standing under less grand trees. Some of the younger natives were even perched high in the branches to escape the heat shimmering from the dusty clearing, or maybe just to get a better view of this historic moment.

The two sides had bargained back and forth for the past two weeks. There were visits by the leaders to both villages with plenty of arguing and squabbling over what would constitute a fair and reasonable agreement.

Dancing Fish was clearly troubled during the long debates. The pain from losing his daughters was etched on his grave face. Marie knew that look and understood it well, having lost her own child. On top of that, he was constantly distracted by trying to care for Willow, who had been seriously injured and was also grieving, but who was also ready to give birth at any moment.

Dancing Fish did his best amid these pressures and the ever-present heartache. He was the Sachem of the Manahates, and he stoically tried to represent his people in the negotiations.

It was decided that all compensations from the Indians for thefts, animal killings, or debts incurred from gambling or drinking would be forgiven and included in the overall bargain. This enraged Jacob, of course, but Director-General Minuit threatened to banish him from the colony if he didn't accept it.

A defensive alliance was pushed hard by both High Limb and Dancing Fish. And in the aftermath of the Canarsee raid, where not only hers but other settler farms had been ransacked or destroyed, the director-general had no alternative but to agree to this term.

Then there were the trade goods and tools to add to the contract price. The knives, hatchets, axes, awls, and kettles originally offered by Verhulst were still included, with only the exact number of each fought over. There were also a few new and unusual requests by the natives.

High Limb had not only demanded a horse as part of the trade—and a plow, which they would be taught to use—but he also focused on "the shoes of the horses," as if they were especially valuable in some way. Minuit was only too happy to agree to eight horseshoes to go with the one horse, four sheep, and one cow they could offer.

But High Limb had drawn the line on pigs. "None of those filthy animals," he said over and over.

By Marie's counting, it all came to a value of sixty guilders in goods and tools for the natives. There was general agreement that this was fair to both sides.

But the main sticking point had continued to be the idea of "selling" the island. Regardless of how hard Director-General Minuit pressed his position on this point, Dancing Fish would not change his mind. Land was to be shared, not given up entirely.

The colonists could clear and settle the land they needed, but the Indians would also maintain their own. This was probably the most important negotiating point of all, and Dancing Fish never wavered on it. The director-general—and the Company—would simply have to accept it if they wished to come to agreement with the natives.

Once, when she was alone with Minuit, Marie had asked, "Land is land, and it has to belong to someone, doesn't it?" He had explained that in some cases, as with the legal idea of *usufruct*, land could be shared and used by others.

"But who will *own* the land?" she asked.

Minuit grinned and raised his eyebrows high. "We will."

The formal ceremony started when the sun reached its peak. Marie could sense the symbolic moment of change. The calendar's passing to shorter days would also match a shift in the colony's future.

The director-general had been under enormous pressure from the Company to conclude a bargain for land with the Indians, and he had finally succeeded where Director Verhulst had not. Minuit had even invited the disgraced Willem Verhulst and his ever-complaining wife, Phaebae, to attend, although they did not have a place of importance at the event—a point not overlooked by the scowling Phaebae.

For the occasion, an empty barrel, to function as a table for signing the contract, stood upright a short distance from the oak's massive trunk, and two sets of logs had been rolled in to form a V-shape that flared out on each side of the barrel. This is where the leaders of both groups sat.

On the Dutch side were Director-General Minuit, Sheriff Lampo, Verbruggen, Jacob, and Marie. On the other side: Dancing Fish, High Limb, Willow's aunt, Wawamis—the ranking matron—and two new faces. These were the leaders from the island's two other groups Marie had heard of but never seen before. And there were native priests and Holy Men aplenty, but they sat on the ground near the end of the native's logs along with other clan and family matrons from the three island tribes.

And as was now typical and expected, Dancing Fish gave a running translation of the different languages of the speakers from his prime seat.

First came the obligatory gift exchange. The Indians had brought bags of dried corn and fish, and a bundle of the special tobacco cigarros. Director-General Minuit, already sweating in his heavy clothes, presented Dancing Fish with a fine steel hatchet and several Jew's harps. Seeing the puzzlement of the natives, Minuit attempted to make music with one, but his skill was so poor that everyone on both sides started laughing, and he finally gave it up, his face red with embarrassment.

Next came the prayers and invocations. The settlers still had no priest, so Minuit offered a short prayer entreating God's presence and calling for a successful conclusion to the event. The native priests then took advantage of their positions by droning on about spirit beings, prophecies, and other pagan concepts that had little meaning to any of the settlers.

Marie, quietly absorbing the activities of the two groups, noticed that whenever the priests spoke of a prophecy, Dancing Fish fingered the glass button he always wore around his neck. It seemed to be a charm of some sort. It was said that Hudson, himself, had given it to him when he was a child.

Then out came the ceremonial pipe and the ritual smoking of tobacco. The pipe passed from hand to hand, with each person puffing and muttering a few words. When it finally reached her, Marie took two puffs of the sweet blend, offered her thanks for being alive and being able to witness what she knew would be a turning point for the colony, and blew the smoke to the cloudless sky.

Marie hoped for short speeches while she fanned herself and felt the sweat trickling between her breasts. There had been so many discussions leading up to this day that there was not much left to say. Or so she thought. But their director-general couldn't help himself and pontificated endlessly about the importance of this and that. The words barely registered with Marie, who kept busy swatting away the always ambitious flies.

Then it was Dancing Fish's turn. He stood and the murmuring stopped. The only sounds came from the birds and the far-off rumbling of waves crashing against rocks at the point.

The elegant native wore only his white breechcloth and the same beautiful, feathered cloak tied around his neck. His dark skin and the long hair of his high status glistened, and every-one's eyes were turned to him while he spoke in a firm voice that echoed from the surrounding tree trunks. Whatever loss or turmoil he felt was well hidden.

"At first, I was against this agreement," he said, speaking each line in his much-improved Dutch and then in his own language. "The land—this island—is our summer home. It is where we plant and harvest our crops. Where we fish and hunt. Where we gather our berries and oysters." He looked down at the ground. "Where we bury those we love."

His head sunk lower for a moment, then raised, his eyes circling the crowd.

"But it is the will of our people to have this agreement," he said, looking at the director-general. "To live in peace with you and your people."

Everyone could see the tears in his eyes. He was doing what his people wanted, but it seemed to Marie that he did not, him-self, want it. She had watched while he had, during the contract discussions, stricken through each instance of the word *sell* and written in the word *share*. Every *purchase* became *trade, acquire* became *use; ownership, custody; possession, holding*. Minuit was initially against these changes, but he had no option. And in private, he boasted that these changes would do nothing. The Company would not bow to the words of Indians over their own claims and desires.

Finally, it was time for the signing.

Director-General Minuit stepped to the barrel with the vellum contract, a goose quill, and a bottle of black ink. Standing over the barrel, he looked over the crowd, nodding for effect, then signed his name with a flourish at the bottom of the agreement. He left the vellum and writing implements on the barrel and stepped away, allowing Lampo his turn.

Once all from their side had signed, it went to the natives. Dancing Fish shook his head and waved up High Limb, who awkwardly signed with an *X* in a huge scrawl. Then followed Willow's aunt and the two other Sachems, who were even more clumsy in signing their *X*'s.

At last, it was Dancing Fish's turn. He walked up behind the barrel, looked down at the contract, then hesitated, seeming unsure. He lifted his amber eyes to look directly at Marie.

She smiled at him and waited for his smile in return. But none came. Only a vacant look, on a face empty of emotion.

Then he dipped the quill, scribbled something, and quickly sat back down.

It was done. They had bought the island of Mannahatta.

▶◀

Dancing Fish walked back to the village without speaking. Others were jabbering about the tools and trade goods and what they would do with them, but he was in his own world, merely putting one foot in front of the other. Wondering about what they had just done, and what it would mean for the Manahate band. And for the other bands.

Could he have gotten more in the agreement? Could he have stopped it completely? Shreds of visions and dreams careened inside his head. He didn't know what to feel.

"Sachem!" came the pressing small voice. "Sachem!" It was one of the young curing women. No more than a girl, really—the older curers and healers had mostly died off in the fevers.

"What is it, little one?" he asked. "What's so urgent?"

"It's Willow. You must come quickly."

A fear like he had never felt shot through him and hollowed out his stomach. Willow. The baby!

He ran back at full speed and ducked into the longhouse. He made his way through the main room where a small crowd waited and went into their private chamber.

The first thing he saw in the dim light was the baby, being

cleaned by one of the healers. It was a boy, and he let loose a piercing shout. His heart leapt at the sight of the boy, but it fell straight down like a rock when he saw Willow. She was on the sleeping platform, moaning. The smell of vomit was strong.

He knelt next to her and tried to get her attention, without success. She was taking rapid breaths and pulling every skin and fur on the bed around her. Her eyes were closed, and she was shivering and sweating at the same time. And mumbling words he couldn't understand.

"What's wrong with her?" he asked the oldest curer, who knelt next to Willow, feeling her forehead. "Is it the Beast Fever?"

"Not that. It's the other kind."

"What other kind?"

"From the injury." She opened the fur, and he could see the angry red swelling that consumed her upper arm. "It can happen like this," she said. "When someone is wounded. Or distressed. And she is both," she said, indicating the baby.

"And the cures?" he asked, panicking with the worst of thoughts.

"We've tried them all." The woman looked into his eyes. "You must prepare yourself."

Dazed, he put his left hand on Willow's head and his right on her shoulder. He could feel both the heat and the agitation coming from her.

Suddenly, she opened her eyes to him and shouted, "Meekak! Sunshell!"

He sighed. "No, it's me, your husband, Dancing Fish. The girls are fine," he lied.

She closed her eyes and started shaking and mumbling again.

"Husband," she said finally without opening her eyes.

He reached to one of her hands, cold like snow, and squeezed it. "I'm here."

Her words came out in pieces, between short breaths and shivers.

"Promise me."

"Anything."

"Promise me you'll watch over the People."

"I will."

"You belong to them now. You are Sachem."

"I know."

She shuddered. "And protect our girls and our son. No matter what."

He held her trembling hand. "No matter what."

She rolled onto her back and started moaning again.

Before the second sunset after the Turning of the Days, Willow began her journey to join the stars.

Sixty-one

End of July, 1626

MARIE WAITED ON THE ROCKY BEACH WITH THE OTHERS AND watched the ship's launch approach. The sun bore down relentlessly while a stiff wind created whitecaps on the narrow strait that separated them from the opposite shore. They were around the tip of the island where it flattened slightly and started its contour back to the north. Some optimistically called this area of beach and water "the harbor," which only made her laugh.

When would they ever build a proper dock? It had been more than a year since their arrival, and there was still no easy way for the ships to unload. They used small boats that ferried in and out and skidded up the pebbly beach, only to have passengers get their feet wet and sometimes twist their ankles in the holes between the rocks.

They were the official welcome committee—the council. And with them was the new man: Isaack de Rasière, the province's first secretary and commissary. He had arrived while the director was upriver and would be working as his assistant.

Director-General Minuit had wasted no time after the land agreement signing. He had immediately left to travel up Hudson's river to gather all the settlers he could locate and convince them to move down to their little village at the southern end of the island. This was now the official center of New Netherland. And with an honorable and grand new name: *New Amsterdam.*

Marie could make out the silvered head of Minuit at the bow of the launch, which was filled to overflowing. Seagulls and other birds screeched and dove around the boat, no doubt sensing these were newcomers who might throw up a morsel for them to fight over.

As usual, Jacob was irritated. "Just what we need," he snarled. "More people to look out for and make our lives complicated."

"But also more people for our oats and tobacco," co-councilor Tonis Verbruggen said. "And for your rot-gutting oat spirits," he added. The brewing of liquor from sprouted grain was now an ongoing enterprise for many, including Verbruggen, which was a constant complaint from Jacob. He felt that he was the pioneer of this effort, and only he should be doing it.

"It's only *your* spirits that rot the gut, Tonis," Jacob countered. "And I'm still waiting for you to pay me for the recipe."

"What? Pay you for a way to make alcohol from grain that any idiot knows?!" He poked Jacob in the arm. "You're a fool if you think that."

Jacob slapped his hand away and started to swing when De Rasière grabbed Jacob's arm.

"Stop this bickering," De Rasière snapped. "No one should be wasting time on spirits when there's plenty more important work to do. The making of alcohol drinks and imbibing is not on the approved list for this colony."

Jacob scoffed. "The *approved list*. Typical from a man who knows nothing but numbers. We'll be out there sweating while you're sitting in the counting house doing what?"

"Counting," De Rasière said defiantly, staring right back at Jacob. The secretary was oddly clean-shaven and wearing spectacles. And with a receding hairline, he looked older than his thirty years. "It's my job," he continued, "and you would do well to keep that in mind as I track the accountings."

"Well, you just keep yourself busy doing that," Jacob said, sneering and walking away.

Marie stepped forward. "I apologize for my husband, Meneer De Rasière. He has his own mind, and usually speaks it."

He looked at her and attempted a warm smile that was anything but, although it did show off the large gap between his front teeth. "You need to remind your husband that this colony is an enterprise, not a wild place without rules."

She smirked inwardly. That was exactly what New Amsterdam was becoming: a wild place full of misfits and individualists. Maybe New Amsterdam was officially a company town, but in reality, it was a messy community, an odd mixture of people looking out for themselves. There was an adventurous feeling of self-sufficiency and initiative about the place, and the people—who, more and more, were coming from different places and speaking different languages—all had different ideas of what they wanted this colony to be.

Minuit joined them on the beach, and the launch headed back to ferry more settlers from ship to shore. After quick welcomes, De Rasière introduced himself and handed over a packet of papers to the director-general. "My orders for assisting you," he said in explanation, bowing his head slightly. Then he looked to the crowded ship and added, "I see you've made a convincing argument to have the colonists join us on the island."

Director-General Minuit nodded and appraised his new assistant from top to bottom before giving him his first order. "I want a plan by tomorrow for how we are to feed, house, and settle 100 more of our people."

Minuit threw the papers back at De Rasière and turned to walk away. "I'm tired. I need a drink."

▶◀

Dancing Fish knew that the Souls of the girls, and now Willow, were traveling to the Sky World, if they had not already arrived. But sitting by their graves at the burial ground north of the Great Pond—his face blackened in sorrow, breathing in the smoke from the fire he always made, and talking to their curled-up cold bodies—gave him comfort.

The tears that streaked his face came less regularly, but the grief seemed always present. He frequently found himself filling his head with visions of them together: picking strawberries, laughing, or telling jokes around the cooking fire. And when he dreamed at night, it was often of making love to Willow.

"We're almost ready to harvest the tobacco," he said out loud to her while he threw bits of last season's crop on the small fire. "And the corn is up to my head. I'm not sure there will be enough hands to do the work, but we'll do the best we can. And at least I'm not completely alone in the living chamber," he added. "I have Little Perch to remind me of happier days." He let the smoke waft over him and looked up at the summer sky with its puffy white clouds, painfully remembering the cloud-guessing game with the girls.

He tried to smile. "Little Perch is a good boy and so full of energy, just like his sisters. He has your bright eyes and already your long black hair. The old women who are left say it's a good sign. A sign of a long life." He pondered the twist of that statement, considering where he was sitting and who he was talking to. "Thankfully, both his eyes and skin are dark. I'm not sure I could stand being reminded each day of the whiteness that moves through his blood. And mine." He took a deep breath. "And, honestly, I feel that white part of me leaving. Like a sickness that is slowly forgotten.

"Raspberry and Wawamis watch over the boy. They love him nearly as much as I do. Raspberry has found another new mother to give him her breast, and with no living uncle, your aunt fills that role. And sometimes even High Limb comes around to play with him as a man."

He allowed himself a half-smile. "High Limb and I are much closer now. No longer the rivals of the past. Friends, even.

"And we both understand what Owl told me long ago: that the visitors are the true enemy of us all—even more than the Canarsee or the Iroquois. But the white settlers are not a regular enemy. There are no clear lines of battle. At least not yet. Instead, they have a way of slowly pressing against us, day by day, like a stream that eventually cuts a groove through the rock. You can't always see it, but then afterward you look back and wonder: how and when did that happen?"

He sighed. "Mar-ee was right. They want what we have. Especially the land. And there are many more of them now. Always more, coming in ships that bring them to Kapsee.

"The little village is growing with the constant building of their strange houses. And all these settlers need room to live and grow their crops. So they take what they can from us. Any abandoned house or field is seized, most times without even asking. They just *take*."

He leaned forward. "You are wondering about the gifts and tools?" He shook his head and snorted. "Yes, those wonderful gifts. Some trade them back to the Whites for the burning drink or for duffel cloth to make blankets and sleeping skins.

"And remember the horse, sheep, and cow? Well, we ate the sheep and the cow. There are too many who are hungry. And the taste was good!

"The horse—and they are not Holy Dogs, I can tell you that—is still with us. He pulls the plow when we clear more land, which isn't often, and I've learned how to sit on his back. Oh, it's such a thrill. Almost as good as swimming, which I continue to do around the Point. But it's so busy now with all the ships and boats. Kapsee used to be a place to be alone with my Manitto perch and the oysters, but now I keep running into settlers wherever I turn. So I stay close to Werpoes more. Tending to the crops."

He put more dried strawberries on the grave mounds. "So we're still here, my lovely Willow and dear Meekak and

Sunshell." He glanced at the small mound that held the puppy's body next to that of his old friend, Kong. "And you, too, little Run-Run. But there are fewer of us. And so many of them."

He hung his head and ran a hand through his hair, as if smoothing his thoughts. "Honestly, I'm not sure of what to do anymore. I was so careful to change the words in the agreement, but it has little effect on them and their hunger for the land."

He decided it was time to do it. He took hold of the glass button strung around his neck and pulled hard. The thong snapped and he held the button up high in his hand. He spoke to it. "The great glass button," he said. "You were the symbol of the Fourth Fire Prophecy. You represented the great question at the time of Hudson: *Are the Visitors from the East good or bad for the People?* My task was to find out, remember? All the years of holding you and trying to determine the answer from you: good or bad? Are we to be brothers with these strangers or not?

"Well, I've had enough time with you. Years of holding you in my man's apron or having you bang against my chest. Waiting for an answer that I now know."

He spit on the dirty, four-holed button and rubbed off as much dried grease as he could, letting the sun glint from it. Then he placed it on top of Willow's grave. "I'm finished with the wondering," he said with a louder voice than needed.

"Well, it's about time."

A surprised Dancing Fish turned to the familiar voice. It was High Limb. "How long have you been listening?"

"I heard the very end."

"I thought you liked these people," said Dancing Fish. "Wanted what they had."

"I *only* wanted what they had. I never liked them. In fact, I hate them. If I could kill them all, I would. But it's too late for that now."

"Much too late," Dancing Fish agreed, then he looked up at his friend. "Although there is one . . ."

Sixty-two

HIGH LIMB HAD HEARD THE SOUND ALL DAY WHILE HE hunted. With one doe and one buck down, it was time to find out what was causing it.

"Finish gutting these two," he instructed one of his young warriors, "then take them back to the village for butchering." He pointed to Green Leaf, the one who had gambled away his moccasins, and said, "Follow me. I want to see what this noise is."

They walked silently through the trees, arrows nocked, the full heat of summer pressing on them from all sides. The closer they got, the quieter were the calls of birds and the whining of insects. And the louder the strange sound.

They suddenly stood at the edge of a clearing where there had been none before. This was the hunting and gathering land of his family lineage, and yet, here in front of him were white settlers making a clearing! Trees were down, with cut branches scattered over a wide area. What was once a fine canopy of green leaves over sturdy trunks was now open to the sky.

He motioned to Green Leaf to take a few steps back with him into the shadows. He wanted to inspect and understand what he was seeing.

He counted three of the Whites. All had their shirts off— something rare for them—and their cloud-white skin was already turning red from the sun. The noise had stopped, and they were picking up branches and piling them to one side.

They joked and laughed with each other and stopped frequently to wipe the sweat from their faces with cloths tied around their necks.

Then two of the men leaned over and lifted a long piece of shiny metal with a handle on each end. High Limb listened carefully while they spoke.

"Keep the saw level this time, you idiot," said one. "No twisting. And keep the movement steady. Push, pull. Push, pull. Is it so hard to understand? And you," he said, pointing to the third man, "keep those wedges coming so we don't bind the kerf."

High Limb knew the voice of the man speaking. It was Jay-kub. He had not recognized him without his shirt, but now he saw the thin body and his thick beard, and he heard the angry way he spoke to the others.

But what he saw next almost stopped his heart. The two men stood on both sides of his Guardian Tulip Tree and were preparing to use the metal to cut into it. They were going to cut down the sacred tree!

"Follow me!" High Limb shouted to Green Leaf as he leapt into the clearing and sprinted toward the men. While he ran he released an arrow that struck the wide tree just above the men's heads. They immediately stopped their cutting, dropped the long metal tool, and turned to see where the arrow had come from.

High Limb came to a halt two body lengths away from the closest man, in a position to see all three. Keeping his eyes on them, he motioned for Green Leaf to move around his right side. With both bowstrings taut, they had the men covered and could respond with speed.

"What's this about?" Jay-kub demanded, aiming his question at High Limb. "Why are you interrupting us, you—" He stopped himself, realizing who he was addressing.

High Limb took a moment to stare into the challenging

eyes of the ugly man. He felt like striking down this hateful being right on the spot, but he needed to think this through. Dancing Fish always told him to think before acting, but it was so hard. He took a deep breath through his nose to calm himself. "Who gives you permission to cut trees, clear more land?"

"Your land?" Jay-kub replied, his voice giving away his hatred for anything to do with the People. "It's our land. We have an agreement." He smirked. "Which you, yourself, signed. Or have you forgotten?"

Stay calm. Steady. "The agreement is that we share the land. We have our land, you have yours." He glanced at the ground. "This is our land. You can have land to north, not here."

He could see Jay-kub thinking, putting together in his mind what he would say next. So he used the pause to explain even more and get to the point.

"Do you know what this tree is?" High Limb asked in his softest voice, trying his hardest to control his anger.

"This tree?" Jay-kub pointed to it. "This exact tree?"

"Yes. This tree."

The vile man stepped back and looked up. "It's a tall one. Tall like you." He chuckled at his clever joke and the others joined him.

High Limb waited for the laughter to end. "Is more than tall tree. This tree is named Tulip Tree. It is straightest tree in forest. We use tree to make canoes. Do you know this?" He was speaking in the voice of a teacher, as he had heard Elders speak all his life. But he knew he was no teacher. He was a hunter and a War Chief. A man of movement, not of words.

"Congratulations!" Jay-kub said. "You can make a canoe from this tree. And I'm sure there are many of these trees, all good for making your canoes." He grinned at High Limb. "But this *particular* tree—this Tulip Tree—is now in our way, and we are going to cut it down." He leaned over to pick up his end of the thin metal. "With this saw."

"Wait!" High Limb shouted, and the three white men stopped.

"There is more you not know about this tree."

"And what's that?" Jay-kub asked, obviously growing weary of the conversation.

High Limb released his right hand from the bowstring and moved it slowly to the handle of the sword. He already knew how this would end. A War Chief always knew.

"This is Guardian Spirit tree for me," he said to the skinny white man he hated.

"Your what?" Jay-kub asked, his eyes no longer laughing but drifting down to the sword that hung from High Limb's waist.

"I teach you now, settler. Pay attention."

High Limb nodded to Green Leaf and started to walk very slowly around the third man and toward Jay-kub. He talked as he walked.

"When we are to be a man, we must find our Guardian Spirit. It acts like a guide for our lives. Protects us. Shows us the right way. Our Manitto."

Jay-kub sneered. "This is nonsense. This—"

"Quiet!" High Limb said forcefully, his eyes narrowing and focusing on the face of this dreadful man. "I speak. You listen."

He continued, all the while moving imperceptibly closer to Jay-kub.

"As boys, we receive our Guardian Spirit in dreams or in visions. For some, it is a bear or wolf. For others, a fish or bird. For one boy, it was even the lowly ant."

"An ant?" Jay-kub howled with laughter. "You have an ant for a Guardian Spirit?"

High Limb stepped closer. "Not the ant for me." He tightened his grip on the sword handle. "Guardian Spirit for me"— he looked down into the man's eyes and inclined his head slightly—"is this tree." He jerked his head toward it. "Sacred tree. This one. And you cut it. Which means you cut me."

No one moved and no sound was heard for the longest time. Then—

"To your muskets, men!"

Jay-kub had barely taken two steps before High Limb closed the gap and without hesitancy drove the blade of the sword hard into the man's back. So hard and so deep that the handle was buried in the sweaty white skin on one side while the bloody point protruded out the other.

Jay-kub landed with a thud on the thick leaf mold of the ground.

High Limb could hear shouting and screaming, but only after he heard Jay-kub's final death breath did he look back to see Green Leaf standing with his bloodied knife over the two white men who were still alive but moaning and writhing on the ground.

Dancing Fish will not like this was the only thought that entered the War Chief's head.

▶◀

Dancing Fish walked slowly back to the village from the burial site. The lowering sun splintered through the trees and lit up leaves and patches of ground. It reminded him of how much there was to do with the crops. But he was in no mood to do it. He felt drained. And alone. Without Willow and his girls, he was heartsick. And with no button hanging at his chest, he felt even more naked.

Pull yourself out of this sorrow, he urged himself while he followed a small path, matching his footsteps to the sound of a woodpecker busy tapping high in a tree. The sharp sounds gradually woke him from his numbed unhappiness. He remembered Little Perch and also what he had promised Willow. To watch over the People and to protect their son.

But how? The band was small now, and everyone had his or

her own concerns. Each was protecting self and family, trading and dealing with the new white settlers for his own purposes. The sense of the Manahate band being a community—all working together—seemed to be disappearing.

And he was the Sachem. He was their leader. Why was he failing? Why had he let things become so splintered? The land agreement had done little to stop the settlers from doing as they pleased: clearing more land, building more houses. What had he really accomplished?

Dancing Fish pondered these confusing thoughts while he walked south.

He passed a dead oak lying on its side when he heard the buzzing. He stopped to listen and watch. The end of the old log was flared open, and a shaft of late sunlight lit up the bees flying in and out of it. He bent down very slowly to get a better view. He didn't dare to move more.

He could clearly see the honeycomb that the bees were building. He smelled it, too: earthy but sweet—the smell of life.

Then he spotted the big wasp. It was moving around the log's opening, inspecting, and chewing up a few single bees in the process. The other bees seemed to pay no attention.

This wasp was a scout. It would drop its scent and fly back to the nest to bring a swarm of wasps that would destroy the entire bee colony. At least, that was what was supposed to happen. But these bees had a different idea.

Dancing Fish watched with fascination as the bees crowding over the comb suddenly began wiggling and moving in a defined rhythm. It was like a wave passing through them. Then, without any warning, they massed into a group over the wasp and soon had it completely covered with their squirming bodies.

Some of the Elders and Matrons in the band thought the bees stung the wasp to death, but others believed that the bees heated up their prey with their body vibrations and basically cooked and suffocated the wasp. Whichever was the true reason, after some time these bees moved off the now-dead wasp. It would not be alerting any others.

Dancing Fish slowly backed away and was soon trotting down the path away from the bees. And thinking. Was this not a sign? A direct proof given to him by the Animal Spirits of how to protect the group by truly acting as one? Not as individuals following what tradition said was right for a hunter, a fisherman, a woman—but as one body, acting with the same goal in mind. Working together to protect each other.

Yes! That was the answer for the band facing the white settlers. To be more united, not less. And if sacrifice was required by some—like with the few bees—then sacrifice it would be.

He was feeling much better when he crossed over his corn-field and walked into the darkening village. Waiting for him at the central fire was High Limb, a look of deep concern on his face. His mouth was turned down, the space between his brows furrowed.

"*Hè-yó,*" Dancing Fish called out in greeting.

High Limb grunted in response. "We need to talk. Something serious has happened."

Something more serious than everything else? Dancing Fish gestured to one of the logs ringing the fire that was being built by a young fire tender, its sparks flying up to meet the night sky and the first stars. "Tell me."

He listened carefully while High Limb explained what had happened with Jay-kub. This was a likely outcome that everyone could see coming. Eventually. But why now, in the midst of so much bleakness and struggle? The deliberate killing of a white settler—

They both heard the unmistakable sound at the same time and looked to the edge of the clearing. The man Lampo, behaving like a soldier leader, was marching toward them with four more men. Each carried a musket and a determined look.

"You," Lampo said, pointing at High Limb with the end of

his musket. The fire flickered in his bearded face when he stood on the opposite side of it. "Did you kill the settler named Jaykub, married to the woman Mar-ee?"

High Limb nodded without pause. "I did."

Lampo stepped around the fire with two of the men. "Under lawful authority, and in the name of Pieter Minuit, Director-General of New Netherland, I arrest you for murder."

Dancing Fish placed a hand on High Limb's shoulder and stood, slowly, all the while keeping his eyes on the muskets. "Then you arrest me, too," he said, carefully watching the man.

Lampo frowned. "Why? Why you, too?"

"Because I was also there."

High Limb gave him a puzzled look as the men closed in on them. But all Dancing Fish could see were the bees, united and working together.

Sixty-three

THE THUNDERSTORM CAUGHT HER BY SURPRISE. MARIE HAD learned that storms usually swept over the island in the afternoon during the summer months, but this one came in early. It was hard enough to load Jacob's body into the cart by herself, but doing it in the rain made it that much worse. With every thunderclap, the new horse either bucked or kicked—which made the cart tip and pitch.

Wearing the large deerskin from the natives for a rain cover over her black mantle—the only thing she had to signify her mourning—she finally managed to get Jacob's body, wrapped in a double layer of linen and duffel cloth, into the slippery bed of the cart and tied down for the journey.

The rain had eased off to a light drizzle by the time she snapped the whip, and the horse started off on the slow walk to New Amsterdam. She stood in the front of the cart, the reins in her hands, the steady plodding of the horse's feet concentrating her mind on the fight it was having with itself.

The man she had married was lying dead behind her. Murdered. Someone had to be punished. On the other hand, whatever had provoked the natives to kill him was probably of his own doing. By most measures, he was not a good man. He had beaten her more than once. He cheated the Indians every chance he got. The man deserved it.

But Jacob was her husband. He had helped get her to the

island. And he was one of the settlers—on the council, even. They were under contract to the Company and obligated to work for its advancement. Creating a thriving colony on the island was the primary goal.

And though she wanted to believe they could share the land in peace with the natives, she doubted it could really happen. And that was despite the agreement they had all signed to accomplish just that. She believed it was a fairy tale. Whether they knew it or not, the Manahates were surrendering control of the land they so treasured.

Yet . . .

As much as she needed to be on the side of the settlers, she also wanted to help the Indians. She liked them. Even if they ran around half-naked and practiced their strange beliefs. Making an offering before an animal is killed or a tree is cut? Believing in strange spirits and not the Holy Trinity? Despite how much she tried, she could not understand that a rock had a spirit to be regarded.

But with few exceptions, the natives were good and trustworthy people. Could she say the same of her own? Really? So many were barely tolerable. Braggarts, drunkards, brawlers, and self-interested connivers. Like Jacob.

The natives she had come to know best were not like that. Maybe the real questions were: who did she mourn more? Was it her husband? Or was it poor Willow and her two beautiful girls she had attached herself to, now all dead? Who would she grieve the most? Who did she truly miss? Could she answer without hesitation?

Apparently not.

And what of the leaders? Which one did she want to follow? The obvious answer was Director-General Minuit and the others with the Company. She was still legally their employee. But the natural leader, the one who spoke with such honesty and caring, and who made her small life more pleasurable, was

Dancing Fish. The savage.

Although she felt sad and bewildered about her own life and her future, she was even more pessimistic about the future of the natives. What would happen to them? Maybe they could just give up the lower end of the island and move elsewhere. There seemed enough room, either farther north on the island or even off it.

With tall trees on both sides of the path as witness, she made herself a promise to help the natives however she could, while still remaining loyal to her own people. She was not a native, and never could be. Even if she sometimes caught herself fantasizing about it, she was her father's daughter. She was a Boucher. From Liège and Amsterdam. A European.

Her place was with her people. But she would aid the Indians.

The rain had stopped when the path finally widened and the cart rumbled toward the fort. She could see the beginnings of the earthen berm that would be the fort's walls. A windmill was being erected just beyond to catch the gusts at the tip of the island. The gray sea churned with waves, but off in the distance the leaden skies were breaking to reveal streaks of blue.

She turned to the east in front of the fort and entered the village proper. Already, she could see more tree clearing and building along the strand. She passed the newly built stone counting house that was the Company's new office and storage center for pelts. Hogs and dogs roamed the open areas, now turned to mud by the rain. She heard sheep bleating and horses neighing, and the smell of manure mixed with the briny scent of the sea to form a potent aroma.

With a dead husband lying in the cart and a bustling little village forming all around her, she hoped to God that things would get better for everyone. And she meant *everyone* while she acknowledged those who stopped what they were doing to tip their heads or hats as she passed by.

"What's your plan?" asked High Limb.

"Plan?" Dancing Fish replied, trying to wiggle the rope that tightly bound his wrists to the post in the dark room. They were in the counting house, the only building made of stone in the settler's village. He had watched it being built and was impressed by its sturdiness. He had often dreamed of building such a house himself when he was younger, but he didn't see the purpose of it. Now he did. It not only stored the skins and furs brought in from trading, but he had heard a soldier call it a *jail*. A place to keep a person who went against the laws.

"You let yourself be taken with me for a reason," came High Limb's deep voice. "What is it?"

"Because we are the same, you and me."

"Why do you say that? I'm the one who killed the white man, not you."

"But we are both of the People. And we are both leaders. We should both set an example for the band. I've been thinking about this." He heard High Limb laugh even though he couldn't see him in the darkness. He was tied to a different post.

"You always surprise me with how crazy you are, Little Eel," High Limb said. "Always with your strange ideas. Or maybe it's your white blood. Is that what makes you so peculiar?"

"My white blood is gone. I no longer recognize it. It has left me just like steam leaves a boiling pot."

"So, you're not going to use your white blood to get us out of here?"

Dancing Fish smiled, even though his action couldn't be seen. "I don't need white blood to remove us from this place. I am the Dream Maker, the Inventor. I will find a way. Our time is not over yet. There is still work to do."

He could hear his old rival chuckle. "I admire your confidence. But how will you take the torture?"

"They won't torture us."

"No? All people torture their enemies or those who break their laws."

"Not these. They like the whipping post, or something they call the *pillory*, where they lock your head and hands in wood blocks. But mostly, they'll want compensation."

"Ah, like we do. Make payment to the living family for the loss of the dead." High Limb sighed. "But my family has nothing to pay. What then?"

"Then they hang you by the neck from a tree limb."

"And you'll be hanging beside me." High Limb laughed softly, enjoying this. "I'll finally be rid of you."

"Then our problems will be solved, and we'll be on our way to the Sky World to join our ancestors and loved ones."

They both laughed together. Two old rivals now becoming friends with their hands tied in a dark, damp room full of animal furs—Dancing Fish could pick out the distinct smells of beaver, otter, and mink—with the sound of wind and waves coming from outside the thick stone walls.

"Then I might as well give you this," High Limb said.

Dancing Fish felt something slip over his head. He knew instantly that it was the glass button on its thong. "But how—"

"These witless people don't know how to tie knots well. I slipped out of mine awhile ago and just wanted to see how long it would take you. Here—"

His wrists were quickly freed from their ropes, and he reached to touch the glass button. "How did you find this?"

"I saw it on Willow's grave and knew you'd need it back. A Dream Maker who invents the future cannot be without his prophecy charm."

Dancing Fish found High Limb's chest in the dark and patted it. Then he held the button in his hand, rubbing its smooth surface. He would need all the help he could summon to deal with these settlers.

Sixty-four

BEFORE THE SUN BREACHED THE LAND TO THE EAST, HIGH Limb made sure their rope fastenings were retied to the thick posts. Let the Whites think they know how to secure captives.

There was just enough light coming through cracks in the thatched roof that he could see where they were being held. It was a large, single room with no openings, except for a door, which was closed. He had tried pushing and pulling it during the night, but it was secure.

The animal furs High Limb smelled in the night were piled on one side of the chamber. Mink, otter, and beaver, all neatly stacked. Their binding posts, in the middle of the room and firmly buried in the dirt floor, supported the roof.

He was looking for weak spots that could help with their escape when the door suddenly opened, flooding the room with light. He turned his head to see bright sunlight—the rain had passed.

Led by the leader Minwee, a group of the settlers came and stood in front of the furs, facing Dancing Fish and High Limb, each tied to his own post. Two of their warrior soldiers stayed at the open door, hands on the muskets propped against their sides.

Minwee, sweat glistening on the part of his pink face not covered by hair, unrolled a piece of paper, glanced at it, then addressed the two of them.

"This is a trial, an official court proceeding of the West India Company." He nodded first to High Limb and then to Dancing Fish. "Dancing Fish will translate my words if any are not understood by you."

The small man lifted his chest and head to appear taller. "As Director-General, I am the judge and sole jury in this matter, and these—he glanced to both sides at the others with him—are witnesses of the Company." It was the same group of faces—their council—only now with a new face replacing Jay-kub. Mar-ee wore a black mourning covering, and he tried to avoid looking at her.

"Do you understand?" asked Minwee.

Dancing Fish whispered a few words of translation and High Limb nodded without speaking.

Minwee looked down at the paper again. "You both—High Limb and Dancing Fish—are accused of murdering one of our settlers, the man known as Jay-kub De-witt, husband of Mar-ee Boo-shay De-witt."

He saw the white Sachem glance at Mar-ee, who stood still as a tree and showing no emotion.

"Did you commit this crime of murder?"

High Limb studied Mar-ee's eyes and saw the sadness in them. This was one outcome he had not thought of—although he doubted he would have done anything differently.

"I did," he said simply.

"And what was your role?" Minwee asked Dancing Fish.

"I am his helper."

"But were you there?" asked Minwee, staring at his fellow captive. "Did you participate in the act of murder upon Meneer De-witt?"

Dancing Fish took a moment before speaking. "It does not matter if I am there. I am Peace Sachem of the Manahate band. I am responsible for all actions of Manahate members. I am guilty like I use my own hand."

The Whites starting talking to each other, pointing and arguing. Minwee finally turned back to face them. "It is the opinion of this court that you, High Limb, War Chief of the Manahate band, are guilty of murder and shall be hanged by the neck until death. As our Bible instructs: *an eye for an eye, and tooth for tooth.*"

High Limb had not heard of this *bible*, but the logic was sound. Although he was surprised to hear nothing said about torture.

Minwee turned his eyes to Dancing Fish. "And you, Dancing Fish, Sachem of the Manahate band, are guilty of assisting in this crime and are to pay compensation for it. The amount of land, food, or wampum is to be determined."

Just like they thought.

"You will both stay here for the day and night until punishment is rendered tomorrow. This court is adjourned."

Again led by Minwee, the group turned to leave the room. But Mar-ee lingered, the last to go. She stepped close to Dancing Fish as she made her way to the door and whispered something in his ear. High Limb was too far away to hear it, but he saw the sly smile cross the tied man's face while Mar-ee walked quickly to join the others before leaving the house.

One of the soldiers shot them both a fierce glance and said, "Enjoy a peaceful night." He laughed then stepped out and closed the door solidly behind him.

▶◀

Marie wasn't sure why she was doing this. If anything, she should have been pleased with the verdict. They had buried Jacob the afternoon before, and her husband's murderer was going to receive the harshest possible punishment. But even when they had discussed it in the counting house, she was silently opposed. While she prepared the horse, she grappled with her conflicted feelings.

She had watched how, over the past year, the small band of natives had shriveled, both in size and in spirit. The once-proud people her father had written to her about seemed so much weaker. Their vigor and energy were leaving them. The devastating diseases had caused much of that, but now, with what they—the settlers and traders—were doing, there was even more pressure on these simple people of the island.

She was young and certainly no expert or leader, but even she could see the damage being inflicted. The local fur animals were almost depleted; they now came from farther up the river or from other directions. So there was less to trade. Food, tobacco, and wampum were always valued, but over time the settlers had found other ways to produce or find these things. It appeared to her that the Manahate natives had lost much of their importance and influence. And with it, their standing as equals with them, the Europeans.

And she noticed something else that had changed. The Indians had been self-sufficient in every way she could imagine when she first met them in the spring of 1625. Her father had also written about this amazing quality of an active, full life he had witnessed in his time with them.

But now, the complex and rich web of their existence seemed broken. They relied more on foreigners' pots, knives, and cloth than on their own ways. She had heard this from Willow but had not fully understood its importance. She was now beginning to. The natives seemed less in control of their own lives.

The land agreement had not helped them. She had always known they did not understand the true meaning of the Company purchasing the island, and slowly, bit by bit, the director-general—and by extension, even the lowliest of the settlers—had assumed a sense of dominance and authority over the land. The natives had not left, but there was a subtle shift in power between the two groups. Each day, the Company was more in charge, and the Indians were . . . well, what were they, exactly? Neighbors? Co-inhabitants? Subjects?

Whatever they were now, the natives were not equal. They were somehow in a lower position. And this bothered her in a way that was hard to put into words or coherent thoughts. She only knew that she felt the need to be on their side.

Then there was the alcohol. The natives seemed particularly susceptible. And she blamed herself—or at least Jacob—for having started that trend. But the making of spirits was now a common activity by many of the settlers, and they took advantage of the Indians' thirst for it at every opportunity. So it was fitting that she would now use liquor to help them.

It was late when she calmly walked up to the counting house with the two flasks. After the murder, she was frightened of being away from the village by herself and was staying with another family on the strand.

The stars dazzled brightly against the black sky and provided just enough light by which to make her way. The moon was starting to rise, and it cast its yellow reflection across the water that sucked and splashed around the rocks at the island's tip.

"Who is it?" one of the guards called out. He was sitting with his companion, their backs to the wall on opposite sides of the door.

"Just a lonely widow with more brandy than she can drink herself." She stopped in front of the soldiers, saw them grin, and pointed to a spot in front of them. "May I?"

They both smiled and gestured for her to sit.

Although she was only pretending to drink from her flask, they were not, and soon they were singing and leaning against each other for support. Then they were passed out and snoring.

She stepped around them and rapped on the heavy door four times. That's what she had whispered to Dancing Fish.

Now she walked quickly to the opposite end of the counting

house where the horse and the cart waited.

▶◀

Dancing Fish stood on High Limb's broad shoulders and waited. They had already pulled down, piece by piece, the reed matting between the heavy horizontal logs of the roof. They had tried moving the logs by hand but had failed. Dancing Fish marveled at how strong the house was made, but then this was the place that held all the valuable furs between ship arrivals, so they had put all their civilized skills to it. He was impressed. But now he would use his own skills to undo it.

The knotted rope finally cleared the roof and fell over the edge and into his waiting hands. He wrapped the rope around the last two support logs and pulled on it with rapid tugs.

He heard the sound of the whip and then the horse cart creaking as the rope pulled taut. He could hear the horse straining and Mar-ee's voice urging him on. Unlike her other one, this horse was healthy with a lot of strength.

Finally, there was a cracking while the roof supports were pulled free from the tops of the walls. The logs clattered to the ground at the same time he heard noises coming from outside the front door. The soldiers were awake.

"Hurry!" he shouted to High Limb as he pulled himself through the narrow opening where the logs had been. With the moon casting a strong glow, Dancing Fish looked down and saw Mar-ee waiting in the cart, her face contorted with worry. "You must go," he yelled down to her. "Don't wait. They cannot find you helping us."

She continued to look up at him, frozen in fear or doubt, her white face reminding him so much of her father.

"*I say go!*" he shouted. "Go now before too late." And a final thought: "Take care of my son if something happens to me."

Mar-ee snapped out of her trance, nodded, turned, and

whipped the horse. The cart jerked and they were gone in an instant.

"Hey, don't forget me!" came the voice from below. High Limb had pulled over some of the furs and was standing on them. He reached his hand up and Dancing Fish grasped it in his. Bending his knees and trying to balance, Dancing Fish pulled up against High Limb's weight with all his strength, and the giant man was able to grab the top of the wall and muscle himself up onto it.

They heard the shouting of the soldiers who were running around both sides of the house.

"Now," Dancing Fish said, and he and High Limb both jumped off the wall, landing hard on the ground and rolling to a stop.

"Stop there!" came the words of the first soldier to round the corner of the house. "Don't move!"

Dancing Fish saw him fumble with the musket while another man came into view from the other side. This man wasted no time, dropping his musket to pull out his sword and run toward them at full speed.

"Let's go!" Dancing Fish shouted at High Limb, who was gripping his knee and grimacing. "I fell wrong," he said.

High Limb then reached into his apron and pulled out one of the horseshoes. Steadying himself on the ground, he pulled his arm back and released the metal with full force. There was a loud *smack* when it hit the charging man square on the chest, knocking him off his feet and onto his back.

Dancing Fish grabbed High Limb under the arm and pulled him up. "You and your horseshoes. Come on. To the woods!"

The two ran and hobbled together and reached the treeline just as the musket sounded. The ball whistled by the ear of Dancing Fish, and they plunged into the forest they knew well.

Sixty-five

THEY HAD MANAGED TO STAY AHEAD OF THE SHOUTING SOL-
diers and work their way to the salt marsh on the eastern shore.
The moon was bright, but the thick forest canopy blocked the
light and offered them the gloom and shadows they needed to
avoid their pursuers, now multiplied in number judging by the
sound of the voices.

Dancing Fish stopped at the edge of the marsh to listen.
"How's your knee?" he asked High Limb, who had struggled
to keep up.

"Don't worry about me. Let's just get away from these soldiers. I'm out of horseshoes!" They both laughed at this. They
had no weapons left.

"Follow me into the marsh," Dancing Fish instructed.
"We'll be exposed, so stay low in the reeds."

"Where are we going?"

"Into the water, of course."

"And then?"

"You'll see."

Dancing Fish bent down and stepped into the muck, using
his hands to move the grasses and reed stalks to the side. The
reeds were stiff and soon covered him with stinging cuts on his
arms and chest. High Limb, following close behind, was cursing. Only wearing their aprons would make moving through
the marsh painful, but the benefit would come when they were

in the water with nothing to slow them down.

The soldiers must have seen them. They were firing their muskets, but the balls never landed close. As soon as they reached open water, both dove under and swam like frogs until they were well into the middle of the waterway and out of musket range.

Dancing Fish stopped to tread water and orient himself. By looking at both banks, he could see that they were slowly moving south. The tide was ebbing. He brought a handful of water to his mouth. Mostly fresh. They were moving out into the Great Lake. Just what he needed.

The water of summer was the warmest it would get, so there was no danger of chilling. They could stay in it all night, if needed. But he had a different plan.

"Will they send out a boat to find us?" asked High Limb.

"Not at night. They'll wait until daylight. And by then, we'll be gone."

"Gone where?"

Dancing Fish spotted a large log that bobbed high in the water several body lengths from them. "Not far. Come," he said while he silently stroked to it.

Once they were on the side of the log away from the island, holding onto its rough bark and broken limbs, they could relax. Anyone looking for them in a canoe or swimming in the waterway would only see a log slowly moving out to sea.

"Remember when we were last on Pagganck?" Dancing Fish asked, his head tilted back in the water, looking up at the stars.

"Ah yes. In the snow with you. Spying on the Point."

"And remember when you joked about how the strangers could cut as many trees as they wanted and build as many houses, and it wouldn't matter? Remember?"

High Limb muttered his remembering.

"Well, take a look now."

They were floating past the eastern flank of the island's tip, and the two peered around the ends of the log. There were bonfires lit with people running and shouting. No doubt blaming each other for their escape.

In the strong moonlight, Dancing Fish could see how much more clearing had been done from the time of their winter spying. The number of houses had at least doubled or more, and he could make out the rising form of the fort to the west.

"Do you still believe the land cannot change?" Dancing Fish asked.

There was only silence from High Limb while the log slowly drifted past the island under a full Sturgeon Moon.

▶◀

They waited until they were on the far side of the small island before swimming to it. The sun would soon crest the bluffs to the east across the narrow channel, and the clear sky was already thickening with the haze of summer.

Dancing Fish led a limping High Limb through the dense mix of nut trees and oaks—from one side of Pagganck to the other.

Once they came to the edge of the treeline facing north to the Point, each sat behind a different tree. A blackberry thicket—only a few of the ripe berries not eaten by foxes and birds still remained—provided another screen between them and the far shore of Mannahatta. They would not be seen from the village of the settlers.

"So this is your great plan?" High Limb muttered, plucking a few of the dark berries and popping them in his mouth. "To hide like two scared rabbits?"

Dancing Fish glared at High Limb. "I didn't murder a settler," he said, looking for his own berries to eat. "Would you prefer swinging from a tree limb, kicking and choking until

414

your long neck breaks?"

"At least I would be closer to home than on this deserted piece of rock."

They both looked in silence at Kapsee Point, so close across the water. The changes made by the settlers were even more obvious now in the growing dawn light. The entire tip of the island, from west to east, was cleared of trees. Everywhere Dancing Fish looked, there were houses or other buildings being made, with fires burning and people moving.

"Have we lost our beloved Point?" High Limb finally asked.

"I fear we have," said Dancing Fish, thinking of all the memorable times he had spent either swimming around the rocks, fishing, or just sitting and gazing out at the wide and deep waters. He pointed. "See the largest rocks at the tip, just south of that fort they talk so much about?"

High Limb peeked around his tree.

"That's where I spotted Hudson's ship," Dancing Fish said. "Remember how amazed we all were when we first saw it? The Great White Bird floating to us. And the strange Spirit Beings?"

High Limb laughed. "Yes. And I remember how you almost pissed your apron when you were called to meet the red-coated leader on the beach. I thought you were going to faint right onto the sand."

Dancing Fish remembered it well. In fact, he remembered almost everything from the time of first meeting the Salt People. From Hudson's arrival to this hot day in summer so many years later. And in those years, what had he learned about the strangers? How had he answered the question of whether they were good or bad for the People? That had been his mission, his task from the beginning. And the answer was not a happy one.

He reached instinctively for the glass button hanging at his chest and rubbed it between thumb and forefinger. He believed he had been chosen by the glass button itself to discover the truth about the Visitors from the East. To understand the prophecy. He was now Sachem and White Seer of the band. It was up to him to see into the future. A future that was based on the past.

He rubbed the button again and closed his eyes. The warm southern breeze caressed his skin and made a swishing sound through the treetops that mixed with the screech of an osprey somewhere on high looking for its next prey. He saw himself sitting with Owl, looking over the water just like he was now with High Limb. And he heard the conversation again, as clear as on that day, as if the man were right there with them:

"It's just the beginning with the white strangers, isn't it?"
"Yes."
"And will I play a part?"
"You will play the most important part of all."

He sighed. Owl had spoken the truth. And it was still not over.

"So I ask you again," High Limb said, interrupting his memory vision, "what are we to do? We can't stay here forever."

Dancing Fish blinked himself back to the present. "We go north."

"But we just came south!"

He clucked his tongue. "Great War Chief, you've never heard of fooling the enemy?"

High Limb looked at him and grinned. "What do you have in mind?"

"We'll take the next flood tide up the Great River, swimming at night if needed. When was the last time you held a good basket from the Wiechquaesecks in your hands?"

"It's been some time. And I like that they're on the opposite end of the island from this white village. But we'll be gone for how long?"

"For as long as it takes. Eventually, with time, we'll find a way to rejoin our people."

Dancing Fish looked across the water at the tip of Mannahatta and studied the gentle rise of land beyond the village of the Whites. That's where the great pond of Xitkwe and their summer longhouses waited. Where his son waited, being held by . . . Who?

"The settlers will not move north from the Point in large numbers," he said. "There'll be other pockets of them on the island, yes, but they'll leave Werpoes to us. And we must give Kapsee to them. That is what I see coming."

"But if you're wrong, and they try to fill the island?" High Limb asked.

Dancing Fish didn't hesitate. "Then we fight. We fight for our future."

Part Four

The Warriors

1640–44

Sixty-six

March 1640

DIRCK VAN OST WAS SURPRISED BY THE WILDNESS OF THE land outside New Amsterdam. While the village at the bottom of Manatus island was crowded with more than 80 buildings and hundreds of people including the soldiers garrisoned at the fort, the rest seemed almost uninhabited. There were farms close-in and scattered about the narrow island, but for most of their march north they had seen nothing except the sodden path at their feet and the occasional stream, rock outcropping, and of course, all the trees.

So many trees! None, except the occasional evergreen, were leafing out yet, but the serviceberries and wild cherries were in full bloom. Their delicate white blossoms dotted the broad trail on both sides. Sweet smells he couldn't identify loaded his nose while the sounds of birds and rustling leaves filled his ears. And the warm sun was a welcome break from the cold and gray of the fading winter.

"Keep a close eye out for any savages until we get there," said the tax collector—the *commies*, Paulus de Sille, as they walked with purpose along the well-worn path. "They'll do anything to slow us down or find a way to trade for alcohol or a bit of cloth. I want to reach the village before the sun sets."

Van Ost glanced and nodded at the short, squat man who was breathing hard to keep up with the pace of the group. The commies had a disdain for the natives that nearly equaled that of Director Kieft. But the man's job was to collect the imposts and fees due the Company, so he supposed a certain wariness and distrust was normal. That's why he was there with the four soldiers and an empty cart: to provide protection for the group going to meet the famed Dancing Fish in their summer village at the top of the island.

Since coming to New Amsterdam only months before, Van Ost had heard a lot about this Indian leader, who was supposed to have an intelligence to match their own. Based on his experiences with natives in prior postings—Brazil, Suriname, and Guyana—this seemed a fanciful idea, but he would keep an open mind. His main duty, besides protection, was to help the commies collect the levy—the corn tax—the director demanded. But he was mystified. "Why are they still here?" he asked. "Didn't the Company purchase this island?"

De Sille snorted. "Supposedly, yes. That was back in '26 under Director Minuit. But here we are 14 years later, and we can't seem to be rid of them. At least there are fewer now. And thank God for that."

Without breaking stride, Van Ost bent to pick up a dead tree limb and throw it to the side. "Tell me about these particular natives. I've been waiting out the winter at the fort, and I'm curious. I've heard stories. What is their character?"

De Sille loosened the long coat at his neck and stopped. Van Ost signaled for the group to halt next to a fast-moving stream that sloshed with melting snow.

"Like all of them," the commies started between slowing breaths, "they're a lazy, thieving, Godless bunch. But this group is especially difficult. Their other leader—he's called High Limb, the War Chief—murdered one of our own years ago."

"I heard that. Why wasn't he shot or hanged?"

"Oh, they put him in jail and threatened retribution, but in the end that crazy Walloon woman defended him. Said the killing of her husband was justified. Can you believe it?"

He could. Women had the power to turn a man's mind. He knew that firsthand. "And now they refuse to pay the director's levy, is that it?" he said.

"Yes, and more than once. This time, we need to make it stick." The commies looked directly at him. "So you have to assert some authority to make that happen. Understand?"

"Of course," Van Ost said quickly. But this was the problem. He personally thought the demand from Director Willem Kieft for the Indians to pay a tribute for basically nothing was a bad idea. But he was Ensign of the army here—second in command of all soldiers—with an obligation to carry out his orders. He couldn't risk his progression through the ranks. Being named Captain-Lieutenant was his goal, and if he kept his head down and performed as expected, he would achieve it. And that would prove his worth to Kathrijn's wealthy family back home.

He was waiting for De Sille's reaction when he heard a splash and sudden cry: *Help!!*" A quick look sent a shudder down his spine and raised the hairs on his arms.

One of the soldiers had fallen into the stream, which was bad enough with its ice-cold water, but what was coming at him from out of the treeline was the real problem. A huge black bear was moving at great speed toward the struggling soldier. And he saw why. A small bear cub was standing in the water and giving off a sound not unlike a crying baby. Surely this was the mother coming to protect her cub.

"Jan!" he shouted to the dazed soldier who now saw the moving mass charging him. "Get up! Run back! Fast!"

Jan was frozen in place.

"Now!" Van Ost shouted at the top of his voice while he frantically prepared his musket.

The soldier got to his feet and started to stumble toward them but it was too late. The bear was soon upon him, and it roared and swiped the man with his right paw, sending him back into the water, face down.

Van Ost didn't wait. Taking quick aim he fired a buck-and-ball load at the bear. The shot landed squarely and stunned the animal, which now looked away from the downed soldier and directly at their group. This was what Van Ost wanted. He pulled out his pistol and shouted his orders to the others: "Close up! Pistols ready."

The bear cocked its head, trying to decide what to do. Then it roared and charged them.

"Fire!" he shouted, and the simultaneous discharge of pistols followed.

The bear stopped and shook its huge body, roared once more, then turned. It lumbered away from them and back into the trees, the cub yelping and running behind.

▶◀

Dancing Fish pulled a cluster of oysters from the muddy bank and started tapping with his steel knife. As each live oyster imperceptibly moved, he broke it off and placed it in the reed bag slung around his neck.

"Don't forget to put the young ones back," High Limb said.

Dancing Fish stopped to look at his old friend who stood at the edge of the oyster bed, both of them in knee-deep water. "You're telling me how to harvest oysters? Someone who knows more about this river and its animals than you ever will? Ha! You spend a finger of time to hunt one deer then take a nap for the rest of the day." He smiled at his insult while he scooped his gloved hand and splashed cold water on his companion.

High Limb splashed him back, laughing. "Yes, me. Someone who was smart enough to show you how to put cattail leaves inside your leggings to keep you and your balls from freezing." He straightened up and grinned. "I know how to invent, too," the War Chief said smugly.

The tide was low with the sun high in a clear sky, and they were collecting from the great oyster flat under the ridge of The Wart. The same bulge on the island's upper west side that had witnessed the bloody battle with Hudson's crew so many years before.

It was the equinox, and it was that time again: the start of the good months when they moved from their winter home to Mannahatta. When fish migrated up the Great River, and they were busy at their new summer village, Shorakapkock, repairing their wigwams and rekindling long-dead fires.

Dancing Fish stepped back from the oysters and regarded the War Chief. His one-time rival was still tall and imposing, even after so many winters. His black hair was braided long and hung behind his broad chest, and his arms still bulged with power under the wet hunting shirt. The arrogance and pride had never left him, but time had softened his bullying and violent streaks.

"Do you regret killing Marie's husband back then?" Dancing Fish asked, thinking of all that had happened in the seasons after the settlers arrived.

High Limb narrowed his eyes, wrinkling the tattoos on his forehead. "What I regret is that we didn't kill and drive off all the Whites when we had the chance." He paused. "Then, you had to appease them even more."

Dancing Fish shook his head. "You're not serious. If I hadn't sold the other islands to that drunken Director Twiller they would have hunted you down and hung you. Or worse. You spent only one moon in their jail." He was now using the European way with their names and titles.

High Limb grunted. "I can take their worst any time. They don't even know how to torture correctly. They're still just as ignorant as before."

"Maybe, but look what these ignorant people have accomplished. Their village at Kapsee is bigger than anything we have.

And with more of the settlers spread all over the island. And the Manahates now number, what—maybe 50?"

"If that many," High Limb said dejectedly.

Dancing Fish climbed onto the mudflat so the sun could warm him. He heard a fish splash in the river but didn't turn to look. The strong, briny smell of sea and seaweed triggered a cascade of images and thoughts of the changes the passing of time had brought them.

After the settler named Bronck bought the land near Achqueehgenom, they had moved their winter home farther up the Aquehung river to Cowangough. The Wiechquaesecks had sold Bronck the land and had then made an offer to Dancing Fish that he, as Sachem, could not ignore.

The years had not been kind to the three bands who made Mannahatta island their summer home. The Rechgawawanks had already been swallowed into the Wiechquaeseck band, and the proposal was for the Manahates to do the same. The Wiechquaesecks were the largest and most powerful band between the Great River and the waterways that separated the eastern lands from the island.

Over many seasons the fevers had killed even more of the People, and the Whites had continued to fill the island just like he had predicted. So the offer by the Wiechquaesecks for the Manahate to join with them was a generous and logical one. And he had agreed for the sake of the band's future. But not before being promised they could keep their band identity, as Manahates. And while they would use—and he would lead—the northern village of Shorakapkock for their summer home, they would still visit and make use of the land around Werpoes for hunting, gathering, and corn planting. And for visiting the graves of their ancestors just north of the Great Pond.

"So we will continue to oppose this new Director's demand for *contributions*?" High Limb asked, studying the opposite shoreline of the river.

"Of course. It's a foolish idea. But like we planned—"

"Father!" a voice sounded from the trees. The speaker, Dancing Fish's son, Diver, abruptly appeared, excited and breathing hard.

Dancing Fish watched his son of 13 winters compose himself when he saw the War Chief and him together. Now initiated into manhood—and long having left his Little Perch baby name behind—he stood erect and earnest. The Turkey Clan tattoo cut into his right shoulder was still raw and puffy. But seeing it was a welcome reminder of Willow, Dancing Fish's long departed wife. He briefly closed his eyes to bring the memory of Willow back, but this was getting harder to do with the years.

"What is it?" he said, coming back to the present.

"A group of Whites is in the village," Diver said. "They're asking for you. They have an injured man, and they look serious."

"They're always serious," High Limb said, spitting into the water. "Serious and stupid."

Dancing Fish ignored the War Chief and nodded to his son. "Then let's go see what they're so serious about."

▶◀

A lowering sun cast shadows from the surrounding hills while High Limb carefully studied the Whites. The central fire snapped and popped, and the Salt Men stood on one side, warming their hands. The injured one had already been taken away by the curing women. He would survive the bear clawing.

Two of the men looked like officials: a short one like a tree trunk standing by an empty cart, the other tall and appearing very much like a Soldier Chief. They both wore the silly leg stockings and their strange flat-topped hats. The rest were ordinary soldiers who wore heavy clothes with straps and belts, and they all had muskets or pistols at the ready. This was what interested High Limb most.

"What is the reason for visit on this nice day?" Dancing Fish asked in his easy way of talking to these people. Many now knew the tongue of the Whites and could even write bits of it—their important names and words—on their paper, but Dancing Fish was the most skilled in its use. He understood how to apply either humor or subtle anger when it was needed.

The short, fat man stepped to the side of the fire and spoke, pulling a paper from his coat. "We have come again to ask for the contributions required of you."

"What 'contributions'?" Dancing Fish said in an innocently mocking way.

The man frowned. "You know very well what I'm talking about. Here, I will read the directive to you again so there is no doubt." He lifted the paper and read:

> As the Company has to bear great expenses, both in building fortifications and in the upkeep of soldiers and sailors, we have therefore resolved to demand from the Indians around here, whom we have until now protected from their enemies, some contribution, like pelts, corn, and sewant. And if there is any nation which is unwilling to agree in friendship to contribute, we will seek to bring them to this by the most justified means.

The man folded the paper and put it back in his coat and waited while the fire crackled and sent wisps of white smoke skyward.

High Limb had heard enough. His anger rising, he started to speak but felt a hand against his arm as Dancing Fish took a step forward.

"With much respect, sir. What authority do you have to make this demand on us?"

The fat man blinked his eyes several times before answering. "We've been through this before. I am the Commies of New Netherland, responsible for all fees, levies, and taxes. I'm here representing our esteemed Director Kieft." He nodded to the Soldier Chief. "This is our Ensign, Dirck van Ost, second in command of the army. Surely you know all this."

Dancing Fish took his time answering. "Here is what I know." He stopped to turn and look over all who stood on their side of the fire—the village leaders and others who were curious—then turned back to the man. "We live in these parts for many generations. And we protect ourselves in all that time. Yes, we have enemies—Mohawks, Mahicans, others—and this is why we have agreement with your Director Minuit about this island. For defensive alliance. But where is defense? Where is alliance? What do you do?

"You have a fort. You have soldiers with guns and other weapons who sit in the fort doing what, sleeping?" Dancing Fish glanced at High Limb, who grinned and then studied the muskets and pistols again. "In truth, you do nothing to explain these contributions, this tax."

The face of this short man, the part that was not covered by a wide straw beard, had turned from white to the color of a cherry. "You dare question our help and protection of you?" He was angry now, almost shouting in a high, whining voice.

"Yes, I question you," Dancing Fish said. "You do not help us at all." The Sachem's face turned serious, and he pointed his finger at the man whose eyes were wide with shock or fear, High Limb wasn't sure which. "Our troubles only start when you come to our lands. You are the problem. And now you want us to pay you for this . . . this protection and friendship." Dancing Fish laughed and shook his head.

The Soldier Chief now moved and stepped closer, his hand on his pistol. He was tall with a dark beard cut closer to his face. And those bright blue eyes that were a mark of these strangers.

The man looked at both of them in turn before speaking with a surprisingly soft sound that reminded High Limb of rustling reeds. "You have heard the demand. We must return with something." He pointed to the empty cart. "Pelts, corn, or sewant—your wampum. Your choice."

High Limb watched as the other soldiers moved slightly forward behind their leader, their hands also on the pistols at their waists.

"Pelts, corn, or wampum," Dancing Fish repeated before turning his head to High Limb and dipping it slightly. He turned back to the Whites with a big smile. "To agree in friendship, we offer you something."

High Limb nodded to one of the young warriors. The boy sprinted off and soon returned with a bundle wrapped in deerskin. High Limb walked with the bundle and handed it to the Soldier Chief, never breaking eye contact.

The man set the bundle down at the feet of the Commies, who squatted and started unwrapping it. He suddenly shrieked and fell back on his rear end.

While others crowded around, High Limb heard Dancing Fish chuckle and he joined in.

Their contribution was a pile of rat skins.

Sixty-seven

July 1640

MARIE BOUCHER LIKED WORKING WITH KOFI. HE HAD A sense of humor and a head for figuring things out. But he wasn't always good at knowing when to slow down and work easy in the heat. Like now.

They had been topping and weeding the tobacco when he suddenly sat down between the chest-high rows. "I don' feel so good," he said in his odd way of talking as he lay back on the dirt.

She bent down to feel his head. It was burning, but there was no sweat. "Stay down," she said, looking up at the sun's position in the sky. "The crops will shade you here. When did you last drink?"

"Mornin'," he mumbled.

She shook her head. She had told him time and again to keep drinking water when it was hot. She had already learned the lessons of taking frequent breaks, and of wearing short and loose clothing, like the natives. But Kofi was a good worker, and he just wanted to work. Unlike a lot of slaves, he worked more than needed. And drinking took time away from work.

"I'm going to the house to get some water and something to cool you down. Will you be alright here?"

"Miss Marie, where you 'spect me to go?"

She laughed while she watched his teeth flash against the dark skin that reminded her of her favorite chocolate drink as a child in Wallonia. She patted him on the arm and started walking fast to the house.

While she poured water in a bottle and searched for large cloths to soak, she thought about how important Kofi was to her. She had bought him from a Dutch sea captain five years earlier and never regretted it. The farm's business in tobacco and oat brandy was good. So good, in fact, that she was one of the richest women on the island. Only one or two lady tavern owners, and maybe the top prostitute, were more successful.

But she was also alone. Which made the work that much harder. Nonetheless, she preferred it this way. She was a widow, and that's how she liked it. No devious and lazy men were ever going to slow her down again.

As she walked back to the tobacco field with the water bottle in one hand and the dripping cloths over her shoulder, she realized: she needed Kofi. And she would do whatever it took to keep him around. Even if it meant hearing more talk from the villagers about how "scandalous" it was for an unmarried woman of her age to be sharing a property with a single man. And a 25-year-old Negro slave, no less.

She smiled as she stepped over the furrows of a fallow garden, her shortened duffel dress catching the heat from the ground. *Let them be scandalized. What do I care? He has his own hut away from mine.* Not that she hadn't let her mind drift to more sensual thoughts when she was lying alone in her empty house, knowing he was only a dozen steps away.

When she reached him she immediately opened his work shirt and laid the wet cloths over his stomach and chest. "There, that should help. Now drink some water, but only in little sips." She pulled his head up from the back and put the bottle to his large lips. "Small sips," she repeated while he took in the water.

She lowered his head and sat back on a dry cloth she had brought, shading her face and listening to the droning of insects on all sides. He would be fine.

After a time, she saw his eyes angle down to her. He asked, "Miss Marie, why you not marry ag'in? You got lotta men after you."

She stood and pulled off the cloths, moving them in the air to cool them down. Then she put them over his body again and poured more water on top. "They're only after my money. My success. I'm not making *that* mistake again." She thought of Jacob and involuntarily shook like she had a chill. No, no more of that.

"Uh huh," he said. Then, "But I be wantin' to marry. You know that."

"I know. Juba's her name, right?"

"Juba Angola. Livin' wit' all them others. Up on East River."

She looked up at the pink tobacco flowers that hadn't been topped yet. They moved in the light breeze and surrounded her with the sweetest scent. Then she spotted a hornworm and cursed.

When the topping was done she would go south to the village and ask Director Kieft and Minister Bogardus about Kofi wanting to marry. No African slave had been married on the island yet, but no slaves had been owned privately before Kofi either. She was used to being the first to do things. And to getting her way.

▶◀

Van Ost stood with the director and the captain at the southwest bastion of Fort Amsterdam and stared out at Staaten Island through the summer haze. A steady wind from the south made the waves crash on the shore, throwing up a spray that sometimes reached them in a fine mist.

"This is most upsetting," Kieft said, jabbing his thumb at the far-off island. "These Raritans won't pay the levy, and now they dare drive off an official trading party?"

The man was enraged, but this was nothing new. Kieft was well known to all for being a tyrannical man who was quick to antagonize people. Even his body and appearance bore out an imperious manner. His aquiline nose implied superiority, firmness, and power. And everything from the fine stockings to his broad-brimmed hat—complete with a white ostrich plume—communicated a haughty, high station.

This man ruled the entire colony with an iron fist, although he rarely left the confines and safety of the fort, such as it was with its crumbling sides, dismounted cannons, and houses and magazines in disrepair. He was the master of an unruly and raucous society, but he was determined to make it bend to his will.

"And then there's the De Vries pigs," Captain Beeckman said with a slight slur in his speech. His love of drink was no secret, and Van Ost wasn't surprised to smell it on his breath now. But Beeckman, like Kieft, had family connections to the Company, and the two shared an arrogance that their high positions afforded. And a willingness to overlook each other's offenses.

"Exactly!" Kieft shouted. "They kill the hogs of the settlers, refuse to pay reparations, drive off our ships, and continue to withhold their fair contributions. This is intolerable." The man was working himself into a frenzy while he held tightly onto his hat to keep it from flying away in the stiff breeze.

Van Ost kept his face immobile, but he was concerned. He knew that rigid authority was what the Dutch States General wanted for managing the other colonies, but this one, New Netherland—especially this strange mix of traders and settlers in and around New Amsterdam—seemed different. This was now a true colony, but a military dictatorship didn't feel to him like the most fitting way to run things. But he was only a soldier and maybe not the best judge.

"Ensign Van Ost," Kieft said, turning his back to the wind, "what do you think? You're second in command here. Can we accept this insolence from the savages?"

Now he had to answer. He started carefully. "I've only been here some months—"

"And what have you observed?" Kieft asked quickly, cocking his head slightly.

"It seems that the Indians—the savages—have very different ideas from ours."

"Yes, yes. And?"

"Well, sir, they seem to respond more to the carrot rather than the stick, if you get my meaning." He considered his next words. "I would suggest showing our side to greater advantage—what we can offer them."

Kieft stepped back and raised his eyebrows at him and shot the thin and wiry Captain Beeckman a quick glance. "Well, well, it seems we have a politician here in the army." He pulled at his graying beard that was cut short on the sides but grew longer at the chin. "And what would you have me do? If you had any say in the matter. Which you don't," he added. "But I'm curious. Give me your opinion."

He was ready. "I would keep applying pressure to the Wiechquaesecks and this Dancing Fish in the north, maybe with a stronger promise of mutual defense, but I would focus on the Raritans and what's happening there." He tipped his head in the direction of Staaten Island. "That seems of more immediate concern."

The director stared at him without moving, then said to the captain, "I believe the ensign is right. At least on the last part." He clapped and rubbed his hands together. "Let's pay a visit to these Raritans and teach them a proper lesson. Give them a chance to agree to our demands. And if they don't"—he grinned in a wicked sort of way Van Ost was becoming familiar with—"we'll cut down their corn and take as many prisoners as we can. We'll not allow them to make fools of us."

"I'll prepare the men," the captain said without pause,

clearly looking forward to a fight.

"No," Kieft said, turning again to look out across the white-capped water and sniffing at the sea smell. "Let's send the new man here to lead the party with the secretary. You stay with me, Captain. I want to see what kind of soldier our ensign really is."

▶◀

Dancing Fish made a point of taking Diver south on the island whenever possible. Not just for help in checking the corn and tobacco crops—there were older women assigned to that—but to stop at the burial ground and remember their departed family.

As they approached the gravesites north of Werpoes, Dancing Fish immediately saw the breaks in the thorn fence, and then the dogs. They were digging in the mounds!

"Come!" he yelled to his son while he sprinted to the fenced-off area and vaulted over the bramble fence.

Most of the dogs took off running, yipping and whimpering, but a couple stood their ground and bared their teeth, growling. That was their last moment of defiance when the round end of Dancing Fish's walking stick smashed into the largest dog's head, sending it sprawling to the dirt where it lay still. Diver did the same to another, and the remaining two took off running to find and slink through the closest fence opening.

Dancing Fish clubbed both motionless dogs in the head again and threw them over the fence. He loved dogs, but these were less than dogs. They were cowardly, soulless beings that only the Whites could abide.

He walked back to the grave mounds and motioned for Diver to sit near him while he carefully filled in the holes the dogs had dug. "You didn't know your mother or your sisters," he said quietly. He had not remarried, choosing to live with the memories of Willow and his two girls instead.

He pressed lightly on each grave, working hard to pull the images of Willow, Meekak, and Sunshell to a point behind his eyes where he could see, hear, and touch them.

"What were they like?" Diver asked, not for the first time.

He sighed. "They were my life. They—and now you—were and are the reason to greet the sun each morning and the stars each night. They, and the others in the band, give the reason to breathe each day."

"Tell me again what happened to them," Diver said in his deepening voice.

Dancing Fish heard the buzzing of the first mosquitoes at his ears. He saw that the sun was gone, and a purple glow now filled the sky to the west. As he applied grease to his arms and legs he told his son the story of their family. And he intertwined that with the larger story of the People and how things started to change after the coming of Hudson.

He liked to tell the story as much as possible. He felt it was important to keep the memories alive and to make sure the younger ones understood their history. He had tried writing it down on the paper of the Whites, but it was better to tell it in their way, gesturing and taking the roles of each person in the story. He sometimes did this in front of the entire band, especially in the winter months, but he also made a point of doing it for those in the family—Raspberry, Willow's sister, was now married and lived with her mother, Wawamis—and especially for Diver. Diver would be dealing with the Whites after he was gone.

While he spoke of the past, he examined his son. He had Willow's muscled legs and wide shoulders. His hair—still long and not yet plucked in the style of a warrior—was almost as black as hers but he could see glints of the reddish color that was his own. But Diver thankfully had her darker eyes, which pleased him. He wanted no reminder of the whiteness that came from his own mixed blood.

When all the color from the sky was gone he pulled the pouch of tobacco from his neck. He pinched a small amount of it between his fingers and put it to his nose. The familiar scent of blending two tobaccos and red willow bark made him close his eyes so the memories and visions could flood in.

He instinctively felt for the glass button with his other hand and pulled it from his apron. The button was worn smooth, and it shone in the growing light of the stars. He held the button out for Diver, who took it.

His son repeated the learned words: "The prophecy asked the question: are the Visitors from the East good or bad for the People?" He rubbed it and handed it back.

"And the answer was not good for us," Dancing Fish said simply, putting the button back in its place. He sprinkled the tobacco over Willow's grave and then those of Meekak and Sunshell, and also where his dogs Kong and Run-Run rested. And he saw how large the burial ground had become, with mounds in every direction.

"But we are still here," he said to his son. "And we have our honorable lives to live so long as the rivers flow and the grasses grow." He smiled at Diver. "Why don't we go to the pond? Let's see if you still know how to dive and swim. If you can live up to your name."

"I've already reached the bottom, and I'm younger than you were," Diver boasted.

Dancing Fish chuckled as they got up and started to walk south. He looked up to the shining stars and spoke to the one that was Willow. *We have lost much, but we are still strong,* he mouthed to himself. He watched Diver's back while he strode in front, eager to get to the pond and prove himself. *The future is always with the young, isn't it?*

Sixty-eight

THE TWO SHIPS HAD ANCHORED IN THE WATERWAY THAT SEP-
arated Staaten Island from the western mainland where the
Raritans lived. As the 40 soldiers and sailors worked their way
through the towering forest, Ensign Van Ost couldn't stop wiping the July sweat off his face with a rag. And wondering how
this day would end. They were supposed to come to an agreement with the natives, but he had his doubts.

"Beastly hot and sticky," he said to Secretary Van Tienhoven,
who was trying hard to keep up with the pace of the march in
search of the village.

The grossly overweight man just grunted and kept fanning
himself with his right hand.

"That's not going to help," said Van Ost, feeling sorry for
the red-faced and bloated secretary who was Director Kieft's
second in command.

"How soon do you think?" Van Tienhoven asked, stopping
to rest in a clearing.

"Not far now. The scouts say it's close." He looked up at a
perfect blue sky and a scorching sun. Then he noticed that all
sounds and movement around him had stopped.

The Indians suddenly appeared from out of the trees. They
were a group of four tall men clad only in breechcloth aprons
and armed with bows and clubs.

"Who is leader?" the tallest one asked in broken Dutch.

Van Ost took a step forward. "I am Ensign of the army, and this"—he opened his arm to Van Tienhoven—"is Cornelis van Tienhoven, Secretary of New Netherland and emissary of Director Willem Kieft." He waited for the secretary to step forward and say something, but the gasping man just flapped his hand toward him indicating he should continue.

"We come to meet with your Sachem and to ask for payments and reparations," Van Ost said. "We wish to come to an agreement." He saw the natives look and mentally count their numbers. He added, "Peacefully and without violence."

The tall Indian spoke quickly with the others and turned back to him. "You, you, you," he said, pointing at him, Van Tienhoven, and the corporal at his side, "come. Others," he spread his hands wide, "stay."

After another march, stopping several times to let Van Tienhoven catch his breath, they arrived at the Raritan village. Like all the native villages he had seen, it was a collection of long and short wigwams clustered around a central fire that blazed and smoked, even in the heat. Dogs and children darted here and there, but everything stopped when they came into full view.

To the side of the fire waited a small group of what he assumed were the leaders. The one in front wore a mantle of brightly colored bird feathers, and he had even more stuck in his long hair that draped over one shoulder.

"Greetings, Sachem," Van Ost said, bowing his head slightly after they had stopped at the fire. "We come—"

The secretary suddenly pushed him aside and spoke. "We come to collect our settlement for what is owed us. You have not treated us correctly, and we seek your payments." Van Tienhoven spent a moment to take in the village. "We have many men behind us, but there will be no violence if we can come to an agreement."

The main leader cocked his head slightly and said, "Do not

440

understand. You want payment? For what?"

"To begin with," the secretary said, "you have not paid the corn tax. And now, you've killed the pigs of one of our important settlers back on Staaten Island. There must be reparations for that."

The leader stared at Van Tienhoven for a moment and then started laughing. The others around him were soon laughing, too. "We don't know what you talk," the leader said. "We kill no pigs. We pay you nothing."

The only sounds came from the crackling fire, the omnipresent insects, and a calling of far-off birds. He saw the secretary open his mouth to speak, but before he could, muskets began firing behind them. Van Ost swung around and saw many of their men charging into the village from three sides.

"Stop this!" he ordered as he stepped toward the main group rushing forward. But the soldiers weren't listening or stopping.

He turned back to the secretary, but to his shock, he was gone. Vanished.

The assault was swift and vicious with shootings, sword stabbings, and hand combat coming from their side. The soldiers seemed caught in an uncontrolled state of madness.

"Soldier!" he shouted when he grabbed and pulled one man back by the arm, "What are you doing? There was no order to attack."

Seeing the stripes on his jacket, the man stood up straight. "We've had it with these savages, sir," he said. "They disrespect us, they steal from us, they . . . they . . ." The man slammed the butt of his musket on the ground. "We own the land and only want what's ours. They're not our equal, sir. They're just wild people. They don't deserve to be here."

Van Ost reached for the man's collar and jerked him close. "Listen to me," he said, smelling the man's sweat and putrid breath. "We have an assignment and a job to do. And we have order and rules." He pushed the man away. "This is the army, not a gang of pirates."

But it was no use. He could only watch as soldiers and sailors ransacked the village and attacked any native too slow to flee into the woods. There were bodies on the ground and wigwams burning. Screams mixed with cries for help while Van Ost stood in a daze next to the fire. What were the director and the captain going to say about this? It was not going to help his career. Nor his prospects for marriage to Kathrijn.

▶◀

"This rabbit stew is excellent," Dancing Fish announced while he breathed in the tasty aroma and held the bowl up to show his appreciation. He kicked High Limb's leg.

"Yes, very good," High Limb said, giving him a stern, sidelong glance.

The Hackensack leader, Oratam, raised his bowl in return and smiled. "We are happy to offer a good meal to our friends and cousins of the Manahate band, now with the Wiechquaesecks. Let's enjoy the night's food and drink before we turn to more important matters." He raised his bowl again, then signaled to a young helper to add more wood to the slowing fire.

Dancing Fish nodded and went back to his steaming stew. A short log was added to the blaze, and he watched sparks fly up and out of the smoke hole of the Council House to a black sky pricked with stars.

They had made the journey to the Sachem's village with several objectives in mind. The first was to visit with relatives who had moved west across the river to the land everyone now called *Pavonia*. High Limb also wanted to trade for more guns or, failing that, for some powder and shot for the one lonely musket the band possessed. It was against their law for the Dutch to trade muskets to them, but a few of the weapons had trickled in from northern traders who valued wampum even more than furs. The limitation was the black powder and lead shot, which was much harder to acquire.

But the main goal for Dancing Fish was to finally convince Oratam to join with him in creating an alliance of nearby bands to work together in opposing the Salt People. There was already a loose covenant for this when facing Mohawk or Mahican hostilities, but this was different, more complex. And Oratam was known to go along with the Whites. An appeaser. A submitter.

The Wiechquaesecks and the Hackensacks—and the Tappans just to the north—were large and powerful Lenape bands, occupying both sides of the Great River. They weren't enemies—the Mohawks and the Mahicans were—but they didn't work together in the way Dancing Fish was hoping for. And even though the Manahates were now part of the Wiechquaesecks, and paying a small tribute to them, all knew that Dancing Fish had the most insight into the Whites and was the best go-between for the different groups.

After the food bowls were cleared, the tea served, and the tobacco pipes and rolls pulled out for smoking, it was time to start the serious discussion.

Dancing Fish stood to speak. He first met the eyes of all who were seated or standing at the edges of the large, warm room. The sounds of murmured conversations gradually faded, and when he was sure he had everyone's attention, he began.

"We live in a world influenced more and more by the Europeans." He started a slow walk around the fire, making sure he could feel Mother Earth under his feet with each step.

"We have lost many important things since their arrival. The beavers are gone, and the deer are fewer. The trees have been cut, and so have our numbers from the fevers the Whites bring." He heard the sobbing start as he knew it would. "We have less and less, and they have more and more."

"But we have more tools and weapons!" shouted out a

young warrior to his left side.

Dancing Fish turned to look directly at the youth. "Yes, we have more tools and weapons—you are right. But these are *their* tools and weapons. We have become reliant on them." He pointed at the youth. "When was the last time you chipped a stone knife? Or made a bear robe to keep you warm? Do you even know how?"

The young man dropped his eyes to the ground.

Dancing Fish pressed him. "And how many canoes have you made from the tulip tree? Where is our ancient way of life? Where are the original Lenape ways?" He sighed. "I will tell you where. They are being lost. And when I say lost, I mean lost forever. More and more, we have to grow the corn to trade for steel knives. We have to catch the fish or the deer to trade for kettles. We have to make or find the wampum to trade for duffel cloth that is not one-half as good as an animal hide."

He waited for this to sink in before continuing. "Do you not see what is happening? We are losing everything that the Creator Kishelemukong has provided to us. And for what?"

Oratam pounded the Sachem's staff on the ground. It was his turn to speak.

"You make good points, Dancing Fish, like you always do. But what do we *do* about this? What is your solution?"

Dancing Fish was ready. "We resist them. And we resist them *together*."

"What do you mean together?"

"The bands must cooperate more. If one is attacked, the others come to the defense. We must work more . . . " He searched for the right word. "Collectively." He looked at the Sachem on his fur-covered stump. "You remember, Oratam, the way the wolves fell upon a fawn when we were young?" He looked back at the youth. "When there were wolves."

"Yes, I remember," the Sachem said, closing his eyes to bring the memories back. "They attacked in a group, signaling and helping each other."

"Exactly," he said. He held up his two hands and pushed them together, interlacing the fingers. "Together. That is what we need more of now."

A young warrior on the other side of the fire jumped to his feet. "We don't need other bands to help us. We are Hackensack. We can fight for ourselves. This is the talk of old men. Dream Makers as they call you. But what good are dreams, and why do we need you? I can kill any White whenever I want. We now have guns!"

The youth held up a musket, and Dancing Fish could feel High Limb stir at his side. He shook his head in both acceptance and disappointment. The arrogance of youth.

"You and another friend can certainly kill a Dutch man. Or a woman. But how will you do against a company of Dutch army soldiers? With a cannon that can blow this entire Council House apart with one shot. How will you defend against that, young warrior?"

Dancing Fish fixed his eyes on the young man. "You are brave, and that is good. But you also don't understand what you're facing." He looked to Oratam. "Which is why we must confront them first with a different kind of power."

Oratam leaned forward on his stump. "What do you mean by *different power*?" he asked. "Like giving them rat pelts for the contributions?" He chuckled and the room joined in.

"The rat pelts were a symbol," Dancing Fish said. "To show that we will not submit to every foolish request. That we have brains and know how to use them. To make them think twice."

"So what are you suggesting, specifically?" the Sachem asked him.

"We start with the corn tax, refusing to pay it. All of us. If none of us pay, then the idea will fail."

"And then?"

"And then we start to turn away from other influences they

hold over us. Like the burning drink. We must stop yielding to it. I know it's hard. But we must resist. Otherwise, we lose everything that it means to be Lenape." He heard murmurs of approval until Oratam pounded his staff again.

"But my goal with the Salts is peace," the Sachem said, aiming a hard glance at the youth with the musket. "To not—"

There was a sudden stirring behind them, and a man—Hackensack by his tattoos—stumbled to the center of the room and sprawled on the dirt next to the fire. He was covered in cuts, blood, and leaves.

"What is this?!" Oratam demanded. "What's happened to you?"

The man came to his knees while water was brought to him. He drank deeply, then spoke.

"I was trading with the Raritans. Suddenly, a large group of Whites—soldiers—started attacking the village. They wouldn't listen to our pleas. They just kept coming and stabbing and ..." He put his hand to his eyes and took several deep breaths before continuing. "I was only able to escape by the help of the Spirits."

High Limb jumped to his feet and pointed to the bloody trader. "You see! There is your peace."

Sixty-nine

August 1641

Marie Boucher sat in a tall chair in front of the director's desk. She was in the living room of his house, which doubled as a meeting space. There were two small windows high on the wall to let in light and air, but the room felt even hotter than the outside, if that was possible. She could hear the sounds of waves on the shore mixed with seagulls squawking.

The director's house was one of several buildings inside the walls of Fort Amsterdam. If you could call them walls. Pigs, dogs, and people regularly climbed over the earthen mounds to enter or leave the fort, even though there was also a main gate, which seemed more for show than an actual entrance.

She caught Director Kieft studying her attire with a turned-down mouth. "Should you really be dressed like an Indian?" he said, disapprovingly. "A woman of your stature?"

Marie fingered the edge of her low-cut, sleeveless jerkin. "It's made of duffel cloth, from the company store."

"Yes, but most ladies wear a bodice from neck to waist, do they not? To ... to ..." he stammered, "cover their delicate parts."

She laughed while she watched summer sweat glisten on the forehead of the man who controlled all of New Netherland. "And tell me why I would want to cover myself up in his heat? I think going naked from the waist up like the natives would be more practical, don't you?"

She watched his face redden and his lips quiver.

447

"Do not speak like this!" he said, raising his voice, which, she had to admit, did have a commanding, if irritating, quality to it. "You are a Dutch woman of prominence—"

"A Walloon woman," she corrected him. "Speaking Dutch."

"Yes, yes, alright," he acceded. "But still, a New Netherlander. And not a savage." He shook his head as if trying to dislodge a dangerous thought. "Can we please get to the matter at hand and end this talk of clothing?"

Marie enjoyed sparring with Kieft but didn't want to overly anger him. She knew the Indian situation was volatile. After the Dutch attack on the Raritans west of Staaten Island the previous year, there had been reprisals by the natives and escalations by Kieft and his soldiers. Tensions between the two sides had risen over the past months with no easy peace in sight, and she didn't want to inflame things further.

They seemed to be sitting on a powder keg where one spark could set off the explosion. There were even rumors that Kieft might require all the outlying settlers to move closer to the fort for protection. That would be a big inconvenience for her and her growing business. She had to watch what she said.

She had tried talking to the director about Kofi many times, but he was always too busy with the natives or some other urgency. But with Kofi's repeated pleadings, she could wait no longer. "It's about my slave, Kofi," she said in a calm tone.

"What about him?" he asked, flicking away a fly.

"He wants to marry. Another slave. A Company slave."

Kieft narrowed his eyes and, leaning forward, put his elbows on the table and crossed his fingers. "First, you press me to allow the colony's only private slave, one not available to do the work of the Company, and now you ask that he be allowed to marry." A grunting sound came from his throat. "Do you never stop pushing, woman?"

She smiled. "You should be thankful I'm not asking that he marry a Dutch lady."

The director closed his eyes and covered his ears with his hands. "Do not speak such heresies. Please, Madame Boucher, quiet that tongue of yours. For both of our sakes."

"But I'm not finished with my requests." She watched him roll his eyes.

"What is it?"

She softened her voice. "Although legally I do not need to ask, I respectfully request Kofi's manumission. That he be freed and set at liberty."

Kieft leaned back in his chair. "I see you've been keeping up with the laws. Then you should know that a private slave is your property, you can free him as you please." He smiled. "But your asking for my permission is a good action on your part."

Now she knew she had used the correct strategy.

He leaned forward again. "Here is what I propose to you, Madame Boucher." He extended one finger from his right hand toward the ceiling. "Provided Reverend Bogardus is in agreement, your slave may marry. But only to another Negro slave owned by the Company. And that slave and any children will still do the Company's work."

She had anticipated this and nodded once.

"Second"—another finger went up—"let's not talk of manumission and freedom now. I'm too occupied with other matters. The Indians are causing me—us—quite a problem."

"Which leads to my third request," she said, watching him start to quiver again. "You are building a burgher guard and want us all to assist in defense of the colony."

"Quite so."

"And every male is expected to be in possession of a firearm."

"Every male *immigrant*," he corrected.

"And slaves are not immigrants?" she asked innocently.

Kieft slammed his hand down on the table. "You're really asking too much, you know that? Maybe you should spend more time finding a good Dutch husband to marry rather than worrying about these details."

Marie didn't hesitate. "There are no good Dutch husbands. I've already tried one."

He threw up his hands. "Fine. Your Kofi may have a musket for our mutual defense." He pointed at her. "And he may be called upon to use it."

"And powder and shot," she immediately added.

He stood abruptly, knocking over his chair. "Very well. Go to the company store and purchase what you need." He gave her a final, pleading look. "And leave me in peace. Please!"

▶◀

Reverend Everardus Bogardus was already at his spot outside the church greeting each person when they emerged from the Sunday service. Van Ost shielded his eyes from the summer glare on exiting the small building and waited patiently in line. He heard the rough sea roaring on the other side of the fort's walls as he turned and spotted the Walloon woman and her slave. Most of the women were shocked by this unusual involvement, and more than a few single men were simply puzzled by it. He met Marie Boucher's pale blue eyes and nodded to her, but she turned her head away. Strange woman.

"Move along, man," the captain prompted behind him. "Don't want to be standing in this heat longer than I have to."

But there was nowhere to go. "It's the director and the minister arguing again," Van Ost said over his back, indicating the heated argument going on between Kieft and Bogardus at the front of the line. The two had been at loggerheads almost from the beginning. The reverend was sympathetic to the needs of the settlers and the natives, where Kieft's main concern was the trade business. The settlers—and the Indians—were either a nuisance or a hindrance to that goal.

The two voices grew in volume and anger. "We should be

saving the natives and their souls, not killing them!" the stout Bogardus shouted at Kieft.

"And you should mind to your own affairs, Reverend," the director replied forcefully. "I'm the highest authority here, and I will decide what's best."

The minister, clad in his long-sleeved cassock and black clerical hat, was having none of it. "The Dutch Reformed Church has the moral authority, and we answer directly to God." He snorted. "Not to you."

The director gave him a menacing look. "Mind your tongue or I'll make a complaint to the Company, and they'll recall you."

"If anyone is recalled, it'll be you," the reverend retorted before taking a step toward Kieft. "If you're not going to recognize the right and honor of the church, then maybe you shouldn't be attending our services."

Kieft smiled as he lifted himself over the smaller minister. "And that is the first reasonable thing you've said all day."

Secretary Van Tienhoven, seeing the escalating conflict, quickly stepped between the two men and urged the director away by the arm. "Let's not get into a fight with the church," he said while the director kept looking back and scowling.

"It'll only get worse between those two," the captain said into Van Ost's ear, the smell of brandy evident. "You watch."

He didn't doubt it. There were so many different factions fighting for power in the colony, it was hard to keep up with them all. But what he had to do was focus on his job—being a good Company soldier—and not get dragged into these squabbles for dominance and control. He needed to have a mind to his future, no matter what.

Captain Beeckman whispered, "Just remember that we report to the director, not to the church. Never forget that."

Van Ost nodded without speaking. If only it were that simple. Kieft had congratulated him on the raid against the Raritans, which he considered a disaster. He still had much to learn.

Seventy

DANCING FISH SAT ON A FLAT ROCK, HIS LEGS DANGLING IN the warm, shallow water. He watched the maple trees on the other side of the waterway that separated the northern part of the island from the mainland. Gusty winds from the approaching summer storm blew the branches this way and that, turning the leaves from dark green to gray and back again. And with each turn, the trees made a swishing sound that reminded him of the wind whistling past the sails of Hudson's ship all those years ago.

The sky was darkening, and he could hear the rumble of thunder coming from the south. He was hoping to catch fish in the weirs with the ebbing tide, but he knew the storm would make the fish hide under submerged logs and avoid the traps.

"Let's stop for today!" he shouted to Diver and Takokwsu, who were checking the weirs farther along the water. He stood and motioned for them to join him.

While they walked back to Shorakapkock, Dancing Fish noticed that the short, thin Takokwsu seemed preoccupied. He had never really liked the eldest nephew of Stands Tall, the Wiechquaeseck Sachem who had recently passed over to the Sky World. Where the Sachem had been wise and deliberate, Takokwsu, who had joined the Manahate band through marriage, was moody and quick to anger. He seemed mad at life. He didn't have the graces and dignity of a seasoned man, even for someone with his advanced age of 27 winters. And he didn't show enough respect or attention to his wife and two small children. That was maybe his worst failing.

"Takokwsu," he asked gently, "what's on your mind? You're quiet today."

"I've been thinking about the Whites," he answered after a long pause. "About what they have and what we don't."

A familiar topic of conversation. "But much of what they have is not good for us."

"Easy for you to say. You're a Sachem, a leader."

Dancing Fish stopped and the other two followed suit. He studied Takokwsu's face and the unkempt hair—half braided, half not—that framed it. The man called himself a warrior but he certainly didn't look or act like one. "Do not speak foolishly. You know well that a Sachem has less than others. A Sachem is more concerned with his people and less about himself. Did you not see that in your uncle?"

Takokwsu snorted. "Stands Tall was not mad enough at the Whites. And he died because of it."

"No, your uncle died of the fevers, like many others."

"But did you not say, yourself, that the fevers came from the Whites?"

"Yes, I did. But being mad or not mad at them is a different matter. Some die from the fevers and some don't. We're both lucky to be alive."

"I don't feel lucky. I feel we need to do something about these strangers."

"They're no longer strangers, and we *are* doing something. We're resisting in our own way." He looked intently at the man. "And you can be a part of that. You can start by giving up the strong drink. You trade things of value for what, a few fingers of time lost to the clouds? What kind of way is that?"

"It's a way to forget what is happening to us."

Dancing Fish knew it was hard to counter this idea,

expressed by many. But he had to try. "You know the forgetting is temporary with the drink. And afterward, you're worse off than before. And so is your family."

A hard look came into Takokwsu's eyes. "My family is not your concern, Elder."

He stepped quickly up to the man and slapped him across the face with his open hand. Takokwsu shrank back for a moment and started to reach for the knife at his waist but thought better of it. He did not move.

"Everyone in the Manahate band is my concern," Dancing Fish said. "Even you. I'm opposing the Whites, too, but not by drinking their burning water. This requires thinking, not drinking."

They stood motionless, staring at each other until Diver stepped forward. "Do you want to come with us tomorrow, Takokwsu?" he asked the man in a voice that was changing from the high of a boy to the low of a man. Diver was already showing his leadership skills at a young age.

Dancing Fish smiled at his son. "An excellent idea." He turned to Takokwsu. "We're going south. Why don't you come? We can talk more and maybe do some good trading along the way."

The man suddenly came to life. "South? On the long path?"

"Yes. To Werpoes. And I can show you the right way to trade."

Takokwsu returned to his gloomy mood. "And what would I trade for? A black kettle?" He scoffed. "I'm not a woman. I am a warrior. I live to fight."

But not much of one. "There are other things to trade for that will help us—help you—that are not the dark pit of drink."

"Like what, muskets?"

Dancing Fish shook his head. "The Salt People will not trade openly for muskets. You know this. But they will trade for wampum. And with wampum, you can trade for whatever you

454

like, with them or with the People."

Takokwsu seemed lost in thought.

Diver asked him, "Do you have something to trade? Skins? Meat? Fish?"

The man's eyes suddenly opened wider. He dipped his head. "I will join you."

▶◀

The storm had passed, and the sun was high in a cloudless sky when the three of them reached the house of Claes Swits. It sat just off the path all now called the Wiechquaeseck Trail, where it bent in toward a half-moon-shaped bay on the eastern waterway.

Roughly one-third up from the island's tip, the house was a popular place for Whites to rest their legs and talk with Swits while they drank his beer and brandy for a small price. It was also a stopping place for any of the People traveling north or south on the island. And open to trade.

Dancing Fish knew the old Swits man well and liked him. Unlike many Whites, Swits always had a kind word for the People passing by his house. It wasn't much of a house by New Amsterdam standards—more like a rough cabin—just some logs stacked up with a roof of brush, reeds, and dirt, but it was a well-known spot to spend some time off the trail.

When they arrived at the house, Swits was sitting in front under the shade of a broad hickory. The sound of a woodpecker's drilling bounced through the tree trunks of the forest, and the smell of roasting meat came from the door.

The old man with his white hair and big belly stood to greet them. "Welcome, travelers," he said, raising his arm in sign. "Who have you brought with you?" he asked.

Dancing Fish nodded to his two companions. "You know Diver, my son, and this is another from band: Takokwsu." He watched Swits smile warmly, but when he glanced at Takokwsu he saw no smile, just a determined look with jaws tightly locked. It was an odd reaction, but he was an odd man.

"We are on way south, to Great Pond at Werpoes," Dancing Fish said, "and want stop to rest and trade." He pointed at the deerskin hides Takokwsu carried over his shoulder. "Maybe for few strings of wampum?"

Swits smiled warmly. "Of course. Come in and have something to eat or drink, and we'll talk trade."

They started to step into the house when Takokwsu turned to Dancing Fish. "Why don't you stay here so I can watch Diver begin the trading? Let him be on his own more."

Dancing Fish thought it an unusual request, but he also saw the wisdom in it. "Yes, why not?" he said to the man. "Just bring me some water when you can."

He settled into the same chair Swits had been sitting in and tried to locate the woodpecker in the surrounding trees. The bird would be high up on a dead limb, probably at the top of the canopy.

He was scanning and listening when he heard a strange thumping noise inside the cabin.

Diver suddenly came running out with a wild look in his eyes. "Father!" he yelled, "come quick, inside."

Dancing Fish jumped to his feet and sprinted to the house, passing his son and entering the dim room. And what he saw froze him in place.

Takokwsu was standing over the old man, holding an axe and breathing hard. "Now I have my revenge," he said in gasps, eyes fixed on the man's body on the wooden floor.

It took Dancing Fish a few moments to realize that Takokwsu had cut off the head of Swits with his axe! The head had its eyes open, and it lay a short distance from the body, which oozed blood from its torn neck.

"What ... What have you done?!" Dancing Fish questioned

in a panic. "Why have you killed this man who is liked by all? What has happened here?"

Takokwsu dropped the bloodied axe and turned slowly toward him while Diver entered the room. "I have waited 15 years for this. This is my revenge."

He explained that as a boy, he had been with a different uncle and others on a trading trip when they were stopped by a group of Dutch men who robbed them of their furs and then killed them—he was the only one able to get away.

"And you've kept this inside you all this time?" Dancing Fish asked him, stunned.

"Yes," he said, dropping to his knees next to the body and swaying in a circle.

Dancing Fish slumped to the floor and buried his head in his right hand. His mind was filled with the depth of the problem this violent act by Takokwsu had just created. By their ways, Takokwsu had legitimately avenged the killing of his uncle. An eye for an eye. But the Whites would not understand this. They would see it as the simple murder of an innocent old man. A murder that would have to be met by severe punishment.

He looked at Takokwsu. "You've just made our lives much, much harder."

Seventy-one

THE DIRECTOR'S HOUSE WAS A TWO-STORY, STEP-GABLED building—the first in New Amsterdam—inside the fort, up against the eastern wall and directly opposite the barracks. And Van Ost could hear shouting and angry words from it all the way from the other side of the parade square.

A heavy rain had fallen the night before, and he had to step carefully to avoid puddles while he crossed the muddy ground to the house. The sun had long set, and fireflies blinked on and off in the muggy August air.

He knocked on the main door and was met by Secretary Van Tienhoven. "They're already arguing and half-drunk," the bulky man said as he led him back to the first-floor meeting room where the others were.

Director Kieft had called together the heads of the most prominent families soon after the murder of Swits, and he had selected twelve men to advise him further on what to do about, not only the murder, but the escalating problems with the Indians. This was the first meeting of The Twelve to work on a plan. But while Van Ost scanned the crowded room, which smelled of sweat, beer, and the fishy odor of whale oil burning from a few lamps that offered only faint light, he knew it would be hard to get this group to agree on anything.

"We need to work with the natives," settler David de Vries was imploring. "We want them on our side, not as enemies."

458

"And what of Claes' murder?" another settler shouted, sloshing beer from his tankard. "We must answer force with force."

A cheer erupted along with more tankards raised in the air. One of the nearby tap houses was providing drink for the meeting. At a reduced price, of course.

A farmer from north of the village stood. "I'm worried for my farm and for my family. We can't have savages roaming over the land and killing and destroying whatever they like. We have a right to protection." He looked over to Kieft, who sat in the far corner of the room in a chair slightly higher than the others. "I want to know what the director thinks. Why doesn't he just send out the army"—the man pointed to Van Ost and the captain who now stood next to him—"to stop these outrages against us?"

Kieft rose from his chair and the room quieted. The director pulled at his beard while he looked around the stuffy room. He seemed to study the crowd as a general would survey a battlefield. Except these were the ordinary people under his charge in New Netherland.

Van Ost knew that if Kieft had his way, he would not have a council of men at all and would simply give orders to do whatever he pleased. But he was under instruction from the Company to be more open to advice from others. Kieft was surely gnashing his teeth about having to put up with suggestions from simple farmers, merchants, and traders. He was an official with higher responsibilities. He was the king of his kingdom.

"First, I want to thank you for your good advice," he began, to several snickers and muted laughs. No one believed that the director valued opinions other than his own. "I have been listening to your words carefully."

One man jumped to his feet. "Why won't the savages simply hand over Claes' murderer so we can hang him and be done with it? His death must be paid for in blood."

A chorus of "Ayes" filled the room.

Van Ost glanced at Kieft and stepped forward. "I and the captain have asked this of the Wiechquaesecks more than once," he said, turning to Captain Beeckman, whose bloodshot eyes and slow manner spoke of a long night with the bottle. "And they have refused each time."

Angry shouts and the banging of tankards on wooden tables was the instant response to this. Then another stood. "I've heard that one of the savages said he was sorry 20 Christians had not been murdered instead of just one."

The room broke out in enraged shouting and yelling. "If we don't do something soon," the man continued, raising his voice over the din, "this whole village will be ruined. With all of us dead like our friend Claes." Many in the room nodded solemnly at this thought.

Kieft raised both hands and eventually silenced the room. "Do not worry, my friends," he said in a strong, serious voice. "God's intention will be made manifest." He paused. "And I'll make sure it is."

The director smiled and stepped toward the door. This was the signal that the meeting was over. "I think we are done here, but I wish Captain Beeckman and Ensign Van Ost to stay to discuss some details with me. Have a safe journey back to your homes."

The men's murmurs mixed with the scraping of benches when they rose and slowly left. When they were finally alone, Kieft turned to the two of them. "Forget these ignorant farmers. We will punish the savages for what they've done, and do it in our own way." He rubbed his hand over the top of one of the tables that had been made by slaves. "I want you to organize more expeditions against the Indians. It's time for more pressure."

"Gladly," the captain said, sounding more sober. "And will you be leading these expeditions?" he asked with an imperceptible smile.

"Oh no. You're the soldiers. That's your job. I must stay at the fort."

"Of course you must," said the captain, barely containing his disdain.

Kieft let the affront pass. "I want you to go after them and extract what you can: Swits' murderer, or failing that, bring me the tax contributions, or a tribute. Use whatever force is necessary." Kieft looked right at Van Ost. "Don't disappoint me, Ensign."

Van Ost winced. Those were the exact words his father had always used to encourage his own self-doubts. And he had plenty of them.

▶◀

The Green Corn ceremony marked the start of the fall hunting season. The Balance of Days had passed, the leaves were turning, and while the women, old men, and children prepared for the corn harvest, High Limb led his hunting warriors south and to the eastern waterway.

They met Takokwsu near the abandoned village of Shawkequa, where he had been told to hide away from the Whites. The settlers had not made their way to this part of the island yet, and he would be safe so long as he stayed out of sight.

Not that many knew Takokwsu had killed the old white man, but the burning drink was known to loosen too many lips, so putting distances between Takokwsu, the Whites, and the band was the smart thing to do. His family had been told he was on an extended hunting trip, and High Limb knew the three warriors with him could be trusted to make no mention of seeing the man.

"I have something that might interest you, War Chief," Takokwsu said between bites of sizzling deer flesh. They had gutted several bucks and were letting them hang to bleed while tasting some of their kill. They sat on rotting logs around a fire that glowed bright as darkness slowly folded around them.

A small blaze was all that was needed this late in the year, with the mosquitoes asleep for the winter and their hide coverings to keep them warm in the cooling nights.

"What do you have?" High Limb said, reaching for his tea near the fire.

"In my time away," Takokwsu said, "I've been exploring and watching the Whites from a distance. And I discovered an interesting place not far from here."

He changed his position to kneel next to one of the logs and to pull out a small pouch from his leggings. "I found this in Swits man's house and took it." He opened the end of the pouch, tilted it, and let a dark powder fall onto the log.

"Their black powder," said a surprised High Limb, who had only examined it once before. He bent closer and rubbed the powder between his fingers. It was like charcoal mixed with grains of sand.

He sniffed it. Then he tasted it. "It tastes like burnt wood but with piss mixed in."

"Yes, and I know where they store it. In a house south of the big pond near Werpoes."

"Where exactly is this house?"

With the sun low in the west the next day, High Limb and the three warriors hid behind a laurel thicket with a good view of the powder house. It was square and small, and it stood between two narrow strips of swamp water. Far enough away from the Dutch village, it was a good place to put a house that could blow up. While High Limb didn't know everything about the magic of this fire powder the Whites used in their muskets, pistols, and cannons, he knew enough to understand the danger it presented if handled incorrectly.

And his plan was to steal some of it.

Only a hint of yellow colored the western sky while High Limb crept closer to the powder house. He had instructed the warriors to stay back and find other places to hide themselves. They would give warning and assistance, if needed, and he'd go to the house alone.

The sky was almost dark when he walked in a low stoop up to the small door. Pausing first to listen carefully, he pushed against it. It was locked but creaked slightly each time he pushed.

Feeling and judging the resistance offered, High Limb stepped back and then rushed forward, slamming his full body weight against the door that made a cracking sound and then flung open. He fell to the dirt floor from his effort but rolled swiftly to his feet and stood in a defensive crouch.

He was studying a pile of small barrels in the weak light when a voice startled him. "Don't move, or I'll shoot you," came the invisible command.

High Limb strained to find the owner of the voice. The man suddenly stepped out from the shadows with his musket aimed directly at the War Chief. He had obviously been left inside the house as a guard, and High Limb cursed himself for not having considered this possibility.

With the two men frozen in position, High Limb quickly went through every option in his warrior mind and came to his only course of action: he turned and ran for the open door. But he was too slow. The musket's loud firing filled the house, and he instantly felt the shock and then the pain from the ball striking his left leg. He collapsed to the ground.

The next morning, with his leg tied tightly, he was forced into a long, limping walk in front of the man holding his musket until they reached New Amsterdam.

High Limb's arrival caused an immediate clamor in the

village, and before long, he found himself in a shameful position on the northern side of the fort: kneeling on a platform with his hands and his head sticking out through three holes in a framework of wooden blocks. He—a War Chief—was in the pillory!

▶◀

Dancing Fish had never seen anything like it. In front of him was the respected High Limb, a War Chief known to bands across many lands. And he was being shamed and debased not only by being put into the pillory stocks, but even more by the people of the village who had gathered around the wooden structure and were hurling, not just insults, but also eggs and other pieces of food aimed at his head. And the War Chief was fighting back with the only thing he had: his unmoving and unemotional silence. His dignity.

Dancing Fish was unsure of what to do. He, Diver, and the three warriors who had told him what had happened all stood together in an open area just north of the fort, staring at their war leader with the crowd to their left and the fort directly ahead. Behind them rested a small wheeled cart loaded with ripe corn and two beaver furs. Dancing Fish was prepared to negotiate for High Limb's release.

He heard the main gate of the fort open, and soon a small group approached. He recognized three men whose names and positions he now knew: Director Kieft, Commies De Sille, and Ensign Van Ost. The others he didn't know. And each wore an overabundance of clothing for such a bright, pleasant day.

"Make way!" Kieft commanded, scattering the crowd in front of the stocks. He motioned to Dancing Fish and the others in his group to move forward.

"How is his injury?" Dancing Fish asked, looking at High Limb, who threw him only a quick glance. The War Chief was clearly embarrassed to be found like this.

"He will be fine," Kieft said. "The bullet passed straight through the upper part of his leg without hitting bone. He'll be walking normally soon enough."

"Why do you put him like this, in these wood blocks?"

De Sille, standing next to Kieft, said, "He's a thief. We caught him in the powder house."

Kieft gave the man a hard glance. "Quiet!"

High Limb suddenly chuckled and all turned to look at him, his face covered with drippings of egg yolks and bits of shell pieces. "Not big secret, your powder house, is it?"

"Nevertheless," Kieft growled, "we found you there, sneaking around and obviously trying to steal something."

High Limb struggled against the stocks, making them rattle and squeak, but he soon gave up and just grimaced. "I steal nothing. Only curious."

Laughter tumbled out the mouths of the Whites. "A curious savage, eh?" the Commies said, grinning. "We have a way of dealing with those of you who are curious." The people all laughed at this, but Dancing Fish observed that the soldier Van Ost was expressionless and studying him carefully.

Dancing Fish had heard enough. "No matter what you think War Chief did or did not do, I now negotiate—to trade—for his release. He injures no one." He shot a hard look at Kieft and waited.

The Director pulled at his pointed beard. "What do you have in mind?"

Dancing Fish turned and pointed to the cart. "I bring your contribution—your tax."

Kieft smiled. "Do you now? Finally." He indicated with his hand that De Sille should go inspect the trade goods.

"A good load of corn and two beaver pelts," the Commies declared before moving back to his group.

Kieft tipped his head and looked first to High Limb and

then at Dancing Fish. "Well, this is a satisfactory start. But we still demand the murderer of Claes Swits."

Dancing Fish stepped aside for two of the younger Whites to start rolling the cart in the direction of the fort. At the same time, Van Ost lifted the top piece of pillory wood and helped High Limb to stand up. He wobbled on his legs but soon limped over to join the group from the band.

High Limb put his hand on Dancing Fish's shoulder and murmured in their own tongue. "I was stupid. I'm sorry."

"Yes, you were," Dancing Fish said. "And you are forgiven." He smiled at High Limb. "That is, if you tell me more about the black powder."

High Limb grinned at the same time he grimaced from his leg injury. "All in time."

"We are done here," Dancing Fish announced to the white leaders in a loud voice. He turned and all of them started walking north up the broad path that he remembered used to be edged with tall, green trees. Now, there were only small garden plots and strange-looking houses.

He heard the demanding words of Kieft behind him. "We still must have this murderer, do you hear? And we will get our justice."

Dancing Fish stopped and turned back to stare silently at Kieft.

The Director returned his stare and narrowed his eyes. "One way or another."

Seventy-two

Winter 1641–42

MARIE COULD SEE THE SNOW PILING IN THE CORNERS OUT-
side her small windows. It had started soon after the minister
and his assistant arrived. The snow was wet and heavy, and she
worried about the weight of it on the roof when the sound of
creaking came to her ears. But she trusted the sturdy framework
built by the best of the colony's carpenters, for which she had
paid handsomely. And this was not a day of worry. It was a joy-
ous day. A good day for a wedding at her farm.

It had taken awhile for the proper church items to be set up
in her small living room. Reverend Bogardus was very particular about each piece and where it should go. He wasn't used to
performing the wedding ceremony outside of the church, but
there really was no other option. Marrying two Negroes—one
a slave, no less—inside the fort would have caused a riot. But
it helped that Kofi was now a baptized member of the Dutch
Reformed congregation.

A white linen cloth covered the table, and the two gold can-
dlesticks were in place and lit. Their scent conjured up memories for Marie of going to church with her family in Wallonia.

Bogardus held the silver chalice with one hand while he
poured brandy into it with the other. Then he couldn't help
giving it a big taste. "It's fine," he said, making a soft smacking sound with his mouth before putting the chalice down on
the table next to the ornate cross. Marie was sure she saw his

inner struggle to keep from taking another taste. Bogardus was a hard-drinking Calvinist who, without acknowledging his own hypocrisy, could rail against drunkenness at one moment and drain a full tankard the next.

"Are we ready?" he asked, turning to face them.

Marie stepped back and proudly surveyed the scene. In front of the table stood the minister in his long white cassock and black hat. Facing him was the happy couple: Kofi and his intended, Juba Angola, whose almost-black skin and white teeth battled for attention. They each wore their best clothes. New Amsterdam's elite would have snickered and considered them mere rags, but for Kofi and Juba, these were their equivalents of the finest silk doublets and dresses, even if they were made of coarse duffel cloth.

The assistant, who was also the horse cart's driver, stood off to one side, and she, to the other. They were the witnesses.

Marie had instructed the reverend to make his speech short, and after giving him more than one stern look, he finished his discourse on human weakness and the power of a loving God in record time. He then had the couple each drink from the chalice—a ritual she was sure he had invented—and asked about the rings.

In a somewhat different way than was her background, the couple had already been wearing their wedding rings—simple gold bands—but on their left hands. The reverend now asked them to move each other's ring to the right.

"And by this act and in front of these witnesses, I declare you, Kofi and Juba, to be man and wife in the eyes of God."

The two turned and hugged each other, beaming. "Tank you, tank you," Kofi said ardently, taking the reverend's hand and shaking it over and over until Bogardus was finally able to pull it away.

"The next step is for Juba to be baptized into the church, like you. You know this?" he asked them.

"Oh yes, Revint," Kofi said, still smiling broadly. "I know that, certain."

A sudden frown wrinkled the reverend's face. He asked Kofi, "And where will you two be living? She has been at the slave camp on the East River. But now?"

Marie stepped forward. "They'll both be living here, on the farm. Kofi has his own hut. It's small, but they won't mind."

Kofi nodded his head vigorously at this.

"No, I suppose not," Bogardus said, letting out a low laugh.

The ceremony over, Marie invited everyone to take a seat at the table. She had loaded it with a plate of honey-infused bread balls and several tankards of beer. Now they could relax.

With Kofi and Juba chatting animatedly to the young assistant, Marie pulled her chair over to sit next to Bogardus. "Shall we talk?"

"About what subject?"

Marie eyed the short man, who had taken off his hat and unbuttoned the top of his cassock. He was well into his second beer, and she saw that the silver chalice was now empty. "There seems to be only one subject coming from your church sermons these days," she said, watching for his reaction. "Your differences with Director Kieft."

He gave her a tired look. "Yes, unfortunately. And the Indians, of course."

"Of course. But they're related."

"Indeed they are."

"Can you not prevail on Director Kieft to be more open-minded about the natives? That they have a place on this land and should not be treated so harshly?"

Bogardus sighed. "I have tried to instill in him the idea that we are all God's creatures, Indians included. But our director doesn't seem interested in what God thinks. About anything."

The reverend then leaned close to Marie and lowered his voice. "I fear not only about the native Indians but also about

469

the colony itself. I'm not optimistic."

Marie leaned back in her chair and pondered the minister's words. She glanced at the window and saw that the snow had stopped. Snow was always a problem, but what Bogardus was hinting at was different. And potentially much more serious.

▶◀

The New Year had finally come, but the identity of Swits' murderer had not. Dirck van Ost knew everything moved more slowly in winter, especially one this cold, but that was not an adequate excuse for Director Kieft. He continually complained about his taxes not being collected and the general non-compliance of the Indians to his way of thinking. They owed him fealty, and when it was not forthcoming, he became angrier and angrier. His will would be asserted without regard to the weather or time of year.

So it was with an emotional heaviness that Van Ost found himself setting out again on another mission at Kieft's order to extract something from the natives. This time it was a short distance north to the large pond that supplied much of their fresh water.

Van Ost knew the Indians moved the bulk of their numbers off the island to more sheltered areas in winter, but some were often left behind. And there were the winter hunting parties that passed over Manatus, which the natives continued to call "Mannahatta." It was one of these that his small company of soldiers met on the south side of the deep pond.

The surface of the pond was frozen solid, and the hunters were inside a large wigwam covered with snow, blue smoke spiraling out of the hut's central roof hole. Strangely, there were no guards posted—most likely because of the extreme cold—so their approach was unobserved.

"Come out and show yourselves!" Van Ost commanded, his

soldiers positioned behind him, muskets ready.

There was instant disturbance inside the wigwam, and the door flap soon opened and one man stepped out. He was a tall, strong warrior in full leggings and with a fur cloak wrapped around him to ward off the bitter cold. His head was plucked in the warrior style, leaving only the central crown of pitch-black hair. Tattoos covered his forehead, but they looked different than the ones Van Ost was used to seeing.

"Who are you?" the ensign asked, lifting his right arm up in a questioning sign while cradling his musket in the other.

The native leaned his head to one side and conveyed a puzzled look. Strange words in a guttural voice came out of his mouth. Van Ost recognized none of the language and shrugged his shoulders to indicate as much.

The man nodded and turned to speak to those waiting inside the wigwam. Soon, a younger, shorter native came out of the opening. After a quick exchange between the two, the new man asked in halting Dutch, "What you want here?"

Van Ost, carefully noting the knives that protruded from both native's waists, spoke slowly. "We seek the murderer of Claes Swits."

The two men looked at each other and spoke rapidly. "We not the ones," the younger man said. "You want Manahates."

"Manahates." Van Ost repeated. "You are not Manahates?"

Both men shook their heads. "No. Wiechquaesecks. North." The better speaker pointed in the direction. "No Manahates here now."

While Van Ost absorbed this information, more Indians started to appear from inside the wigwam. Their group was growing and spreading out to both sides, and Van Ost was surprised to see that the natives soon outnumbered his group.

"Sir," his corporal said with a worried tone, "I don't like this. And we are under orders to bring back something to the director. What should we do?"

471

Van Ost thought fast while he took in the smell of food cooking. It came from inside the wigwam. "You have food." It was more a statement than a question, but the native nodded.

Then Van Ost remembered something. He raised his voice. "Where are the buried food stores?"

The two central Indians looked at each other then turned to him and lifted their hands at the same time. "Do not know."

"Yes, you do," Van Ost said firmly, lifting his musket higher and reaching for the pistol with his right hand.

The eyes of every native simultaneously followed his movements as they started whispering among themselves.

"Men," he said in his most powerful voice, preparing the fire command. "Muskets!" Every musket was now raised and pointing directly at the native group in front of them. "At my command."

And then, in one movement, like a flock of birds reacting to a loud sound, the entire group of Indians turned and started running away.

Van Ost was about to give the order to not shoot and let them go when, suddenly, one of the men fired his musket at the backs of the fleeing natives. Others quickly joined in. "*Cease Fire!*" he shouted, but it was too late. Through the smoke of the volley, he could see that several natives were on the ground, bleeding and writhing.

Angry about his men but also gauging the situation and looking for an opportunity, Van Ost turned to his corporal and pointed at the wigwam. "Use their fire and set that wigwam alight."

"Alight, sir?" the corporal asked, confused.

"Yes," he said forcefully. "Burn it down. Now."

After the ashes had cooled, and after the wounded natives had either died or crawled off into the leafless trees leaving streaks of dark blood, Van Ost ordered his men to dig into the now-warm dirt. Soon, they were rewarded.

With the weak sun setting, and the scent of burnt ashes still hanging in the cold air, they were able to find several buried food pits full of salted fish and meats as well as corn, dried roots, berries, and nuts. Now he had something to bring back to the director. Something to make him look like a good soldier and leader. He was doing his job.

▶◀

Dancing Fish poked through the ashes and studied the empty food pits. Then he stepped back and surveyed the entire scene. The largest of the wigwams, including the old Council House, had been burned to the ground. Most of the small individual wigwams were untouched.

"What happened here?" Diver asked. "Who would do this?"

He had brought his son south for their yearly winter hunting trip, which included visiting the burial grounds and the old village at Werpoes next to the pond.

A round object caught his eye and Dancing Fish walked over to inspect. He bent down and picked up a lead musket ball, rolling it between his fingers. "The Whites did this," he said, shaking his head. He sniffed the air. "And not that long ago."

Diver said, "But weren't we going to eat the food in the pits? I'm hungry."

"I know. Me, too." He stood for a moment listening to the wind moving through the bare tree trunks. Then he looked at the bodies of the rabbits and two foxes they had killed that morning: one gray and one rare red fox.

"We'll take the red fox to Marie," he said. "We'll trade it for some food so we can continue to hunt. And she'll have other food." He smiled at the thought of seeing her again. They were good friends, and she would help them.

The sun was a low, dull blur in a gray sky when they came to Marie's farm, two fingers walk northeast of the pond. Her black man, Kofi, first confronted them but then led them to Marie's rambling house, and they were soon in its warm interior.

"This fox is too valuable to trade for food," an older but still-strong-looking Marie said, holding the animal up by its tail and looking carefully at its thick, reddish fur. "A few more of these, and you'll have a wonderful robe to present the Wiechquaesecks for tribute."

"But we need food," Dancing Fish softly. "We hope to find hibernating bear but don't have yet. That makes much food and even better robe."

"Oh stop it, you yellow-eyed savage," she said teasingly, flashing a broad smile under the same curly hair and pale blue eyes of her father. "You've done so much for me, the least I can do is offer you some food." She winked at Diver. "And even some very special oat brandy."

"You know how I feel about the brandy," Dancing Fish said, "but the food we accept with gracefulness."

"Gratitude," she corrected.

His Dutch tongue was good, but there were always new words to learn. "Gratitude," he repeated, committing it to memory and thanking her.

After they were joined by Kofi's new woman, Juba, they ate a hearty meal of rabbit stew and cornbread, and then relaxed by a blazing hearth fire drinking tea and smoking tobacco. Dancing Fish talked at length about the running arguments and disagreements with Director Kieft and his army, and he could see Marie and Kofi nodding their heads in agreement. They were not from the land or the People, but they understood the situation well enough.

After some moments of silence, Marie announced, "Kofi wants to show you something." She signaled with her head, and he stood and walked into another room. Soon, he was back with a musket and two pouches. He opened one pouch, reached in, and pulled out a fistful of black powder that he spilled onto the dirt floor. He then started shaping the powder into a long, thin line.

"He's found a way to split large logs with the powder," Marie explained.

Kofi reached for one of the pieces of wood stacked by the fire and showed it to Dancing Fish and Diver. It was singed with black. "Dis one," he said before going back to his powder line.

"Did you know that black powder can burn on its own?" Marie asked. "Just watch."

Kofi grabbed a small sliver of wood and put its tip into the fire. Then he pulled it out and, urging everyone to step back, touched the flaming end to the start of the powder line. Suddenly, the black powder started to burn brightly. The sparking ball of flame moved quickly down the line, hissing and consuming the powder as it went along. When it reached the end, the flame shrank and disappeared, leaving nothing but a black line of soot on the ground.

Dancing Fish was impressed but not surprised. "It burns," he said simply. "Like in matchlock pan before musket shoots."

Kofi nodded, smiling.

"But not just in muskets or pistols," Marie said with a mischievous grin.

Dancing Fish sat back on his heels and pondered this a moment. Then he understood.

He rocked forward, reached for the powder pouch and shook it. "Powder burns like a fire by itself," he said, speaking out loud while he thought. "But if the powder is held"—he tightened his fist around the top of the pouch—"then it goes nowhere." He looked at Marie and Kofi. "And it explodes."

"Boom!" Kofi shouted, his mouth wide and laughing.

"Boom!" Dancing Fish repeated, grinning like a boy who had just caught his first rabbit.

Seventy-three

November 1642

HIGH LIMB WAS AT THE WATERWAY NORTH OF SHORAKAPKOCK with the older men of the band, practicing with the new weapons. With time, he had slowly turned Dancing Fish to his way of thinking, of being more aggressive toward not only the Whites but to the enemy bands in the north.

The Mahicans, who had acquired many more firearm weapons from the French and the Mohawks, had grown steadily in strength and in their demands for tribute from their southern neighbors. Using threats and violent attacks where they killed men and took women and children captive, the Mahicans now received regular tribute payments from the Wiechquaesecks, who themselves received small tributes from their own Manahate band.

Dancing Fish's ideas of a "different kind of power" were gradually giving way to the only tool High Limb fully understood: raw power. Their world was becoming one of constant struggle, and the only way he knew of winning a struggle was to fight back, and to fight back hard. Over the past months, they had acquired a small stockpile of three muskets, two pistols, and the needed black powder and ball shot for them by trading with different bands and by more than one gift from Marie. This, of course, was against Kieft's orders, but High Limb could not have cared less. Their survival was at stake.

So on this gray and storm-threatening day with the leaves

already starting to fall, High Limb instructed the men on how to shoot the muskets and pistols, and he let Dancing Fish explain how to make and use gourd bombs.

High Limb felt pride in discovering a method of filling a hollowed-out pumpkin with a mixture of black powder and warmed whale oil. A thin cord of braided fiber rope saturated with the thick liquid was then inserted into a hole in the pumpkin skin and sealed with mud. The cord was lit with a flame, and the pumpkin exploded with a loud bang and threw the burning mix over anything near it. One of their favorite entertainments at night was to float these pumpkin "booms"—that was the favorite word—on water sitting on miniature rafts, and watch while they blew up and spread the flaming oil over the surface in all directions.

They were busy firing their weapons at targets when the word came from the scouts: the Mahican delegation was on its way. This was the gathering both High Limb and Dancing Fish knew would come.

It was a tribute meeting—when the threat of hostile attacks by the stronger group was met by offers of gifts and submission by the weaker. And although High Limb hated to admit it, their little band was the weak one. The corn harvest had been poor. They barely had enough to store for themselves without thinking of offering it for tribute to the powerful Mahicans. And pelts were also scarce. Wampum was the only trade item left to offer, but they had to protect their dwindling supply of that as well. Dancing Fish would have to handle this meeting with extreme care.

After the Mahicans arrived there was a short exchange of minor gifts. The two sides silently eyed each other across the central fire in the main Council House while wind from an approaching storm rattled the bark strips of the wigwam.

The Mahican group included their Sachem, a priest, the War Chief, and several warriors, clearly their biggest and strongest. Their attitude and the number of weapons they carried were an obvious sign of their warring intentions.

The Sachem, Chansomps, a muscular young man with long braided hair and pox scars on his face, started things off. Standing slowly, he reached into a large bag and pulled out the severed head of the Wiechquaeseck's current leader, known to all. He tossed it in the fire, where it blistered and hissed loudly. The awful stench of burning flesh soon followed. Still not having said a word, he then stared at Dancing Fish, who gave away no hint of shock.

"What is it you seek?" Dancing Fish asked from his place at the head of the circle after Chansomps had returned to the ground, legs crossed.

"What do all powerful leaders seek from all subservient tribes and bands?" Chansomps said quietly in his accented Algonkian tongue that closely resembled their Munsee.

"I don't know, we've never been one," Dancing Fish replied to chitters from all sides.

Chansomps smiled. "You have a good attitude, Dancing Fish. Your fame for quick thinking is well known, even among our people. And, of course, your knowledge of the Whites."

High Limb, who sat to the right of Dancing Fish, was already counting the muskets the Mahicans had brought. And he guessed at the pistols he couldn't see under their coverings. This group could not be taken lightly. They were dangerous.

"But we know the Whites, too," Chansomps continued. "The French from the north and the English in the east."

"For their weapons," High Limb interjected, but he soon felt Dancing Fish's hand against his arm. A sign that he should be silent.

Chansomps didn't miss the sign with his dark eyes and said, "Your War Chief is partly right, of course." He pulled out an elaborate pistol and placed it on the ground where it caught the firelight on all its intricately carved surfaces. "But our Whites give us more. They bring trade, and they bring security. Is it not the same with you?"

Dancing Fish took a moment before speaking. "*Our* Whites—the Dutch—are not the same. And they are led by someone unlike the white leaders you know."

"You talk of this man Kieft?"

"Yes. And he is not a good man."

"Are there any good white men?" Chansomps replied to laughter.

Dancing Fish leaned forward on his Sachem's stump and looked around the gathering. "Oh yes. I have met them. But it doesn't matter how many good ones there are." He paused and turned his head to listen to the growing strength of the storm outside. "Like a giant boulder rolling downhill, the bad ones will leave destruction in their path. It cannot be otherwise."

Dancing Fish then stood and started to walk slowly around the fire. His shoulders were more hunched than High Limb remembered, and his movements were stiffer, but the man he had known his entire life still commanded the attention of anyone within his presence. All eyes in the Council House were on him. And when he reached Chansomps on the opposite side of the fire, he stopped and crouched next to him.

High Limb saw several Mahican warriors reach for their knives or pistols in expectation of a trick, but Dancing Fish immediately lifted both of his hands to put them at ease. Then he nodded his head slowly at their Sachem. "Let's not waste more time," he said firmly. "You've come to demand submission and tribute of us. We understand this." He then spread his hands apart and opened his fingers. "But we have little to offer you. Our harvest is poor, our fur animals are gone, and the little wampum we have cannot even make a full belt."

Chansomps sat motionless, not responding.

Dancing Fish then slowly stood and looked down at the Sachem of the Mahicans. "Let us stand together, Chansomps," he said, lowering his hand as an invitation.

Chansomps ignored the hand but also stood. The two Sachems were now face to face.

"A young wolf submits to an older one," Dancing Fish said before taking a step back. "The one with more experience. But here"—he turned in a full circle with his arms out—"*we* are the experienced ones." He stopped and looked again at Chansomps. "We are the Real People of the Algonkian. We are the Lenni Lenape, the grandfathers of all the tribes."

Dancing Fish turned and started to walk back to his stump, still speaking. "We will give you our friendship and our wisdom, but that it is all." He sat down. "We are finished here."

▶◀

The Mahicans attacked without warning at the height of the storm. Not that the attack was unexpected, but the timing was. The Manahate were water people. They had lived around the waters of Lenapehoking all their lives. If a raging storm was a good omen, Dancing Fish thought, they would accept it. And they would use it to their advantage.

It was unusually late in the season for a northeast-heading tempest of this strength, but Dancing Fish took it as a gift from the Spirits. That and the extra Hackensack warriors Oratam had sent in response to his urgent request. He had taken a risk by offending and not submitting to the Mahicans, but his War Chief had backed his decision. They would fight force with force. And cleverness. They were ready.

The shallowest part of the waterway that isolated the island from the mainland was at the Wading Place, one finger's walk north of Shorakapkock. And that's where High Limb had placed his warriors with the best musket aim.

The Mahicans may have assumed an easy crossing with the ebbing tide, but the storm had raised the water level so high, the enemy had no choice but to swim across with weapons held up over their heads. Not only did this fatigue and disorient them in the cold water, but it made them easy targets when they emerged and faced musket fire from all sides. The rain of lead balls against them was so powerful that those not struck down at once turned and fled back across the channel for safety and regrouping.

But the Mahicans were not easily turned away. From his vantage point behind a large boulder near the water's edge, Dancing Fish could see Chansomps on the opposite shore cursing his warriors and hitting them with his Sachem's staff. Meanwhile, the pelting rain and driving wind only increased.

The waterway made a tight curve farther west, and High Limb guessed this would be their next crossing point. He was right, and so, they were prepared.

Fierce wind still roiled the waterway, but the Mahicans had adjusted their tactics. This time they came in small groups, with each group pulling a floating raft that carried their weapons. It was a good plan, but theirs was better.

When all the enemy was in the water, Dancing Fish signaled Diver, and he and his team of younger warriors unleashed a number of gourd bombs into the air just upwind of the approaching men. As each pumpkin hit the water, it burst apart into a ball of flame that quickly spread and overtook the makeshift wooden rafts. Soon, most were burning out of control, and the swimming Mahicans could do little but watch while their weapons sank. But even then, they didn't count on what happened next.

Diver, true to his name, was at home and accomplished under the water, able to hold his breath for a long time. And he had recruited others who were also strong in this way. While the Mahicans were deciding whether to swim forward toward the enemy or back to safety, Diver's little group was busy dropping to the bottom and gathering up all the weapons they could

481

find in the murky waterway. One by one, they came out from their side of the water carrying armfuls of muskets, pistols, clubs, and hatchets.

"Well done!" Dancing Fish shouted when Diver ran past him to the village with his dripping cache. Another group— mostly older women and men—waited in Shorakapkock, ready to dry, clean, and prepare the weapons for their own use.

And so, the Mahican-Manahate battle ended much as it began: with both sides basically intact. There was still much distrust and ill-feeling between them, but while Dancing Fish stood on the waterway's shore, watching a hard rain being driven horizontally by an angry and roaring wind, he knew that this conflict was actually of little importance in the long run. The two groups—all the tribes and bands, in fact—had much bigger challenges ahead of them.

Seventy-four

HIGH LIMB LOOKED APPROVINGLY AT TWO BUDS WHILE SHE stirred the succotash pot hanging over the fire. His wife had lost the shape of her trim body long ago, but she had been a good wife, delivering his two twin sons and standing by him at all times. Not that they hadn't had their problems.

"You're a bully," Two Buds had told him one day after a nasty fight when he struck her. She didn't speak to him or allow any warmth or passion for an entire moon phase. He finally apologized and promised to be more considerate in the future.

And with that admission, High Limb gradually started to change his thoughts about himself and his ties to those around him. He was still the strong, powerful War Chief, but the attentive and respectful side of him he had always considered a weakness had now become an unusual comfort. He felt more complete somehow. He found himself thinking of others: the family, of course, but also the whole band, and finally, all the People. And that there was more to this life on Mother Earth than just selfish ideas.

She had brought that out in him. He was lucky to have her.

Two Buds spooned the steaming succotash into his gourd and started humming. It was a song to the Spirits, and he couldn't help humming along with her. But his mind had already shifted elsewhere, reflecting on all that had happened during the past two moons.

Shortly after the Mahican battle, the band had moved to its winter home at Cowangough. For a brief time heading into the Turning of the Days—the Solstice, Dancing Fish was now fond of calling it—life seemed almost normal. There were the usual moonlight hunts, time for tool and weapon repairs, and band gatherings in the Council House for feasting and story-telling around warm and comforting fires.

But the bad news soon reached them. The Mahicans, no doubt angry over their embarrassment at Shorakapkock, had intensified their raiding on the northern bands. Wiechquaesecks and Tappans were the primary victims of their fury, which brought the battle straight back to them. Their two sons had both married Wiechquaeseck women and had moved north to their households as was the custom. But when both families had suddenly appeared at Cowangough in fear for their lives, a decision had to be made.

Most of the Wiechquaesecks who had escaped the violence wanted protection from the fort at New Amsterdam, and many had already started gathering near there. But both High Limb and Dancing Fish were against this. They didn't trust Kieft to help any of their people, much less their own family members.

And so it was decided to divert anyone fleeing the Mahican attacks to go either to the rarely used and remote hunting camp at Nechtanc, west of the Hook on the eastern waterway, or to Pavonia across the Great River to be with their Hackensack friends. These were determined to be safer. At least, they were some distance from the Whites at the fort.

"When will we see them?" Two Buds asked while she smoked a tobacco roll and rested her other hand on his knee.

"Soon," High Limb said, listening to the hissing fire and sniffing his own cigarro before he lit the end with a flaming twig. "Dancing Fish and I will organize a hunt and bring the meat to them at Nechtanc. And then we'll be able to see how they're doing."

She clutched his knee. "And you really think it's safer for them there, and not here with us?"

"There are Whites filling in all around us. This village is known to them. Nechtanc is still isolated. Especially in winter." He drew in a mouthful of tobacco smoke. "The Dutch will eventually expand to the Hook and to Nechtanc, no doubt, but for now, it's a good place for them to be." He held his wife's hand. "Don't worry, we'll see them before the Snow Moon is full."

►◄

Dancing Fish smiled when the light of the rising sun struck his closed eyes. He was back on the lower part of the island—his true home.

He had left Nechtanc alone in the dim morning, trudging through the snowdrifts and rounding the Hook to find a sturdy log where he could sit to watch the new day start, and to let his mind soar. The only sound was the slightest of winds moving across the ice of the eastern waterway and whispering through the bare trees behind him.

As the light grew stronger, he felt for and grabbed the powdery snow with his hands and put it to his mouth. The snow's cold dryness soon melted away, and when he swallowed the water the image of a great wave came to him. An enormous wave that advanced north from the Great Lake and grew and grew in size the closer it came, scattering his Manitto perch before it. It finally rushed forward and completely covered the island of Mannahatta.

Before the dreadful wave could retreat, he shuddered and opened his eyes, only to be blinded by the sun directly in front of him. He had to steady himself on the log with both hands while he waited for his rapidly beating heart to slow.

He ate a small portion of pemmican to settle himself. Then he closed his eyes again, concentrated on his breath, and waited for another vision to form.

He felt the sun move higher in the sky and grow stronger on his face. He remembered the day when Marie had explained to him the most astonishing thing. That Father Sun did not walk his path across the sky each day, but instead, that Mother Earth turned like a wheel while she moved slowly around the sun. It had taken him days of thought and observation to understand this idea. Mother Earth moving but the sun and the stars not? It had overwhelmed him. As had the ideas that the priest Bogardus had talked about with so much energy.

Their holy man had taken to traveling to the villages and speaking about his God. A God of Gods. A Spirit of even higher rank than the great Kishelemukong. This Spirit was the son of their God, and he promised everlasting life to those who believed in him. And those who didn't would not enter into an afterlife that floated somewhere near the Sky World.

These were extraordinary notions to him, but he was used to that with the Whites. He remembered how he had looked forward to the new ideas of the Europeans when he first met them with Hudson. How the strange concepts excited him, energized him. But now, he mostly saw how the ideas were more proof of how different these people were.

Could such differences ever be resolved? Could one set of beliefs be so wrong in the face of another at odds with the first? Could these vast differences be melted together, much like the snow that melted in his mouth? Could the Europeans—and he knew there were many kinds of Europeans, not only the Dutch—really coexist with the Real People of Lenapehoking? He was doubtful. Things were moving so fast now, and with much of it feeling out of balance.

When he heard the sound of someone moving through the snow, he opened his eyes again.

"So here you are," High Limb said, lowering himself to sit on the log. "All the food is distributed. The bellies of my sons and their families are full, but their eyes are worried. They are full of fear."

"Of the Mahicans or the Dutch?" he said, watching the clouds of his breath dissolve in front of him.

"Both." He was quiet, then asked, "Are you seeing things again?"

Dancing Fish stared straight ahead at the ice-covered water. "Yes. And nothing good."

"You see trouble ahead?"

He turned to look at High Limb and asked, "What happens when a large wave breaks on a shore full of rocks?"

The War Chief looked at him for a moment in silence. "The wave covers the rocks and scatters them."

"That is what I'm seeing."

▶◀

The slaves cleared away the food from Kieft's dining table, and the men lit their pipes at the fire before sitting back down. The small room was a comfort against the bitter cold outside, and Dirck van Ost was ready to let the brandy warm his insides. Although the heat from the debate would have worked equally as well.

With The Twelve long since disbanded, the director now relied on his inner circle for advice: Secretary Van Tienhoven, Sheriff Cornelis van der Hoykens, Commies De Sille, the influential settler De Vries, Captain Beeckman, and himself. But their views were far from uniform.

"We cannot allow another murderer to go unpunished," Van Der Hoykens said forcefully, speaking of the recent killing of a colonist by the Hackensacks across the river. "And again, as with Swits, they refuse to turn over the murderer."

Voices muttered and heads shook at this frustration.

"They are not going to hand over someone to us if they feel

the killing was justified," De Vries said in his usually calm voice. "It's just not their way."

"And I don't care about their ways," Kieft insisted, slamming down his glass and spilling the brandy. "We have our laws and require justice."

"And what about all these Indians near the fort," Captain Beeckman added. "They're seeking our protection from the hostile northern tribes, and we don't have enough soldiers to safeguard them all."

"Nor do we want to," Kieft said. "I am not risking our men and our resources for that."

Van Tienhoven, who had spoken little, cleared his throat and looked at the director. "I have some news." The secretary, as unappealing as he was in his corpulence, was known to indulge his lustful urgings on many of New Amsterdam's female citizens, whether married or not. And beyond them, native women who were willing to exchange their nightly affections for trade goods. He was a sponge of information.

"What news?" Kieft demanded.

"I've heard a rumor regarding the whereabouts of the Claes Swits murderer."

"*What?*" Kieft cried out. "You know this? From whom?"

"From whom doesn't matter," Van Tienhoven said. "Do you want to know?"

Director Kieft lurched up from his chair and thrust his face to within inches of the secretary's. "Of course I want to know, you fat fool. Where is this savage criminal?"

"At one of the refugee camps."

"At Pavonia?" Van Ost asked. He knew there was a large camp of Tappans and Wiechquaesecks there.

"No." Van Tienhoven smiled and emptied his glass. "There is another camp of fleeing natives not far from here on the East River. And full of Wiechquaesecks. They call it 'Nechtanc,' just west of Corlaers Hook."

"Then that settles it," Kieft said, his fists tightening on the table. "We're going to wipe the mouths of these savages. We're going to attack them!"

"But wait—" De Vries started.

"I am not waiting," Kieft said, trying hard to control his voice. "Some of the colonists want us to be more aggressive in stopping these Indians, and that's what I intend to do."

Kieft looked at Beeckman. "Captain, you will take the main army force across the river to Pavonia." He turned to Van Ost. "And you, Ensign, will round up as many colonists as you can and attack this Nechtanc camp with a smaller detachment." He paused and lifted an eyebrow. "And try to show the same leadership you did last time. Think of your career." He gave him a suggestive look. "And your cherished Kathrijn."

Van Ost looked down at the floor, sure he was blushing. "When?"

"In one week's time. We recently passed the persecution day of Saint Valentine." Kieft fixed his gaze on both men and broke into a devilish grin. "I want you to surprise them in their sleep. Let's show them our own brand of persecution."

▶◀

Dancing Fish was dreaming of giant waves when he heard the first scream. Then came the sounds of musket fire. Then the shouting and shrieking.

He quickly crawled to the door flap and opened it. What he saw in the light of the filling moon shocked him. Whites—some soldiers, many not—were running across the camp's main space firing muskets and pistols, and swinging their long swords.

A mother, holding her baby close, ran past the central fire but was grabbed by two bearded men not wearing uniforms. One held her tight while the other wrenched the infant from her arms. With the mother fighting and screaming, the man dropped the child to the ground and started hacking it with his sword. The sounds of the blade slicing into bone and flesh were overshadowed by the hysterical wails of the mother, who the other soldier was holding back with a knife to her throat.

The attacking man was starting to throw the pieces of the baby into the fire when Dancing Fish struck him head-first. They both rolled and grappled on the snowy ground. The man tried to slash with his sword but Dancing Fish pinned his arm down with his knee and drew out his steel knife. He drove it hard into the man's gut then pulled the blade upward with all his might. The man gasped and tilted his head back, eyes open and unmoving.

Hearing a new noise behind him, Dancing Fish turned to see High Limb driving his war club down onto the other man's head, caving it in. The man sank to the ground while the mother rushed to what was left of her baby, gathering up the bloody pieces.

"Come on!" shouted High Limb as he lunged for the next closest attacker.

Dancing Fish, using his knife in one hand and a fallen sword in the other, fought one raider after another. He and High Limb both stood back-to-back and challenged every enemy fighter they met. But the Dutch—led by the determined-looking Soldier Chief, Van Ost—were in a frenzy of violence and brutality. They struck, shot, and stabbed every one of the People they could, even entering wigwams and killing everyone inside.

The Manahate and Wiechquaeseck warriors were fighting back hard. Dancing Fish had short glimpses of men he knew—High Limb's sons and Takokwsu, who had joined them in the camp—clashing and battling the best they could. But they had been caught off guard and were outnumbered. And they had few firearms or the time to use them. He thanked the Spirits he had ordered Diver to stay at their winter home to help guard it.

The battle raged on, but they were losing. He saw lopped-off hands and arms being thrown into the fire, now smoking black and spewing the odor of burnt flesh.

When he spotted the Whites lining up and preparing their muskets, Dancing Fish called out to High Limb: *"Run!"*

"Two Buds! My boys!" he said, shaking his head. "I have to find them!"

High Limb sprinted away in search of his family while Dancing Fish signaled everyone around him to head for the woods to save themselves.

They had just entered the treeline when he heard the musket explosions and the sounds of the lead balls striking the trees and bushes on all sides. Everyone was weaving and dodging the tree trunks and snow-covered limbs to escape in the near-darkness.

As soon as they had enough distance from the camp, Dancing Fish stopped and listened, his heart hammering in his chest. He could still hear far-off wailing and howling, but no enemy sounds were approaching. He turned to the others who had also stopped to catch their breaths.

"Everyone split up," he ordered. "Do not go back to Nechtanc; there is nothing we can do there to help. The dead will have to wait. Keep moving but not in large groups. Work your way home to Cowangough. We'll meet there and have a council when we can."

Dancing Fish wiped the tears from his face with the back of his hands. He could see the others watching him in silence. Their faces showed a combination of shock and fright. "We'll not forget this night," he said with all the confidence he could gather. "We will avenge what has happened here."

Seventy-five

HIGH LIMB HAD WATCHED AND WAITED FROM THE TREES around Nechtanc until the Dutch were gone. The sun was up, but there was no heat to melt the ice in his heart. He walked over snow trampled and turned a deep brown that mixed mud and blood. The bodies of the People—the Dutch had taken their bodies with them—were strewn over the ground. The cold thankfully kept the flies away, but vultures were already circling high overhead.

He had walked through many killing fields in the aftermath of battles before, but it was the sight of these dead that so angered High Limb now. Many had not just been killed but mutilated, too. Arms and legs were broken. Heads had been cut off and were now missing. He saw no single body that was not either burned, disfigured, or hacked apart. And that included the youngest children and the women. In the raiding among the bands, the women and children were usually taken captive. They were a prize to be kept or used for bargaining. Here, they were nothing but animals, slaughtered and butchered like the pigs of the Whites.

He was nauseated by the sight.

And then he came to a group of bodies that immobilized him. Froze him to the ground as if he were a tree rooted to it. There was his beloved Two Buds, lying on her back with her legs at odd angles. Both hands had been cut off, and her throat was slashed from one side to the other. Thankfully, her head was intact, but her open eyes and mouth showed the terror she must have felt in the last moments of her life on Mother Earth.

Averting his eyes, he quickly picked out the bodies of his two sons and their families lying in a close group. They were killed trying to protect and comfort each other. But they did not face a merciful or dignified death. The heads of his sons were gone, sliced and ripped from their bodies, while the wives and children were carved and split open like one would gut a fish.

High Limb sank to his knees, pitched his head back so far it felt like his neck would break, and let out a cry that scattered the vultures in mid-flight. His anger and misery were mixed in a heavy stew that threatened to crush his heart. The taste of his despair rose like acid in his throat.

He placed both hands on the cold earth and dropped his head down to take long, slow breaths to calm himself. He tried to clear his mind to think. He would overcome this tragedy. He would take his family to the burial ground and send them off to the Sky World. Then he would make his way back to Cowangough to meet up with Dancing Fish, if he had survived.

Together, they would take their revenge.

▶◀

The cleaved heads of more than 80 Indians were arranged on sharpened stakes behind the small stage. Much of the village was crowded into the fort's parade, and a bright sun looked down from a clear sky as if in affirmation of what they had done. But Van Ost could sense that the feelings of victory were not shared by all.

"This is very unchristian," Minister Bogardus whispered to him while they waited with the other high-ranking officials for the director to mount the stage. "Showing off the heads like they are trophies?" They both glanced over at the grisly display that was starting to smell despite the cold air. "Disgusting. Goes against all decency. How can the bodies be buried? Even the savages have their own form of interment."

Van Ost nodded but said nothing. They had buried their own dead only that morning, and all with heads intact. He had not counted on the crazed violence unleashed by the civilians under his command at Nechtanc. Somehow, the raw feelings of the men had taken over their senses. He was ashamed of what they had done. He knew he had to prove himself in Kieft's eyes, but he was still discomfited by the level of violence. And Captain Beeckman's raid at Pavonia had been no different. Pure savagery and brutality had ruled there, too. And now the captain stood near him with a smug smile on his face.

"We found our Hackensack murderer," Beeckman said, pointing to the head, beaten and bloody, with one eye missing from its socket. "How about you?

"We, as well," said Van Ost. "We forced one of them to point out this Takokwsu at gunpoint."

"And you killed the informer, too?"

"Yes," Van Ost said, looking sadly at the heads of both men on their poles.

"Oh, cheer up. It was our job and we did it." The captain chuckled without a hint of regret. "And a fine job it was."

Just then, Director Kieft climbed the few short steps to the top of the platform and gazed out at the crowd filling the square. He held up his right hand for silence. Then he turned to look at the skewered heads behind him. He took his time turning back and lifted both arms up high in a sign of victory. As if he were the bloodied hero back from the battlefield.

There was scattered cheering and applause but not nearly what one would expect from a crowd of this size. It was as though the boiling bloodlust had had time to cool down and consider the vengeance they had wreaked.

Kieft, however, heard only the applause, and he started to

speak in his strong voice. "We have done it!" he proclaimed. "We've taught the savages a lesson they'll not soon forget."

He walked over to the heads of Takokwsu and the Hackensack murderer and tapped both their bloodstained skulls with the blade of a small silver dagger. "Two murderers brought to justice," he said proudly.

"And the others?" someone shouted from the crowd. "Were they all murderers, too?" There were mutterings of agreement from the crowd. Perhaps some had begun to wonder just who the savages were here.

Kieft stood still, a frown clouding his face. "I am tasked with keeping all of you safe and secure. And what we have accomplished here"—he looked down at his advisers—"is exactly that. We are doing what is required."

"But will there not be retaliations?" asked a farmer Van Ost knew from Staaten Island. "My sister and her family are at risk. What do you intend to do about that?"

"And I have relatives in the north," cried out another. "What about them? How exactly are you going to protect them now? What is your plan?"

"My plan?" Kieft screeched. "You ask for my plan?" He turned and pointed to the exhibition of heads. "There. You can see the result of my planning on those stakes. The natives have seen our strength and our power. They will not dare to cause more harm. They now see what the conclusion will be."

David de Vries had quietly appeared behind Van Ost and Bogardus. The ensign turned round to him. "And what is your opinion, Meneer De Vries? You know these Indians better than most."

De Vries signaled for both of them to lean in closer. "Our esteemed director is playing a dangerous game. He has attacked isolated and disorderly groups of natives." The settler nodded to the beheaded examples behind the stage. "If the Indians ever decide to organize themselves behind a strong leader, our heads could easily be sitting at the ends of very similar stakes."

▶◀

Dancing Fish discovered that word of the attacks at Pavonia and Nechtanc had spread rapidly. So he and High Limb decided to travel together to the winter villages to explain what had happened and what was sure to come. And in every place they visited over the next weeks they were met with spellbound concentration, as if they were prophets. Surely, this was helped by Dancing Fish having plucked and scraped his head clean, leaving only a graying hair lock on its crown. His fame was already widespread throughout the region, but no one could ignore a Sachem-turned-Warrior.

Across the lands of the Hackensack, Tappan, Wiechquaeseck, Siwanoy, and other groups in Lenapehoking, local Sachems and War Chiefs listened intently and young warriors screamed their support for taking action against the Whites.

Dancing Fish usually started by speaking first about his visions and dreams. And his belief that they—the People—had the right and the duty to not only defend themselves but to actively resist the Europeans. And if that meant attacking first in response to recent events, then so be it. It was *their* land being taken. It was *their* sovereignty, *their* connection to Mother Earth, and *their* very history and unbroken link to their ancestors that was at stake. Would they stand by and let the white occupiers slowly destroy them? Or would they stand up as men—as warriors—and fight back?

Then, just like in the days when they were young traders with each taking turns, High Limb, his head now also stripped clean, followed and explained the best ways of surprising the Whites in their homes, burning their farms, destroying their crops, killing their important animals, and if any stood in their way, killing them, too. And he urged the bands to consolidate all the muskets, pistols, powder, and shot they had and make sure only their most skilled experts used them to attack the enemy. High Limb ended by showing how simple gourd bombs could be made from black powder and pumpkins.

"Remember," Dancing Fish said at the end of each village gathering, "this is war. Each of you has a duty to the others." He held up his open right hand. "Separately, we are like the fingers of this hand." Making sure every eye was on him, he slowly closed his fist and balled it tight. "Together, we are unbeatable!"

The counterattacks started almost immediately. Farms were set afire and settlers killed on both sides of the Great River. Although they were separate groups, the different bands were like one in their minds and in their rage. Even Oratam was convinced to release his hot-headed warriors and attack Dutch farms and villages spread over Hackensack land.

Dancing Fish heard from multiple sources that terrified European survivors were streaming south for the safety of Fort Amsterdam. "Good," he said to High Limb while they organized Cowangough and prepared to move back to the island for the warm months. "Let them come together at the fort. It'll be much easier to watch them if they are in one place."

"Being close also has disadvantages," High Limb said. "They can get to us faster and in force, even if we're at the top of the island."

"That's why I suggest we not stay only at Shorakapkock through the planting and harvest. Some of us—you, me, the better warriors—should keep moving. Let's not spend more than a few nights at any one location. We both have no wives to protect. And our children are either gone or grown and can take care of themselves. Let's keep a warrior force moving together and go where we're needed."

Dancing Fish pressed his lips and silently scolded himself for what he had just said. He had seen High Limb's shoulders slump after he spoke of wives and children. The great War

Chief was now truly alone. At least he still had his son, Diver.

"So now we're just killers?" High Limb asked him, surprisingly.

He looked at his oldest friend. "No, we're not only killers. We're also protectors."

"But only of those who are worthy of protection."

"Exactly. And I've been thinking about one white settler who has helped us many times. And who we should visit to make sure she is safe."

High Limb smiled and threw a bundle of skins on the two-wheeled cart. "I understand. Go on alone, and I'll meet you later. I have much to prepare for Shorakapkock."

▶◀

"Miss Marie," Kofi pleaded. "Everyone goin' to fort. When we goin'?"

Marie stopped her writing and looked at Kofi's face, noticing the first sign of fear she had ever seen in it. He was standing with his arm around Juba on the opposite side of her worktable, and both were staring at her, waiting for her reply. In the silence she heard robins singing in the trees outside. Spring had finally arrived.

She gently shook her head. "No, Kofi. We're not going anywhere. We will stay here. This is my home and we'll be fine." She looked at Juba holding onto Kofi with both arms. "Besides, we have to finish the clearing and planting of the new crops. Those seeds are not going to plant themselves, now are they?"

"No, ma'am," he said reluctantly. "Guess they an't."

"No, they an't," Marie said, smiling. "And when that's done, there are more barrels and hogsheads to build for the trading. Now, you two start the work, and I'll join you shortly. It's a fine day out there. But I need to finish this paperwork first."

She listened to the pleasant sounds of birds chirping while

she moved through the pile of papers, studying invoices and signing contracts. Suddenly, dogs were barking and she reached under the table and pulled out the pistol she kept there just in case. It was one of the new ones that used the flint ignition mechanism. She had paid a high price for it, but a woman of means living in the woods had to be careful.

The dogs stopped their barking, and a knock on the door was followed by a familiar voice calling her name.

"Come in," she said warmly, sliding the pistol back into its hidden bracket.

The door opened, and it was her old friend Dancing Fish, wearing his traditional full leggings and a deerskin hunting shirt. He carried a bow, and she saw the large knife handle protruding from his waist. At his age—she guessed he had long passed 40—he was still a handsome man with only a slight slowing of his movements.

She stepped around the table and walked to meet him. He started to offer his hand but she ignored it, throwing her arms around him and hugging tightly. He leaned back in surprise but she just laughed, letting her hands slide down to hold both of his.

"Come on, now," she said. "You and I don't need to be formal with each other. We've seen too much together."

He smiled. "Yes, we have. But I'm not used to European woman giving me bear hug." He laughed and she joined him.

Finally, she could hold in her surprise no longer. "Your hair! This is the plucked head of a warrior."

His welcoming face suddenly changed, and he gave her a stern look that would have frightened her if she didn't know him well. "You know about the troubles."

"Yes, of course. Everyone is telling me to leave here and go to the fort for safety."

"But you do not go."

"How can I?" She looked down at the papers scattered

across the table then nodded her head toward the windows. "I have a business to run. Crops to tend. Trades to make. And this is my home." She looked again at his warrior head. "Should I be worried?"

He motioned to the chairs, and they both sat. "I tell you this. You have nothing to fear from Manahates or Wiechquaesecks. I can control them. But other bands . . ." He started shaking his head. "I know you are not the enemy and you respect the People. But not all know you like I do. Some warriors act first and think later. There is anger on all sides." He reached for one of her hands. "Safer if you go to fort. But I know no one tells you what to do—you have your own mind." He smiled. "So I have different idea that can help you and me."

"And what idea is that?"

"I pick two warriors to protect you and farm. You do not see them, but they are there. And when you bring in harvests, you go to fort to trade and do one thing for me."

She smiled and cocked her head. "You're planning something, aren't you?"

He let out a soft chortle. "I say only this: if you go to village over many days, you can learn things I do not know. And then you tell me those things."

"Ah," she said. "You want me to spy."

"Not sure if 'spy' is right word. My Dutch—"

"Come now, Sachem," she said, teasingly. "You speak Dutch—and English, and even some French—as well as anyone on this island. If 'spy' is not correct, how about 'observe' or 'notice'?"

He smiled broadly. "Notice and observe is good."

"I will do it on one condition."

He peaked an eyebrow and waited.

"When the harvest is ready, you let those invisible warriors help me bring it in."

He laughed. "Just like your father. Always trading."

Seventy-six

DANCING FISH HAD TAKEN TO CALLING THE YEARS BY THE numbers the Europeans gave to them. And the summer of 1643 passed by bloodily. The warrior group Dancing Fish and High Limb had assembled—they had been nicknamed the "Fighting Flock"—grew larger every time they ventured out from Shorakapkock to make war with settlers who were the most hostile to them. On their return, and after the injured were attended to, or the dead buried, the warriors would go out again in search of houses, barns, and stacks of grain to burn.

One of their target areas was to the east of their winter home under supervision of the neighboring Siwanoy band. Dealings with the Wiechquaesecks—to which the Manahates were now affiliated—and the Siwanoys were often stormy. Sometimes allies, sometimes enemies, the friction between the two groups had ebbed and flowed like the tides for as long as anyone could remember.

But now, a call came from their supreme Sachem, Wampage, to Dancing Fish. In fact, he had seen Wampage in a dream motioning for him to come to him from the opposite side of a creek. So when a runner arrived at Shorakapkock with an urgent request from the Siwanoy Sachem, Dancing Fish did not delay in complying, and he decided to bring along the flock.

With Diver insisting on coming, and High Limb, as War Chief, agreeing, they reached the village of Asumsowis with the sun still high but glaring through a white haze that marked the hottest and stickiest part of the summer. The village sat at the very bottom edge of a neck of land jutting south into a body of water that connected all the way back to Monatun.

The day's heat forced the meeting to take place outside, but thankfully near a rocky point open to sea breezes on two sides.

Wampage, who sat on a raised stump closest to the point, was a powerful man with a broad chest and bushy eyebrows. His strongest warriors, heads plucked clean except for their crowning crests, sat near him, leaving room for Dancing Fish and his flock to sit opposite. Turtleshell bowls of warmed fish and roots were offered to all while squawking seagulls wheeled above them looking for scraps.

"Why do you call for our help?" Dancing Fish asked in time.

"There is a large family of English," Wampage said, "headed by a willful and wicked woman, and they have settled near here." He tapped his Sachem's staff on the ground. "We have asked for payments many times, and each time this crazy woman with many children refuses. Says she was given the land by the Dutch leader on your island."

"Kieft," he said.

"Yes, that's the name. You know him?"

Dancing Fish nodded. "He is the enemy of us all. He is our greatest problem."

"But he is far from us, and this group—*Hutchinson* they call themselves—is now a thorn stuck to our feet."

"And you want me to talk to them, these Hutchinsons? In their tongue?"

"Yes. They must show us the proper respect. They must pay us in gifts if they are to stay on the land."

Dancing Fish immediately saw the problem, and it was the same one as always. The Dutch thought they had purchased exclusive use of the land, even beyond Mannahatta island, and the People thought differently. It had been like this since 1626 with Minuit. And he had signed the parchment himself. He was partly to blame. So he had to do what he could.

"You will take me to this place of Hutchinson," he said, "and I will talk with them. I'll try to make them understand."

"Good," Wampage said. Then he gave him a serious look. "But if you fail, I will kill them all."

"And maybe we'll help you," High Limb added, stretching out his long legs and smoking his tobacco roll.

They arrived at a clearing near a river that flowed feebly north to south, much like their own Aquehung stream to the west. A large group of maybe 15 Whites was assembled in front of the Hutchinson house, its walls built of stacked logs and a roof made of bark and sod. It seemed hard to believe so many could fit inside this one dwelling.

Dancing Fish quickly identified the Matron, a woman in her middle years, small with dark hair and wearing the usual full dress of European women that covered them from neck to ground. Surrounding her were several children—who clearly resembled her—along with younger men and what looked like servants or slaves, most with black skin. And all except the youngest held muskets or pistols.

"What do you want with us?" the Matron said in a strong English voice that didn't match her size. "I am Anne Hutchinson, and this is our land."

Dancing Fish stepped forward and spoke in the same tongue. "I am from Manahate band. I am here to help understanding with the People who live near you." He nodded to Wampage, who stood in front of his dozen warriors.

"You speak English!" the woman said, obviously surprised.

"Yes. We sit and talk?"

The Hutchinson woman moved her eyes over their group carefully, then shook her head, lifting her musket at the same time. "No. We will stand and talk."

Dancing Fish struggled for the English words but managed

to explain how important compensation was if they were to live on this land of the Siwanoy. "There must be gifts of food and tools from you. This is expected. If you do this, you can stay."

"We have already received a land grant from Director Willem Kieft," she said defiantly. "Nothing more is owed."

Wampage touched his arm and asked, "What is she saying? I don't see friendship in her eyes."

Dancing Fish was now caught in the middle between two groups who had very different ideas about the situation. Feeling in his gut that this would not turn out well, he turned to check over his men. Diver was missing!

He spoke to Wampage and explained that the woman was standing hard by her opinion.

"Then," the Sachem whispered to him, "I suggest you not move and let us handle this. You and your men stay back. This is our fight."

In what was no more than an instant, the Siwanoy attacked the Whites with total surprise and in full fury. Dancing Fish counted only two firearm blasts before Wampage's men were upon them with hatchets and knives.

Dancing Fish turned and held his arms out wide to both sides. "Stay back!" he ordered the others. "It's their battle."

He pushed against High Limb, who was ready to join the attack, and soon he had the flock at the edge of the clearing where all they could do was listen to the screams and watch the slaughter.

▶◀

Dancing Fish was relieved when he saw Diver enter the edge of the Hutchinson clearing to his left, but he was surprised to see that his son was leading a young girl by the arm. She had passed no more than eight or nine winters, and when she saw the dead piled in front of the house she screamed and tried to pull away from Diver. But he held firm, wrapping both arms around her while she kicked, clawed, and cried.

"I found her picking blueberries near a large split rock," he said as he tried to control her. "We both heard the musket shots, and I tackled her when she started running to the house."

Wampage, covered in blood, walked over to Diver and the girl. "Give her to me," he ordered Diver, who looked at Dancing Fish with questioning eyes.

Dancing Fish nodded and the girl was released. She quickly eluded Wampage's grasp and sprinted to the pile of bodies and started crying out, touching each in turn and calling out their names. When she came to the Hutchinson Matron, who could only be her mother, she sank to her knees and shrieked. The woman's left hand was separated from her body and lay some distance from it.

Wampage walked over to the girl and roughly pulled her up by her long hair. "We'll take this one captive." He laughed. "She will be our payment."

"No, she is mine!" Diver suddenly announced, walking to them. "I found her. I claim her for the Manahate." He stuck his hairless chest out and started to reach for the girl, but Wampage slapped his arm down.

"You are a boy," Wampage said. "And this is not your business." He looked to Dancing Fish and raised his heavy eyebrows, waiting for a response.

Dancing Fish saw an opportunity. Glancing at High Limb, he stepped closer to the dispute. "My son did capture the girl and brought her here." He stared at Wampage. "You cannot disagree with this."

"No, but—"

"So this is what I propose," Dancing Fish said, making a subtle movement with his head in High Limb's direction. "We will trade the girl to you in exchange for four muskets of the Whites."

High Limb had already crossed the space and was inspecting the weapons.

Wampage, handing off the girl to the closest warrior, smiled and crinkled his eyes. "Ah, the trader is back to his old game." He quickly surveyed the bloody heap of bodies and weapons and faced Dancing Fish. "Two muskets and one pistol."

Dancing Fish responded without delay, "Two muskets, one pistol, and the powder and balls that go with them."

Wampage considered this, looking at the squirming girl and no doubt calculating the years of work and pleasure she would provide them. He dipped his head. "Agreed."

The tension between the groups was instantly relieved. High Limb gathered up the weapons, and the different warriors congratulated themselves on achieving the better outcome.

"Put all the bodies into the house and set it on fire," Wampage ordered his men. "Burn it all!"

He then walked over and picked up the hand of the Hutchinson woman. "I will now adopt the name of this Matron to honor the day and my role in her death," he said, lifting her severed hand high. "From this day forward, I am to be called *Wampage Ann Hook*."

Everyone clapped their hands and stamped their feet on the ground while Wampage Ann Hook tossed the hand into the house that was burning in a great, smoking pyre.

▶◀

September's crystal days had arrived at last. The heavy air of summer no longer clung to Dirck van Ost's skin. He felt lighter on his feet when he came out of the barracks and started to cross the square of the fort, heading to the southwest bastion. The sky was a brilliant blue with no cloud in sight.

But as he weaved past the bunches of colonists who had taken up residence inside the fort, Van Ost was brought back to reality. These were the displaced people from the Indian attacks that had destroyed their farms and upturned their lives. They were crowded together in family groups, speaking in low tones, some sitting on mats and others merely on the packed dirt. He avoided their eyes at the same time he held his breath to keep from smelling their foul odors, for he knew not where they relieved themselves, nor did he want to know.

He felt better when he climbed the steps to the rampart that looked out over the Upper Bay, sparkling in the bright light and offering a refreshing breeze from the south. This was the same bulwark where the decision to attack the Raritans had been made three years earlier, which had started the native revolt. And here he was, looking out again at Staaten Island and standing with the same two men who had participated in that fateful decision.

"The Eight are pressuring me to do something," Director Kieft said. He had called together another council of advisers from the citizenry, this time from eight of the most powerful burghers of New Amsterdam. "We cannot support these displaced people indefinitely," he said, turning and shaking his head at the sight of his fort full of impoverished colonists.

"And our army is ill-equipped to defend them if the savages choose to attack us," Captain Beeckman said. "We have only 200 men fit to fight, and our supplies are low. And I've heard rumors that there are more than 1,500 Lenape warriors ready to march on us."

"Fifteen-hundred?" the director said in surprise. "Can this be?" He looked at Van Ost. "What do you know?"

"I don't have the numbers, but I've heard of groups of natives organizing themselves, and that Dancing Fish is in the middle of it."

"You should have killed him when you had the chance at Nechtanc," Beeckman said, glaring at Van Ost.

"We tried," he replied stiffly, taking offense at the criticism.

507

"He outsmarted us and got away."

Kieft stared at them both and shook his head. "Well, we now have to outsmart them. We have to take action. We cannot just sit here and wait for an attack."

The director lifted his head and looked north, up the island. "I have heard that a Captain John Underhill is having good success against the savages in New England. You know of this, too, no doubt."

Everyone in the army knew of Captain Underhill and his role in turning the tide in the Pequot War of 1637. And especially his brutality against the natives there.

"I'm told he's English and married to a Dutch woman," Beeckman said. "And he gives no quarter when it comes to the savages."

The director smiled. "Then he is the man we need."

Seventy-seven

Winter 1643–44

HIGH LIMB AND HIS MEN MOVED SILENTLY THROUGH THE naked trees and ankle-deep snow. He was excited about the flint muskets they had recently captured. Instead of the burning rope of the matchlock, these newer weapons used a flint-striking system that worked in all types of weather, even in rain. And they were lighter and easier to carry.

The group he was leading—he was again in northern Siwanoy territory with half the fighting-flock warriors while Dancing Fish had gone south to Hackensack and Raritan lands—had only two of the muskets and one pistol, but these were the latest European weapons, and they gave him all the confidence he needed.

What was disheartening was the palisaded village that now greeted him. The Siwanoy leader Wampage Ann Hook had again asked for their help but also warned that the northern Siwanoy had their own ideas about fending off the Whites who were now starting to fight back. But what he saw in front of him when they came out from the treeline was a disaster in the making.

Their flock of warriors had been successful against the Europeans in the last months by using the irregular tactics of strike-and-go that High Limb had perfected. They would hide behind trees and come out from different sides to attack and then disperse back into the forest. The goal was to never be caught in a single mass that could be surrounded by the enemy. Since that terrible defeat at Nechtanc, where he had lost his family, they had not been bested by any group of Dutch soldiers. But what faced him now was the exact opposite idea: a small village crowded behind a high circular wall of standing logs with pointed tops.

"You have to get out of this trap," High Limb said to the local Sachem after the greetings and pleasantries were exchanged inside the Council House.

"We thank you for coming to aid us in our defense," the fur-covered leader said, "but we've studied how the English fortify their villages, and we think this is best."

"But you are not English," he said bluntly, chewing on the leg of a winter hare while the central fire crackled and meat-scented smoke rose to the ceiling. "You do not have their war weapons." He withdrew the flint pistol from his waist and handed it to the leader, who turned it over and marveled at it.

"But we have our good bows, clubs, and spears," a warrior said smugly. "We know how to fight." Several of the others grunted their approvals. They were not going to be told how to defend themselves by an outsider.

"Then we will not join you in this decision." High Limb looked around at his warriors, who were eating but also paying close attention to his words. "Instead, we will form a perimeter around your wall but well back so we're not seen. If an attack comes, we'll be your security ring. We have promised Wampage Ann Hook to help you, and that is what we'll do."

"As you wish," the Sachem said, handing the pistol back. "We hope you don't get bored sitting and freezing in the snow."

"I'd rather be bored than dead," High Limb replied.

The attack came two days later, as the white ground turned first blue then gray under the last of the sky's spent light.

High Limb saw the dark shapes of the Europeans arrive in a large group, then split apart to form a circle around the village at the very edge of the forest. He had thankfully positioned his warriors farther back in the trees, and none had been discovered by the new arrivals.

High Limb watched with fascination while the leader of the attackers, a tall, thin man with a small beard and an odd-shaped hat, shouted a loud order in heavily accented Munsee tongue to "come out peacefully and you will be spared." He also thought he saw the Dutch soldier Van Ost at his side, but in the fading light he couldn't be sure.

There was immediate commotion inside the palisaded wall, and High Limb could only imagine what the villagers were thinking and doing. He had instructed his warriors to do nothing and to keep still and silent if unprovoked, and they were doing exactly that. He couldn't see them, but he knew they were intently watching this unfold.

Gloom turned to darkness with no movement on any side. Then there was a sudden shouted order of *Fire!*, and the night was immediately ablaze with musket blasts from all sides of the village. The Europeans were firing directly at the palisade, and he could hear the musket balls striking and splintering the circular wall. He also heard a rising sound of screams from inside the enclosure. As the firing continued, the howling increased.

All at once, the muskets were silent and only the wailing could be heard. Then came the loud voice again: "Come out, or we will burn you out!"

High Limb reacted instantly. Shouting first to one side and then the other, he ordered his men to attack the Whites. The next moments were confused while he and his warriors fell upon the Europeans from behind, and the battle changed from one of remote distance to close combat, fighter against fighter.

High Limb dispatched the first enemy with a shot from his pistol. He then pulled out his long steel knife and began attacking and moving closer and closer to the white leader who now stepped into the clearing with a burning torch in his hand.

"Set it afire!" the man shouted at the same time he launched his torch over the wall. Immediately, other flaming torches were flying into the village.

It didn't take long before orange flames and black smoke could be seen between the cracks in the wall and then soaring above it. The Whites now entered the clearing and closed the circle around the burning village, shooting at any who tried to escape the blazing firestorm.

High Limb, outraged by what he was seeing, jumped into the clearing. The villagers and warriors he had met only days before were now being cooked alive while the flames leapt higher and the intense heat melted the snow around the wooden wall.

Suddenly finding himself out in the open and stunned by the massacre he was witnessing, High Limb saw the European leader turn and look directly at him. And there was Van Ost standing next to him and whispering in his ear.

In what seemed to pass at the pace of a turtle, both the leader and Van Ost raised their pistols and aimed them at him. At the same moment, High Limb had already turned away and was sprinting toward the trees. He heard two blasts. One ball struck a sapling he was running past, but he then felt a sharp pain in his left arm. The force of being shot knocked him down, but he was on his feet quickly and lurching into the forest. He didn't stop until he was far away from these evil men who had just destroyed an entire village of the People.

▶◀

Marie wanted to know if the rumors were true. She had heard that the soldiers were starting to fight back against the Indians. And now, winning. Thankfully, her farm had been spared from native attacks, as she knew it would be based on her talks with Dancing Fish. It was time to see if she could help him in return.

The stated reason for her visit to New Amsterdam was to

bring in hogsheads of stored tobacco and barrels of oat brandy for sale. The village would welcome the comforting merchandise at the start of January, and she would be able to learn what she could.

After selling the tobacco and brandy at the company store, she and Juba went to meet with Director Kieft on the other side of the fort's square. The air was cold but the sun bright, and Marie could feel its frail heat as she sidestepped around the displaced colonists who sat in tight groups to keep themselves warm. She felt herself lucky she was not one of them. Then she stopped and grabbed Juba's arm.

At the edge of the square, a group of children were playing a game and laughing. When she looked more closely, Marie could see they were kicking balls to each other. But these were not balls. They were heads! Indian heads. Warriors, by the look of their clean scalps, but not only warriors. There were also heads of women and even of children.

She had to turn away and grip her chest to keep from vomiting. Her heart was racing, and her mind reeled with outrage. "Let's go," she said to Juba, pulling her hard to leave as fast as they could.

She had partially regained her composure once inside the director's house. "Wait here," she instructed Juba in the hallway outside Kieft's office, pointing to a row of chairs and handing her the leather pouch full of clinking guilders from the sale. "Count them again just to make sure."

The door opened and a secretary of some sort smiled at her. "He's ready for you."

Once inside, the director motioned to the chair in front of his cluttered desk. "I hear you've brought in some good trade merchandise to the store," he said.

She nodded, sat, and glanced around the room.

"And I see you have an actual office to work from now," she said, looking for any distraction to calm her.

513

"Well, unfortunately, I've had to give up space in the larger room for housing some of the refugees. It's a bad business."

"Yes, it is," she said, holding in her tension until she finally couldn't. "But I was shocked by what I saw in the square outside. Kicking the heads of natives as in a game? It's disgusting."

"No more disgusting than savages destroying our farms and killing farmers, wouldn't you say?" He looked at her intently. "I've noted that your farm is one of the few that hasn't been struck by the Indians. Are you that lucky?"

She had to be careful now. "Lucky, and I have trusted servants who know how to handle muskets."

"Hmmm . . ." Kieft murmured, picking up a quill and running his finger along the feather. "And your connection to Dancing Fish has nothing to do with this?"

"I have not been threatening in my dealings with the natives, if that's what you mean. I treat them with respect."

"Respect?" Kieft said with incredulity. "How can you possibly respect a savage that has no appreciation of civilization or our moral standards?"

She laughed. *"Moral standards?* You speak of moral standards when you burn down entire villages and use the heads of the captured for amusement? Have you no sense of decency?"

The director abruptly stood up from his chair and thrust a pointed finger at her. "You are an important person in this community so I will allow you some leeway. But you should be very careful about what you say and how you say it. Our forces are fighting back, especially now that we have the help of Captain Underhill. He is winning battles, and he'll be doing so again when he returns here in February after his campaign in the south. He means to clear out the entire island of Manatus once and for all. And not a moment too soon, I say."

He stepped around the desk and drew close to Marie— close enough to where she could smell his sweat and see a gleeful gleam in his eye.

"The tide of this war will be changing," he said, "and anyone who sympathizes with the Indians will end up on the wrong side of things." He stared at her. "Regardless of how important he—or she—thinks they are."

Marie filed the threat away but focused on the detail she had just learned. The dreadful English captain would soon be marching up the island. She needed to warn Dancing Fish.

Seventy-eight

Diver was indecisive. "Are you sure?"

Dancing Fish grinned. "Of course I'm sure. I've done this many times. It's good for you. It thickens the blood, which is what you need in winter."

His son stood naked on the ice, bent over, arms wrapped around himself, shivering. They had cut the round hole earlier, and it was already starting to freeze again. The sun had started its downward journey, and the smell of the sweat-hut fire had drifted over the pond of Xitkwe.

"If you don't get in now, you'll never be a true man," taunted one of the warriors they had brought along. Each of them had already plunged into the heart-stopping water, and now only Diver remained to take part in the ritual.

Another said, "And if you are to keep your name, you must do it now."

Finally, Diver straightened up, put his arms to his sides, and jumped in feet-first. For a long moment he was gone from sight, but then his head burst out of the water, yelling at the top of his voice: "*Ow! It's cold!*"

Everyone laughed while Diver reached up and found a helping hand that pulled him back up onto the ice. A long fur robe was offered, and soon, they were all walking back to the shoreline, chatting and joking.

Dancing Fish had decided to include two of the flock's

toughest warriors on the once-a-year, winter hunting trip. The back-and-forth battles with the Dutch had raged over the winter, but February—the days of the Snow Moon—was the time for this tradition of going south to the pond and burial grounds, and it was important to continue it. Diver needed to understand his link to the past, and no European soldiers were going to stop that.

The Whites had started winning more battles with the new Soldier Chief, Underhill, but the People had been gaining strength, too.

More of the bands had come together and sent their best warriors. These were men who were willing to fight for the land, and they were willing to lose their heads in the process. Some already had, and Dancing Fish's stomach turned at the thought of what Marie told him she had seen at the fort. He had promised himself to use all the skills he had to prevent that kind of desecration from happening again.

They had rebuilt the wigwams at Werpoes and now sat inside the largest, finishing the otter they had killed, and smoking their tobacco. The cooking fire had warmed them, and they were taking turns going to the sweat hut to cleanse and purify.

"Tell us about your latest visions, Sachem," the warrior who had just returned from sweating asked. "Mine are usually confusing and seem to be of little consequence." He smiled. "But yours . . . Yours are the ones everyone wants to hear."

Dancing Fish looked at the young man, his body solid with muscles and already an experienced fighter at an age only slightly greater than Diver's.

"My visions are also confusing," he said as he threw the end of his cigarro into the fire and heard it sizzle in the flames. "But I try to connect them to my life and to the life of the People. The Spirits decide the consequences."

"And what do the Spirits say now about the Salts and our war with them?" Diver asked him.

He didn't answer right away, letting the vision of the large wave breaking on a shore of rocks reappear behind his eyes.

"They tell me we must stay together and fight them with all our strength. More will be coming soon." He did not mention the wave covering the rocks and scattering them.

▶◀

When they reached Shorakapkock the next night, the usually empty village in winter was buzzing like a thousand cicadas. Dancing Fish learned that warriors from the surrounding bands had been arriving for days after the warning from Marie had gone out in all directions.

The white soldiers were coming, and there was much to do in preparation. Wigwams were full with warriors sharpening knives, restringing bows, and organizing their weapons. Others stood around the central fire, swapping war stories and trying to out-boast each other.

"How was your trip south?" High Limb asked Dancing Fish, who sat close to the fire in the Council House that was half-buried in snow. The War Chief was carefully filling pieces of hollowed-out stag antler with black powder. Through trial and error, they had determined that antler was superior to skin pouches for carrying the powder used in their precious muskets and pistols.

"Not so good for hunting, but," he chuckled, "Diver's getting used to jumping into freezing water." He turned serious. "And the visions were clear."

High Limb stopped his work and looked up. "Tell me about them."

"The large wave is coming. It can only be the soldiers with this new Underhill chief."

"And you think it will be soon?"

"Within the next two nights."

High Limb straightened his back with a cracking sound and moved his bare head around in circles to loosen his neck. "We'll be ready." He pointed to a stack of the small lead balls.

"Do we have enough?"

"We have what we have. The Spirits will tell us if it's enough."

Dancing Fish nodded, then asked, "And your arm? How is it healing?"

High Limb held out his left arm to show off the scar. "It's fine."

"And the women and children back at Cowangough. Have they been instructed?"

"Yes. If the soldiers keep moving to our winter home, the People will all disappear into the trees in small groups. No one will find them."

"Let's hope it doesn't come to that."

"The Spirits will protect us, Sachem." High Limb grinned and inclined his head toward him. "And, of course, your whiteness."

"My whiteness?" He snorted. "From a white grandfather named Jacq who I know little about? It means nothing. It is gone. A mist burned off by the sun. If it ever existed." He looked hard at his old nemesis. "Listen, I'm no better than you. And you're just as clever." He pointed at the weapons surrounding the War Chief. "Look at all you've done, all you've invented and made. We are no different, you and me."

"And them?" High Limb tilted his chin toward the south, in the direction of Fort Amsterdam. "Are we different than them?"

He hesitated only a moment. "We are *better* than them."

Dancing Fish instinctively reached up to touch the glass button that hung around his neck in the winter season. He tapped it several times. "We should move the men before the night is over. How many do we have?"

"From the Navesink, Raritan, Hackensack, Siwanoy,

Wiechquaeseck, and our own Manahate . . ." He tilted his head and moved his lips in counting. "I think almost 100."

"And from just the Manahate?"

"Every man who is a man and who can fight. I say 15, including us."

Dancing Fish shook his head slowly. "Only 15. Do you remember when we could have brought so many more warriors together for battle?"

"I do," said the War Chief quietly. "And I remember other things that were more plentiful and more . . ."—he paused in deep thought—"more magnificent."

Dancing Fish reached out and put his hand on High Limb's shoulder. "Let's not think of the past. Send the warriors out into the forest to wait. The time has come."

▶◀

The village was eerily quiet when they entered it. The only sound Van Ost heard was the crunching of snow under their boots and the heavy breathing of the men who had marched all morning through the island's bleak landscape. Not a soul could be found, but evidence of them was all around. Fires still smoked from warm embers, and footprints had packed down the snowy paths between the wigwams.

He watched Captain Underhill pick up a gourd bowl near the central fire and stick his finger in it, then put it to his mouth to taste. "Stew. Not bad."

Underhill was supposed to be co-leading this march up the island with Captain Beeckman, but Van Ost had seen the tall English captain gradually take over the command to the point where now, at this topmost village of Shorakapkock, there was no question about who was in control of the combined Dutch-English force.

"You men," the Englishman said, pointing at a group of

Dutch soldiers, "form a perimeter around the village. Make it 100 steps out and pay close attention to your surroundings. There could be savages waiting behind any tree or rock."

This was the same village where Dancing Fish had humiliated them with his bundle of rat skins during Van Ost's first spring in New Netherland. As they had discovered, most of the natives were off the island in the middle of winter, but one couldn't be too careful when the clever Sachem was involved. So now he studied the terrain from a soldier's point of view.

They were in a valley between two hills that roughly lined up north to south. He could see to the north the curving waterway that separated the island from the higher mainland. Because of the moving water, it was only partially covered in ice in spite of February's frigid cold. To the south was a low-lying area that was normally marsh but now hardened with frost.

After the scouting parties sent to follow any tracks returned and reported seeing nothing, they settled in for the night. They built a large fire where the former one still smoldered and took up residence in the various wigwam shelters scattered around the central fire pit. There were no stars showing through the flat gray sky, but a dim half moon rose to cast a feeble light over them. Marching through snow was hard work and many were soon asleep. But not Van Ost. He knew something was coming.

It took only one shout from a perimeter sentry to rouse the camp, and they quickly formed into close units circling the fire, looking outward. He was in command of his section of two units aimed directly north.

"Muskets!" Underhill called out, and the men frantically loaded their powder and then ball shot.

"Direction out!" came the next command. Everyone had their muskets up, although not all pointing the same way.

The next order would be the range, but there was no command. Because there was no range. Because there was still no sign of the enemy in the weak light.

They were drilled in forming battle lines and engaging the other side, which would be doing the same. Close up ranks, open fire with a mass volley on command, then fall back and let the next group take the following action. But these tactics weren't effective in a situation where the enemy attacked randomly from erratic positions. So they had tried to adjust their strategy more to how the natives fought. But their training was ingrained.

Van Ost looked back nervously at his fellow soldiers while they looked at him. Where were the Indians?

The answer arrived when flaming arrows suddenly came out of the darkness at them from all sides. Men shrieked and cried out when they tried to put out the fires spreading to their clothes. Others simply fell over gravely injured or dying.

The ordered ranks rapidly disintegrated with men running every which way and firing muskets at phantom targets.

"My command!" Van Ost shouted, forcing his unit, like a school of fish, back into some kind of orderliness. "Stay together and march directly north until you see the enemy. Then fire at will."

More sure of his leadership than ever, he led the charge into the night's gloom.

They hadn't gone more than a dozen steps before firearms were shooting at them from two directions. "Fire at the muzzle flashes!" he yelled. Soon, the thundering of musket and pistol blasts mixed with the sounds of men screaming in pain. And from both sides of the battle.

Captain Beeckman's unit was on his left flank, and in the brightness of the musket flares he saw the captain hit and fall to the ground. He didn't move.

Then, soon after it had started, the firing from the natives stopped.

With the smell of gunpowder enveloping them, Van Ost realized they still hadn't seen the enemy. But he sensed their next move. "Fix bayonets," he ordered. *"Now!"*

He waited for the sounds of metal attaching to muskets to end then called out his next order: "March forward!" If he couldn't find the enemy then he would make the enemy find him. "To the waterway," he instructed while the first hint of day began to lighten the sky.

The curving stream was in sight when they attacked. Natives swinging clubs and knives came at them from the left and right shouting their piercing war cries. Soon, all were entangled in one brawling mess, fighting hand-to-hand. The ice and snow reflected back just enough light so they could make out who was on their side and who wasn't.

Van Ost had just finished bayoneting one of them in the stomach when he suddenly came face-to-face with Dancing Fish across a small distance. Surprised to see a native Sachem fighting as a warrior with a shaved head, he hesitated for a moment. Which was just enough time for the Indian to lunge forward, holding a knife in each hand.

Van Ost, who was trained in close combat, stepped nimbly to the side and landed a sharp blow of his musket butt to the native's side.

Dancing Fish fell but was upright in an instant, holding his ribs. "Very good, Sir," he said, shaking his head and lifting up both arms to show his two knives. "But maybe you are not so skilled at throwing a blade, are you?"

Van Ost had been backing up slowly and realized he was now at the edge of the waterway, which was only frozen in spots. "Throwing knives is not worthy of a soldier," he said with distaste. "Fighting at close quarters requires skill and strength, something an old rat catcher does not possess." He threw his musket down and pulled out his sword. "Shall we determine who is the most skilled?"

Dancing Fish grinned. "An old rat catcher has many skills." He took a step closer. "And punishing rats is one of them." The native suddenly sprang forward with both knives swirling.

At the same time, Van Ost retreated into the ice-cold water and then executed a classic fencing lunge, kicking his forward foot up while pushing off his back foot. The two men made contact when he thrust the point of his sword into the native's chest just below the collarbone near the left shoulder.

Dancing Fish, apparently confused by the complex move, had built up so much momentum that the stabbing didn't stop his forward motion. Instead, he teetered and swayed into the water, clutching his chest and looking bewildered. "I have not seen this skill," he muttered weakly as he fell backward with a splash.

Van Ost stood quietly, his feet in the icy water, and watched while the body of Dancing Fish floated away.

Seventy-nine

THE FACES OF HIS FAMILY AND KIN COMPETED FOR HIS ATTENtion, all trying to speak to him. Hard Stick scolded, Thunder Cloud instructed, Meekak and Sunshell giggled, Willow cursed the worms on the corn, and Diver just laughed and laughed. He yearned to talk back to them but couldn't move his mouth or get any sound out. He was crippled and helpless.

They started calling his name. *Dancing Fish! Dancing Fish!* Louder and louder the words blared until a slap to his head made him open his eyes. He was staring up at High Limb, his face streaked with dried blood.

"We thought you were gone," the War Chief said somberly, lifting his eyes. "To the Sky World. But you came back."

He tried to move his legs but couldn't. He was in a wigwam and could feel the scorching heat of a fire on his face. But the rest of him was cold. So cold.

"What happened?" he asked in a raw voice.

"We found you floating in the waterway, one arm around a log and the other holding a piece of wood you had stuck deep into the wound. You were badly injured, but the cold water helped you. Every part of you was stopped. Frozen. Like a piece of ice."

Dancing Fish was suddenly aware of a searing pain on the left side of his chest. He moaned and shifted his right arm under the mound of furs that covered him. He felt the wet bandage and sucked in a tight breath from the throbbing.

"Try not to move," High Limb said. "We're bringing you back slowly."

He now saw other faces in the firelight looking down at him. Also covered in blood. He saw worry in their eyes. "What happened in the battle?" he asked.

High Limb tightened his lips. "We lost many men. But so did they. There was no victor."

"And where are they now?"

"Gone. Some to the south. Some north."

Dancing Fish forced his mind to understand. Then he moved his head from side to side, scanning the faces around him. *"Where's Diver?!"* he asked, a sudden fear overcoming him.

High Limb put a hand on the good shoulder and squeezed. "They've taken him. He's been captured."

▶◀

"You lost all those men? *And* your own captain?" Director Kieft was pacing furiously behind his desk and waving his silver dagger in the air to emphasize the questions. There was no one else in the room except him and the sheriff, Van Der Hoykens.

Dirck van Ost was exhausted and angry. They had spent a long day dragging back to the fort, and he had passed a restless night without much sleep. He had cuts and bruises on his arms and one on his back, and they were all hurting. But he was proud of his efforts in the battle. He had taken decisive actions that resulted in the removal of Dancing Fish and the capture of his son. There was nothing to be ashamed of. Yet here he was being reproached again for some sort of failing.

"Where is Captain Underhill?" he asked, trying to deflect the criticism.

"I've sent him north," Kieft said. "There are new troubles up there." He scowled at Van Ost. "But we have more than enough here on this island." He pointed the dagger at him. "With Beeckman dead, I'm now naming you Captain, and I want you to finish what's been started."

Tipping his head to the director while holding in a smile, Van Ost said, "I'm sorry about Beeckman, but thank you." He wasn't sorry at all, and he was finally a Captain! That made up for the director's unfounded rebukes and reprimands. "And the Sachem's son?" he asked.

"He's in the fort's prison," said Van Der Hoykens.

Kieft touched the tip of his dagger. "Until he isn't. We will hang him. Along with the others captured."

"Sir, if I may . . ." Van Ost started. "There could be a better use for the boy." He had thought of this during the fitful night.

"What?"

"We could use him as bait, or as a hostage. He's the only son of the Manahate leader."

"But you killed Dancing Fish, didn't you?"

"Yes, but family ties are important to these natives. They'll want him back regardless of who the new leader is. We could trade him—"

"I don't want to trade him! I want to kill him and every other savage he's connected to. Do you not understand?" To illustrate his point he thrust the dagger into the wooden desktop where it stuck fast. "For us to succeed in New Netherland, and especially here in New Amsterdam, we need to reduce the role of these Indians."

"Reduce their role?"

Kieft calmed his voice. "We must make them accede to our ways. They must accept our law and order. But first, we have to end this war with them. We cannot have our colonists intimidated and even killed by these heathens. One way is to take the life of this leader's son as an example."

"Sir," Van Ost said, "and with respect, another way is to return the boy as a goodwill gesture. An overture, if you will."

"An overture?"

"Yes. Of peace."

The director sighed. "I know what you're thinking, Captain, but I have a different mind about this. We'll make it known that we plan to hang this boy for their daring to resist us. To show our power and resolve." He looked at Van Der Hoykens, who nodded back in agreement and added, smiling, "And maybe torture him while we're at it."

"And then we hang him along with the others for all to see," Kieft said to finish his idea. "That will make them come to us and consent to our demands."

"And what are our demands?" the new captain asked.

The director glared at him. "That they end their armed resistance. That they follow our laws and yield to our dominance. They must live within *our* system, not theirs."

"And if they don't?"

The director grabbed the dagger and stuck it again into the table where it vibrated with a ringing tone. "Then we destroy them once and for all."

▶◀

Dancing Fish had worked his way down along the Great River and had not, so far, been identified. He wore the oldest, smelliest skins he could find, and he had smeared wound salve over his face and neck to cover the tattoos that marked him as a Sachem. That and an insect-eaten deerskin hood over his plucked head would hopefully disguise him. His chest wound ached and was still sore, but the injury was healing after several days of rest.

It was the start of the month of March for the Whites, and even though the ground was beginning to soften, the mornings and nights were still cold. But to help the illusion of being a destitute native, he had thrown his moccasins away at the river and approached the fort in bare feet.

High Limb had wanted to come, too, but he had talked him out of it. He was there to get information. He had to know the fate of Diver and the other captives. And it would be easier alone.

While the light faded in the west, he slipped unnoticed into a large group of the People who stood around a fire near the north wall of the fort. It was mostly men, but there were a few women with their children close by. All looked as dirty and desperate as he did, and many were drinking from the bottles he saw empty and scattered everywhere. Possibly Marie's oat brandy. She sold it in barrels to the drinking houses who put it into glass bottles with their own markings.

He listened carefully to what was being said. From the accents, none were Manahate, which was good because he would have quickly been identified. And he didn't know what they had heard about the Shorakapkock battle.

"Where are you from?" the man next to him asked, his voice slurred from the strong drink. The powerful smells of body odor and brandy assaulted Dancing Fish and forced him to breathe through his mouth.

"From the south," he said vaguely, lifting his chin toward the earthen wall with the beginnings of a palisade on top.

"You look familiar to me." The man stared at him. "Your eyes. Yellow like an eagle. Are you sure—"

Dancing Fish lowered his head and pulled down on his hood. "Several in my band have the same eyes. It's common. And I'm no eagle."

He moved away from the man and shuffled to a different side of the group, listening all the while. He stopped next to two men, both drunk, who were talking.

"They're going to hang 'em," said one.

"Fine with me," the other said. "There'll be a crowd. More chance for food or drink."

"Or stealing!"

Both men laughed and drank from a shared bottle.

He needed to enter this conversation. "Wh-when? Wh-when is the ha-hanging?" he asked, intentionally stuttering and trying to change his voice.

The closest man turned to look at him. "Soon, I hear." He reached out and grabbed his left arm, which made him wince in pain. "Do you have brandy for us?"

"Wh-what do I look like?" he said, ignoring the shooting pain and pretending to stumble more over his words. "A Sachem?"

"A Sachem!" Both men started laughing loudly and punching each other on the arm. "I wouldn't want to be the Sachem of the Manahate band in a few days," the close man said.

"Why is that?" Dancing Fish asked, terrified.

The other man grinned. "Because it's his own son who's hanging first."

▶◀

Dancing Fish walked slowly into the water of the pond, washing the dirt and smell from his body, being careful around his healing chest wound. The water was still bitterly cold, but he paid no attention to that. He needed to cleanse himself as well as his Breathing and Dreaming Souls.

The Great Pond at Werpoes at night was like he remembered it by his senses. He could see the black shadow of the cliff looming over it, hear the sound of a solitary owl hooting, taste the water's freshness, and feel its iciness against his bare legs. But he knew things were not the same in other ways. The Whites had been visiting the pond. Not just for its good water, but to linger. Even to build. A few of their lean-tos and rough huts had started to appear along its edges.

He used to think of the pond as his very own. A place to be alone with his thoughts and visions. A place to dream of his inventions and to imagine his future. A future without limit and focused—he now admitted—mostly on his personal needs. But over the many years and seasons, he had gradually let go of his own satisfactions and yearnings. He had willingly taken on the destiny of the People, and especially of the Manahate band as their Sachem. He had slowly turned from thinking only of himself to thinking of others, of everyone's happiness and safety. And he was glad of this.

But he was failing. The Europeans continued to settle the land. And with the unfortunate help of the People, they had depleted the fur animals. They had spread their tools and trade goods over Lenapehoking to the point where the People's old ways were disappearing. And they had started a war. Now, they were ready to hang his own son along with others.

How had it come to this? And what could he do about it?

He had a feeling the answer surrounded him, in the water of the pond in which he now stood, naked. He would let the water inspire him. He would give himself to the water. And the water would reveal what he must do.

He pushed off the muddy bottom, turned over on his back, and floated toward the center of the pond. The sky was a black dome pricked with a shower of lights. The stars winked and twinkled as he filled his lungs with cold air. He took a few more breaths, then gradually let the air out, letting himself slowly sink under the surface. Adjusting the angle of his body, he found a point of balance where he was underwater but no longer sinking. He closed his eyes and emptied his mind of all thought. And he waited.

A blurry image of his old mentor, Owl, came to him. He saw the long, gray braids and the dark wrinkled skin. And the chuckling in the man's raspy voice.

You will play the most important part of all, Owl said again.

I know you said that, but are you sure? he answered back to the vision.

Owl grinned in his special way. *Of course I'm sure. I'm in the Sky World. I see all.*

Can you see this battle, this war? Who are the winners, and who are the losers? What do you see?

No one wins or loses the battle of life. Rivers flow and grasses grow. There is life, and there is death. You can't have one without the other. Death is inevitable. You don't battle it.

He was trying to think of another question but Owl's shape began to waver and fade, just as his body started to tell him he needed to breathe. He opened his eyes and saw the fuzzy stars above him.

Dancing Fish sculled with his hands until his nose and mouth broke clear of the surface. Sucking the sharp air into his drained lungs, he realized what he had to do. He stroked to the shore and quickly put on his coverings. It was time to visit Marie again.

▶◀

High Limb had been summoned by the dark-skinned Kofi and now rode with him in the horse cart to meet Dancing Fish. While they slowly made their way south on the Wiechquaeseck Trail, they passed blooming serviceberries and heard the angry chatter of red squirrels marking their territories. They did not speak. Each had limited skills with the Dutch tongue, and High Limb had given up trying to understand where Kofi's homeland was and what he was doing on the island. Marie respected him, and that was good enough.

But he was more than surprised to see Dancing Fish and Marie waiting for them at the burial site just north of the Great Pond. This was sacred ground. It held the bones of their ancestors. And visitors were not permitted.

"Why are *they* here?" a troubled High Limb asked, pointing at the two.

"Because they understand what's at stake for us," Dancing Fish said. He nodded to the small white woman and the strong black man. "And they've agreed to help."

"Help with what?" he asked while looking unhappily at the grave mounds around them.

"They will help us free Diver and the others." Dancing Fish walked up to another cart near Marie and pulled back the cover. "Take a look."

High Limb stepped to the cart and peered in. The distinctive black powder barrels and many small, dark bottles stared back at him. "What's in the bottles?"

"Whale oil," Dancing Fish said, picking one up and handing it to him. "With a little black powder mixed in."

High Limb pulled out the wood stopper and smelled the familiar fishy odor.

Dancing Fish asked, "Do you remember your pumpkin booms?"

He grinned. "Of course. They worked well against those Mahicans, didn't they?"

Dancing Fish laughed and gave Marie and Kofi a short history of the Mahican attack. Then he took one of the bottles and placed it against a stick he picked off the ground. "Now imagine an arrow with one of these being shot against a wooden target," he said, looking at High Limb. "What would happen?"

High Limb chuckled. "Boom and fire again?"

Dancing Fish smiled and nodded. "Boom and fire again."

They spoke for another finger of sun, then Marie and Kofi disappeared with their carts on their way first to Werpoes and then to New Amsterdam, leaving High Limb and Dancing Fish alone among the burial mounds.

After each had spent time at the graves of his family, they came back together in a round clearing that had been made long ago for moments of reflection. They were face to face, tears dripping from their noses.

Dancing Fish reached out and put both hands on his shoulders. High Limb repeated the motion, and they both stood, arms attached, eyes locked. If Dancing Fish's chest wound still bothered him, he didn't show it.

High Limb started to sing softly. The Green Corn song. He shuffled his feet to the rhythm, turning slowly in a circle with Dancing Fish, who joined him in the song and the movement. Grabbing each other's forearms, they performed their slow, spinning dance like two beetles clenched in combat.

High Limb tightened his fingers on his old nemesis. "You were once my rival," he said in a high prayer voice.

"You were once *my* rival," Dancing Fish repeated.

"Now, you are my friend."

"You are *my* friend."

High Limb suddenly stopped the dance, but their arms remained linked. He looked down into his friend's yellow eyes. "We are the Real People," he said with a new, powerful voice that came from deep within his belly.

"We are the Real People," Dancing Fish repeated.

"Of the Manahate band."

"Of the Manahate band."

"And we are warriors."

"We are most assuredly warriors."

High Limb smiled at his friend. "And now, we will finish our task together because you have a plan that goes far beyond what you told them, don't you crazy Dream Maker?"

Dancing Fish opened a grin that stretched his face. "Of course I have a plan. Do you want to hear it?"

Eighty

Mid-March, 1644

TWO LARGE PILES OF TIMBER LOGS PROVIDED THE PERFECT hiding place at the harbor. Dancing Fish saw that the sun, nearing the time of the spring equinox, was just starting to set in front of the fort to their right. The wind was light, and the sky was aflame with pink and red clouds.

"Ready?" he asked High Limb in a hushed voice.

Three enormous ships were anchored less than an arrow shot from the dock the colonists had built to unload cargoes of trade and people. And the landing was empty, which would suit their purpose well.

They picked up two bags and walked unhurriedly to the dock. Covered in worn skins and leggings, the two would go unremarked by the Salt People. Just another couple of needy Indians with nothing to do.

Once at the end of the landing, Dancing Fish reached into the top of his leggings and pulled out the whale oil bottles. They needed to be warmed to turn the oil from solid to liquid, and packing them inside their aprons had been High Limb's smart idea.

They crouched and replaced the stoppers with oil-soaked cloths, then tied the bottles to arrow shafts with thin hemp cord. Scraping his steel knife against a small flint, Dancing Fish lit the first of the two wicks.

"Now!" he said, standing up and quickly nocking the arrow

to his bowstring. He pulled back with his eye on the center ship and let the arrow with its heavy bundle fly.

High Limb was only a breath behind him, and both watched as their burning arrows soared to the large target that rocked gently in the sea swell. They followed this with arrows to the other two ships and then stood back to observe.

There was a whooshing sound after each bottle broke, but Dancing Fish heard nothing more in the dimming light. Then, all at once, men were yelling, and the orange glow of fire began to appear on each of the ships.

After gathering up their supplies, they walked back to their hiding spot and Dancing Fish watched with satisfaction while the fires on all three ships grew. The men on board were shouting and running around in their frantic efforts to do something, but he hoped it would be useless.

He turned to High Limb. "Good. The first step is done. But now there's a change of plan."

High Limb cocked his head. "Change of plan?"

"You can't come with me."

His eyebrows pinched. "What do you mean? I'm the War Chief. I fight."

"Not this time, my friend," Dancing Fish said. "You have a more important task."

Dancing Fish stepped close and spoke with a careful seriousness. "You will save my son and the others remaining in the fort. Kieft wants *me*. I'm the prize. And he'll be fixed on that. Which means he won't be looking for someone leading the others away. Someone getting to safety across the Great River." He touched his arm. "And that someone is you."

High Limb frowned. "It's too uncertain to split up like this."

"Don't worry, I'll only lead them away to where we agreed and then rejoin you later. Just like we talked about."

The War Chief muttered under his breath but soon nodded his agreement.

"And one more thing." Dancing Fish pulled off the thong and glass button that hung around his neck. In the lowering light, the button looked well-worn and polished to a glossy shine. The four holes were completely filled with dirt and dust. "You see. The holes are full. The prophecy is coming to its end."

He held out the button to High Limb. "Take this to remember me."

"No!" High Limb said, forcefully pushing the hand and button back. "You keep it. You are the Dream Maker. You are the White Keeper. You were the prophet all along. And the prophecy is revealed through your button. Keep it with you for strength. I'll see it again when we meet up later."

Dancing Fish pressed the glass button to his lips. "May it give us both courage."

▶◀

Marie waited with Kofi and the carts in the empty marketplace outside the north gate of the fort. A full moon had risen in the twilight, and it illuminated the panic around them. They had to calm the horses while soldiers from the fort mixed with colonists, all shouting and running toward the harbor and the ships. A light veil of smoke now covered the tip of the island, and the smell of burnt wood permeated the air.

A soldier suddenly appeared. "What are you doing here?" he asked nervously while he kept an eye on the alarmed crowd surging past him.

"We're here for trade," Marie said calmly. "We have gunpowder and whale oil. Would you like to see?"

The man shook his head. "No need. I recognize you. But the market doesn't open until morning."

"We know." She pointed to the carts at the same time she opened her shawl to expose the flint pistol. She patted it. "We'll be safe. We'll sleep under the carts."

The soldier cast a suspicious eye at her and Kofi. "As you wish. But with all this going on, I'm not sure how much sleep you'll get."

"What *is* going on?" she asked.

The man angled his head in the direction of the harbor. "Someone has set fire to the ships. When we catch whoever it is . . . Well, I wouldn't want to be that man."

"How do you know it's a man?" Marie said indignantly.

The soldier stared at her while stealing glances at her shawl. "A woman would not do this. They know their place, and they're thankful for it." He leaned in closer to where she could smell his bad breath. "Do you not agree?"

Kofi started to step forward, but she stopped him and then looked up at the man. "Oh, I most certainly agree. A woman's place is with her man." She circled her arm around Kofi's and winked at the soldier. "Especially a *strong* man." She was crossing a line and she knew it. And she didn't care.

The soldier blinked and stepped back, unsure of what to say.

Marie smiled warmly. "I hope you catch him."

She watched the confused soldier join the stream of people heading south to the harbor. Just when the man rounded the fort's bastion, she spotted him.

Dancing Fish was walking slowly against the crowd, keeping close to the wall of the fort. She saw him look their way and then approach the single guard stationed with a bayoneted musket at the main gate. They were too far away to hear, but she could make out that they were arguing about a piece of paper he had handed the guard. Earlier, Dancing Fish had asked her for paper, ink, and a quill.

All at once, Dancing Fish wrestled away the guard's musket, then bayoneted a long coat sleeve, pinning it to the wooden doorway.

The guard pulled frantically at the musket, but Dancing

Fish had already fled, running at top speed away from the gate.

He stopped when he reached them. "High Limb is waiting," he said, breathing hard. "Near the wall." He gave them both a long, curious look, and it was with an emotional expression Marie had never seen on him before. He reached for her hand and squeezed it. "Thank you," he said quietly.

Then he was gone, bolting up the broad Wagen Wegh trail that led north out of New Amsterdam.

▶◀

Van Ost crowded with the others—Kieft, Van Tienhoven, Van Der Hoykens, and the commies, De Sille—on the southeast rampart and stared in disbelief. The ships were burning out of control. Men jumped overboard while flames crept up the masts and started to ignite the furled sails. The dull roar from the fires mixed with yells from those still on the ships and from those onshore shouting out advice. Boats with more men were being rowed out to lend assistance. To do what was unclear.

"Why can't they put the fires out?" Kieft bellowed. "Did you send the soldiers?" he asked, directing his attention to Van Ost, who watched in the half-light while columns of black smoke rose from each ship, partially obscuring the moon. The reek of charred wood was strong in the captain's nose.

"Of course, director," he said, irritated that he was somehow being blamed. "All the soldiers we can spare are down at the harbor, helping. Only the ones needed to guard the prisoners are here."

"Shouldn't *we* be doing something?" De Sille asked, his eyes reflecting the glow of the fires.

"We *are* doing something," Kieft said with impatience. "We're commanding."

Van Ost would have preferred being down there with the men, maybe with a bucket in hand, but he was now Captain and needed to stay close to the director and to the other leaders.

"Who could have done this?" Kieft said. "These ships hold cargo and are essential for the trade. This is a disaster."

"Maybe it was an accident," Van Ost offered.

"This was no accident," Sheriff Van Der Hoykens shot back. "All three ships? And when I find out who started this, hanging will be much too lenient. Burning them alive or quartering them would suit me better."

They were discussing the most appropriate retribution when a soldier who Van Ost recognized as a gate guard suddenly appeared holding a folded piece of paper. "Beg pardon, Director, sir," he said with deference, holding the paper out to Kieft, "but this letter is addressed to you."

"Who gave this to you?" Van Ost asked the man while Kieft took the letter and started reading it under an oil lamp.

"A savage, sir," the soldier said. "And he was very demanding."

Kieft crushed the paper in his hands and hurled it sharply to the floor. Then he turned to Van Ost. "I thought you said you killed this Dancing Fish!"

"I . . . I did!" he exclaimed, confused. Then he picked up the crumpled paper and unfolded it. He read the simple Dutch words out loud in growing disbelief:

I start fire on ships.
I not pay your tax.
I kill Claes Swits.
I am enemy.
If you are warrior you come alone meet me at Great Pond.
Battle like men.
Are you a man?

– Dancing Fish of Manahate band

He was stunned. How could this be?

Kieft grabbed the paper out of his hand and held it above

his head. "He has gone too far!" he shrieked. "And he will pay dearly for this."

The director balled up the paper again and threw it to the ground. "We will end this now," he said, his eyes bulging, his nose flaring with rage. "Captain Van Ost," he ordered, "pull some of your best men away from the ships and march to the pond as fast as you can." He paused to look at the sheriff. "And take Van Der Hoykens. He will put this Dancing Fish in irons and bring him back to the fort."

"But he says to come alone," Van Tienhoven said.

"Don't be ridiculous," said Kieft. "We're not fighting a duel. We're sending a force to cut off the head of the snake. We are finally going to kill this leader."

Van Ost asked, "And what about the prisoners?"

"We'll stay here to safeguard the prisoners," Kieft said, his eyes burning with anger. "You have one objective. Now go!"

▶◀

Dancing Fish sprinkled a layer of leaves over the branches and stepped downhill to study his concealed trap. There were many large rocks and gaps on the trail that curved up to the cliff overlooking the pond, and it would be easy to miss this hole that could break a soldier's leg. Or two, if he was lucky.

The light from the full moon was screened by the smoke that had now reached Werpoes. It was still strong enough to see by, but not so strong as to make visible the different ambushes he had prepared. He knew Kieft would send several men for him, but how many, he wasn't sure of. His goal was to slow them down and give High Limb more time.

He moved up to his next snare while a gentle wind rustled the treetops and a nearby male woodcock made its lonely *peent* call. The path was flanked here by pines of all sizes, and it was easy enough to notch their trunks with the small hand saw he had borrowed from Kofi.

He cut V-shaped hinges on the inward side of several trees and carefully sawed in from the opposite edge to a point where only a quick pull on ropes hanging from each pine would bring them down across the trail. The soldiers would be forced to climb over the choked branches or attempt to scramble around the trees on the steep-sided path. And that would stall them.

He rushed up to the final surprise. He had placed two of Marie's black-powder barrels on opposite sides of the trail. They were six paces apart and well hidden. The long, slow-burning fuses—another High Limb creation made from hemp cord saturated with bat dung—would hopefully be easy to fire but stay concealed from those approaching. He didn't like thinking about what these explosions would do to the men near the barrels, but this was the cost of the war Kieft had started.

Dancing Fish only hoped that Marie and Kofi would not be caught. Kieft would not be easy on anyone linked to this plot. But Marie was a smart one, and he felt sure she would know how to keep herself, Kofi, and Juba safe.

He was thinking about Marie when the woodcock's calls stopped, and in the silence he heard the unmistakable sound of men on the march. They were coming.

Dancing Fish raced down to the pines, turned, then tugged on the ropes while he ran back uphill, hearing the trees fall behind him. When he reached the barrels he stopped again to listen. Suddenly, a cry of pain rang out. They were at the first trap.

He concentrated on scraping his flint to spark the fuse. It burned and slowly started sputtering toward the barrel. He moved to the second one across the path but could not get the fuse to light, as much as he tried. He was frantically sparking the flint when he heard a shout: *"There he is!"*

Dancing Fish gave up and started running up the trail with a single thought in his mind: delay them as long as you can for High Limb.

Eighty-one

HIGH LIMB, WEARING A LONG BEARSKIN ROBE AND HOOD AS A disguise, helped Kofi move the carts to a position near other traders in front of the company store. With Marie's coaxing and the offer of a full bottle of brandy, the gate guard had allowed them early access into the fort, and he had slipped in with them.

While the traders slept or sat in small groups and talked about the burning ships, High Limb and Kofi moved through the crowd of displaced people in the fort's open square. They quietly persuaded them to move away from the small prison house that sat to the side of the store and near the main gate. They needed the area clear.

Marie had already left the fort with the excuse of finding food for them, and now High Limb carefully ferried two powder barrels under his robe to the corner where the prison met the earth wall. The moon was full and high, but the pall of smoke and bits of ash from the ships made seeing difficult, which was to their advantage.

After a signal between them, Kofi walked to the center of the square and started shouting and howling in the strange tongue of his home, turning himself around in circles like a man possessed. This drew everyone's attention and fixed the eyes of the guarding soldiers in his direction.

With this diversion, High Limb stood next to the prison wall and called out with his Munsee words, "Diver! Are you there? Do you hear me?"

After a moment, he heard faint words back, "High Limb? It's me. What are you planning?"

He cupped his hands around his mouth. "All of you! Listen closely. Move away from the outer wall where I stand. Get down low and cover your heads. Protect yourselves and be ready."

He heard sounds of movement from inside, and then the soldier who was guarding the door came around the corner to see what noise was about.

High Limb acted immediately, pouncing on the guard and driving his knife into the man's neck while covering his mouth. He then moved to the barrels, placing one at the middle of the prison wall and the other next to the closed front gate.

Crouching, he held the flint and repeatedly struck it with his knife until one fuse, then the other, was burning. He jumped up, ran across the square to Kofi, and pulled him roughly by the arm to the opposite side.

Two loud blasts sent a shockwave through the fort's interior. People were screaming as bits of wood and earth pelted them, and two plumes of smoke billowed up into the night sky. The strong smell of black powder was everywhere.

High Limb and Kofi had already run back to the prison and were helping all who could walk leave through a ragged hole in the wall. Stepping over the bodies of those who had not moved far enough away, High Limb frantically searched for Diver and finally found him dazed in a corner. "Come with me!" he yelled, putting his arm around him and helping him to his feet.

They had just stepped through the hole in the prison wall when a loud voice rang out. *"Stop them! Don't let them get away!"* It was the leader Kieft standing in front of his house under a lamp and pointing.

Releasing Diver, High Limb picked up the musket of the guard he had killed and aimed it at the evil man. Kieft dove to the ground just as High Limb pulled the trigger. The shot did nothing but blow out the light of the lamp.

"Next time, I no miss," he yelled in Dutch tongue while he grabbed Diver, and they both fled out the ruined front gate.

▶◀

Dancing Fish stood at the edge of the cliff and listened. He couldn't see the soldiers, but he could hear them grunting and swearing while they worked their way up the trail that led to him. It wouldn't be long now.

He glanced up at the moon, which was at its highest, small and hazy from the smoke of the burning ships and a thin scattering of clouds. It was the Worm Moon, when the earthworm castings brought out the songbirds, and the world woke from its winter slumber. The night air was cold and still, but it would soon be alive with the smells and sounds of another spring.

Looking down at the pond in the murky light, he recalled when he was a young man standing at this same spot. Ready to dive into the deep water and touch the bottom. Before he had known that Europeans existed. Before he had learned about their ways. And before he and the People had lost so much.

He lifted his eyes to the sky and searched for the stars of his long-dead parents, his Willow, his children, and all his friends and family who had moved on from Mother Earth. They were hard to see through the blur of smoke and clouds, but he knew they were there, winking and approving of what he was doing.

Dancing Fish thought of his manitto—the silvery perch— who still guarded over his two Souls. *Well, Spirit, here we are again, at another point of decision.* He smiled to himself. A lifetime of decisions, some good, some not. But always, he hoped, for the right reasons.

He stared down at the surface of the pond that reflected the moon and the entire Sky World above. An inner voice whispered something to him. He heard it again and nodded.

He slowly began removing his skins, leggings, and moccasins. Then he tightly rolled up the two hanging ends of his apron. He stood exposed, as good as naked, and opened the paint pouches he had hidden earlier.

Hoping the long barrel fuses were still burning, Dancing Fish worked swiftly, using his fingers to paint the front of his body in stripes from top to bottom. One stripe was red from the bloodroot, the color of war and turmoil. The other, made from clay, was white, the sign of peace. He had faced these two choices—these two ways of being—ever since the coming of the strangers. And now he would show his dilemma for all to see. But he needed one more thing to complete his display.

He reached down and picked up the glass button with its thong, slipping it over his head. The prophecy was sealed into the button's hard surface. The questions had been answered.

Suddenly, he saw a flash of light below and heard a loud bang, immediately followed by screams. His powder barrel had exploded and sent some of the Europeans to the Sky World. Or to their version of it.

He turned in a circle and searched the night for the sign. Seeing nothing but blackness in the direction of Sapokanikan and then Ishpatena, he kept circling left until he saw the glow of the burning ships far off in the harbor. The smell of their scorched wood had drifted all the way to the pond. But there was no signal from High Limb. Not yet.

Dancing Fish heard the rattle of metal behind him and spun around. Coming out of the dark treeline and into the clearing were the soldiers. There were only six, but all had determined looks on their faces. Some were holding their arms, and others had blood streaked over their uniforms and skin. All had one or more weapons at the ready. And all were staring at him.

▶◀

"This way!" Marie shouted when she saw them coming. She

had found a large rowboat tied to a private dock on the far west side of the harbor. The owner was more than happy to lend it out for the night for six guilders in hand and two promised barrels of oat brandy. She didn't tell him it would be a one-way trip, but Marie would reimburse him and buy his silence later.

It was a ragged group that approached in the semi-darkness. High Limb was holding onto Dancing Fish's son, and Kofi brought up the rear. In between them was a muddle of native men, women, and children. Some were limping, others bleeding, but all were covered in black soot, which must have been the result of the blasts she had heard. The getaway had worked. So far.

"Hurry," she said, balancing in the boat while helping them into it, one by one.

"Where go?" a young native girl asked her in broken Dutch. Her face was black but her eyes shined in the dim light, showing a combination of fear and excitement.

"Away from here," was all she could think to say.

As soon as the boat was full, Marie extended her hand up to Kofi who pulled her back up and onto the dock.

"Any trouble?" she asked him.

"No, Miss Marie," he said, then smiled. "People like me dancin'."

Marie released a small laugh while she scanned the harbor. There was a crowd on the main dock, and she could see that the fires were almost out on the burning ships, or what was left of them. They were reduced to low hulks, consumed down to the water line where they hissed and smoked relentlessly.

"We ready," said High Limb, looking around intently.

They were an odd bunch, Marie thought, regarding the two men. A white woman settler, an Indian warrior, and an African slave. Somehow, that seemed to sum up what New Amsterdam had become. A mingling of different people, cultures, and beliefs. A rough place where ambition, greed, love, and hate all came together at the tip of the island she now called home. Marie wanted the moment to last, but she saw the impatience and concern in High Limb's eyes. It was time.

"You there!" came the abrupt challenge from behind her. She whirled around to see two soldiers running toward them with swords and pistols drawn. "Stop where you are!" came the command. "Don't try to escape."

She was fumbling with her own pistol when Kofi reached down and picked up one of the boat's long oars. "I do it," he said to her.

Just when the men were almost on them, Kofi swung the oar and smashed it into the closest soldier, knocking him off his feet and into the water. At the same time, High Limb had avoided the second man's sword arm and grabbed the other. In one swift movement, he pulled the man off balance and hurled him onto the sharp boulders that formed the base of the dock. Then he jumped into the boat.

Kofi threw the oar and an unlit torch to High Limb, who caught both and gave the two of them a final look. "We go now," he said before he set the oars in position.

Marie stood next to Kofi, and both watched as the packed boat pulled away. High Limb knelt at the stern, holding eye contact while another man rowed. The warrior's body was proudly erect and impassive, but his smooth head was nodding, and he was smiling at them.

High Limb raised one hand and gave it a quick movement to the side. Marie knew this was a final farewell for this group. They could not come back to the island. They were abandoning their home.

As the boat melted into the night, she thought of the one who remained. The one she knew best. Who was, at this moment, facing his own farewell decision.

Eighty-two

Dancing Fish started to shiver. A westerly breeze had come up, and his naked skin was exposed to it.

"Why are you without skins or clothes and painted like this?" Van Ost asked him in his thin, reedy voice, standing in the middle of the soldiers. They held pistols or muskets, some aimed at him, others at their sides. All had their eyes on him, some with their mouths open, others snickering.

"I am as a boy. The way I am when new to this world. The world before you come." He reached up to touch the glass button that hung from his neck. The sound of muskets cocking was immediate.

"Hold your fire," Van Ost said, raising one arm in the air.

Dancing Fish closed his hand around the button and pressed, feeling a warmth and a subtle vibration from it.

"I thought I had killed you at Shorakapkock," the man said.

"The Spirits protect me. More to do."

"More?"

He nodded and gripped the button with a firmer hand.

"What is that?" Van Ost asked, standing his musket on the ground against his leg.

"My button. From Hudson."

The Soldier Chief gave him a strange look. "Hudson? You knew him?"

He tipped his head. "One of his men give it to me."

"And what's the button for?"

He smiled inwardly. "It tells me the future," he said. He noticed he was no longer shivering. He was no longer cold.

"We already know your future," said the man standing next to Van Ost, smirking. Dancing Fish didn't know this man, but from his clothing he looked important. And dangerous.

"Who is this man?" Dancing Fish asked, pointing with his head.

"I'm the sheriff," the man said, stepping forward and pulling out two metal rings linked together. He shook them so they made a jangling sound. "And I'm taking you back to the fort." He grinned. "Where things will become very unpleasant for you."

No, you're not, he thought, sure now that what he was doing was right.

Van Ost took a step forward to join the man. "You have killed several of my men tonight, and that letter you wrote—"

"You like my letter?" He chuckled. "It is good? I learn over years how to write your words."

"This is not funny," Van Ost said, his face tightening. "Is what you wrote in the letter true?"

He pondered the question and said, "I see your leader Kieft is not here. That is true."

The man with the rings took another step. "You're wasting our time!" he said angrily.

Can you not see how that's my plan?

Now alert to everything around him, Dancing Fish sensed the musty smell of the serviceberry and heard the sweet cooing of a mourning dove. He turned his head in its direction and could see from the corner of his right eye that light was forming on the eastern horizon. But the west and south were still dark. And it was to the southwest where he spotted the light. A small lone blaze just starting to move across the blackness of the Great River. Hudson's river.

It was the signal. It was High Limb!

▶◀

Something was amiss. An Indian leader—a Sachem no less—
with almost no clothes on. And painted as though he were a
Commedia clown. Van Ost was frustrated with this native he
thought he had killed, and who now stood defiant and unafraid
in front of them. The man was obviously stalling for time and
was staring at something in the distance.

"What are you looking at?" he demanded of the naked,
painted man.

"I look at the future," Dancing Fish said calmly over his
shoulder. "A future without you."

Van Ost had no idea what the man was talking about, but
now he saw it, too. A small light—a lamp or torch—was moving away from New Amsterdam across the dark river toward
Pavonia. "Is that . . . " No, it couldn't be. There were plenty of
men left to guard them.

"Your prisoners, yes," Dancing Fish said, turning back to
face them. "Your great fort and your many men fail. That is my
son and others who leave this place and go to safety. Away from
you. And now, you have no time to stop them."

Van Der Hoykens snorted and jangled the irons again. "You
don't understand, do you?" he said, the combination of anger
and contempt clear in his voice. "There is no place you can go
to be safe from us. We are in charge. We—"

The next moments were as if in a slow motion to Van Ost.

The native reached down to pick up a knife concealed behind a rock and launched it toward them. The knife thumped
against the sheriff's chest directly over his heart and buried itself up to the hilt.

Van Der Hoykens clutched at his breast, and the irons clattered to the ground. The sheriff's eyes were wide, his mouth

wordlessly opening and closing like that of a fish. He first sank to his knees, then fell face-first onto the dirt with a loud groan.

Van Ost hesitated. His job was to bring Dancing Fish back to the fort. His own future as Captain depended on it. But he knew what would happen to the man there. He would be hanged and possibly tortured. Was this the way to treat a leader of men? There was something admirable about this Indian. He had acted like a warrior, not much different than himself.

But Van Ost had to do what he was trained for, and to erase any question of his commitment, ability, or worth. He would stop the immediate threat: a knife-throwing, half-naked savage. He would finally end it. Now.

In a steady, nearly unconscious series of movements, Van Ost lifted his musket, cocked the hammer with his right thumb, and took quick aim. His finger found the curve of the trigger, and he pulled it back firmly. The flint struck the frizzen and sparked the powder in the pan. The discharge—accompanied by a thunderous blast and a cloud of white smoke—shot out the lead ball that struck the native somewhere above his stomach with a hard *thwack*.

The Indian leader's mouth gaped wide like a dark tunnel as he started to stumble backward.

▶◀

The force of the musket ball crashing into him was stronger than expected. Dancing Fish knew what an arrow strike felt like, and this was much more powerful. Like a giant war club to the chest.

There was no pain, but the impact knocked him back. He reeled over his feet and instinctively tried to catch his balance. He was at the edge of the precipice, waving his arms in two circles in a last effort to regain his footing. But it was no good.

Just before he fell, he grabbed at the thong around his neck and snapped it off, holding tight to the glass button. As he went over the side, he squeezed the hard disk with all the strength his shocked body could summon.

▶◀

Dancing Fish didn't remember hitting the water, but it must have knocked the wind from his lungs because he was descending fast, head down. His ears burst in an eruption of agony, which overwhelmed the burning now coming from his chest.

The jolt had also released the glass button from his hand, and he watched, emotionless, while it slowly tumbled and twirled into the soundless depth, glinting as it spun away. He felt no sadness about losing it. He had no more use for it.

With the button gone, a calmness enveloped him, and all pain stopped. There remained only a great peace. His son was safe. His people were safe. High Limb would lead them. The plan had worked.

Dancing Fish turned his sinking body with one last effort and looked up through the clear water at a brightening sky he knew was filled with stars. The Sky World sparkled beyond him, waiting. Waiting for him to take his place among those who preceded. He would soon be joining the others.

I'm coming, he mouthed silently. *I'm coming.*

Eighty-three

HIGH LIMB STOOD ON THE ROCKY SHORE OF THE HACKENSACK land with Diver at his side, both looking back to Mannahatta. In the growing light, a smudge of smoke from the burning ships was visible around the Point at Kapsee. Across the water, he could make out the rise of land that surrounded the Great Pond. He wondered what was happening there. If Dancing Fish had somehow—

"Will we see my father soon?" Diver asked, his words quiet and with a slight tremble to them.

"I'm sure we will," High Limb said, hoping it was true. But knowing in his heart it was not.

"So we wait for him here?"

High Limb put his arm around the young man and pulled him tight. "No, we must keep moving. The Salts will be coming for us. Your father will catch up."

"But where are we going?" Diver asked, gently releasing himself from High Limb's hold. "Are we leaving the island?"

High Limb turned his head and looked to the west, which was beginning to catch the light of the rising sun. "We will follow the sun west. That is our destiny." He paused. "And yes, we are leaving the island behind."

"But father—how will he find us?"

He used his most confident voice. "Don't worry, your father will know how to find us. We'll be together again."

Diver asked, "War Chief, will everything be alright now? I mean, for us and for the People?"

High Limb turned back and studied the boy's eyes that caught the new light of the sun. Dark eyes but with small flecks of yellow like his father, and with the same curiosity and intelligence. He also saw a trace of the ruddy color in Diver's hair. Then he smiled with a certainty his inner feelings betrayed.

"Everything will be fine," he said. He bowed his head respectfully to the Great River that moved steadily and silently just below their feet. Then he looked across the water to the island one last time.

"So long as the rivers flow and the grasses grow, we will be fine."

Afterword

NEW YORK CITY—AND ITS CENTERPIECE ISLAND, Manhattan—is a hub of commerce, finance, media, and culture. A metropolitan colossus on the global stage. The world's first megacity. And with its titanic reputation, a question emerges for the curious. That is, as environmental historian William Cronon succinctly puts it: *How did things get to be this way?*

When confronted with the complexities of modern New York City, the question seems almost unanswerable. Yet the seeds of this change were firmly planted in the early 1600s. And *New York 1609* tells one version of that formative story.

So what happened in those intervening 400 years? What were the fates of the characters in this tale, both historical and fictional? And what of the location itself?

Needless to say, it's difficult to summarize four centuries of history in a few paragraphs, but let's start with the city.

After a peace treaty ended Kieft's War in 1645, hostilities between Indians and Dutch settlers and officials continued to flare up in New Netherland until the English finally took over New Amsterdam (and New Netherland) in 1664 and renamed it "New York" after its new proprietor, James Stuart, Duke of York (and younger brother of King Charles II).

The Dutch briefly tried to take it back, but the English reclaimed it for good in 1674. The doubts expressed in this book by Reverend Bogardus and others about the future of the

Dutch colony proved to be well founded in the end.

The next three centuries witnessed a vibrant New York City's expansion and increasing influence in world affairs as the United States grew from a marginal colony into an international powerhouse.

Regarding the historical (real) characters last visited in Part Four of the book, David de Vries continued to oppose many of Director Kieft's policies, which ultimately led to Kieft's being dismissed and recalled back to Amsterdam to face trial.

In a bizarre twist of fate, the constantly arguing Willem Kieft and Everardus Bogardus both drowned on their voyage home in 1647.

Cornelis van Tienhoven continued his notorious ways in New Netherland, becoming New Amsterdam's *Schout* (Sheriff) in 1652 until he was fired by new director Pieter Stuyvesant in 1656. Van Tienhoven disappeared that same year with only his hat and cane found floating in Hudson's river.

Influential Hackensack sachem Oratam lived a long life helping to negotiate truces, treaties, and land deals between the Lenapes and the Europeans. Siwanoy sachem Wampage was one of the signers of the treaty that sold 50,000 acres of Bronx/Westchester County land to Thomas Pell in 1654.

Using the author's imagination, the fictional Marie Boucher would have died the wealthiest woman in New York in 1686, and her private slave Kofi would likely have been manumitted to half-freedom by the close of 1644. Dirck van Ost would have returned to his homeland and married his beloved Kathrijn.

And High Limb and Diver would have followed the sun west on one of the migratory routes explained below—and with Dancing Fish forever in their memories.

▶◀

While the story of America's Indians is superficially well known in its broad and tragic outline (depopulation, forced relocations, state-sanctioned killings, broken agreements, dispossession, and westward migrations), there are many historical details about the indigenous peoples of the northeastern United States that have remained hidden from general view.

One myth to bust is that the Lenape people (renamed "Delaware") died out. While it's true this group eventually lost its vast ancestral homelands centered around the Hudson and Delaware river valleys by the eve of the American Revolution, it's nonetheless remarkable they were able to hold onto some of their lands for as long as they did (almost 150 years) in the face of continuing colonial expansion. They accomplished this by becoming knowledgeable and calculating in the complexities of land deeds and usage, which all started with the "purchase" of Manhattan in 1626, as dramatized here in Part Three.

Over time, the majority of the Lenape-Delaware people created a diaspora of living communities in Oklahoma, Wisconsin, and Ontario, Canada. Other, smaller descendant groups also exist in New Jersey, Pennsylvania, and Kansas. At this writing, there are 573 officially recognized Indian tribes in the United States, and three are Delaware-Lenape: the Delaware Tribe of Indians (Bartlesville, Oklahoma); the Delaware Nation (Anadarko, Oklahoma); and the Stockbridge-Munsee Community (Shawano County, Wisconsin). In addition, there are three First Nations reserves in Ontario, Canada, that are also home to the Lenape-Delaware (see Acknowledgments).

The surviving fictional characters High Limb and Diver (and their descendants) could have taken two migratory routes to their present-day locations. One was north to western Massachusetts (Stockbridge) then over to the Oneida lands in northwest New York before ending up at the Stockbridge-Munsee Community in Wisconsin. The other, and more likely, path was west through Pennsylvania, Ohio, Indiana, Michigan, and ultimately turning northeast into southern Ontario, ending up in the Chatham-Kent/Moraviantown/Brantford area between the U.S. cities of Detroit and Buffalo.

Curiously, the Munsee-speaking Lenape formerly living on and around the island of Manhattan, New York City, have largely been forgotten in their own homeland. With some exceptions—*Mannahatta/Manhattan, Gowanus, Canarsee/Canarsie, Maspeth, Hackensack, Raritan*—few Indian place names exist, and there are only a handful of commemorative signs or plaques to remind today's residents and tourists of the role American Indians played in shaping the local history of this important city.

One of the author's goals in writing this story is to bring this history into the light. As author and anthropologist Herbert Kraft notes in his book, *The Lenape: Archaeology, History, and Ethnography*: *"Kwëlahaapchìch wëmi awèn mwëshalawoo yuk Lënapeyok."* Or, "Let us hope that the Lenape will be remembered forever."

Notes About the History

THIS BOOK IS A WORK OF HISTORICAL FICTION. MEANING—
and I follow author Ken Follett's guiding principle—the events
depicted either *did* happen, or they *could have* happened. For
example, as described in Part One, a Mahican warrior actually did climb up the stern of Hudson's ship and take several
items from the master's cabin for which he was subsequently
killed by the crew. In Part Three, Willem Verhulst did try to
buy Manhattan island but failed, whereas Pieter Minuit finally
succeeded (there is no surviving deed or bill of sale). In Part
Four, Claes Swits was murdered by a grudge-holding native,
the massacres at Nechtanc and Pavonia did occur, and the heads
of massacred Wiechquaesecks were literally kicked around like
footballs in the winter of 1643–44. (Note: although this book
includes significant violence, this is based on reality; it was a
violent time.)

So while there are some historical facts from this early period to rely on—and I've tried to be faithful to the historical
record of major events—I've also taken the fiction writer's pre-
rogative of filling in the gaps with my creative powers.

And the same Follett guideline applies to the characters
of this story. Their words either *were* spoken or written (taken
from journals and letters), or they might have been, keeping
in mind that the text is written in English and not all characters spoke it. But even our knowledge about the historical

figures mentioned or featured in this book is incomplete. There are large holes in their biographies, and I've attempted to plug those holes. All other characters are fictitious.

Circling back to the Indian point of view, while I've read many of the backward-looking accounts of this era by Native American writers, we ultimately run into a wall of unknowns. One reason is that the American Indians depicted at this time period (at this New York location) had no written language; they had an oral storytelling tradition. Consequently, most of the contemporaneous (and subsequent) written histories are from Europeans: the explorers, traders, settlers, travelers, and officials. So I've stepped in, hoping to balance the equation.

One can even question basic terms to describe the native peoples. For example, the tribal name *Lenape* and linguistic name *Munsee* only emerged in the 1700s. And even though *savages* was indeed a word used at the time to describe the Indians by first-contact Europeans (though not exclusively), I have chosen to apply the word cautiously—and only by characters who would logically use and say it.

The bottom line is that any historical errors in the telling of this story are entirely my own, with the excuse that while some things can be known, others cannot. Such is the nature of historical fiction.

But in this mix of historical uncertainty, there is one thing I can say for sure: when I was treading water at the tip of Manhattan island during my nonstop swim around it in 1983, waiting for the ebbing tide to change, I looked up at the tall buildings crowded together and asked myself the key question: *How did things get to be this way?*

— Harald Johnson
Charlottesville, Virginia
Spring Equinox, 2018

Acknowledgments

THIS MULTI-YEAR, HISTORICAL FICTION PROJECT (INCLUDING the four short ebooks and the consolidated and expanded omnibus edition) brought me into contact with so many wonderful sources of inspiration and information. As I zeroed in on my concept, time period, and location, I proceeded to devour all the books, articles, and other references I could consult or get my hands on (some are in special libraries or collections).

Mannahatta: A Natural History of New York City by Dr. Eric W. Sanderson was an eye-opening book and one of my early inspirations. In fact, it is one of The Mannahatta Project's amazing seventeenth-century image reconstructions by Markley Boyer that you see on the cover of the books. The encyclopedic *Gotham: A History of New York City to 1898* by Edwin G. Burrows and Mike Wallace was a valued resource along with its associated online sites and groups. *The Island in the Center of the World: The Epic Story of Dutch Manhattan and the Forgotten Colony That Shaped America* by Russell Shorto was another go-to reference book for me. Paul Otto's *The Dutch-Munsee Encounter in America: The Struggle for Sovereignty in the Hudson Valley* provided a good overview of the clash of material cultures between the Europeans and the native Lenape people. *A Description of New Netherland* by Adriaen Van Der Donck is a primary reference from the mid-seventeenth century (both 1968 and 2008 editions). The 1921 *Religion and Ceremonies of the Lenape* (from

Indian Notes and Monographs: A Series of Publications Relating to the American Aborigines by M.R. Harrington was found in delicate condition in a special protective box at the University of Virginia library and provided important guidelines on such topics as spirit guides and the male initiation practices of the Lenape. *Half Moon: Henry Hudson and the Voyage That Redrew the Map of the New World* by Douglas Hunter added key information about Hudson's route and the nautical challenges he faced with the complicated tidal estuary that influences the entire New York City area. And no acknowledgments section regarding Henry Hudson's 1609 voyage would be complete without shipmate Robert Juet's actual log chronicling the adventure (most of Hudson's log has been lost).

Other key historical reference books include: *The Munsee Indians: A History, The Lenapes,* and *Native American Place Names in New York City* by Robert Steven Grumet; *The Lenape: Archaeology, History, and Ethnography* by Herbert C. Kraft; *The Iconography of Manhattan Island: 1498–1909* by I.N. Phelps Stokes; *New Netherland: A Dutch Colony in Seventeenth-Century America* by Jaap Jacobs; *The Barbarous Years: The Peopling of British North America: The Conflict of Civilizations, 1600–1675* by Bernard Bailyn; *Lenape Women, Matriliny and the Colonial Encounter: Resistance and Erosion of Power, 1600–1876* by Regula Trenkwalder Schoenenberger; *Manhattan in Maps: 1527–1995* by Paul E. Cohen and Robert T. Augustyn; *The Last Algonquin* by Theodore Kazimiroff; *Gotham Unbound: The Ecological History of Greater New York* by Ted Steinberg; *Hudson Tercentenary: An Historical Retrospect (1909)* by Frank Chamberlain; *The Historical Atlas of New York City: A Visual Celebration of 400 Years of New York City's History* by Eric Homberger; *The Hudson: A History* by Tom Lewis; *A Sweet and Alien Land: The Story of Dutch New York* by Henri and Barbara van der Zee; *Guns, Germs, and Steel* by Jared Diamond; *Changes in the Land: Indians, Colonists, and the Ecology of New England* by William Cronon; *The Saltwater Frontier: Indians and the Contest for the American Coast* by Andrew Lipman; *Fur, Fortune, and Empire: The Epic History of the Fur Trade in America* by Eric Jay Dolin; and *Indians, Animals, and the Fur Trade: A Critique of Keepers of the Game* edited by Shepard Krech III.

Also, selected historical readings from: Nicholas Jean de Wassenaer, Edmund Bailey O'Callaghan, David Zeisberger, John Heckewelder, and the Moravian Church Archives; and contemporary readings from: Joyce D. Goodfriend, William A. Starna, and Charles T. Gehring.

As I mention in my Notes About the History section, contemporaneous references from the American Indian perspective in this time and at this location are nonexistent. However, I studied key, backward-looking books from Native American authors such as: *As Long As the Grass Shall Grow and Rivers Flow: A History of Native Americans* by Clifford E. Trafzer (whose emotion-packed title I gratefully adapted and used in my text); *Native Universe: Voices of Indian America*, edited by Gerald McMaster and Clifford E. Trafzer for the National Museum of the American Indian; *The Inconvenient Indian: A Curious Account of Native People in North America* by Thomas King; *Red Ink: Native Americans Picking Up the Pen in the Colonial Period* by Drew Lopenzina; and the books of current Native American author Evan T. Pritchard: *Native New Yorkers*, *No Word for Time*, and *Henry Hudson and the Algonquins of New York*, which provided a framework of the Seven-Fire Prophecy. Also, these biographies and historical accounts: the *Neither Wolf Nor Dog* trilogy by Kent Nerburn and *Black Elk Speaks* by John G. Neihardt.

Two essential Lenape-English dictionaries were: *Delaware-English Dictionary* by John O'Meara (first pointed out to me by Yeya Takenha Theresa Johnson of the Delaware Nation at Moraviantown), and the online *Lenape Talking Dictionary*, a project of the Delaware Tribe of Indians.

Organizations that supplied useful insights include: New Netherland Institute, New Amsterdam History Center, the National Museum of the American Indian (both Washington, D.C., and NYC locations), The Gotham Center for New York City History, and the New-York Historical Society Museum & Library. Plus, these American Indian and First Nations tribal communities: Delaware Tribe of Indians, Delaware Nation, the Stockbridge-Munsee Community, Delaware Nation at Moraviantown, Munsee-Delaware Nation, and Six Nations of the Grand River.

I also enjoyed reading other fiction books about this location and time period: *New York: the Novel* by Edward Rutherfurd; *City of Dreams: A Novel of Nieuw Amsterdam and Early Manhattan* by Beverly Swerling; and *The Mevrouw Who Saved Manhattan: A Novel of New Amsterdam* by Bill Greer. Moving farther away in distance and time, but not in relevance: *Tidewater: A Novel of Pocahontas and Jamestown Colony* by Libbie Hawker; *Will Poole's Island* by Tim Weed; James Michener's *Chesapeake*; the *Contact: Battle for America* series by W. Michael Gear and Kathleen O'Neal Gear; *Black Robe* by Brian Moore; *The Orenda* by Joseph Boyden; and, of course, the classic *The Last of the Mohicans* by James Fenimore Cooper.

My many research trips to New York City to "get a feel for the place" were invaluable. Not only did I spend time on the waters that encircle Manhattan island (around which I had swum years earlier), but I met helpful influences including: Michael Ryan and his research staff at the New York Historical Society, Wayne Cahilly and other staff at the New York Botanical Garden, Untapped Cities tour guide Justin Rivers, the aforementioned Eric Sanderson and Bill Greer, and others.

I also want to thank the individuals who had a direct hand in helping me create this book series. Margaret Ryan contributed her professional editing skills to most drafts, and importantly, gave me the first affirmation that I could, in fact, do this.

Fiction is different from the nonfiction I was experienced in, and her encouragement kept me going. Likewise, Jim Dodds added his own valuable, developmental- and line-editing expertise—and confidence—about the story as it unfolded. And William Van Doren, author and editor as well as artist, gave the final full manuscript his careful attention and added his own excitement for the project.

More personally, Richard Marks family, Martin Smith, and Jim Curl—all old friends—also offered important inputs. Additional feedback (and support) came from my enthusiastic Founding Fans "street team," early readers like author and historical fiction blogger M.K. Tod and author Winifred Morris, and all the followers of my website and Facebook page.

There were also several writing and publishing experts who personally helped me along my path: Larry Brooks, K.M. Weiland, Jennifer Blanchard, Libbie Hawker, CS Lakin, Dan Blank, Jason Kong, and Joel Friedlander.

Plus, I thank all the indie-publishing bloggers and authors I've had the pleasure to interact with in this new world of independent publishing. Their advice and friendship is much valued.

And, of course, a great deal of appreciation goes to my current and future readers. Without you, there wouldn't be much to talk about.

Finally, my deepest thanks go to my wife and partner, Lynn, who continues to believe in me.

About the Author

HARALD JOHNSON IS AN AUTHOR OF BOTH FICTION AND NON-fiction, a publisher, and a lifelong swimmer—who actually swam all the way around Manhattan island. He loves standing at important locations from history and feeling the way they still resonate in our lives today. Harald is the first contemporary novelist to write about the birth of New York City (and Manhattan) from its earliest beginnings. He lives with his wife deep in the woods of central Virginia.

Website: http://haraldjohnson.com